ONE OF US

ALSO BY
MICHAEL MARSHALL SMITH

SPARES

BANTAM BOOKS
NEW YORK / TORONTO / LONDON
SYDNEY / AUCKLAND

ONE OF US

MICHAEL MARSHALL SMITH

ONE OF US

A Bantam Book / August 1998

Book design by Laurie Jewell

Library of Congress Cataloging-in-Publication Data
Smith, Michael Marshall.
One of us / Michael Marshall Smith.
p.   cm.
ISBN 0-553-10605-8
I. Title.
IN PROCESS PR6069.M5225 0
823'.914—DC21   98-10580
CIP

Published in the United States

Bantam Books are published by Bantam Books, a division of Bantam
Doubleday Dell Publishing Group, Inc. Its trademark, consisting of
the words "Bantam Books" and the portrayal of a rooster, is Registered
in U.S. Patent and Trademark Office and in other countries. Marca
Registrada. Bantam Books, 1540 Broadway, New York, New York 10036.

PRINTED IN THE UNITED STATES OF AMERICA

BVG   10   9   8   7   6   5   4   3   2   1

FOR TRACEY,
SISTER, FRIEND

─────────────────────

AND FOR THOSE WHO HAVE BECOME INVISIBLE:
SUE, PEGGY, BETTY, CLARICE, AND MABEL

T H A N K S   T O . . .

NICK ROYLE, WHO HAS BEEN THERE FROM THE BEGINNING WITH FRIENDSHIP, ENCOURAGEMENT, AND STRANGE SQUEAKING NOISES; TO MY AGENTS—RALPH VICINANZA, NICK MARSTON, BOB BOOKMAN, CARADOC KING, LINDA SHAUGHNESSY, AND LISA EVELEIGH—FOR THEIR VARIOUS GOOD WORKS ON MY BEHALF; TO JANE JOHNSON, JIM RICKARDS, STUART PROFFIT, KATE MICIAK, NITA TAUBLIB, AND DAVE HINCHBURGER; TO ALISTAIR GILES, SUSAN CORCORAN, JACKS THOMAS, FIONA MCINTOSH, AND BEATWAX; TO DAVID BADDIEL; TO ARIEL AND THE GUYS AT DEANSGATE, AND TO THE BFS; TO ELLEN DATLOW AND ED BRYANT: TO COLIN WILSON FOR LONG-TERM INSPIRATION, AND ERIC BAZILIAN FOR A SONG; TO TIM AND SUZY AND NOT JUST FOR CAT-SITTING; TO HOWARD FOR GRADUALLY DESTROYING OUR HOUSE; TO SARAH AND RANDY AND PETE AND DANA AND CHRIS AND LORRAINE—AND THE USUAL SUSPECTS IN LONDON; TO ADAM SIMON FOR SEEING THE INVISIBLE MORE CLEARLY THAN MOST, AND TO STEVE JONES FOR OCCASIONAL SANITY CHECKS; TO DON JOHNSON AND CHEECH MARIN FOR GETTING US THROUGH THE LONG, DARK NIGHTS OF AN ENGLISH SPRING, AND TO PAULA, AS ALWAYS, FOR BEING MY REAL LIFE; AND TO MY PARENTS WITH LOVE.

THE INVISIBLE IS THE SECRET
FACE OF THE VISIBLE.

———

—M. MERLEAU-PONTY

ONE OF US

P R O L O G U E

Night. A crossroads, somewhere in deadzone LA. I don't know the area, but it's nowhere you want to be. Just two roads, wide and flat, stretching out four ways into the world: uphill struggles to places that aren't any better, via places that are probably worse.

Dead buildings squat in mist at each corner, full of sleep and quietness. It seems like they lean over above us like some evil cartoon village, but that can't be right. Two-story concrete can't loom. It's not in its nature. The city feels like a grid of emptiness, as if the structures we have introduced to it are dwarfed by the spaces that remain untouched, as if what is not there is far more real than what we see.

A dog shivers out the end of its life meanwhile, huddled in the doorway of a twenty-four-hour liquor store. The light inside is so yellow, it looks like the old guy asleep behind the counter is floating in formaldehyde. When she was younger, the woman would have done something to help the dog. Now she finds herself unable to care. The emotion's too old, buried too deep—and the dog's going to die anyway.

I don't know how long we wait, standing in the shadowed doorway, hiding deep in her expensive coat. She gets through half a pack of Kims, but she's smoking fast and not wearing a watch. It feels as if this corner in the wasteland is all I've known or ever will see; as if time has stopped and sees no compelling reason to start flowing again.

Eventually the sound of a car peels off from the backdrop of distant noise and enters this little world. She looks, and sees a sweep of headlights up the street, hears the rustle of tires on asphalt, the hum of an engine happy with its job. Her heart beats a little more slowly as we watch the car approach, her mind cold and dense. It isn't even hatred she feels, not tonight, not anymore. When the cancer of misery has a greater mass than the body it inhabits, it's the tumor's voice you hear all the time. She's stopped fighting her unhappiness now. All she wants is some peace.

The car pulls up thirty yards along the street, alongside an address she spent two months tracking down, and ended up paying a hacker to find. The engine dies. For the first time, she glimpses the man's face through the dirty windshield. Seeing him isn't climactic, and comes with no roll of drums. It just makes us feel tired and old.

He takes an age to emerge, leaning across to pick up a pack of cigarettes from the dash. I don't know for sure that's what he's doing, but that's what she decides. It seems to be important to her, and what she feels about this man is far too complex for me to interpret. She is calm, mind whirling in circles so small you can't see them at all, but now her heart is beating a little faster, and as he finally opens the door and gets out of the car, we start to walk toward him.

He doesn't notice, at first, still fumbling with his keys. She stops a few yards from the car, and he looks up blearily. Drunk, perhaps—though she doesn't think so. He was always too much in control for that. Probably just tired, and letting it show while there's no one around to see. He's older, grayer than she was expecting, but the slightly hooded eyes are the same. He looks early fifties, trim, a little sad. He doesn't recognize her, but smiles anyway. It's a good smile, and may once have been quite something, but it doesn't reach the eyes anymore.

It's about now that the other car first appears, way off down the other road. I didn't notice it the first time, and she never does. She just stares at the man, waiting. A generic smile isn't enough. We want him to know who we are. The bond operates in two directions. She cannot break it alone.

"Help you?" he asks eventually, peering at her. He stands by the car, back straight. He's not frightened, sees no need to be, but he's beginning to sense this is not a run-of-the-mill encounter. All he sees is a skinny woman in a good coat. But there's something about us that disturbs him, reminds him of someone he used to be.

"Hello, Ray," she says, and then nothing else, waiting for him to remember.

Maybe it's something in her face that does it, puts him in mind of a grin long ago. His eyes open wider. Some measure of confidence returns; his face relaxes a little. A picture of reliability. They look at each other for a while, but by now my attention is on the sound of the car. I know it's coming, big and silver and fast.

"It's Laura, isn't it?" Ray asks eventually. Her name is still there, near the front of his mind. Maybe it always has been, the way his has been in hers. He nods. "Yes, it's you." He gives a short, bewildered laugh, sticking a cigarette in his mouth. "I never forget a face." He clicks the wheel of his lighter and starts bringing it up to his face. His left eyelid droops slowly.

The wink is like returning to a childhood playground, and finding a swing still rocking as if you had only just that moment climbed down. It's enough.

The first shot goes straight through his left eye, blatting a baseball of shit out of the back of his skull. He's still trying to back away as the next bullet tears through his groin, and as another splashes through most of his throat. But then he's on the ground, legs spastically twitching as we step forward to stand over him.

The dog watches it all from its patch by the wall, but it's got problems of its own, and Ray's going to die anyway.

She doesn't stop firing until the gun is empty. The body is still by then, and has nothing worth speaking of above the neck. The cigarette alone is almost intact, clamped between lips that look like something out of an autopsy wastebasket. She decides to leave it that way.

I put my hand in her pocket and pull out another clip. Her hands are trembling a great deal by then, and I think she already knows she has failed. While she's still fumbling to reload, she finally notices the sound of a car hurtling toward her. Her head jerks up.

I know immediately that it's not the cops, and that I've seen the car somewhere before. Laura doesn't. She doesn't know what to think. Her mind is too empty and fractured to make a decision, so her body makes it for her.

We back away, stumbling and dropping the gun. Then we turn and run, expecting to die and asking only why it has taken so long.

We glance back for an instant, and see the car has pulled to a halt in the middle of the crossroads. The doors are open; two figures are standing over Ray's remains. The men are of identical height, wear matching light gray suits, and have eyes that don't look right.

One picks up Laura's gun; the other shouts "Shit! Shit shit *shit!*" in a voice so deep and loud that I wonder how the buildings around us remain standing. He turns slowly toward us, a streetlamp directly behind his head casting a nimbus of yellow light.

We disappear around the corner before he sees us, and run until we fade into black.

PART ONE

REMtemp

CHAPTER ONE

I was in a bar in Ensenada, drinking a warm beer quickly and trying to remind myself that I hadn't murdered anyone, when my alarm clock caught up with me. Little bastard.

Housson's was jammed to the rafters and noisy as hell, and not just because everyone was talking very loudly. Two local alfalfa barons had come into the bar to celebrate some deal, perhaps a merging of their cash-crop-related dynasties, and an eight-piece mariachi band had joyfully latched on to them and settled in for the night. The rest of the bar was a Jackson Pollock of local color: seedy photographers trying to charge tourists for pictures, leather-faced ex-pats peering around the place like affronted owls, and Mexicans setting about getting drunk with commendable seriousness. Housson's looks like it was last redecorated forty years ago, by someone who had the more functional end of the Wild West in mind: dusty floorboards, walls painted with secondhand cigarette smoke, chairs stolen from some church hall. The only nod in the direction of decor is the fading sketches of ex-bartenders, renowned alcoholics, and similarly distinguished local characters that adorn the walls. One of these had already come crashing to the ground, the casualty of a bottle hurled by a disgruntled drunkard: All in all the atmosphere was just one step short of chaos.

I was tired and my head hurt, and I shouldn't have been there in the first place. I should have been out on the streets, or checking different bars, or even heading back to LA. Anywhere but here. She was nowhere to be seen, and as I hadn't had the time to go to a co-incidence dealer before I left LA, I didn't expect her to just wander in. I was still pretty confident the Chicago lead was a deliberate false trail, but didn't have any particularly good reason to believe she'd have run to Ensenada either. I was there just to drink beer and avoid the problem.

The older of the two businessmen looked like he consumed a fair amount of his alfalfa personally, but he'd obviously done a bit of singing in the distant past and was now working steadily through his repertoire, to the delight of the assembled henchmen and underlings. One of these, a slimy little turd I pegged as the accountant son-in-law of one of the principals, was busy eyeing up a group of young women who were cheerily clapping along at the next table. As I watched, I saw him signal to the non-singing baron, who turned and clocked the girls. His smile broadened to the kind of leer that would make a werewolf look bashful and charming; he beckoned the leader of the band over, more money already in his hand.

I was sitting to one side of a table crammed with tourists, the only seat that had been free when I'd entered over two hours before. The girls were red-faced from the day's sun, and fizzing with margarita-fueled bravado; the guys sipping their Pacificos sullenly and panning their eyes around the bar probably trying to work out which of the locals was going to come and try to steal their women first. I could have told them that it was much more likely to be another American, probably one of the boister- ous frat rats who were in town for some damnfool motorcycle race, but I didn't know them and couldn't be bothered. In fact, they were getting on my nerves. The girls were dancing in their seats in that way people do when they're letting themselves off a very short leash, and the nearest one kept banging into my arm and causing me to spill beer and cigarette ash onto jeans that hadn't been that clean when I'd pulled them on two days earlier.

When I felt the tap on my shoulder, I turned irritably, expect- ing to see the waiter who was working that corner of the room. I like attentive service as much as the next man, but, Christ, there's a limit to how fast a man can drink. In my case that limit is pretty high, and yet this guy was still hassling me well before I'd finished each beer. It was good that the waiter was there, be- cause the only way I could have gotten to the bar was with a chainsaw, but I felt he needed to calm down a little. I was in the middle of deciding to tell him to go away—or at least to do so af- ter he'd brought me another drink—when I realized it wasn't him at all, but a fat American who looked like he'd killed a dirty sheep and glued it to his chin.

"Fella asking for you!" he shouted.

"Tell him to fuck off," I said. I didn't know anyone in En- senada, not anymore, and didn't wish to start making new acquaintances.

"Seems pretty insistent," the guy said, and jerked his thumb back toward the bar. I glanced in that direction, but there were far too many people in the way. "Little black fella, he is."

In those parts this could mean the guy was actually black, or an indigenous Mexican Indian. Didn't really make much difference—I still didn't want to talk to him—but it surprised me that my fellow countryman hadn't felt qualified himself to tell him to fuck off. The guy with the beard didn't look the type to run errands for ethnic majorities.

"Well, then tell him to fuck off politely," I snarled into a mo- ment of relative quiet, and turned back to face the mariachi band.

They immediately and noisily embarked on yet another song, which sounded eerily identical to all the others. It couldn't be, though, because it got an even bigger cheer than usual, and the singing businessman clambered unsteadily onto a chair to give it his all. I took a sip of my beer, wishing the waiter would hurry up and hassle me again, and waited with grim anticipation for the alfalfa king to pitch headlong into the table of girls. That should be worth watching, I felt.

Then I became aware of a sound. It was quiet, and barely audible below the baying of voices and barking of trumpets, but it was getting louder.

"Told him, like you said," the American behind me boomed. "Didn't take it very well."

A beeping sound. Almost like . . .

I closed my eyes.

"Hap Thompson!" a tinny voice squealed suddenly, cutting effortlessly through the noise in the bar. Then it went back to beeping, getting louder and louder, before sirening my name again. I tried to ignore it, but it wasn't going to go away. It never does.

Within a minute the beeping was so loud that the mariachi band began turning in my direction. Gradually the musicians stopped playing, the instruments fading out one by one as if their players were being serially dropped off a cliff. I swore viciously and ground my cigarette out in the overflowing ashtray. Heads turned, and a silence descended on the bar. The last person to shut up was the singing businessman. He was now standing weaving on the table with his arms outstretched. He would have looked quite like an opera singer had his face not been more reminiscent of a super-middleweight boxer who'd thrown too many fights.

Taking a deep breath, I turned.

A channel had cleared in the crowd behind me, and I could see straight to the bar. There, standing carefully so as to avoid the pools of spilt beer, was my alarm clock.

"Oh, hello," it said into the quiet. "Thought you hadn't heard me."

"What," I said, "the *fuck* do you want?"

"It's time to get up, Hap."

"I am up," I said. "I'm in a bar."

"Oh," said the clock, looking around. "So you are." It paused for a moment, before surging on. "But it's still time to get up. You can snooze me once more if you want, but you really ought to be out and about by half past nine."

"Look, you little bastard," I said, "I *am* up. It's a quarter past nine in the *evening*."

"No, it isn't."

"Yes it is. We've been through this."

"I have the time as nine-seventeen precisely. A.M." The clock angled itself so that I—and everyone else—could read its display clearly.

"You've *always* got the time as A.M.," I shouted, standing to point at it. "That's because you're *broken*, you useless piece of shit."

"Hey, man," protested one of the tourists at my table. "Little guy's only trying to do his job. No call for language like that." There was a low rumble of agreement from nearby tables.

"That's right," agreed the clock, two square inches of injured innocence on two spindly little legs. "Just trying to do my job, that's all. Let's see how you like it if I don't wake you up, huh? We know what happens *then*, don't we?"

"What?" asked a woman at the other side of the room, her eyes sorrowful. "Does he mistreat you?" With my jaw clamped firmly shut, I grabbed my cigarettes and lighter from the table and glared at the woman. She stared bravely back at me and sniffed. "He looks the type."

"He hits me. He even throws me out the window." This was greeted by low mutters from some quarters, and I decided it was time to go. ". . . of moving *cars* . . ."

The crowd stirred angrily. I considered telling them that having a broken A.M./P.M. indicator was the least of this clock's problems, that it was also prone, on a whim, to wake me up at regular intervals through the small hours and thus lose me a night's work, but decided it wasn't worth it. Trust the little bastard to catch up with me in the one bar in the world where people apparently cared about defective appliances. I pulled my jacket on and started shouldering my way through the people around me. A pathway opened up, lined with sullen faces, and I slunk toward the door, feeling incredibly embarrassed.

"Wait, Hap! Wait for me!"

At the sound of the clock's little feet landing on the ground, I picked up the pace and hurried out, past the pair of armed policemen moonlighting as guards in the passageway outside. I clanged through the swinging doors at the end, hoping one of them would whip back and catapult the machine back over the bar, and stomped out into the road.

It didn't work. The clock caught up with me, and ran by my side down the street with little puffing sounds of exertion. These were fake, I believed, little sampled lies. If it had managed to track me down from where I'd flung it out the window (for the last time) in San Diego, a quick sprint was hardly going to wind it.

"Thanks," I snarled, "Now everyone in that fucking bar knows my name." I swung a kick at it, but it dodged easily, feinting to one side and then scuttling back to face me.

"But that's *nice*," the clock said. "Maybe you'll make some new friends. See: Not only am I a useful timepiece, but I can help you achieve your socializing goals by bridging the gulf between souls in this topsy-turvy world of ours. *Please* stop throwing me away, Hap. I can help you!"

"No, you can't," I said, grinding to a halt. The night was dark, the street lit only by stuttering yellow lamps outside Ensenada's various bars, restaurants, and rat-hole motels, and I felt suddenly homesick and alone. I was in the wrong part of the wrong town, and I didn't even know why I was there. Someone else's guilt, my own paranoia, or just because it was where I always used to run. Maybe all three—and it didn't really matter. I had to find Laura Reynolds, who might not even be here, before I got shafted for something I hadn't done but remembered doing. Try explaining that to a clock.

"You've barely explored my organizer functions," the clock chimed, oblivious.

"I've already got an organizer."

"But I'm better! Just tell me your appointments, and I'll remind you with any one of twenty-five charming alarm sounds. Never forget an anniversary! Never be late for that important meeting! Never—"

This time the kick connected. With a fading yelp the clock sailed clean over a line of stores selling identical rows of cheap rugs and plaster busts of ET. By the time I was fifty yards down the street, the mariachi band was at full tilt again behind me, the businessman's voice soaring clear and true above it, the voice of a man who knew who he was and where he lived and what he was going home to.

I'D ARRIVED IN MEXICO late the previous evening. That, at least, was when I'd woken to find myself in a car I didn't recognize, stationary but with the engine still running, by the side of a patchy road. I switched the ignition off and got out gingerly, feeling as if someone had hammered an intriguing pattern of very cold nails into my left temple. Then I peered around into the darkness, trying to work out where I was.

The answer soon presented itself, in the shape of the sharply defined geography surrounding me. A steep rock face rose behind the car, and on the other side of the road the hill disappeared abruptly—the only vegetation bushes and gnarled gray trees that seemed to be making a big point of just what a hard time they were having. The air was warm and smelled of dust, and with no city glow the stars were bright in the blackness above.

I was on the old interior road that leads down the Baja from Tijuana to Ensenada, twisting through the dark country up along the hills. There was a time when it was the only road in those parts, but now it's not lit, in bad repair, and nobody with any sense drives this way anymore.

Now that I was out of the car, I was able to recognize it as mine, and to dimly remember climbing into it in LA much earlier in the day. But this realization faded in and out, like a signal from a television station where the power is unreliable. Other memories were trying to shoulder it aside, clamoring for their time in the spotlight. The memories were artificially sharp and distinct, and trying to hide this by melding with my own recollections, but they couldn't, because the memories weren't mine and they had no real homes to go to. All they could do was overlay what was already there, like a double exposure, sometimes at the front, sometimes merely tickling like a word on the tip of your tongue.

I walked back to the car and fumbled in the glove compartment, hoping to find something else I knew was mine. I immediately discovered a lot of cigarettes, including an opened pack, but they weren't my brand. I smoke Camel lights, always have: These were Kim. Nonetheless, it was likely that I'd bought them, because the opened pack still had the cellophane around the bottom half. It's a habit of mine to leave it there, which has given my best friend, Deck, hours of fun taking it off and sneaking it onto the top half of the pack when I'm in the john. The memory of Deck's trademark cackle as I yanked and snarled at a pack after such an incident suddenly bloomed in my mind, grounding me for a moment in who I was.

I screwed up my eyes tightly, and when I opened them again, I felt a little better.

The passenger seat was strewn with twists of foil and a number of cracked vials, and it didn't take me long to work out why. A long time ago, in a past life, I used to deal a drug called Fresh. Fresh removes the ennui that comes from custom and acquaintance, and presents everything to you—every sight, emotion, and experience—as if it's happening for the first time. Part of how Fresh does this is by masking your memories, to stop them grabbing new experience and turning it into just the same old thing. Evidently I'd been trying to replicate this effect with a cocktail of other recreational pharmaceuticals, and had ended up blacking out. On an unlit mountain road, in Mexico, at night.

Great going.

But it had evidently worked, because for the time being I was back. I started the car and pulled carefully back onto the road, after a quick mental check to make sure I was pointing in the right direction. Then I tore the filter off a Kim, lit her up, and headed south.

I passed only one other car along the way, which was good, because it meant I could drive down the middle of the road and stay as far as possible from the precipitous drops that line the route. This left me free to do a kind of internal inventory, and to start panicking about that instead. Most of the last six hours were missing, along with a number of words and facts. I could recall where I lived, for example—on the tenth floor of the Falkland, one of Griffith's livelier apartment houses—but not my room number. It simply wasn't available to me. Presumably I'd remember by sight: I hoped so, because all my stuff was in there and otherwise I'd have nothing to wear.

I could remember Laura Reynolds's name, and what she'd done to me. She'd evidently been with me for some of the trip down, in spirit at least: It must have been her who bought the cigarettes, though I opened the pack. I didn't really know what Laura Reynolds looked like, only how she appeared to herself, and I had no idea where she was. I'd probably had a good reason for heading for Ensenada, or at least a reason of some kind—assuming, of course, that it had been I who made the decision. Either way, now that I was here, it seemed I might as well go on.

I made good time, having to stop only once, while a herd of

coffeemakers crossed the road in front of me. I read somewhere that they often make their way down to Mexico. I can't see why that would be so, but there was certainly a hell of a lot of them. They came down from the hill in silence, trooped across the road in a protective huddle, and then headed off down the slope in an orderly line, searching for a home, or food, or maybe even some coffee beans.

I reached Ensenada just after midnight, and slept in the car on the outskirts of town. I dreamed of a silver sedan and men with lights behind their heads, but the message was confused and frantic, fear dancing through an internal landscape lined with doors that wouldn't open.

When I woke up, more of my head was back in place, and I got it together enough to contact Stratten, patching the call through my hacker's network so it looked like it originated from LA. I said I had a migraine and wouldn't be able to work for a couple of days. I don't think Stratten believed me, but he didn't call me on it. I spent the rest of the day fruitlessly searching taco stands and crumbling hotels, or driving aimlessly down rotting streets. By the evening this had led me to an inescapable conclusion.

She wasn't here.

FROM HOUSSON'S I headed straight for the street where I'd left the car. In late afternoon this particular area behind the tourist drag had seemed charmingly authentic. By mid-evening it resembled a do-it-yourself mugging emporium. Knots of alarming locals stood and stared as I passed, their feet wet from the pools of beer, urine, or blood that flowed from each of the bars, but I made it back to the car in one piece. It was parked down a dead end, away from prying eyes, and it was only as I pulled my keys from my pocket that I realized shadows were moving on the other side of the street. The light was too patchy for me to tell who it might be, but in any event I didn't want to meet them. I'm like that. Not very sociable.

Three men were soon distinguishable, heading toward me. They weren't hurrying, but that wasn't reassuring. Particularly when the glint of a tarnished button confirmed what I already suspected. Cops. Or the local equivalent, which was even worse.

Could be they were just out walking their wallets, shaking down the bars; could be they'd just spotted a *turista* and decided to shake me down instead.

Or it could be that their colleagues outside Housson's had passed the word to them that someone suspicious had just been hounded out of the bar by a lunatic timepiece, someone whose name had been clearly articulated. There was no reason that name should mean anything to anyone, not unless stuff had happened back in LA that I didn't know about, but I wasn't going to take any chances. I quietly opened the car door and waited, listening to the sound of their boots scuffing on the ragged road surface.

"Hi," I said steadily. "What can I do for you guys?"

They didn't reply, but merely looked me up and down, as is the wont of such people. The third cop hung back a little, casting a glance at the license plate of my car.

"It's mine," I said. "The papers are in the glove compartment."

Too late I remembered what was next to the papers and under a map. A gun. It was mine, licensed, legal—with a serial number and everything—but it would still be a very bad thing to have cops find. The Baja peninsula isn't bandit territory, but it's heading that way. Twenty years ago it had looked as if fleeing Hong Kong money might claw the Baja up into respectability, but the cash had kept on moving, and now the dark country was taking over again, seeping down from the hills and turning the eyes of the people inward. The cops are very keen that it's them pointing the guns at people, not the other way round.

"Mr. Thompson?" the middle cop said. I tightened my grip on the door.

"Yes," I replied. There was no point in lying. Any part of my body had it stamped there in amino acids. "How'd you guess? I just look like a Thompson, or what?"

"Someone who sounds like you just had a little trouble in Housson's," he said, something that wasn't really a smile moving his lips. "With a clock."

"Well, you know how it is." I shrugged. "They get on your nerves occasionally."

"I couldn't afford such a thing," the middle cop said. "Mine still runs on batteries."

"Probably works properly, then," I said, trying to be comradely. "And you don't have to feed it."

"What are you doing in Ensenada?" the third policeman asked abruptly.

"Vacation," I said. "Few days off work."

"What work?"

"Bar work." Used to be true. I've done most things at one time or another. If they wanted to test me on pouring beer and making change, they were welcome to it.

They all nodded together. Little, uninterested nods. The fact that this was all so chummy should have made me more relaxed. It didn't. It made me feel tense. No one had asked me for money. No one had asked for my papers. No one was hunting through the cavities of my car or body for drugs.

So what were they doing? I hadn't done anything, after all. Not really.

Then I heard it. Quietly at first, the sound of a car approaching in another street. Nothing exceptional about that, of course: I'm familiar with the internal combustion engine and its role in contemporary society. But I couldn't help noticing that the cop in the middle, the one who appeared to be leading this crew, glanced toward the end of the block. I followed his eyes.

Initially there was nothing to see except tourist couples walking hand in hand across the intersection, their cheery voices calling as they pointed out souvenirs to each other. For a moment I had a flash of the first time I came to Ensenada, many years ago. I remembered realizing that every bangle and every rug, every copyright infringement and Day of the Dead vignette, had been stamped out somewhere in a factory and that no one here was selling anything unique or genuine. Realizing that, and not caring. Spending days eating fish tacos at two for a dollar, loaded high with fixings and chili, down by the fish market, where the world's most disreputable pelicans battled for scraps in a flurry of brown feathers. Cruising in the late afternoon, country on the car stereo and Indian kids on every street corner, selling subcontracted Chiclets to support their mothers' habits. And nights of shadows and distant shouting, patterns of light on water and wood fires in run-down chalets; cold breezes on the rocks at the waterfront, the warmth of someone who loved me.

That's why I used to come back to Ensenada. To remember those times, and the person I was when they'd happened.

But the car that slowly moved into position wasn't a beat-up old Ford, and there was no one in it that I knew. It was a squad car, and that's what the cops around me had been waiting for. It was a trap, either because they knew who I was, or because it was a slow night and they just felt like it. Either way, it was time to go.

I braced my hands against my car door and whipped it out quickly, catching two of the cops in the stomach and sending them stumbling painfully backward. The remaining cop scrabbled for his holster. I swung a kick at his hands, smacking into his wrist and sending his gun skittering along the pavement. It had been a big night for kicking. Lucky I kept in practice.

The cops in the car saw what was happening, and the vehicle leapt up the street toward me. I jammed the key in the ignition and had my own car moving before I'd even shut the door. There were shouts from the cops behind as I yanked the car around in a tight bend, scattering grit like a line of machine-gun fire, heading straight for the police vehicle.

I kept the car on course, flooring the pedal, but I knew I was going to have to turn. You don't play chicken with the Mexican police. They tend to win. I caught glimpses of tourists watching as I hammered down the road, their mouths falling open as they realized there was local color in prospect, and that the color was likely to be red.

In the front, the faces of two cops stared back at me through their windshield as they got closer and closer. Their passenger looked a little nervous, but one glance at the driver told me what I already knew. If there was going to be a domesticated egg-producing squawker in this confrontation, it sure as hell wasn't going to be him.

At the last moment I yanked the wheel to the right and went caroming off down a side street, narrowly avoiding rolling the car into a storefront. People scattered in all directions as I cursed my luck and tried to figure out what I was going to do next. Behind me I heard the scream of tires as the cops performed an inaccurate U-turn, cracking a few parked cars in the process. I hoped everyone had the proper insurance. It's false economy not to, you know, and there's a place about fifty yards from the border where you almost believe that what you're being sold is worth something. I forget the name, but check it out.

There weren't that many options available to me—you can either leave Ensenada up the coast or down. I figured on going up, but I had to try to convince the cops I was heading the other way. I made a series of hard turns toward the southern end of town—ignoring lights, screaming over the main drag at seventy, and in general displaying extremely little concern for the finer points of road safety. Cars ended up swerving onto the sidewalk, the drivers shouting after me before they'd even come to a halt. I could see their point, but didn't stop to discuss it.

After a couple of hectic minutes I couldn't see anyone in the mirror following me, so I made a sudden left and slowed the car down, pulling in to park neatly between two battered trucks by the side of the road. I edged far enough forward that I could see the crossroads, and then killed the engine. Heart thumping, I waited.

It worked. People don't really expect you to park in the middle of a car chase. They sort of assume you'll keep on driving. After a few seconds I saw the police car go flying over the intersection, but I stayed put a little while longer, wiping the sweat off my palms onto my jeans.

Then I very sedately reversed out of the space and pootled off up the street.

ON THE WAY BACK to the border I tried to call a friend of mine on the Net, a guy called Quat, but there was no reply. I left a message for him to get in touch with me as soon as possible, and just concentrated on not driving into the sea. I was pretty calm by then, telling myself the Mexican cops had just been fishing, rousting a conspicuous Americano for kicks.

Outside Tijuana I stopped to get some gas from a run-down place by the side of the road. I could have waited until I got to the other side of the border, but the station looked like it needed the business. While the attendant was gleefully filling my car up, I took the opportunity to throw the remaining packets of Kims in the trash, and get some proper cigarettes at contraband prices.

I also elected to make use of their men's room, which was a questionable decision. The gas station claimed to be under new management, but the toilets were evidently still under some old management, or more probably governed by an organization that predated the concept of management altogether. Possibly the Spanish Inquisition. The smell was bracing, to say the least. Both of the urinals had been smashed, and one of the cubicles appeared to be where the local horses came when they needed to empty their backs. If so, someone needed to introduce them to the concept of toilet paper, and explain where exactly they should sit.

The remaining cubicle was relatively bearable, and I locked myself in and set about what I had to do. My mind was on other things, like what the hell I was going to do when I got back home, when I heard a knock on the door.

"I'll be out in a minute," I said, zipping myself back up. Maybe the attendant was just worried he wasn't going to get paid.

There was no answer. I was groping through the same sentence in pidgin Spanish, when suddenly I realized it wouldn't be the gas jockey. He had my car keys. I wasn't going anywhere without them.

The knock came again, louder this time.

I looked quickly around, but there was no way out of the cubicle—except, of course, through the door. There never is. Take it from me, if you're ever on the run, a toilet cubicle isn't a great place to hide. They're designed with very little functional flexibility.

"Who is it?" I asked. There was still no answer.

I had my gun with me, but that was no answer either. I'd like to think I've grown up, but it could just be that I've gotten more frightened. I was never a big one for firearms, and encouraging situations in which I might get my head splattered across walls had even less appeal than it used to. The gun's little more than a souvenir, and I haven't fired it in anger in four years. I've fired it in boredom, as my old CD player would testify, but that's not really enough. You have to keep practicing at senseless violence, otherwise you forget the point.

Extreme politeness seemed the only sensible course of action.

So I pulled the gun out, yanked open the door, and screamed at whoever was there to get the fuck facedown on the floor.

The room was empty. Just dirty walls and the sound of three taps dripping out of unison.

I blinked, and swiveled my head both ways around the room. Still no one. My eyes prickled and stung.

"Hi, Hap," said a voice from lower than I would have expected. I slowly tilted my head that way, bringing the gun down with my gaze.

The alarm clock waved up at me. It looked tired, and was spattered with mud.

I lost it.

"Okay, you fuck," I shouted hysterically. "This is it! Now I'm finally going to blow you apart."

"Hap, you don't want to do that . . ."

"Yes, I do."

The clock retreated rapidly toward the exit. "You don't. You really don't."

"Give me one good reason," I yelled, racking a shell up into the breech and knowing that nothing the machine could come up with would be enough. By now we were back out in the lot, and I was aware of the gas guy standing by the car gaping at us, a smile freezing on his face. Maybe it wasn't fair to take the situation out on a clock, but I didn't care. It was the only potential victim around apart from me, and I was bigger than it was. I was also fading big-time. My temples felt like they were full of ice, and a patch of vision in my right eye was turning gray.

The clock knew that time was running out, and spoke very quickly. "I was trying to tell you something down in that smelly place. Something *important*."

I aimed right at the A.M./P.M. indicator. "Like what? That I have a haircut booked at four?"

"That I'm good at some things. Like finding people. I found *you*, didn't I?"

Finger on the trigger, one twitch away from sending the clock to oblivion, I hesitated. "So? What are you saying?"

"I know where she is."

CHAPTER TWO

I got into it the same way as most people, I guess. By accident.

It was a year and a half ago. I was staying the night in Jacksonville, mainly because I didn't have anyplace else to be. At the time it seemed like whenever I couldn't find a road to take me anywhere new, I wound up back in that city, like a yo-yo bouncing back to the hand that threw it away in the first place. I was planning on getting out of Florida the next day, and after my ride let me off, I headed for the blocks around the bus station, where everything costs less. Last time I'd worked had been two weeks before, at a bar down near Cresota Beach, where

I grew up. They didn't like the way I talked to the customers. I didn't care for their attitude toward pay and working conditions. It had been a brief relationship.

I walked the streets until I found a place going by the inspiring and lyrical name of Pete's Rooms. The guy behind the desk was wearing one of the worst shirts I've ever seen, like a painting of a road accident done by someone who had no talent but an awful lot of paint to use up. I didn't ask him if he was Pete, but it seemed a fair assumption. He looked like a Pete. The rate was fifteen dollars a night, Net access in every room. Very reasonable—yet the shirt, unappealing though it was, looked like it had been made on purpose. Maybe I should have thought about that, but it was late and I couldn't be bothered.

My room was on the fourth floor and small, and the air smelled like it had been there since before I was born. I pulled something to drink from my bag, and dragged the room's one ratty chair over to the window. Outside was a fire escape the rats were probably afraid to use, and below that just yellow lights and noise.

I leaned out into humid night and watched people walking up and down the street. You see them in every big city, mangy dogs sniffing for a trail their instincts tell them must start around here someplace. Some people believe in God, or UFOs: others that just around a corner will be the first step on a road toward money, or drugs, or whatever Holy Grail they're programmed for. I wished them well, but not with much hope or enthusiasm. I'd tried most types of MAKE $$$ FAST!!! schemes by then, and they had gotten me precisely nowhere. Roads that begin just around corners have a tendency to lead you right back to where you started.

Though I grew up in Florida, I'd spent most of the previous decade on the West Coast, and I missed it. For the time being I couldn't go back, which left me with nowhere in particular to be. It felt like everything had ground to a halt, as if it would take something pretty major to get my life started up again. Reincarnation, maybe. It had felt that way before, but not quite so bleakly. It was the kind of situation that could get you down.

So I lay on the bed and went to sleep.

I woke up early the next morning, feeling strange. Spacey. Hollow-stomached, and as if someone had stuffed little scratchy balls of crumpled paper inside my eyes. My watch said it was seven o'clock, which didn't make sense. The only time I see 7:00 A.M. is when I've been awake straight through the night.

Then I realized an alarm was going off, and saw that the console in the bedside table was flashing. MESSAGE, it said. I screwed my eyes up tight and looked at the console again. It still said I had a message. I hit the RECEIVE button. The screen went blank for a moment, then fed up some text.

You could have earned $367.77 last night, it read. *To learn more, come by 135 Highwater today. Quote reference* PR/43.

Then it spit out a map. I picked it up; squinted at it.

$367.77 is a lot of nights tending bar.

I changed my shirt and left the hotel.

BY THE TIME I reached Highwater Street I was already losing interest. My head felt fuzzy and dry, as if I'd spent all night doing math in my sleep. A big part of me just wanted to score breakfast somewhere and go sit on a bus, watch the sun haze on window panels until I was somewhere else.

But I didn't. I have a kind of shambling momentum once I'm started. I followed the streets on the map, surprised to find myself getting closer to the business district. The kind of people who spam consoles in cheap hotels generally work out of virtual offices, but Highwater was a wide street with grown-up buildings on either side. 135 itself was a mountain of black plate-glass with a revolving door at the bottom. Unlike many of the other buildings I'd passed, 135 didn't have exterior videowalls extolling with tiresome thoroughness the virtues and success of the people who toiled within. 135 just sat there, not giving anything away. I went in, as much as anything, just to find some shade.

The lobby was similarly uncommunicative, and likewise decked out all in black. It was like they'd acquired a job lot of the color from somewhere and were eager to use it up. I walked across the marble floor to a desk at the far end, my heels tapping in the cool silence. A woman sat there in a pool of yellow light, looking at me with a raised eyebrow.

"Can I help you?" she asked. Her tone made it clear she thought it was unlikely.

"I was told to come here and quote a reference."

I speak better than I look. The woman's face didn't light up or anything, but she tapped a button on her keyboard and turned her eyes to the screen. "And that is?"

I told her, and she scrolled down through some list for a while. "Okay," she said. "Here's how it is. Two options. The first is I give you $171.39 and you go away with no further obligation. The second is that you take the elevator on the right and go up to the thirty-fourth floor, where Mr. Stratten will meet with you presently."

"And you arrive at $171.39 how, exactly?"

"Your potential earnings less a twenty-five-dollar handling fee, divided by two and rounded up to the nearest cent."

"How come I get only half the money?"

"Because you're not on contract. You go up and meet Mr. Stratten, maybe that will change."

"And in that case I get the full $367?"

She winked. "You're kind of bright, aren't you?"

The elevator was very pleasant. Tinted mirrors, low lights; quiet, leisurely. It spoke of money, and lots of it. Not much happened during the trip up.

When the doors opened, I found myself faced with a corridor. A large chrome sign on the wall said REMtemps in a suitably soul-destroying typeface. Underneath it said SLEEP TIGHT. SLEEP RIGHT. I walked the way the sign pointed and wound up at another reception desk. The girl wore a badge that said she was Sabrina, and her hair was done up in a weirdly complex manner, doubtless the result of several hours of some asswipe stylist's attention.

I'd thought the girl downstairs was a top-flight patronizer, but compared to Sabrina she was servility itself. Sabrina's manner suggested I was some kind of lower-echelon vermin: lower than a rat, for sure, maybe on a par with a particularly ill-favored mole, and after thirty seconds with her I felt the bacteria in my stomach start to join in sneering at me. She told me to take a seat, but I didn't. Partly to annoy her, but mainly because I hate sitting in reception areas. I read somewhere it puts you in a subordinate position right off the bat. I'm great at the prehiring tactics—it's just a shame it goes to pieces afterward.

"Mr. Thompson, good morning. I'm Stratten."

I turned to see a man standing behind me, hand held out. He had a strong face, black hair starting to silver on the temples. Like any other tall, middle-aged guy in a sober suit, but more polished: as if he were a release-standard human instead of the beta versions you normally see wandering around. His hand was firm and dry, as was his smile.

I was shown into a small room off the main corridor. Stratten sat behind a desk, and I lounged back in the other available chair.

"So what's the deal?" I asked, trying to sound relaxed. There was something about the guy opposite that put me on edge. I couldn't place his accent. East Coast somewhere, probably, but flattened, made deliberately average—like an actor covering his past.

He leaned forward and turned the console on the desk to face me. "See if there's anything you recognize," he said, and pressed a switch. The console chittered and whirred for a moment, and flashed up *PR/43 @ 18/5/2016*.

The screen bled to black, and then faded up again to show a corridor. The camera—if that's what it was—walked forward along it a little way. Drab green walls trailed off into the distance. On the left-hand side was another corridor. The camera turned—and showed that this hallway was exactly the same as the first. Going a little quicker now, it tramped that way for a while before making another turn into yet another identical corridor. There didn't seem to be any shortage of hallways, or of new turnings to make. Occasional chips in the paint relieved the monotonous olive of the walls, but other than that it just went on and on and on.

I looked up after five minutes to see Stratten watching me. I shook my head. Stratten made a note on a piece of paper, and then typed something rapidly on the console's keyboard. "Not very distinctive," he said. "I don't think the donor's very imaginative. And you lose a great deal, just getting the visual. Try this."

The picture on the screen changed. It showed a pair of hands holding a piece of water. I know "piece of water" doesn't make much sense, but that's what it looked like. The hands were nervously fondling the liquid, and a quiet male voice was relayed from the console's speaker.

Oh, I don't know, it said doubtfully. *About five? Six and a half, maybe?*

The hands put the water down on a shelf and picked up another bit. This water was a little smaller. The voice paused for a moment, then spoke more confidently. *Definitely a two. Two and a third at most.*

The hands placed this second piece down on top of the first. The two bits of water didn't meld, but remained distinct. One hand moved out of sight, and there was a different sound then, a soft, metallic scraping. That's when I got my first twitch.

Stratten noticed. "Getting warmer?"

"Maybe," I said, leaning to get a closer look at the console. The point of view had swiveled slightly, to show a battered filing cabinet. One of the drawers was open, and the hands were carefully picking up pieces of water—which I now saw were arrayed all around, in piles of differing sizes—and putting them one by one into different folders. Every now and then the voice would swear to itself, take out one of the pieces of water, and return it to a pile—not necessarily the one it had originally come from. The hands started moving more and more quickly, putting water in, taking water out, and all the time there was this low background noise of the voice reciting different numbers.

I stared at the screen, losing awareness of the office around me and becoming absorbed. I forgot that Stratten was even there, and it was largely to myself that I eventually spoke.

"Each of the pieces of water has a different value, not based on size. Somewhere between one and twenty-seven. Each drawer in the filing cabinet has to be filled with the same value of water, but no one told him how to figure out how much each piece is worth."

The screen went blank, and I turned my head to see Stratten smiling at me. "You remember," he said.

"That was the dream I had just before I woke up this morning. What the fuck's going on?"

"We took a liberty last night," Stratten said. "The proprietor of the hotel you stayed in has an arrangement with us. We subsidize the cost of his rooms, and provide the consoles."

"Why?" I reached unthinkingly into my pocket and pulled out a cigarette. Instead of shouting at me or pulling a gun, Stratten merely opened a drawer and handed me an ashtray.

"We're always looking for new people, people who need money and aren't too fussy about how they get it. This is the best way we've found of locating them."

"Great, so you found me. And so?"

"I want to offer you a job as a REMtemp."

"You're going to have to unpack that for me."

He did. At some length. This is the gist:

A few years previously, someone had found a way of taking dreams out of people's heads in real time. A device placed near the head of a sufficiently well-off client could keep an eye out for electromagnetic fields of particular types, and divert the mental states of which they were a function out of the dreamer's unconscious mind and into an erasing device. The government wasn't keen on the idea, but the inventors had hired an attorney trained in quantum law, and no one was really sure what the legal position was anymore. "It depends" was as near as they could get.

In the meantime, a covert industry was born.

The obvious trade was in nightmares, but they don't happen very often, and clients balked at buying systems they needed only every couple of months. They'd pay on a dream-by-dream basis, and the people who'd developed the technology wanted more return on their investment. Also, nightmares aren't usually so bad, and if they are, they're generally giving you information you could do with knowing. If you're scared crapless about something, there's often a good reason for it.

So gradually the market shifted to anxiety dreams instead. Kind of like nightmares, but not usually as frightening, these are the dreams you get when you're stressed, or tired, or fretting about something. Often they consist of complex and minute tasks the dreamer has to endlessly go through, not really understanding what they're doing and constantly having to restart. Then just when you're starting to get a grip on what's going on, you slide into something else, and the whole cycle starts again. Anxiety dreams usually commence just after you've gone to sleep—in which case they'll screw up your whole night—or in the couple of hours before waking. Either way, you wake up feeling tired and worn out, in no state to start a working day because it feels like you've already just been through one.

Anxiety dreams are much more frequent than nightmares, and tend to affect precisely the kind of middle- and high-management executives who were the primary market for dream disposal. The guys who owned the technology changed their pitch, rewrote the copy in their brochures, and started making some serious money.

But there was a problem.

It turned out that you couldn't just erase dreams. That wasn't the way it worked. Over the course of eighteen months the company started getting more and more complaints, and in the end they worked out what was going on.

When you erase a dream, all you destroy is the imagery, the visuals that would have played over the dreamer's inner eye. The substance of the dream, an intangible quality that seemed impossible to isolate, remains. The more dreams a client has removed, the more of this substance is left behind: invisible, indestructible, but carrying some kind of weight. This substance hangs around the room the dream has been erased in, and after thirty or so erasures it gets to the point where the room becomes uninhabitable. It's like walking into a thunderstorm of competing subconscious impulses—absolutely silent but impossible to bear. After a few weeks the dreams seem to coalesce still further, making the air so thick that it becomes impossible to even enter the room at all.

Unfortunately, the kind of client who could afford dream disposal was exactly the type who was turned on by litigation. After the company had swallowed a few huge out-of-court settlements on bedrooms that were now impassable, they turned their minds to finding a way out of the problem. They tried diverting the dreams into storage databanks instead of just erasing them. This didn't work either. Some of the dream still seeped out of the hard disks, regardless of how airtight the casing.

Then finally it clicked. The dreams weren't being used up. Maybe if they were . . .

They gave it a try. A client's transmitting machine was connected to a receiver placed near the bed of a volunteer, and two anxiety dreams were successfully diverted from the mind of one to the other. The client woke up nicely rested and full of vim, ready for another hard day in the money mines. The volunteer had a shitty night of dull dreams he couldn't quite remember, but was paid for his troubles.

No residue was left in the room. The dream had vanished. The cash started flowing again.

"And that's what you did to me last night?" I asked Stratten, a little pissed at having my mind invaded.

He held up his hands placatingly. "Trust me, you'll be glad we did. People have varying ability to use up other people's dreams. Most can handle two a night without much difficulty, three at the most. They get up feeling ragged, and drag themselves through the day. Usually they work only every other night—but they still make eight, nine hundred dollars a week. You're different."

"How's that?" I knew this was most likely a stroke, but didn't care. They didn't come along that often.

"You took four dreams last night without breaking sweat. The two you've just seen, and another two—one of which was so boring I can't bear to even watch just the visuals. You could probably have taken a couple more. You could make a lot of money, Mr. Thompson."

"How much is a lot?"

"We pay according to dream duration, with additional payments if the dreams are especially complex or tedious. Last night you erased over three hundred dollars' worth—and that doesn't factor in a bonus for the dullest one. Depending how often you worked, you could be earning between two and three thousand dollars. A week." He closed the pitch. "And we pay cash. Dream disposal is still in an unstable state with regard to legality. We find it more convenient to obfuscate the nature of our business to some of the authorities."

He smiled. I smiled back.

Three thousand dollars is an *awful* lot of bartending.

It wasn't a difficult decision.

I SIGNED a nondisclosure contract. I was leased a receiver, and had it explained to me. Basically I could go anywhere in the continental United States as long as I kept the machine within six feet of my head while I was asleep. I didn't have to go to bed at any particular time, because the dreams booked to me were just spooled into memory. As soon as the device sensed I was in REM sleep, it fed the backlog into my head. When I got up in the morning, my nightwork would be there on the screen like a list of email messages: how long each of the dreams had been, when it started and finished, and whether it qualified for bonus payment or was just hack work.

And at the bottom of the list, the good news. A figure in dollars. I found I could take six or seven dreams a night without too much difficulty. Some days I'd be groggy and find it difficult to concentrate on anything more complex than smoking, but when that happened I'd just take the following night off.

After six months I was recalled to REMtemps's offices and Stratten asked if I'd like to volunteer for a higher proportion of bonus dreams. I said "Hell, yes," and my earnings took another leap upward. I met a hacker called Quat on the Net, and hired him to write me a demon that would circulate my earnings around a variety of virtual accounts: Every now and then the IRS or some other ratfink would close in on one of them, but when that happened I'd just swallow the loss and keep the rest of it on the move. I also paid Quat a lot of money to erase a particular incident from the LAPD's crimebank, which meant I could go back to California.

It was a good life. I traveled from place to place, this time as a person with money instead of someone looking for a score. After a while it seemed natural to wear better clothes, to head for the upscale hotels. I got used to the other things that money gets you, like a modicum of respect, and bed companions who don't issue you with an invoice in the morning. I kept in touch with the few people I cared about through the phone, the Net, and occasional flying visits. I dropped in on Deck in LA a couple of times, and the city began to lose its darkness for me. I began to think of moving back there, of letting it be my place once again.

There were occasional downsides. Boredom. The exhaustion that came after a night full of bonuses, and the emotional flatness from being forever on the move and never having a relationship that lasted longer than a few days. There were periods when I'd go a little weird, and I came to realize that was because I'd spent so many nights having other people's dreams, I hadn't had time for any of my own. When that happened, I'd clock off, let my mind catch up, and do the subconscious boogie. After a few days I'd be fine again.

I'd found some action that was safe, I was good at, and paid big-time money.

That should have been enough.

THEN FIVE MONTHS AGO I got a call from Stratten. It came very early in the morning, and I was crashed out in a king-sized bed on the top floor of a hotel in New Orleans, the debris of a hard evening's pleasure spread all around me. By then I was back more or less full-time in LA, and had an apartment in Griffith which I called home. I wasn't supposed to hang in one place, however, so I took enough trips out of town to convince REMtemps I was still itinerant.

I couldn't remember the name of the woman beside me, but she was a whiz at answering the phone. By the time I'd realized it was ringing, she already had it up out of its cradle and at her ear. When she passed it over to me I sat up, head foggy and full of half-remembered tasks and confusions. I suppressed the urge to look at the receiver to see how much I'd earned. From the way I felt, I knew it was going to be considerable.

"Mr. Thompson," said that voice, and I instantly became more awake. "Who answered the phone?"

"I don't know," I said stupidly. "I mean, why? What difference does it make?"

"I assume she's someone you've met quite recently?"

"Yes." I glanced across the room to where the woman was standing. Candy, I think her name may have been, though she may well have spelled it with an I. At the end, I mean. She seemed nice, and I got the feeling she actually liked me. I was wondering whether she might be interested in hooking up with me for a while. A whole week, maybe, until I went back to LA. At that moment she was making coffee with no clothes on, and I was hoping Stratten would stop talking soon.

"You met her last night, correct?" he asked. I admitted that was the case. "And she's in *your* hotel room. But she answered the phone after a single ring."

I took a sip from the beer bottle by the bed. "So?"

"Think about it."

I watched as Candy stirred just the right amount of sugar into my coffee. I got what he was driving at. "Don't talk shit," I said. Candy winked at me and slipped into the john.

"Get rid of her and come to the office," Stratten told me. "I have a proposal for you." The line went dead.

I got out of bed and put the dream receiver in my bag. The readout said I'd earned over a thousand dollars. I got dressed, and when Candy came back out, spruced up and fresh and ready to play, I said I had to go out for a while. She took it badly, and then well, and then badly again. She tried a lot of things to get me to stay. When it was clear that wasn't working, she said she'd hang in the room and wait for me. For however long it took.

Call me someone with low self-esteem, but women don't usually react that way after a single night in my company. I'm kind of an acquired taste. It wasn't proof, but it was enough to make me gather my things and walk out the door, leaving her standing shouting after me. In the elevator I did what I'd been told to do in such circumstances, and pressed a recessed button on the side of the dream receiver. There was a soft "crump" sound from within, and the readout panel went black. The unit was now dead, logic board fused into inexplicability.

On the plane to Jacksonville it occurred to me to wonder why—if Candy had been some kind of federal agent—she hadn't just done whatever she needed to do while I was sleeping. If there was one thing a REMtemp was guaranteed to do most nights, it was catch some zees. Maybe she'd needed to talk to me, get names or something. I'd only ever worked on the wrong side of the law, so I didn't know how the good guys did things. Perhaps they'd had me pegged as a potential witness against Stratten, in which case they obviously hadn't met the guy. It didn't make much difference. I had to go back to the office anyway now, to pick up a replacement receiver.

Slumped over a table in an upmarket café around the corner, I mainlined a gallon of coffee and a half pack of cigarettes before reporting to REMtemps. Usually the fog faded to a soft confusion after a couple of hours, but this morning it felt like I'd never slept in my whole life. I wanted to be sharp to respond to whatever proposal Stratten had in mind, but in the end I settled for being not actually asleep and just lurched over there.

This time we didn't meet in a side office, but in Stratten's own den. The office was no bigger than your average football field, but luckily we sat at the same end, so we didn't have to shout. I told him I'd done what he told me, and he smiled. I added that I'd fried the machine, also as per instructions, and that I'd need another one. He smiled again. Then he started talking.

Though I didn't know it, a number of the company's most important clients now asked for me specifically. Most REMtemps left vestiges behind, elements personal to the dreamer that the temps couldn't assimilate. I erased the whole lot, every little shadow and whisper. Hence the bonuses. Hence also the fact that Stratten wanted to offer me a more lucrative line of work.

Memories.

As soon as he said the word, I started shaking my head vigorously and at high speed. Memories can be externalized, but it doesn't work in the same way as dreams. They can't be erased because they are a function of something that has happened in the real world. They can merely be blanked or stored somewhere else, on a temporary or permanent basis, and doing so is absolutely and completely illegal.

For a start, it means that polygraphs don't work. If a suspect genuinely has no memory of committing a crime, fooling the lie detector is a breeze. In a way, it isn't even deception. As far as the guy is concerned, the incident never happened.

Plus this: People are their memories. What has happened is what you are. If you remove the childhood incidents where someone learned right from wrong, you end up with a guy who's kind of difficult to deal with. He just doesn't care. Such people don't understand why they shouldn't steal, or rape, or murder—and that makes them better at stealing, raping, and murdering. In the unlikely event they do get caught, another memory dump just before the polygraph will completely blank that line of evidence right away.

A test case eighteen months before had settled the issue. A freelance proxy dreamer who'd agreed to carry a criminal's memory of a certain event during the trial was sentenced to two life terms—exactly half what the real culprit would have received had he been convicted.

In other words, memories weren't a trade with long-term prospects, and I said as much to Stratten. He heard me out, and when I'd ground to a halt, he let a silence settle. After it had gone on so long that it seemed like what I'd said had been to another person on some other day, he began.

"Yes," he said. "The caretaking of criminal recall is illegal."

"Good," I said affably. "That's settled, then. Where do I pick up my new receiver?"

"However," Stratten continued as if I'd said nothing at all, "the memories I'm referring to do not relate to illegal activities. I'm talking about trivial things, and only temporary transferrals."

"If they're that trivial, let the clients deal with them," I suggested. "And if it's only temporary, tell them to try a few beers instead. Nope, and no thank you. Also, no."

"Five thousand dollars a memory," he said. I stopped speaking before my mouth had even framed the next word. "The memory could be a single instant, an individual fact, and you'd never hold one for more than a week. Usually only a few hours. You could score a quarter million dollars over twelve months without breaking sweat. Plus you can still do the dreamwork."

He let that sink in for a while, and I thought about it. About pulling in seven figures a year. The last couple of years had been good, but wealth has a way of operating on a sliding scale. When you've bought all the stuff you can at your current level, you start noticing the things you still can't have. And start wanting that stuff instead.

Looked at another way: a couple years' work, some sensible investments, and I'd never have to lift a synapse again.

"No," I said. I knew where I was, and I was doing okay.

"You'll find the answer's yes," Stratten said, "when you ask me where you pick up your new receiver."

My mind was still dulled from the night's work: I didn't get what he was driving at. I just fed him his line. "Where?"

"Unless you accept my offer, you don't," he said. "You take memory work. Or you're fired."

I stared at him. "You're a fucker, aren't you," I said.

"I have heard that opinion expressed." His smile didn't waver, and I realized it wasn't a smile and probably never had been.

I looked out the window for a while, more to keep him waiting than for any other reason. I understood now that Candy hadn't really liked me, and that she hadn't even been a fed. She'd been nothing more than a manipulation tool hired by Stratten. He would have known that I'd just woken up when he called, and that I'd be unable to judge the situation properly after a night full of heavy bonuses and bed-oriented frolicking. He was right. Candy had done her job well.

At that moment I understood both that I didn't really have any idea what Stratten was capable of, and that I just couldn't tell with women anymore. I'm not sure which was worse.

Stratten had me, and he knew it. Without dreamwork I was back on the streets. I had money squirreled away, spinning around the tracks Quat had laid for it in the ether, but not enough. Too much of it had been pissed away.

With memory work I could buy my own bar if it came to it.

"Okay," I told Stratten.

CHAPTER THREE

At two-thirty in the morning I saw her, walking up the street toward a small hotel a couple of blocks off the boulevard. It was called the Nirvana Inn, but unless that ineffable plane has peeling paint on the outside and no room service after ten, I suspect the name was a bit of a misnomer. I was sitting in a diner opposite, drinking bad coffee and biding my time, and I recognized her immediately. It was Laura Reynolds. No question.

This was the first time I'd seen someone I was caretaking for, and it felt disturbing, wrong. Like remembering you're dead, or seeing a doppelgänger who looks nothing like you. Laura

Reynolds was in her late twenties, thin and wired—trying to remember how to look like drift life after years of learning to forget. Her face was bony, pretty, intense. She walked like someone who'd spent most of the evening in a bar and flash-lit by neon in the slanting rain, and she looked like a computer sprite who had suddenly found itself in the wrong video game, with no instructions.

I sympathized just for a moment. I felt pretty much the same way.

"That's her, isn't it?" said the clock, who was standing on the counter, next to my cooling cup. I'd let him ride back with me in the car to LA. It seemed only fair.

I nodded. "I owe you one." The clock had refused to tell me how he'd known where the woman was, saying it was a timepiece secret. I'd get it out of him sooner or later, but for the time being it didn't really matter. I'd found Laura Reynolds.

I stayed put for a while, in case the flunky I'd talked to in the Nirvana forgot the fifty I'd laid on him and told the woman someone was looking for her. When five minutes had passed without incident, I slipped off my stool, stumbling slightly. I leaned on the counter for a moment, blinking and waiting for my brain to clear.

The clock looked up at me dubiously, still dabbing the mud off itself with a napkin and glass of water I'd acquired for it. "What are you going to do?"

"Just watch me," I said, not really knowing. My first plan was simply to talk to her. Tell her that what she'd done was bad, and get her to take her memory back. I'm an eternal optimist. If that didn't work, then it was going back into her head by force. Either way, Laura Reynolds was coming with me. I had to get her in the same room as my receiver, and get hold of a transmitter from somewhere—hence my call to Quat. If Laura Reynolds needed persuading, I'd use the gun, but I wasn't going to pull it out in this diner. The homeboys holding up the counter all looked far tougher than me: One flash of my piece and my guess was they'd be packing bazookas. If they were on contract, I'd probably be okay, but if they were freelance they might just whack me speculatively and see if anyone was interested in paying after the fact. The sad thing about my life is that some people might well be. I slipped the clock in my pocket, slid a couple of dollars under my cup, and left.

It was cold outside, and I took a second to lay a perfunctory curse on the head of a certain production company. A couple of years ago they were shooting northern Maine on the Mitsubishi lot, and couldn't be bothered with all the sprinklers and wind machines and stuff. So they got permission to change the micro-climate for the afternoon instead. It got fucked up, naturally, and now you can never tell what the weather's going to be like. It's even more like living inside a madman's head than it used to be, but the movie went over big in Europe, so nobody likes to complain.

I jogged across the street, keeping my hands in my pockets and my head down, just part of the scenery, someone wanting to get someplace out of the rain. Up at the next corner I saw a car had been pulled over, a police vehicle angled just ahead of it. Two guys stood with their hands on the hood, legs spread. One of the cops was methodically stamping on something on the ground, and I relaxed. Just a routine cigarette bust.

The hotel's foyer was hushed and dimly lit. A few plants lolled listlessly in pots around the walls, and the carpet seemed fairly clean. It was one of those places where you wonder what the point of it is: not expensive enough to be worth going to on purpose, nor sufficiently cheap to be the only place you could af-ford. Just part of the string of islands that salesmen and other salaried itinerants hop between, every room sanitized and Bible-positive for their protection and comfort. I've stayed in a million such places myself, and they're like their own little country. Drab, anonymous suites; staff bored out of their tiny minds; the restaurant populated each night only by a scattering of men of uncertain ages, sitting at tables by themselves. Hair damp from a shower after a long day's drive, jeans with a crease ironed in, staring into the middle distance as they chew, their eyes dull from a preliminary check on what will be on the porno channels later on. I was always somehow surprised that such hotels didn't have their own graveyards out back, that their customers were evidently allowed to rejoin normal society after they'd finally had their coronaries.

The flunky I'd leaned on was nowhere to be seen, but that was okay. If I had to come back this way with a struggling woman in tow, I needed as little external input as possible. Laura Reynolds had a room on the second floor, so I took the stairs. It doesn't do to make elevators feel too important. More plants lurked at each bend in the staircase, suspiciously motion-less, as if they had been gossiping with each other only seconds before.

The corridor was long and quiet. I stood outside her room for a few moments, but couldn't hear anything inside. I realized then that I should have cornered the flunky after all, got a copy of the key to her room in case she refused to let me in. Probably he would have raised some footling objection, but I'm an old hand at dealing with that kind of thing. Used to be, anyhow. The fact that I was out of practice was demonstrated by my forget-ting about the whole issue of entry to the room. Sure, you can kick the door down, but it's not as easy as it looks and tends to be hard on the feet. Also, it makes a shitload of noise, which is seldom desirable. Muttering irritably, I turned the handle any-way, already reconciled to tramping back down the stairs and making a nuisance of myself.

The door was unlocked.

I stood very still for a moment, waiting for the shouting to start. It didn't. So I carefully pushed the door open.

Inside was the usual stuff, the unnatural flora of mid-range hotel rooms. The corner of a bed. A battered dresser with an old-looking teleputer squatting on it. Beyond, a circular table with a lamp, and a pile of pamphlets that could only be invitations to the local attractions. Whatever the hell they were supposed to be. I still couldn't hear anything, not even the tuneless hum-ming or occasional sighs most people feel obliged to undertake when alone, to smooth the quietness out.

I stepped into the little entryway and closed the door quietly behind me. On my right was an open closet with a few dresses on those hangers designed not to be stolen, presumably on the assumption that people paying seventy dollars a night for a room make a point of stealing a dollar's worth of coat hangers every-where they go. Why would they do that? The next hotel's going to have its own stock, isn't it? And you can't even use them to hang a shirt in the bathroom while you shower, which is as close to ironing as I ever get.

I took a cautious step into the main room area. The door to the bathroom was shut, and I heard a faint splashing sound.

I let go of the gun in my pocket and took a look around the room. A small suitcase lay open on the second bed, the interior a jumble of good underwear. A bottle of vodka stood on the bedside table, already missing about a third of its contents. Other than that, she had made as little dent on the room as a ghost that walked especially lightly and tidied up as it went. A bedside clock-and-teamaker was staring at me with wide eyes, but I held my finger up to my lips and it remained silent.

I padded back to the door and locked it. Then turned to the closet, took the dresses off their hangers with hardly any struggle at all, and folded them fairly neatly into her suitcase. I zipped it up, poured myself a smallish drink, and sat in the armchair to wait. Chances were she'd come out wrapped in a towel—most people do even when they're alone. If not, I'd avert my eyes. I wasn't going to just charge straight into the bathroom. I try to be polite, and anyway, a few minutes' grace would help ensure the cops were gone from the corner outside.

I beguiled the time reading the hotel's literature, learning at some length of the management and staff's yearning to fulfill my every need. Probably they actually meant the person who was paying for the room, but I scrawled a note on the suggestions sheet anyway, asking for some proper coat hangers. I also discovered that the cost of the room included a complimentary continental breakfast, which annoyed me, as usual. Continental breakfast? Continental shit, more like. You sleep for eight hours, traverse great Jungian gulfs of unconsciousness, and what do they offer you on reentry to our dread prison-world?

A croissant.

I mean, *what*? No sausage? No eggs, no fucking hash browns even? What use is a croissant to anyone, especially first thing in the morning? And yet everybody sits there picking at it, pretending it's food, despite the fact that they would never eat it at home. Hotels around the world have seized on the continental breakfast not because it has any value, or because it's what anyone wants, but because it's cheap and requires no effort. If a hotel offers a complimentary continental breakfast, what they're really saying is "There is no proper breakfast" or "There is, but you have to pay for it."

When I realized I was on the verge of shouting, I put the menu to one side and just waited.

AFTER STRATTEN hired me to receive memories, life carried on pretty much the same, superficially at least. I could still go more or less where I wanted, though I took more care to cover my tracks. I gave up the one-night stands, with very little regret. If the only way you can feel alive is with a novel breast in your hand, you're not doing either of you any good. I closed out all my old credit cards, and got new ones under fake IDs. I worked maybe one, two nights on dreams, just to keep my hand in, then a couple of times a week I'd get a call and be told to be somewhere secluded, with my new machine, at a particular time. I had to let them know exactly where I was, because memories have greater weight than dreams and can be transmitted only somewhere specific, but I made sure I was on the road again an hour later. I also made sure I was alone at the moment of transferral, because when you're giving or receiving memories, your mind's wide open, and it wouldn't take much for someone to implant a little suggestion there.

A momentary blackout, and then a part of someone else's life was in my head. Sometimes the fragments were as long as a few hours, but generally they were much shorter. I kept them for an afternoon, a couple of days, a week at the most, and then a similar session would take them away again.

Most of the memories were straightforward. I was never told why the client was leaving them with me, but it was pretty easy to guess. Once a week a guy would lose the fact he was married, so he'd feel less guilty while he was spending the afternoon with his mistress. An executive would obscure an object lesson his mother had given him about morality, so as to make fucking over a colleague a little easier. A woman would forget something harsh she said to her little brother minutes before a car mounted the curb and killed him, just so as to find a little peace.

Adolescent experiments with people of the same sex. Financial indiscretions. Sticky afternoons with borderline-legal prostitutes. The usual trivia of sin.

Other memories were stranger. Fragments, like a cat walking along a wall, leaping safely to the ground, and then turning a corner and disappearing. A girl's face, laughing, with branches moving gracefully in the wind overhead. The sound at night of a stream gurgling past an open window in a bedroom. I never got any context, just those little garments of remembrance, and had no way of working out why someone might pay five large ones for a holiday from them.

It was kind of weird to spend an afternoon, once a week, convinced I'd married someone named David, but I'm a fairly together guy and realized it wasn't likely I would forget something like that if it had really happened. Some of the memory dumps contained strong elements of their owners' more general personality: little parallel universes, sideways glimpses of other possible lives and fates. But most of the memories were already used to being shunted to the side, and didn't really mess me up. I hemmed them in with enough self-awareness to undermine the truths they purported to tell, and after the allotted time the client took them back, and they vanished from my head. I could remember what it was that I briefly held a memory of, but I could easily tell, once it had gone, what was my experience and what had been someone else's.

I don't know if there were any side effects. Maybe a few. I found myself getting tired more easily, and misbehaving less, but that could have been any number of things. I'd been on the road too long. Maybe the time was coming when I needed to settle down again. Doing that would mean giving up the memory and dream work, because a stationary target would be easy for the feds to find. I knew that what I did was harmless, but the authorities would be likely to see it another way. I didn't know if I was ready to stop earning this kind of money yet, and I didn't know whether Stratten would let me. Also there was the small question of who I'd settle down with. I had good friends in LA, like Deck, but nobody significant of the opposite sex. There hadn't been anyone like that, if the truth be known, for over three years. Most men, in their heart of hearts, believe that there's something that they can do, some change that can be made in their lives that will help them find that special person. Find as many of them as possible, in fact, especially ones with cute bisexual friends. For me it was traveling around, but I was looking for only one. The one for me. I guess I believed that if I kept on moving, sooner or later, in some unregarded burg in the middle of nowhere I'd turn a corner and find her—that person who'd always been looking for me, too. It was my version of the trail that must start somewhere, I suppose. I also suspected that I'd already had that person, and that the trail had stopped there.

So I carried on, caretaking pieces of other people's lives, and wishing that once in a while someone would lend me a *good* memory for a change. I toyed with a little smack every now and then, just to dull the noise in my head of other people's bad times. I discovered what it was like to be someone else, and found myself even less inclined to own a gun. I got occasional headaches, bad enough to put me on the bench for a few days.

But for the most part it was okay, and if I needed a reason, I just watched the money flowing into my account.

Until three days ago, it had all been going fine.

I SHOULD HAVE WORKED it out a lot sooner. The unlocked door was a big clue, if nothing else, and I knew better than anyone what it was like inside her head. But I had no reason to expect her to do something stupid—had good evidence to think otherwise, in fact.

After about ten minutes I stood up and waited outside the bathroom door. Sure, women can spend untold amounts of time in the tub, but three o'clock in the morning is rarely the chosen time. Women usually save that kind of indulgence for when you're already late for going out. I was prepared to be accommodating, because I know how important feeling clean can be, but I really didn't have time for this. The cops outside would be long gone, and I wanted to move. I had to talk to people, make arrangements. My head seemed to be fairly stable, but that wouldn't necessarily last. I also wanted to check the news.

Then I realized what was missing. I leaned closer and listened. No humming, not even the smallest swish of water being moved by a lazy hand. I tried the bathroom door. It was locked.

I kicked it down.

Laura Reynolds was lying in a tub of cooling water, still wearing her panties and bra. The rest of her clothes were folded neatly on the toilet seat. Her head had flopped down onto her shoulder, and her eyes were closed. Her sharp, pretty face had gone smooth and still. The water was red, and there was blood all over the tiled floor. Her skin was white, lips blue.

I started moving very fast.

I yanked the plug out of the tub, grabbed a couple of hand towels from the rail. Her right arm lolled just under the water. As I pulled it up, I saw that the cut wasn't as deep as it could have been, and that she'd missed the major tendons. I wrapped it tightly in the towel and hung it over the edge of the tub, then reached across for the other arm.

The cut there was a lot deeper. Probably the opening slice.

Though maybe not: could be the weaker cut had been the first, and when she'd seen the tunnel open in front of her had decided she might as well run down it as fast as she could. Blood was still slicking out of the wrist in major quantities, and once the towel was around the gash I saw this wasn't going to be enough. Hot water and alcohol had thinned her blood, and it was eager to come out and play. A hotel terry robe hung on the back of the door, and I tugged the belt out and cinched it tight around her upper arm. She stirred then, for the first time; one of her eyelids flickered like some bug's sluggish wing.

Bracing myself with one foot on the tub, I bent forward and tried to pull her up. Though she was slim, she was hard to maneuver, and I nearly pitched forward onto my face. Eventually I got her slumped against the back wall, and held her there while I grabbed the robe and wrapped it around her shoulders. I tried getting her arms through the holes, but it was too difficult and I didn't want to dislodge the towels. In the end I just tipped her over my shoulder and carried her into the bedroom.

She moaned quietly as I laid her on the bed, but gave no sign of moving. I reopened her suitcase, grabbed a few handfuls of clothes, and shoved them into the pockets of my coat. Then I hauled her back over my shoulder and carried her out into the corridor. A quick look either way told me no one was there, which was good, because this was going badly enough as it was. It didn't even occur to me that I should have looked for her handbag until the elevator doors had shut behind me, and at that point I decided she'd just have to live without it.

I was halfway across the lobby downstairs, when I heard an exclamation behind me. I turned unsteadily—unconscious and seminude bodies are difficult to manage—to see the flunky staring at me openmouthed, hand already reaching for the phone.

"Private joke," I said.

The flunky eyed the blood-soaked towels. "Excuse me?"

"She's a heavy sleeper. Sometimes I just come along and take her somewhere weird so when she wakes up she wonders where the hell she is."

"Sir, I don't believe you."

"Does this help?" I asked, pulling my gun out and pointing it straight at his head.

"Very amusing," he said, and his hand left the phone and crept back to his side.

"Keep laughing for a while," I suggested. "Or I'll come back and explain it again."

I lurched around the corner to where I'd parked the car, and laid Laura Reynolds across the backseat. Then I got in and drove away, knowing that if I didn't get her to a doctor within a very short time, my life had just gotten even worse.

As I two-wheeled onto Santa Monica Boulevard, I nearly totaled us both, swerving to avoid a small group of freezers making their way across the road. I could have just driven straight at them, but I make a policy of not tangling with refrigerating appliances. They're really heavy.

WHEN WE WERE safely heading in the right direction, I called Deck. It took him a while to understand what I was saying, but he agreed to do as I asked. Then I flipped the phone to the Net and tried Quat again. It rang and rang. I frowned, cut the connection, redialed. Okay, it was late, but Quat was always up, and whenever he was awake he was on the Net. Still no answer.

I left the phone on callback with a redirect to the apartment, and concentrated on the road as we crossed Wilshire into Beverly Hills. You should know that I'm not a big fan of driving. Never have been. I realize this undermines me in the view of any red-blooded American, but so be it. Lots of people still bemoan the fact that kids spend all their time playing computer games: I say it's the only thing that's going to prepare them for real life. Driving equals long stretches of boredom, during which lunatics will randomly pop up and attempt to kill you—interspersed with pockets of hell where absolutely everything is out to get you. They call these pockets "cities," and they're best avoided unless you happen to live there. Give me a fistfight in a bar, and I'll hold my own. Send me around the beltway at rush hour—fuck off. I'll take a cab. Or walk.

After the turn onto Western, I pulled over to get a proper look at Laura Reynolds. She was still breathing, but the rise and fall of her chest was shallow. The blood around the cut on her right arm was congealing nicely, but the other still looked raw and fresh. I loosened the tourniquet, then retightened it before setting off again. I really hoped Deck got hold of Woodley, or I was fucked. The only alternative was taking her to a hospital, in which case I'd lose her. I couldn't stand guard the whole time, and she'd already proved she was determined to escape one way or another.

When I turned off Los Feliz I was happy to see there wasn't much of a line for entry into Griffith. There're only twenty entrances around the entire district, and at certain times of day getting in can be a major pain in the ass. As we approached the wall, I saw a knot of armed guards peering in the direction of the car, and was pleased to note that even at this late hour security was working for the inhabitants' protection.

In 2007 someone decided that Griffith Park wasn't operating to its full potential. They felt the whole "park" thing, in fact, was a little bit twentieth-century. It was all very well having a huge open space with a couple of golf courses and areas for boy scouts to tramp around, but there were other uses the land could be put to. Upscale residential, for example. The nice areas of LA were pretty full by then, and the well-heeled craved some new lebensraum—especially after plate analysis revealed that come the next quake, Brentwood was going to end up in Belgium. Of course there was a pitched battle with the local history fanatics and the poorer people who liked having a place to barbecue, but the problem with those guys is they don't have much money. The developers did. The developers won, more or less. A solution was reached.

An area was marked off, bordered by the Ventura and Golden State freeways on the north and east, and Los Feliz in the south. A hundred-yard wall was built along this entire stretch, and along the boundary with Mount Sinai Memorial Park in the west, creating an entirely closed-in area. The exterior of this wall was painted with high-resolution LED; the whole surface was wired into a central computer. Certain interior features, like Mount Hollywood and small areas of the old wild lands, were left untouched. Even the developers realized the Hollywood sign was sacred. This, along with stored images of how the park used to be before the development, was seamlessly displayed on the videowall—creating the illusion that nothing was there. From wherever you stood in LA, you could still see the Hollywood sign, and the Hills and park to the northeast. Unless you walked right up to the wall and punched it—which the guards were there to prevent you from doing—the illusion was perfect. It was like nothing had changed.

Inside the district the same idea was deployed in reverse, with views of Burbank, Glendale, and Hollywood constantly updated right up to the sky. LA got a whole new district, but kept the same view, and access tunnels leading from the outside to the three preserved areas meant that there was technically still a public park. The environmentalists were a bit pissed about the whole thing, claiming this wasn't the point, but they never have any money at all and weren't even invited to the planning meetings.

As we approached the gate—a ten-by-six-foot hole in the otherwise flawless panorama—I laid my finger over the sensor in the dashboard. This relayed my name, genome, and credit rating to the matrix built into the car's shell, for reading by the entrance computer. The matrix was treble-encrypted with a top-of-the-line government DES algorithm, and thus had probably taken someone a good twenty minutes to crack. I don't believe that all the people you see driving around Griffith have the money to live there. Particularly those who hang around my block.

I passed, and was allowed through the barrier. The outer doors shut behind me, leaving me in the access tunnel through the wall. The car hummed as it was conveyed toward the inner door. At the end the doors opened gracefully, and I drove out into the world again.

I locked the car to Griffith's auto system and told it to get me home as quickly as possible.

On the inside, Griffith looks like it was designed by someone who took acid in Disneyland. The hills provide perching space for split-level houses of high cost and loveliness, but the rest is wall-to-wall fun. The valley areas are split up into regular grids of stores and restaurants, and you're never more than a five-minute drive from a Starbucks or Borders or Baby Gap, the building blocks of Generica. Extensive areas are pedestrianized, and each storefront has been built up into a hysterical shout of commerciality. Restaurants in the shape of food and stores in the style of their products: The shoe stores look like shoes, the video stores are thin and rectangular, and Herbie's Croutons—where the owner, Herbie, sells over two hundred different flavors of small cubes of toasted bread—looks like an enormous crouton. You don't even have to be literate to know where to shop: the perfect post-verbal landscape. There's a spanking new subway, complete with designer graffiti, a cluster of big hotels in the middle, and enclaves of specialty shops nestling in the canyons. Nothing in Griffith is older than ten years: Even the smog is artificial and guaranteed free of pollution.

It's trashy, superficial, and vacuous. I call it home.

When the car turned into my square, I took it off auto and drove it myself. I can get all brave when the parking lot is in sight. My building, The Falkland, used to be one of the choicest hotels in the area, but then one day someone decided that two hundred yards down the road was far cooler. Everyone checked out virtually overnight; some even carried their suitcases by themselves. Within a week The Falkland was abandoned. By the time I opted for having a stable place to hang my hat, the building had applied for and been granted "characterful" status—then turned into private apartments. A SWAT team of interior decorators was called in to make the place look run-down. They did quite a good job, but if you rub hard on the walls in the apartments, you can tell the grime's just color-wash, an environmental laughter track.

I let one of the building's regulars valet-park my vehicle, as always mentally waving it good-bye. I could afford a collapsing car now if I wanted, but I don't really trust them. I've heard too many stories about people who've slipped one into their pocket, popped into a restaurant for some lunch, and then found the car reexpanding at the table. The last thing you want when you're halfway through your tagliatelle is two tons of vehicle in your lap.

Laura Reynolds was still unconscious but also still alive, and I hauled her over my shoulder and hurried into the building. The whole first floor had become a kind of freak-show bazaar, thronged with fun seekers and working girls—with a constant backdrop of noise coming from a hundred different stalls. At first glance it looks kind of cool, in an If-you're-over-forty-this-is-your-worst-nightmare kind of way, but take my advice: The drugs are generally cut to shit and you don't want to tangle with the girls. Most are method prostitutes: The nurses carry catheters, the meter maids give you tickets enforceable by law, and the schoolgirls like awful bands and always come straight from an argument with their mothers. The only highlight is the homeopathic bars, where you can get wasted on just one sip of beer: A healthcare firm has ambulances out the back with engines running twenty-four hours a day.

Deck was standing right inside the door, looking tense. The

antismoking laws are even tougher inside Griffith, and it drives him berserk. He was also alone.

"Where the fuck is he?" I said, heading straight for the elevators on the other side of the lobby.

"On his way." Deck held his arm out to keep the doors open as I maneuvered myself and my charge into the elevator. Luckily by then I'd remembered my apartment number. "He wasn't exactly awake when I called." Two guys tried to get in the elevator with us, but Deck dissuaded them. He's a good couple of inches shorter than me, and on the wiry side—but it would be a mistake to read anything into that. His face is a little wonky, but his ease with his scars communicates an entirely valid confidence in his ability to handle himself. He's kept in practice at the whole violence thing, working occasional muscle for local businessmen while holding part-time square-john jobs. We made a policy of never working together back in the old days, but I know that if I ever needed someone covering my back, Deck would be that man.

As we stood outside the door, he took Laura from me and held her upright while I fumbled with my keys.

"You going to explain this to me at some stage?" he asked mildly.

"At some stage, yeah." I pushed the door open, listened for a moment, then helped Deck drag Laura Reynolds inside.

CHAPTER FOUR

We got her laid out on the sofa, and I was halfway through making coffee, when there was a buzz at the door. I had my gun out before I knew what I was doing, and Deck held his hands up.

"Be cool," he said, squinting through the peephole and kicking aside the small pile of newspapers that had arrived while I was away. "Just the old guy."

Woodley lurched in. "I take it you understand this is going to be double rate?" he rasped, setting his two bags down on the floor. "It's nearly four in the morning."

"Just shut up and get on with it," I told him. "You'll get four times the rate if you understand that mentioning this to anyone could be fatal. For you, not her."

Woodley harrumphed for a moment, trying to hide a satisfied leer. If there's anything the old fart likes more than money, I can't imagine what it would be. He peered at Laura Reynolds: When he saw the blood-soaked towels, he blanched, and waved a hand vaguely at Deck. "Let them out, would you, young fellow?"

Though I'd managed to remain relatively calm during the drive home, seeing Woodley dithering around brought it home just how ill Laura Reynolds was. I grabbed one of his bags and shoved him in front of me toward the bedroom. Meanwhile Deck opened the other bag and let the remotes out—small crab-like machines the size of tarantulas. Attracted by the smell of blood, they clambered straight up onto the sofa and started nosing around.

Deck and I had used Woodley on and off for five years, back in the bad old days. He had once, he claimed, been a telesurgeon for covert army operations—conducting surgery remotely through satellite links. There was no way I'd found of establishing whether this was true, but it was certainly the case that he couldn't stand blood. We'd shown him some once, just to check. He didn't mind the sight of it as long as it was mediated through the remotes' cameras; he just didn't like the reality of the actual stuff. After he was court-martialed (unfairly, so he claimed, though he declined to specify exactly what the unfair charges had been), Woodley couldn't get a proper license, so he hacked out a living catering to people like me. People who every now and then needed something biological sorted out, and who couldn't go to a hospital. Old fool he might be, and I strongly suspected he collected string and slept on the beach somewhere, but, boy, could that guy stitch. Nicely healed scars in my shoulder, chest, and right leg—all of which had once been bullet wounds—were testament to that.

I stood where I could see both Laura and Woodley, and watched as he got down to work. The old man's hands were trembling big-time, but that wasn't a cause for concern: The controls had antishake mechanisms built into them. He put the glasses and gloves on, and within moments the remotes were speeding up and down her arms. After a while one of them hopped off the sofa and delved in the bag, reappearing with a fridgipacked bag of plasma. Woodley clucked and frowned with concentration.

Deck appeared next to me, handed me a cigarette. I fitted a prism filter on the end and lit it gratefully. The filters are a pain in the ass, stealing half the flavor, but it's the only way of smoking indoors without the wall sensors ratting on you. The filters dissolve after use, which is convenient, because possession of them is a misdemeanor. Smoking in LA these days takes more planning than conducting a minor war.

"So?" Deck asked.

"Later," I said.

Deck smiled, settled back to watch the remotes. He's a patient man—far more so than me. You could dump Deck in the middle of Gobi Desert and he'd just look around and say, "Is there any beer?"

"No," you'd reply, obviously.

"Water?" You shake your head, and he'd think for a minute.

"Anywhere to sit?" And then he'd walk over to the nearest fairly comfortable rock and sit there for as long as it took for either beer, water, or a parallel universe to appear.

After a while I got fidgety, and checked the answering machine. This works pretty well, considering, hardly ever telling me that 67°o*3~ has called about the ;,,,t[{+®3, and so I was surprised to see I had no messages. I'd been away for two days. I'm not an especially popular guy, but people tend to call me at fairly regular intervals to bug me about something trivial. I experimentally banged the side of the machine.

"Piss off," it said. The answering machine's been sulking since I threw my coffeemaker out. I think they had something going together.

"Nobody's called?"

"Since midnight, no. Most people tend to sleep sometimes."

I stared down at it. "What are you talking about?"

"Which was the difficult word?"

"When did you last give messages?" I asked very slowly.

"11:58 P.M. yesterday."

"Tonight?"

"I remember it clearly. You pressed the button lightly for once."

"Problem?" Deck asked.

I didn't bother to ask the machine if it was sure about the time. If there was any useful cross-breeding that could have taken place in my apartment, it would have been between the answering machine and my alarm clock.

"Someone's been in the apartment tonight," I told Deck.

"Has been?"

It's not a huge apartment. We checked the few remaining spaces. Deck walked carefully into the spare bedroom, tossed the closets and looked under the bed—and came out shrugging. I did the same in the main bedroom.

"Nearly finished," Woodley said as I passed behind him, expecting me to hassle him. "And for your information, she's an occasional user. Smack—but not for a while—and a little bit of Fresh."

This didn't surprise me. "What do I need to do now? Recovery-wise?" Nothing appeared to have been stolen. You'd have to have pretty specific needs to want to steal something from my bedroom. The memory receiver was still in the closet, and that was all that really mattered.

The old guy shrugged. "Don't ask me. Didn't do that bit. Boys I used to operate on were just given a gun and told to go back out again."

"You're a doctor, Woodley. You must have some idea."

He shrugged again. "Chicken soup. Keep her off the bottle for a few days. Or give her a stiff scotch. Whatever works. Don't let her go bungee-jumping."

"Woodley—" I stopped abruptly, staring at the head of the bed. The sheets and cover had been turned back very neatly, as if by a maid. It was so unexpected, so bizarre, I hadn't even noticed it at first. "Did you do that?"

"Like to think I operate a one-stop service, dear boy, but it doesn't extend to making your bed."

I paid him off, and waited impatiently while he gathered his stuff together. I ran an eye over the living room, and came up empty. Nothing obvious was missing, and trust me—the decor's so austere, you'd notice if anything was gone.

When Woodley had left, I grabbed Deck and pulled him into the bedroom. "The bed," I said, pointing at it.

"We've been friends a long time," he said gently. "But I just don't care for you that way."

"Someone's turned back the sheets."

Deck raised an eyebrow. "Are you sure?"

"Of course I'm sure. Does it seem something *I'm* likely to do?"

"Not unless there was money hidden underneath."

"Exactly."

"So someone's picked up your messages and turned back the bed. You got an imaginary girlfriend or something?"

"Not even a real one."

"Nobody else got a key? The building's super, for instance?"

"The super is in prison for breaking and entering."

"That's a no, then. Anything missing?"

"Not that I can see."

"Okay, so, to recap: Someone's broken into your apartment and done a bit of tidying. You're twitchier than a pig in a tin, and you're waving your gun around like a flag. There's a woman on the sofa with wrists like a roadmap, and you just paid Woodley quadruple rate to keep his mouth shut. Maybe now would be a good time for you to tell me what's going on."

I took my bathrobe off the hook on the back of the door and got Laura Reynolds into it. I stuffed the bloody one in the trash where, knowing my housekeeping, it would probably remain for two years. Laura still seemed to be unconscious, but that was probably due to medication: There was a lot more color in her cheeks, and with a combination of neat stitching and skinFix, her arms looked a little better. Now that the blood had been swabbed away, you could see both that the wrist cuts were fairly manageable, and that they weren't the first. Old white lines in very similar places said that tonight's dive for the tunnel hadn't been the first of its kind. Didn't make it any less important for her, I guessed, or any smarter.

I carried her into the spare bedroom as gently as I could and got her into the bed. I laid a couple of my old coats on top of the bedding and turned the heat up a little.

Then I went back into the living room and got the answering machine to repeat the messages someone had already picked up. There were only three, and they were all from Stratten. The first was polite, the second businesslike. The third said just *Call the office. Now.*

Time was running out. I got a coffee and told Deck the score.

IN THE FIVE MONTHS I worked memory, Ms. Reynolds had been one of my most regular clients. Though I didn't know her name then, she'd dumped the same memory on me six times.

The memory was this: She'd been down by a stream, in a patch of forest behind the house where she lived. I don't know how old she was, but probably early to mid teens. The day was hot and it was late afternoon, and she'd come down into the woods for something important. The main impression I got was of anticipation, and vulnerability, and the memory always made me feel very young.

She was standing there, waiting, when suddenly there'd been a shadow over her, and she'd looked up to see her mom. Her mother was a very tall woman, quite thin, with a mass of reddish-brown hair. Laura had slowly looked up, until she'd found her mother's face. What she needed a break from every now and then was the expression she saw there. A look of fury—mixed in with a little glee.

The memory always ended abruptly at that instant, and I don't know what the look meant or what had happened afterward. I'd always been kind of glad I didn't. It was one of the memories I could understand someone wanting to get away from once in a while.

Then last week I came back from lounging around a hotel pool in Santa Barbara to find I had an email message from an address I didn't recognize. Before I even read it I ran a check on the source: Sometimes people set their mail to send back a RECEIVED signal when it was opened. The domain code didn't set any alarm bells ringing, but even so I got the console to hardcopy without technically opening it.

The mail was from this same woman, the one who wanted to forget that moment down by the stream. We'd never been in contact before—all transactions were brokered through REM-temps on a double-blind confidentiality principle—but her message mentioned the memory, and I worked out who she was. The message said she had something she wanted me to carry, and would make it very worth my while.

I stared at the piece of paper for a few moments, then set fire to it and let it burn out in the sink. I spent the rest of the day around the pool, and the evening in a bar at the beach end of State Street, playing pool and bullshitting with the locals.

When I got back I had another message from the same address. It listed a phone number. It also mentioned twenty thousand dollars.

I watched a movie on the in-house system for a while, but you know how it is. The back brain makes a decision instantly, and no matter how long you put it off, you know what you're going to do.

At about midnight I left my hotel room and went back to the bar. There was a pay phone at the back, out of sight, and I called the number from the message.

A nervous-sounding woman answered the phone. She made me describe her memory in detail. Then she told me what she wanted. She had another memory, one that wasn't usually a problem. Ten years ago she'd gone on vacation with a man she'd just met, to someplace on the Baja she'd known for years. Ensenada. She and the man had stayed there awhile, hanging out, eating seafood, having a good time. Then she'd come back.

"That's it?" I asked.

She'd recently met a new man. She liked him a lot. In fact, she was thinking of getting hitched. But they were going to go away together first, just to make sure. He wanted to go to the same town she'd been to with the other man all that long ago. She tried to suggest going somewhere else, but Ensenada had become a kind of lovers' in-joke between them, and it would have looked weird if she'd insisted.

I still didn't see the problem, and said so. As long as you steer clear of some of the taco stands, Ensenada's a cool place to be.

The woman said she didn't want to go back there remembering what it had been like with the other man. She thought it might make her see things differently this time. She really loved this new guy, and didn't want to compromise their first trip together.

I know it sounds odd, but believe me—that's the way other people's lives work. They're both more bizarre and more trivial than you can imagine. Most clients had far worse reasons for forgetting something for a while: In a way I sort of respected her attitude, and wished I had a woman who took me that seriously.

But all she had to do was ask for me when she booked the storage. I still didn't see why we were doing the cloak-and-dagger stuff.

So she told me. She was going to be away for ten days.

Stratten wouldn't accept a booking for more than a week, I knew that. He seemed to have pretty much cornered the memory market, and I assumed therefore that he was kicking back to a couple of key cops somewhere, but if they heard he was extending the time limit, all bets would be off. Also, the memory the woman wanted to leave wasn't a fragment. It was for the whole period, three entire days.

No one had ever tried anything that long before.

I thought I was going to say no, but instead found myself telling her the money she was offering wasn't enough. I would have to go on leave from REMtemps for a week and a half. I could earn twenty thousand anyway in that time, without the risk of pissing Stratten off.

"Fifty grand," she said.

I have a way of dealing with temptation. I just succumb and get it over with.

Early the following afternoon I sat in my room and waited for the memory transmission. A third of the money for the current job was already in my hands, and on its way to three different accounts. The rest would come later. The woman had found a hacker with a lashed-up transmitter, and this dweeb had been able to acquire the code of my receiver. This spooked me a little. I made a mental note to find some way of hinting to Stratten, when this job was done, that the system wasn't as impregnable as he thought. If he wasn't careful, the black market was going to start cutting into his business. Worse than that, memory temps could find themselves stuffed with all kinds of shit they weren't expecting or being paid for.

I spoke on the phone with the woman and arranged a time for her to take the memory back. It was a different phone number from the one she'd originally given me, presumably the home of the hacker.

Then I closed my eyes and got myself ready to receive.

It came seconds later. A pulse of noise and smell that filled my mind like the worst migraine you've ever had, magnified a hundredfold. I grunted, unable even to shout, and pitched forward out of the chair onto the carpet, hands and legs spasming. I seemed to go deaf and partly blind for a while, but that was the least of my problems. I knew I was going to die.

After a few minutes, however, the shaking lessened enough so that I could crawl to the bedside table and grab a cigarette. I hauled myself up onto the bed and lay facedown for a while, waiting for the pain to go away. It started to, eventually.

Half an hour later I was sitting up and drinking, which helped. My sight was clearing and I could hear once more the sound of people larking around by the pool below my window. I still felt like shit, but at least I was going to live.

The brain is designed to accept life piecemeal not as sights, sounds, feelings, and tactile impressions condensed into a single bullet of remembrance. Our minds are structured by time, and like things delivered sequentially. I hadn't really considered the difference between getting a quick, single fragment of someone's life and taking on three days' worth of experience in one hit. It was like having the world reconfigured as a place where time and space meant nothing, and everything was one. If I hadn't already spent years bench-pressing with my mind, I'd probably have been slumped in a corner, drooling and staring into nothingness.

As it was, my head was still humming and thudding, trying to wade through what it had received and sort it into chronology and types. I could feel countless threads of data squirming over each other like snakes, searching for some kind of order. Sunburn on my shoulder; salt on my lips from a margarita; a flash of sun on a car window. A thousand sentences all at once, some of them leaving my head, others surging in. My brain was lurching under their weight, misfiring like a heart on the verge of arrest.

I reached unsteadily for the phone. Large amounts of room service was what was on my mind, but first I had to call the woman and let her know that the transmission had gone through. I'm quite professional about these things. I dialed the number and waited as it rang, holding the glass of iced gin up against my forehead and panting slightly.

There was no answer. I redialed. This time I gave it thirty rings before putting the phone down again. I knew she wasn't going away to Ensenada until the next day, so maybe it was no big deal. By then it was forty-five minutes since the dump. Probably she was out, making arrangements—or perhaps she'd gone home.

I munched slowly through a burger delivered by an offensively self-confident bellboy, keeping half an eye on what was going on in my head. It felt like a hard drive running optimization software, without enough slack to swap all the data around. Fragments of her golden vacation were lodging into place, but the rest was still jumbled and hazy.

When I had finished the burger, I called the number again. I let it ring for a long time, and was about to put it down, when someone answered. *"Hello,"* said a voice I didn't recognize. *"Who is this?"* There was a weird sound in the background, like a loudspeaker's echo.

"Hap Thompson," I answered, slightly taken aback. "Is my client there?"

"How the fuck do you expect me to know, dickweed?" snarled the voice, and the connection was severed.

I tried the number again immediately. It rang, but there was no answer. I called the operator. She told me there was no problem on the line but wouldn't give me the address.

I called Quat. He said he'd call me back. I stumbled around my room for ten minutes, gobbling aspirin like candy.

Quat called, hack done. The number was from a booth in the first-class departure lounge of O'Hare Airport.

I called the other number I had for the woman. The line was dead. Then I blacked out.

WHEN I CAME TO, I was pretty scared. Two reasons. The first is that it had never happened to me before, except the tiny blips you got immediately after receiving a memory. The second was that my client had obviously fucked me over.

I checked out of the hotel and drove back fast to LA along Highway 1, bolting myself into my apartment. I panicked when I found a note had been stuffed under the door, but it was only from my old neighbors, the Dickenses. They were a nice young couple with three kids, originally from Portland. A year ago someone came up with an idea to sell everyone on how well the country was doing. They invented an imaginary family: parents of a certain age, such-and-such background, current and past employment, recreational habits, kids' sexes, ages, eye color, and SAT scores—they were extremely specific. Then they hung an entire campaign around it, staking their reputation on claiming that such a family was so many dollars better off every week—figuring nobody could disprove it. Problem was, they screwed up. There was such a family—the Dickenses. Some suit in the Statistics Bureau panicked and took a contract out on them, and they'd been on the run ever since. The note from the Dickenses just said they'd seen someone sniffing around, and that they were gone. They left me their keys, and said I could have the milk in their fridge.

I hid the memory receiver in the bedroom and spent the rest of the day in the bathtub, drinking. By the time I climbed out of the tub, I could piece together most of the first two days of the memory. The woman had been down in Ensenada, but she'd been by herself: Mainly she'd spent the time drinking margaritas in Housson's. The first night had been pretty quiet, and by midnight she was back where she was staying, a small, run-down beach resort called Quitas Papagayo, about a half mile up the coast. I'd stayed there myself a long time ago, and even then the Papagayo's glory days had been thirty years behind it. On the second night, drunk, she'd nearly ended up going home with an American sailor. On the whole, I was glad she changed her mind, and bawled him out in the street instead. She kept screaming at him as he hurried away up the street, then she went back into the bar and drank until it closed. God knows how she got home: She couldn't remember. Hardly the vacation of a lifetime, though I've had worse, I've got to admit.

And it hadn't been ten years ago either. She'd taken an organizer with her, and checked her email obsessively—the dates onscreen made it clear her "holiday" had taken place only a couple of days before she contacted me. Finally she got the email she'd been waiting for. It was short. Just an address. She walked straight out of Housson's and got in her car, and was back in LA early evening.

The next part of the memory, the murder at the crossroads, took a long time in coming. I'd never experienced anything like it before. Though it was very recent, it was already distorted, and shot through with darkness. It was as if a process of blanking had already started before she'd decided to get rid of it. I don't know why she wanted to lose the time in Ensenada, too: When you take other people's memories, you don't always get all the thoughts that happened during them. It's like some people's sense data and internal workings take place in different parts of their head, like they've trained a part of their mind to remain distant at all times. All I got during her time on the Baja was a draining feeling of misery, of a desire to be either drunk or dead—mixed with dark elation. Not a good way to feel, sure, but I had the sense that this was how this woman felt about half the time. Ditching two days of it wasn't going to make much difference. Perhaps she'd spent those two days working herself up to what happened—reliving certain things in part of her mind, steeling herself. I don't know.

But in the end I was able to form a coherent idea of that last night in Ensenada, and what had happened, and to learn her name when the guy used it just before she killed him. I told Deck everything I could remember, from the way the crossroads had looked, to the way the man named Ray winked, to the number of shots the woman pumped into his body. The feeling of emptiness as she stared down at the corpse, reloading the gun for the sake of it.

And the numb despair, as she ran away, at realizing that it made no difference.

LAURA REYNOLDS was breathing easy, apparently asleep. Retelling the memory made me feel something new toward her, though I wasn't sure what. Guilty, perhaps. I'd taken something that had previously been only in our heads—hers and mine—and brought it out into the world. I'd never done that before. I'd always regarded the confidentiality of my profession with a kind of half-assed pride. I hedged the feeling now, told it to go away. After all, she'd deliberately dumped something on me that could get me sent to prison forever.

Deck was standing at the window when I got back, looking down at the street. The sky was beginning to lighten around the edges, and somewhere the smog machines were stirring into life. Looked like we were heading for a hot day, unless the chemicals in the sky decided they fancied a blizzard instead. Being a weatherman in LA isn't the joke job it used to be.

When Deck spoke, it was as if he were working up to something, clearing the side issues out of the way first. "Who do you think the guys in the suits were?"

"I have no idea. They weren't cops, I'm pretty sure of that."

"Why?"

"Don't know. Something about them. Plus they looked familiar."

"Plenty cops look familiar to me."

"Not like that. Like an old memory."

"Yours?"

"I think so. I don't think they sparked anything in her at all."

"Could it be them who've been in here?"

I shook my head. "They didn't see me, remember? I wasn't actually *there*. I didn't do anything. It just feels as if I did."

Deck looked at me. "You know what will happen if you're caught with that in your head?" He'd warned me about this since I started memory work.

"Murder One. Or Half, at least."

He shook his head. "You don't know the half of it."

"What are you talking about?"

Deck walked across the room, and rooted through the pile of yesterday's news. I guess I should cancel the hard-copy paper, save a few trees somewhere: But reading it off a screen isn't the same. He found the edition he was looking for and handed it to me.

I scanned the front page:

There might be an earthquake at some stage.

A property entrepreneur named Nicholas Schumann had killed himself in a spectacular way: financial problems cited. I remembered the name vaguely: Schumann might even have been one of the wheels who redeveloped Griffith. Must have taken a piece of spectacular stupidity for him to have lost all *that* money—or spectacular greed.

The weather was still fucked, and they didn't think they could fix it.

"So what?" I said.

"Page three," Deck said.

I turned to it, and found an article about a murder that by then had happened six days earlier. The story recapped the murder of an unarmed man dead from multiple gunshot wounds in the street in Culver City. It implied that the cops had a number of leads, which meant for the time being they had jackshit, but they were working it hard. It gave the age of the deceased, his profession, and also his name.

Captain Ray Hammond, LAPD.

I closed my eyes.

"She killed a cop," Deck said. "Better still, take a look at the last line. I wouldn't even have remembered the article, except for that. Guess who's in charge of the case?"

I read it aloud, the words like the sound of a heavy door being triple-locked. "Lieutenant Travis, LAPD Homicide."

I looked slowly up at Deck, suddenly properly afraid. Up until then the situation I found myself in had merely been disastrous. Now it had sailed blithely into a realm where adjectives didn't really cut it anymore. It would have taken a diagram to explain, one showing the intersection of a creek and some shit, and making clear the lack of any implement for promoting forward propulsion.

Deck stared back at me. "You're fucked," he said.

CHAPTER FIVE

I crashed at six. One minute I was sitting on the sofa talking to Deck, and next thing I was out. I'd been awake for forty-eight hours, and my brain was carrying more than the usual load. I was too exhausted to dream much, and all I could remember when I woke up a little after nine was another image of the silver car from the end of Laura's memory. I was standing by the side of a road, I don't know where, but it seemed familiar. On either side was swampy woodland, and the road stretched out straight to the horizon, shimmering in the heat. Something hurtled toward where I stood, moving so fast that at first I couldn't tell what it was. Then I saw that it was a car, the sun beating down on it so hard, it almost looked as if it were spinning. As it got closer it began to slow down; when it drew level, I woke up.

I didn't know what it meant other than that part of my brain was evidently trying to get some things in order, and had been since Ensenada. I wished it well. My mind wasn't exactly razor-sharp *before* it became a flophouse for other people's hand-me-downs, and I now had far more pressing things to worry about.

"She's moving," Deck said.

I stood at the bedroom door and waited impatiently while Ms. Reynolds stirred toward consciousness. It looked like it was a long journey. Now that I was properly awake, panic was beginning to resurface, but I didn't poke her with a stick or anything. Foolishly, I was still hoping the whole situation could be resolved amicably.

Eventually her eyes opened. They were pretty red, a combination of hangover and the remnants of having been in shock. She stared at me without moving.

"Where?" she finally croaked. I had a glass of water in my hand, but she wasn't getting it just yet.

"Griffith," I said.

"How?"

"I brought you here." She sat up, wincing. When she looked down and saw the stitches in her wrists, her lips tightened and her face fell: a small and private look of sorrow and disappointment. I couldn't tell whether this was because it had happened, or because it had failed.

I gave her the water, and she drank.

"Why would you do that?" she asked when she'd finished.

"You were going to die. As it is, you're not allowed to go bungee-jumping. Doctor's orders. Want some chicken soup?"

She stared at me. "I'm a vegetarian."

"Right—your body is a temple. Full of money changers like vodka and smack."

"Look, who are you?"

"Hap Thompson," I said.

She was out of the bed with a speed I found frankly impressive, though once on her feet, she swayed alarmingly. "The front door's locked, and the windows don't open," I added. "You're not going anywhere."

"Oh, yeah? Just watch me," she said as she pushed past and swished out into the living room. Deck looked up, and she glared at him, face pale and furious. "Who the hell are you?"

"Deck," he said equably. "Friend of Hap's."

"How nice for you. Look, where are my clothes?"

I picked up my coat from the sofa and fished in the pockets. Two bras, a pair of panties, and a dress of some thin green material. I held them out to her. Laura looked at me as if I'd offered to crack a walnut between my buttocks.

"And?"

I shrugged. "It's all I could carry."

"And my purse is where?"

"Back in the hotel room."

"Are you some kind of monster? You kidnap a woman and don't bring her purse?"

Deck grinned at me. "She's real friendly, isn't she?"

Laura turned on him. "Look, fuckhead—do you mind if I call you that?—kidnapping's a federal offense. You guys are lucky I'm not on the phone right now, talking to the police."

"Memory-dumping's a crime too," I said. "Not to mention murder. You and I both know the last thing you're going to do is get in touch with the cops."

Her eyes went blank, and she did a good impression of total lack of recall. "What murder?" she said. For a moment it was hard to believe this was someone I'd fished out of a bloody bath in the wee hours. She looked like the kind of bank officer who could make you shrivel to a raisin with a raised eyebrow. Either Woodley had done a superb job in patching her up, or she was as tough as all hell.

"Nice try," I said, holding her eyes, "but it's not going to work with me. I do this for a living. You lost the event itself, but you still know what you lost. You'll remember seeking me out, and you'll remember why."

"You took the job. You got paid."

"You lied. And I got only a third of the money."

"I'll get you the rest."

"I'm not sure I believe you have it, and anyway, I don't want it. Don't worry—you'll get a refund. Judging by last night, it looks like the memory dump didn't really work out for you anyway."

Laura glared at me, and then marched over to the front door.

She gave the handle a tug. It was, as advertised, locked. "Open this door," she commanded.

"Coffee?" Deck asked me, poised with kettle in hand over in the kitchenette.

Laura kicked the door, nearly toppling herself over in the process. *"Open it."*

"Lovely," I told Deck. "Think I've got some mint mocha left somewhere."

She stomped back to me. I thought was going to catch a slap in the face, but she just snatched her clothes and banged off into the bathroom, where she slammed and locked the door. I decided "tough as hell" was the answer to my question.

"She going to be okay in there?" Deck asked me.

"Unless she can break the window and absail ten floors."

"No," he said patiently. "I mean—*okay.*"

I knew what he meant. "I think so." I suspected that trying to kill yourself first thing in the morning, with a hangover and two men annoying the hell out of you, was different from doing it in the wee hours of the A.M. with no one around.

Deck found the coffee, poured it into a cafetiere. I used to have a coffeemaker like everybody else. You tell them where the coffee beans are, and how to use the tap, and it's ready whenever you want it. But through a design error the hole the coffee comes out of is rather closer to the machine's posterior than you would hope, and after seeing the little biomachine squatting over a cup, grunting with effort, I tend to sour on the idea of a hot beverage. When it goes wrong, as they invariably do, the result tastes very strange indeed. My machine got sick, with what I suspect was the coffeemaker equivalent of food poisoning, and I just couldn't have it in the house any longer. I put it in the alley behind the building late at night and it was gone the next day. Maybe it made its way down to Mexico to be with its comrades. If so, it must have been in a different group from the ones I'd passed on the way to Ensenada. Coffeemakers tend to hold grudges, apparently, and between them they could easily have forced me off the road. Or maybe they just didn't get a good look at my face.

Deck handed me a cup. "She's not going to just take it back."

"No kidding." Having met Laura Reynolds properly, I was now wishing I *had* woken her up with a pointy stick. I was also finding it hard to believe I'd ever expected things might go differently. "So we go with that time-honored favorite, Plan B."

"Which is?"

"Exactly the same as Plan A, except we just have to keep her locked up while I get hold of the transmitter." The sound of water and occasional bad-tempered stomping made it clear that Laura was now taking a shower. I was looking forward to being harangued when she got out, for not bringing her shampoo and cotton balls.

"By the way," Deck said, "that weirdo called. Quat."

My next move, on plate. "Shit—why didn't you say?"

Deck shrugged. "Didn't know it was important, and he was done before I could pick it up. You set a call-back, apparently. Just said he was around, you wanted to talk to him."

I started moving. "Can you do me a favor?"

"Absolutely not. Fuck off." I waited. Deck grinned. "Babysitting, I assume."

"I have to go see him."

"Why not just call?"

"He won't do business that way."

"How long will you be?"

"Very quick."

Deck settled himself on the sofa, pointed a finger at me. "Better be. I suspect Laura Reynolds is a person who's going to take some handling if she gets het up. This is going to take your charm and winning ways."

"Half hour at the most," I said.

THE LOBBY DOWNSTAIRS was quiet, just a few people setting up their stalls. During the day most of them sell arts and crafts—inexplicable things fashioned out of pieces of wood originally used for something else, which you buy and take home and move from room to room until you realize the attic is the best place for them. Someone else's attic, preferably. It is my firm belief that in the afterglow of our civilization, when all we have made is come to naught and our planet slumbers once more, home only to a few valiant creatures—bugs, probably—who have the courage to struggle through whatever nemesis we have wrought on Mother Nature, some alien race will land and do a spot of archaeology. And all they'll find, particularly in coastal areas, is layers of mirrors made from reclaimed floorboards with homespun wisdom etched on them with a soldering iron, or pockets of driftwood sculptures of fishing boats that rock when pushed, and the aliens will nod sadly among themselves and admit that this was a civilization whose time had indeed come.

I quickly located Tid, the guy who'd parked my car, and gave him the usual ten-spot. I like to think this is a voluntary arrangement, showing great generosity on my part, but I suspect that without it I'd never find out where my car had been put. Tid's a small, disreputable-looking man who seems to live solely on M&Ms, but we'd always gotten along well enough. Money's like that: promotes straightforward relationships. This time I slipped him an extra twenty, and asked him to do me a favor, and then ran down to the parking lot under the building.

The car was parked over on the far side, nestled into a dark corner. This was perfect for me, because I wasn't going anywhere. I got inside, set the alarm, and locked the doors.

Most people go on the Net via their homes, obviously. Though my account was now billed to the apartment, I still had the rig in the car because over the last couple of years the car had remained the most stable environment in my life. I'd bought it after my first couple of months' work for REMtemps, and had it fully kitted out. As I accumulated more money, I upgraded and tweaked to the point where even I couldn't remember where all the wires were. Ripping the rig all out and reconstructing it in the apartment was one of those things I never quite got around to, like throwing away pens that didn't work properly. Or getting a life.

The console in the car plays images directly into the brain, so I don't have to wear VR goggles. All I had to do was flip the switch, close my eyes, and be transferred to the other side.

The light changed, and instead of being underground I was in my standard driveway home page, facing out toward a leafy residential district of smalltown America. I put my foot down and pulled out into the road. My netcar looks like a souped-up '59 Caddy, complete with retro fins and powder-blue paint job, but the engine characteristics are bang up-to-date. I don't mind driving fast on the Net, because of the in-built anti-collision protocol—in fact, sometimes I speed straight at other people just for the pure hell of it. It's especially fun if you come across one of those die-hards who refuse to get with the new metaphor, and insist on trawling the Net on surfboards. You see them occasionally, old hippies scraping along the road on boards equipped with little skateboard wheels, complaining about the traffic and muttering about the good old days of browser wars.

I turned left out of my street and tore down the trunk lines for a while, then hung a right and cut up into the personal domain hills on the other side. You have to slog through a lot of cyber suburbia these days—family sites full of digitized vacation videos and mind-numbing detail on how little Todd did in his tests—before you get out into the darker zones. It used to be that you could type in a URL and leap straight to anyone's home page. But when they folded out into three-dimensional spaces and started to look like real homes—and their owners started spending actual time there—things changed. They wanted you to walk up the path and ring a doorbell like a civilized person. With most other places you can still just jump straight to the general district, but not where I was going—and the jams at the jump links are often so bad, you're usually better just putting your foot down and going the long way around. Thus what had started as an alternative reality ended up just being another layer of the same old same old, operating on more or less similar rules.

Humans are like that. Very literal-minded.

I reminded myself, as usual, that I ought to visit my grandparents soon. Now was not the time. It seldom was. They retired to the Net six years ago, about two weeks ahead of the Grim Reaper. Bought themselves a scrabby virtual farm way out on the edge of Australasia.Net just before they died, and had themselves transferred. Unfortunately they were ripped off by their Realtor, and the resolution is fucked. It's just polygons and big blocks of color out where they live, and voices sound like they're coming through speakers that had an earlier life in a thrash ambient band. I guess I could phone them from out in the real world, but that gives me the creeps: too much like pretending they're still alive. They are—were, whatever—good people, and I'm glad that in some sense I still have access to them, but there are barriers I suspect shouldn't be breached. We still don't know as much about the mind as we think we do, and there's something a little off about them now, as if the rough edges got lost in the translation. Show me a person without a bit of sand in their nature, and I'll show you someone a little creepy.

I started to lose speed, which meant that traffic was starting to build—people checking their mail and doing the early morning shopping online. The roads still looked empty, but that's because I like it that way and usually set my gear to filter out all cars except those of people I know.

Deck hates the Net—won't come in unless he has to. Says he doesn't trust mediated experience. I asked him what magazine he got that out of and he admitted it was something an ex-girlfriend used to say. But I quite like it, enjoy the feeling of going places without actually having to get out of the chair, and of there being some other place you can go to in the flick of a switch. Mainly I use it to access people who refuse to do business in the normal way. Quat, for example, who won't make any transaction over a phone. Doesn't trust them, which is a complete pain in the ass when you need something in a hurry.

As I drove, my mind worked overtime, trying to predict the angles now that I knew more about the guy that Laura had killed. The bottom line was simple: There was even more reason for me to get her experience back into her head and out of mine—like immediately. If there's one thing that really ticks cops off, it's people whacking one of their own. I didn't know how much difference it would make that I hadn't been the one who actually pulled the trigger, but I suspected that if they got hold of me, they'd choose not to get mired in metaphysical complexities.

On the plus side, my guess was that the murder case wasn't going to be easy to crack, and that for the time being I remained reasonably safe. The cops' only route to me was through Laura, and something told me that her connection to Ray Hammond wasn't one that was going to leap out at them straight off the bat. The loaned memory of his eyes said Hammond was a man who was good at keeping secrets, and that Laura would be one of them. The wild card was the guys in gray who'd come along at the end of the memory. As I'd told Deck, they didn't strike me as cops—and I was even more sure of that now that I knew who Ray Hammond had been. It was partly their reaction at the scene of the crime and partly just something about them. These guys had nothing on me, and so no action was required, but I'd certainly be keeping them in mind.

It was possible that the cops would roust Stratten for information on his recent clients. Stratten would have no knowledge of my piece of freelancing, but I had to make sure that I behaved in as normal a way as possible, otherwise his brain might start ticking over. In other words, I needed to give him a call and act nice.

I ran back over it every which way, and always came back to the same conclusion. If we could just lie low for a while, and Quat came through for me, chances were I would be okay. Which left only one question, irrelevant but still curious.

What was a ranking cop doing with property in wasteland LA?

Eventually the sky started to darken and my speed picked back up as I approached the adult area. A Net Nanny peered at me at the intersection and let me pass, correctly judging I was of adult age, if not necessarily an adult. The adult zone's not a homey place—perpetual night, gas stations and twenty-four-hour mini-marts, bus shelters with no one standing at them and solitary figures trudging down roads—but I had to drive through it to get to where the wild folks live. Competing banner signs kept pace with the car as I shot through, shouting about the wares of sex sites along the way. Gradually the signs got sidetracked into punching each other out, and started to fall behind. At one point an entirely naked and silicone-enhanced female appeared in my passenger seat, cooing about the things I could see for just $19.95 an hour, but I kept my foot down and got out the other side before it got out of hand. The image pouted and dissolved as I crossed the line into hacker territory, leaving me with the sound of a kiss.

It's individual domains again out there, but the houses are of more baroque design and have Fuckoff Dogs sleeping out front. As you drive past in the twilight, each opens one eye and growls to let you know they're there. The Fuckoff Dogs are basically hack detectors, and can deal with anything short of a supervirus. There was a period when you'd see lions, dragons, and eternal vortexes of death-knives keeping guard, but then the hackers all moved on to some other fad and dogs slowly took over again.

Time tends to seem to slow in the hackers' zone because of the processing requirements of all their little tweaks and hacks. Roads seldom lead where you expect, and unless you know where you're going—and have forward clearance—you'll find yourself burped out somewhere on the other side of the Net.

Eventually I got to Quat's street, and drove up to his gate. His Fuckoff hauled itself to its feet and squinted irritably at me as I approached. He's an old version and getting tired, but Quat's too sentimental to upgrade. I held my hand out and let the dog sniff it, half expecting, as always, to lose my fingers, but he recognized my Preferences File and let me in. It tried to send a cookie back down the link as I passed, and I blocked it, as usual. One of Quat's milder cookies will localize your operating system into Amish, and one time he turned my avatar into a serial killer. I'd whacked fourteen virtual people in cyburbia before the sysCops caught up with me, but luckily Quat had included an Undo function and no lasting harm was done.

I parked in front of the house and ran up the path to the front door. As the buzzer played what sounded like an entire symphony deep in the bowels of the house, I nervously hopped from foot to foot and peered through the window into Quat's living room. It was very tidy. It always is. Quat's so house-proud, rumor has it that even in the real world when he has a party, he insists that everyone is modeled in code and spends the evening in a virtual-reality version of his apartment: Then, when they leave, he can just restore it from a backup, without the wine stains and piles of vomit. I'd never actually met Quat in the flesh, but I could believe it.

"Yo," he said when he opened his door. "You got my message."

"Nice suit, Quatty," I replied. Quat always dresses like a particularly straitlaced FBI agent from the 1950s, which I guess is an ironic statement of some kind. His virtual face, likewise, is a picture of stern respectability—whereas I expect in the real world he looks the usual hacker mess and doesn't spend enough money on clothes.

"Can't stay," I said, and he nodded.

"I guessed a call at three in the morning was unlikely to have been purely social. What do you need?"

"A machine."

"What kind of machine?"

I looked him straight in the eye. "A memory transmitter."

He raised an eyebrow. "Are you serious?"

"Yes. And I need it fast."

He shook his head slowly, still looking at me. "Fast I can't do. To do it at all is going to be extremely difficult. As you know. And expensive. I know only about two people who might be able to lash one up. And they're both doing time with no hope of Net access."

"There's someone around who can do it," I said.

"Got a name?"

I shook my head, wishing I'd thought to ask Laura Reynolds but knowing she wouldn't have told me. "Just trust me, there is. And however much it costs, I need a machine. Now."

"Someone taken a job they shouldn't have?"

"That's about the size of it."

"It doesn't worry you that if Stratten finds out, he's going to be extremely mad? I mean, like, *killing* mad?"

"Quat, I've got no choice. The last lump of money your demon fractalled for me was the first payment for the job. The dump's already in my head. You've got to find this guy, and fast."

Facial reactions don't mean a whole lot on the Net, but Quat's stern face now looked especially stern. "What are you carrying?"

"A murder. A cop-killing. And there's something hinky about it. I need it out of my head."

He looked away, running his eyes over the pristine tidiness of his entryway. In reality he could have been doing anything, and was probably already starting getting in touch with his contacts. "Got to go," I said. "Give me an estimate."

"Twenty-four hours."

My heart sank. "Shit—that long?"

"If you're lucky. Where are you going to be?"

"Wherever I am," I said, and went.

Quat and his house dissolved into a shower of pixels, and I was back in the parking lot again. I was about to leap out and go running upstairs, with that youthful vigor I have, but then decided I could do with a quick cigarette without Laura Reynolds whining at me. Meantime I got the teleputer to flash up the bottom line of today's news. People were doing stuff, or had done stuff, none of it of direct relevance to me. It was going to be a sunny day unless it pissed down later on. There was nothing about the Hammond murder. Life was holding steady, at least for the time being.

I finished the cigarette and slipped out of the car, trying not to let any of the smoke escape.

I KNEW SOMETHING was wrong the moment I closed the apartment door behind me. Rather than knocking, I'd used my key, on the grounds that Laura might be in an escapist mood. Turned out not to be an issue. The living room was empty. No one was in the bathroom either. I quickly walked to both bedrooms, then turned and pointlessly searched the living room again. Deck and Laura continued to fail to be there.

I stopped myself from checking the other rooms again. The apartment was empty. You can tell. The objects in the room looked smug and overprominent in that way they do when they've got the space to themselves. I stood still for a moment, blinking, not sure how to react but suspecting that outright panic was the way forward. I hadn't specifically told Deck not to take Laura out shopping or something, but he's a bright guy. I'm sure he took it as understood. There was a third used cup on the counter, which meant there'd been time for Laura to finish up in the bathroom and doubtless irritably accept a cup of coffee. The readout on the answering machine said no one had called, and the machine itself bad-temperedly confirmed this.

There was no note, and no sign of a struggle in the apartment. There just wasn't anyone there. The place felt like the *Marie Celeste*, except that it wasn't a ship and it was carpeted.

The phone rang. I grabbed it. "Deck?"

"No—it's the Tidster."

"Tid—have you seen Deck? With a woman?"

He laughed. "No. That'd be something to remember, right?"

"You didn't see him leave the building."

"No."

"Then what the hell are you calling for?"

"You still interested in hearing if any official-looking dudes pull up outside?"

My blood ran a little colder. "What are you telling me?"

"Silver car, two guys, ten seconds ago."

"Holy fuck." I slammed the phone down on Tid, who was still talking, snatched my coat, and ran out of the apartment. Dithered for a moment in the hallway, then headed toward the bank of elevators that led down the northern side of the building—judging that the men would come up the central way.

As I ran I asked four questions: How the hell had they found the apartment? Why were they after me, and how did they even know I existed? Who the hell *were* they?

No answers came. Near the end of the corridor I found myself slowing down, and stopped just before turning the corner. I had the jitters big-time, and not just because of the general situation. I felt trapped. I glanced back toward the apartment: There was no sign of anyone yet, but once they entered my corridor they'd see me, and I was too far away to hear the elevator doors. Large and noisy sections of my brain were shouting at me to just keep running, head for the other elevator bank, and get the hell down to another floor. But something else was telling me to be careful. I decided to trust it.

I reached into my pocket and yanked out the clock, shook it vigorously until it woke up.

"Jeez, what time is it?" it said irritably. "I'm bushed."

"Got a job for you," I said.

At this, the clock brightened considerably. "Cool. What?"

"I need you to go around the corner and walk until you can see the elevator doors."

"Why?"

"Just do it. If the doors open and anything danger-shaped comes out, run back here screaming your head off."

I set the clock down on the floor. It peered up at me suspiciously, and I waved it forward. As it toddled off around the corner, keeping close to the wall, I prepared to feel kind of foolish.

For a minute it was very quiet; then I heard the sound of the elevator doors opening. The clock didn't shout.

I was halfway around the corner when I heard something else.

A gunshot.

After a brief pause in which I froze, shocked into immobility, the clock came hurtling around the corner toward me. "Shit," it squeaked breathlessly, and then it was gone. I ran after it as fast as I could, but not quickly enough to avoid getting a glimpse of who had come out of the elevator.

Two men. Dressed in gray.

I hurtled down the corridor, knowing I was trapped. As I

passed the clock, it made a dive for my jeans, clung on, and scrambled hectically up my left leg. When it got to the top, it scurried rapidly back into my jacket pocket and nosed its way into the deepest corner. I sensed it wasn't going to be a great deal of help.

I heard a *ping*, and realized that someone was about to enter the floor via the central elevators. Glancing behind, I saw that the two men were coming down the corridor after me. They were running fast, with a compact running style in exact step with each other. In that second I also flashed on something I hadn't consciously noticed in the memory: Both wore old-fashioned sunglasses, like sloping beetle eyes.

The one on the right scoped me, and a shot rang out, whistling about six inches to the right of my leg. I found my rhythm again, and then some. As I sprinted around the corner, I saw four old people getting out of the elevator in a neat two-by-two formation. All looked pretty alarmed. I banged straight through the middle—knocking three of them over—and into the elevator behind them. I slapped the button and threw myself flat against the side wall as the oldsters squawked and jabbered. The doors closed mercifully quickly, and I just stared across the elevator, panting slightly, not bothering to peek through the narrowing gap.

Then we were heading down. "They shot at me" came a muffled voice from my pocket, sounding genuinely upset.

"Fuckers," I said, pulling out my gun. "I won't stand for that."

"You mean it?"

I slammed a clip in. "Absolutely. You're my clock. Anyone shoots you, it's going to be me."

I decided against screwing around with lower floors and went straight to the basement. Waved the gun around as I jumped out, but nobody was there. I turned and shot out the elevator controls on both sides, and an alarm of implacable vehemence went off.

I ran across the parking lot with the back of my neck tingling, expecting something small and hard to smack into it at any moment, and dived into the car. I left The Falkland's premises at around a hundred miles an hour, for once in my life deciding that anti-collision software was for wimps. I lost the back end for a while as I swerved onto the street, causing a certain amount of disquiet in my fellow road-users, then just put my foot down and headed for the gate.

It was only when I was half a mile away that I remembered I'd left the memory receiver in my apartment.

CHAPTER SIX

I called Deck's house from the car, though I knew it was pointless. He lives out near the beach in Santa Monica, and there was no way he could have gotten there in the time I was on the Net, even assuming he had a reason to. The phone rang for a while, and then his machine kicked in. I shouted something brief and to the point at it, then hung up.

When I was through the wall and back in real LA, I slowed to something approaching legal speed, and retraced my route of the night before back out to the boulevard. I didn't know what else to do. The only thing I could think of was that Laura had somehow convinced Deck to take her back to the hotel to collect her moisturizing creams and exfoliants. Long shot, I grant you, but it was either that or they were still in Griffith somewhere, and I sincerely believed it would be better for me to spend the next couple hours elsewhere. I had no idea who the guys in gray were, or what they wanted—but it was clear they were pretty hot at finding people: even people they'd never seen before. I wanted lots of distance between us. I reasoned that Deck knew my number: He'd call when he could. Assuming no one was stopping him.

I wasn't surprised to see the same flunky behind the desk at the Nirvana Inn, and he didn't seem surprised to see me.

"Chip," I said, reading the name on his badge. "How the devil are you?"

"Excuse me?" he said after a pause.

"Good to hear it. Now, question: Has Ms. Reynolds been back here this morning with a guy?"

"No, sir," Chip replied. "But a guy came with another guy, and they were looking for her."

"What did these guys look like?"

"Medium height. Kind of grim, with matching outfits. Arrived about ten minutes after you left last night."

I stared back at him. "And what did you tell them?"

"That Ms. Reynolds had just been abducted. I gave them a thorough description of you, and read them your registration number from the external security camera."

"I see. Why?"

He shrugged. "They threatened to kill me, too. And they were even more convincing."

That at least explained how the men in the gray suits had tracked me down. "Fair enough. Any cops been by?"

"No," Chip said cheerfully. "Guess I've got that to look forward to."

"Not necessarily. But if they do, will you do me a favor?"

"Maybe. What?"

"Forget I was here."

"And why would I do that?"

I pulled my wallet out. The only big note I had left was a fifty. "Partly this," I said, placing it on the counter. "Mainly just because it would help me out, and right now I'm a person who could use some assistance."

The money vanished. "I'll see what I can do."

"Thanks," I said, and turned to go. The adrenaline that had shot me across from Griffith was turning sour, and I wasn't in the mood to play tough guy any longer. Either he'd help me out, or he wouldn't. Not much I could do about it.

I was a couple of yards from the door when he called out to me. I turned to see him holding something in his hand. "Her bag," he said. "You left it in her room."

I took the suitcase from him, looked inside. The remainder of her clothes, her purse, even the half bottle of vodka.

"How come you didn't give this to the other guys?"

"They didn't ask for it. Plus I don't think you're the only person who needs some help."

I looked at him. He was young, wholesome, firmly of the genus "Hotel Staff Who Rate Their Chances At Making Duty Manager Within Five Years," but evidently more than that.

"What do you mean?"

"That woman. Ms. Reynolds. She seemed nice, but in a jam. Anyone who's skinny and pretty *and* drunk before she goes out for the evening isn't thinking happy thoughts. It's a hard call, but I reckon you're closer to being a friend to her than the other guys. I sure don't think they had anyone's happiness on their minds."

I zipped up the suitcase again. "Thanks," I said. "See you around."

"With the greatest of respect," Chip replied, "I sincerely hope not."

The car was parked in the lot of the diner opposite. I tried Deck's number once more, with the same result. I could either go wait outside his house, or I could go back to Griffith. Someone once taught me that if you don't know where you're going, there's no point hurrying there, so I rooted around in Laura's handbag for a moment, then locked the car and went to get some food.

During the day the diner looked considerably less dangerous, though probably still not somewhere you'd want to take someone of a nervous disposition. Me, for example. It was also empty, apart from a well-dressed guy slumped over a cup of coffee at the far end. The cook nodded at me as I came in, so I felt welcome, which was nice. The way things were going, I would be living in places like this for the rest of my life.

The menu informed me that the pigs that had ended up in the sausage patties had all been organically farmed, and that everyone had been real nice to them throughout their life. It seemed unlikely to me that the diner's clientele would give a shit—these are guys whose hair is still wet from climbing out of the primordial soup. But that's LA for you: Maybe they all practiced mugging without cruelty. Personally, I care only for pigs that have been kept in matchboxes and had people whisper nasty things to them in the night, but I ordered a small breakfast anyway. I could always beat up the sausage on my plate. From the look on the waitress's face, it was clear she was working there only to fill in time before the world ended in the depressing way she'd always anticipated. Taking my order seemed to deepen her sadness.

While I waited for my food to arrive, I took a look through what I'd taken from Laura's purse. Her organizer.

Luckily the unit wasn't finger-coded, or I'd have had no chance. It was password-protected in the conventional way, but that didn't take long to crack—especially as I had a vague idea of what the password was from her loaned memories of Ensenada. I plugged her organizer into my own, which is packed full of software of dubious provenance which I've picked up on the Net. By the time I was halfway through my first cup of coffee, the OS had rolled over and I was in.

The fact that she'd passworded it at all said a lot about Laura Reynolds. Every organizer gives you the option, and the world is divided into those who do and those who don't password. If you do, then every time you turn it on you've got to scribble or type in that sequence of characters before you can even get someone's phone number. A bit of a pain, and no real protection against someone who knows what they're doing. Secrets are difficult to keep, and anyone who runs their life around them is forever teetering on the edge of disclosure. Plus this: Making something secret makes it too important, elevates it to the point where it runs your life from the shadows. If you hide what's at your core from other people for too long, sooner or later you end up hiding it from yourself and waking up with no idea of who you are.

Laura Reynolds's password was 16/4/2003. I worked out she'd have been around fourteen, fifteen back then—assuming I was right in pegging her age in the late twenties. I checked that date in the calendar, but it was blank. Of course, she wouldn't have had this organizer then—it was an Apple Groovy™, quite new—but she could have filled it in anyway. People often do that in the first flush of new organizer joy, sketching in the story of their life thus far. I also did a search for the phrase "My Birthday": Everybody puts them in, privately making the day special for themselves—as if the organizer is their own private world, and they're free to be vulnerable there. Laura's birthday was 11/4, so that wasn't it either. Whatever. It evidently meant something to her.

I knew there'd be no entries for the period when she'd been in Ensenada, and found there was nothing on the day when she dumped the memory of the murder on me either. I trawled through her address book for a while, but nothing jumped out: Then I did a search to see what names were most frequently cross-referenced in the calendar. It seemed Laura hung out with a girl called Sabi pretty regularly, but that was it. The rest was just business appointments and working lunches. I didn't recognize any of the company names. I didn't even know what Laura did for a living.

My food arrived, and as I chomped rapidly through it I set the organizer to do a general search on my name and that of Ray Hammond. The sausage was pretty good, if you're interested, though something about the eggs made me suspect the hens had had a rather harder time of it than the pigs. The guy down at the end now appeared to be asleep, his forehead gently resting on the table. Just looking at him made me want a beer.

Checking the search results didn't take long. There weren't any. Either there'd never been anything about me or the dead cop in Laura's organizer, or, more likely, she'd erased it. I couldn't even find the email from her hacker listing Hammond's address, or any Net addresses with distinctive hacker domains. There were no records in the calendar of the days when she'd used REMtemps's services. Sometime between the memory dump and last night, Laura Reynolds had done a pretty thorough job of clearing out her life, maybe believing that if it wasn't down there to read, then it hadn't really happened.

Finally, much later than it should have, it occurred to me to check the owner information in the organizer. No address was listed—sensibly, but again secretively—but there was a phone number, an email address, and the promise of a small reward to whoever returned the device. I decided to claim it, and dialed the number. It rang a couple of times, and then picked up.

"Laura?" I said, surprised.

There was no answer. I realized it was probably her machine, and waited to leave another fruitless message, promising myself that I'd talk to someone at some point in the day who was actually *there*. I was beginning to feel like I was in a parallel universe where nobody could hear me except machines.

The line remained quiet. "Laura, are you there?" I said, suddenly less confident. "Deck?" I tried. "Can you hear me?"

"Nobody's here," a voice said. It was male, deep.

"Who's that?" I asked, thinking: boyfriend? cops?

"You know who it is," the voice said. The more I heard it, the less I liked it. It sounded too clear, as if it weren't coming into my head via the phone. Something told me this was neither a policeman nor an insignificant other.

"No, I don't," I said. "You going to tell me, or what?"

There was a long pause. "You'll remember," it said.

"Look, is Laura there?" I asked petulantly. My own voice didn't sound at all deep anymore.

"Around the school we went," the voice said. The line went dead.

I remained absolutely motionless for a moment, the phone still at my ear. It felt as though something were going to swirl out of the blackness, as if a word were finally going to make it off the tip of my tongue. A memory. There was so much in the way, other people's and my own, but it was coming.

"You okay?" asked a voice, and the sensation disappeared. I blinked and saw that it was the slumped man who had spoken. He'd raised his head from the table and was looking at me. A little older than me, mid-length wavy fair hair. Strong features, strangely reassuring, and his eyes were clearer than you'd expect in someone who obviously had a hangover from hell. "You look like you've seen a ghost," he said.

I left what was left of my money on the table and ran.

I DROVE AIMLESSLY and fast, not knowing where to go. Just being on the move seemed important. Eventually I turned off the boulevard and pootled through residential for a while, then pulled over to the curb, cut the engine, and sat. As soon as the car was stationary, my hands started shaking.

I hadn't recognized the voice on the phone, but it had sounded familiar. Generically familiar in the same way as the two men who seemed to be chasing Laura were also familiar. But I ran a check on her area code—the phone must have rung on the other side of Burbank. They say that nowhere in LA is more than a half hour from anywhere else, but they also say that the moon is made of cheese and the Empire State Building is a phallic symbol. I didn't believe the men in gray suits could have gotten from my apartment to Laura's house in the time provided, but I didn't know where that conclusion left me.

I'd started the morning with a simple, albeit difficult, task. Getting hold of a transmitter. Not only had I made very few inroads on it, but the problem seemed to be broadening, seeping sideways into areas I had no understanding of. It was as if something were holding me in place, preventing me from going forward. There was a structure here, but I couldn't see it. Without Laura Reynolds to revolve around, nothing that was happening seemed to make sense.

As I sat there, staring out the windshield and wondering what to do next, the door to a house on the other side of the street opened. It was a good-looking house: two-story, not too fancy, nice deck. A youngish woman in a lilac-colored dress peered suspiciously across the road at me: keeping an eye on her neighborhood, keeping the chaos at bay. A tiddly kitten came trotting out of the door from behind her, and the woman called to it. The kitten scooted vaguely around on the deck for a moment, obviously rather taken aback by the magnitude of the space it now found itself in, and then galloped back indoors. I hoped it had a sibling to whom it could spend the afternoon fibbing about its adventures. The woman in the lilac dress took a last look at my car, then followed the kitten inside and shut the door.

For a moment I wished more than anything that I lived there with her. That she knew my name, that the kitten was ours, that I had woodworking tools and knew where I kept them. From the outside, other people's lives always look more rounded than mine, more meaningful, more whole. At least, I hope it's only from the outside.

Sometimes it feels as if reality is streamed, and that I'm sitting in the back of the class that knows nothing but transience, hotels, and takeout food. As if there's some test you have to take before they'll let you move up a grade to where the nice folks live, but I can never find out where it's being held.

For want of anything else to do, I bit the bullet and dialed REMtemps. I still had the dream receiver in the trunk of the car, and I wanted one less thing hanging over my head. Sabrina put me on hold for a little while, and then Stratten himself came on the line.

"You're a hard man to get hold of, Mr. Thompson," he said.

He sounded impatient but not unfriendly. I played it casual. "Man of mystery. Anyhow, I'm back in town, and—"

"Back?" Stratten said quickly, and I realized I'd made an error. I'd patched my calls through Quat's system while in Mexico, making it look like I was still in LA.

"Had to go upstate yesterday," I continued as smoothly as I could. "That's why I wasn't there for your calls."

"Business trip?"

I'm not that stupid. "Personal, of course." I left it there. Extraneous details always sound like lies.

"Next time set a redirect. I've got a lot of work stacked up for you."

"I can't do a memory," I told him. "My head still isn't right."

"Migraine?"

"Yeah," I said, and at that moment it was pretty close to the truth. A sudden gout of Laura's vacation slewed down through my head, filling it with hangover and sour margaritas.

"But you'll do dreams despite that?" Stratten was too polished to let suspicion into his tone, but I knew it was there.

"They're different, as you know. Plus I need the money." Not true. I had around a quarter million hidden in various places on the Net, not including the money I intended to give back to Laura Reynolds. But I figured it would make Stratten happy to think I was beholden to him.

I was right. "Okay," he said, apparently satisfied. "Take one more day off. But make sure it's a restful one. Tonight's going to be very tiring."

You don't know the half of it, I thought.

I DROVE BACK to Griffith, and took a pass in front of The Falkland. There was nothing to see, but I still didn't like it, so I parked on the far side of the square and sat outside a bar, drinking beer on credit. Deck's phone remained unanswered, there was no message on my machine, and a call to Tid's cellular told me there'd been no sign of the two men in gray suits. I didn't try Laura's number again.

I was halfway through my third beer, trying to work out a way of checking out my apartment without laying myself open to the possibility of being killed, when the phone finally rang.

"Where the *fuck* are you?" I shouted, scaring some of the other early afternoon drinkers.

"On the Net, where else?" answered a calm voice. "You running a little tense there, Hap?"

"Quat," I said more quietly. "Thought you were someone else."

"Well, be glad it's me. Got some good news for you."

About time. "What?"

"You lucked out. I found a guy who lashed a part-working device up less than a week ago for a woman who wanted to make a large transferral. Sound familiar?"

"Sure does." Laura's hacker. Had to be. "When can I have it?"

"Guy's in the area. Tonight soon enough?"

Better than I'd dared hope. I felt light-headed with relief. "What's the deal?"

"Thirty thou, one-time usage. Guy delivers, waits, takes it back."

"Can't do it that way. I have some logistical problems." Like not having my receiver at hand. "I need it overnight at least."

"Hold a sec." There was silence, then Quat came back on the line. "Okay, but the price goes to fifty, and the device is back by six A.M. Guy's doing me a favor here. He wants it back in pieces pronto."

"Deal." It was actually less than I was expecting, and in the current situation cheap at the price. "What about the delivery? Time and place?"

"Why not your apartment?"

"I'm going off the color scheme." I thought for a moment. "You know the Prose Café?"

Quat sniggered. "I know of it."

"Tell your guy eight o'clock, there. Will you arrange the money transfer?"

"As we speak. And you might want to go alone, Hap. I think this is a guy who scares easy."

At least he makes it out into the real world sometimes, I thought. "How will I know who he is?"

"You'll know," Quat said, and was gone.

I took a celebratory swig of my beer and beamed goodwill at my fellow drinkers. The most difficult piece of the puzzle was now in place. True, the easier bits—like having access to my own machine, and to the woman whose head the memory needed to go back into—had gone a bit complex to compensate, but at least I was getting somewhere.

I had an idea, and dialed the Tidster's number again. He answered on the first ring. He always does. He doesn't seem to have anything to do except run errands for people like me.

"Got a fifty-buck job for you if you've got ten minutes."

"That rate, you can have half a day. What do you want?"

"I left something that I need in my room. Thought maybe I could give you the key and you could go up and fetch it." For a moment I understood why Woodley would operate only through remotes. Maybe he was more in tune with the times than me.

"Sure. But why can't you go?"

"There are reasons. But listen—when you get to the room, you've got to knock first. Don't just go barging in there."

"Whatever you say, boss. Where are you?"

"Just across the square." Abruptly I stopped, realizing I couldn't do this. Tid could knock on the door all he liked, or more likely he'd ignore my advice and just open it right up. Based on past performance, if the two men had come back to my apartment, they'd shoot him either way. If they weren't there, he'd earn fifty bucks. It wasn't enough. No amount of money was enough for that kind of risk. Plus I remembered I didn't have any cash left.

"Listen, Tid. I've changed—"

"Hey hey hey," he said, voice distant. "Talking to a man who's been looking for you."

"What the hell are you talking about?" I asked, but then realized he wasn't speaking into the phone. Frowning, I listened to a muffled exchange, and then someone else's voice came on the line.

"Hap," it said urgently. "Where the hell have you been, man?"

Luckily my phone was made of the stuff they used to fashion space shuttles from. "Deck? Are you okay? Have you got Laura?"

"Yes and yes, though I'm pretty spooked. Been trying to get hold of you all morning." Deck sounded relieved.

"How?"

"On the phone, Hap. How do you think, spirit guides?"

"Don't go up to the apartment. I'm across the square outside the Twelve Bar. Get the fuck over here."

I stood up, stared across the square. There was a three-second delay, and then the doors to The Falkland opened. Deck came out, Laura's upper arm gripped firmly in one of his hands. She was wearing the green dress and looked nice, though pretty pissed. At least she wasn't bothering to dig her heels in, which would have been merely tiresome.

Deck was talking fast from five yards away. "Jesus H. Christ, Hap. You leave it off the hook or something?"

"No," I said. "And I've had it in reaching distance all the fucking time. You sure you've got the right number?"

He spieled it off like a machine gun.

"I am getting really, really fed up with this," Laura said. "Being dragged around dives by this monkey all morning is my idea of a very dull time."

"Shut up," I said. "I fetched your purse, so be polite."

"Oh, yeah, like that's some big favor."

I ignored her, turned to unlock the car. "What happened?" I asked Deck.

"Don't know," he said, looking sheepish. "Got twitchy. Hap, there's something a little weird going on here."

"No shit, Scully."

Deck helped Laura into the back, then settled in the passenger seat. I locked the doors and set the car on an auto-tourist route, then got their story as we tooled around the neighborhood.

Deck had waited until Laura got out of the shower, then gave her a coffee. They were exchanging unpleasantries, when the phone rang. Deck was going to let the machine take it; then he realized it might be me calling from the Net with a change of plan. So he picked up.

A deep voice came on the line. Asked to speak to Laura Reynolds. Deck said she wasn't there. The voice chuckled quietly, then asked for me instead. Deck said I wasn't there, and was asked to deliver a message. "The wrath of nothing will fall swiftly," the deep voice said.

"Not very nice," I said.

"No, and quite threatening, I thought. Plus a little incomprehensible. So I wait for a few minutes, thinking maybe I should call you, and then I get a nervous feeling. Something about the guy's voice made me think that 'swiftly' might mean not, like, 'tomorrow,' or 'sometime later in the week, possibly Friday.' It might mean actually *now*. So I went to the window, looked down at the street. I didn't see anything unusual, but I didn't know what I was looking for. Then I called you, but the line was busy."

"When was this?"

"Exactly a half hour after you left." At which point I was sitting in the parking lot below The Falkland, smoking a cigarette and not talking to anyone at all. Deck shrugged. "So, well, you know how I get sometimes."

I did. Deck has a sixth sense. Sounds corny, but he does. A while ago he saved the life of someone I cared about, simply by keeping them talking. I wasn't there for a variety of reasons, but I heard about it afterward. My friend and Deck were drinking together in a bar, killing time. She was supposed to meet up with someone and drive out of the city, but Deck got the Fear and kept her there, talking nonsense and pretending to be trying to convince her of something else. He managed to delay her for only ten minutes, but that was enough. The guy she was due to meet got impatient waiting for her, ran to his car to go look for her. Couple of seconds later he was spread in a thin red mist over a hundred cubic yards, and it was raining bits of motor vehicle.

The car had been wired. No way Deck could have known about the bomb, none at all. Make of it what you like, but if Deck gets nervous, I do what he says.

"So I grabbed Little Ms. Charming here and we left." Laura scowled.

"You didn't check in the parking lot under the hotel?"

Deck looked embarrassed. "Er, no. Not then. I forget that when you say you're going to Quat's you aren't actually, you know, *going* there. Anyway, I dragged us around Griffith, keeping on the move. It felt . . . I don't know."

"What?"

He shrugged. "It felt like someone was following us. But I couldn't see anyone. Tried your cellular at like fifteen-minute intervals. Busy. In the end decided I had no choice but to come back. This time I did check the lot, but you weren't there."

"I made about five calls once I was out of the Net, all of them very short. Mainly to the machine at your place."

"Well," he said, "then your phone's fucked. Talk to the weirdo about it. Where you been anyhow?"

"You were right. The guy who called the apartment did mean now. They turned up about five minutes after you left. I must have missed you by seconds."

"Who's 'they'?" Laura demanded.

I looked at her. "The guys in the gray suits."

"What the hell were they doing there?"

"Looking for you, I would guess," I said. "What are the chances of you answering some questions?"

"About what?" she said, digging around in her bag. "How stupid you guys are?"

"About why you blew Ray Hammond's head off. And who these other guys might be."

"Don't know what you're talking about," she said, smiling sweetly. "It never happened. You can polygraph me if you like. I'm clean."

"Yes, but not for much longer." I was on the edge of losing my temper. "I've got hold of a transmitter—from the same guy *you* dealt with." Her smile vanished. "He's delivering it tonight, and ten minutes later all this is going to be back in your head. And guess what? Deck and I get to walk away. But not you. You're the only one the cops will be able to connect to the murder, and that's just the least of your problems."

"So what's the biggie, in your humble opinion?" she asked, eyes hard.

"Those guys in suits. They're a lot tighter on the case than the police are. They dropped by the Nirvana this morning. And I called your house. They were there. Looking for you."

"I don't believe you. How would you know my number?"

"Your organizer. Your best friend is called Sabi and your birthday's in November."

"That's *private!*" she shouted. "That's *my* life."

"So's what I've got in my head, but you didn't mind sharing that. Question is: How did *those* guys know where you live?"

"I don't know. They don't mean anything to me."

"You obviously mean something to *them*. They got to your house far too quickly from the Nirvana, by the way. Either there's more than two of them, or something real strange is going on, which is why I'm not keen on going up to the apartment just now. Whoever these guys are, they're real close on your tail."

"Not just mine," she snapped. "You heard your little friend here. After me, they asked for *you*."

"They're looking for me only because they know I've got you. The flunky at the hotel snitched me under duress."

"Bullshit. You know what I'm saying is true."

We were passing Herbie's Crouton just then, included in the route in its capacity as one of Griffith's finest architectural achievements. I sent the store my customary beat of ill will, but not with much attention. When I turned back, Deck's eyes were on me.

"She right?" he asked.

"Probably. The guy I spoke to said something pretty weird. I don't know what it meant, but it meant something."

"No one just walks away," Laura said quietly. "That's not how life works." I couldn't really disagree. In the rearview mirror she looked small, and alone, and for a little while I wasn't angry at her.

CHAPTER SEVEN

The Hard Prose Café is over in the warehouse district of Griffith.
It's not really a warehouse district, of course, just another chunk
of reality-flavored life. During the eighties and nineties people
got so used to overpriced bars and restaurants being in cavernous
old buildings that they forgot they weren't originally planned
that way. So, when they were laying Griffith out, they built a
couple of blocks of looming edifices and redeveloped them *during* construction—building walls and then knocking them out
again immediately, to get that authentic feel. The block the Café
is on actually has a fake wharf out front: It's only when you walk

right up to it and look down that you realize the "river" is a Plexiglas roof over the subway. Sometimes I think we've gotten so used to chocolate-flavored drinks that real chocolate would make us break out in a rash.

Laura took it hard when we walked into the Café. I guess the place offended her aesthetic sensibilities. The Prose was started by a bunch of Hollywood writers who wanted somewhere dark to sulk between meetings. The service sucks. You have to book a table for about an hour before you actually want it, because the management works on the assumption that the clientele will deliver themselves late. It takes you years to attract a waiter's attention; they'll change your order in the kitchen without consulting you; and if your meal does ever arrive, then someone you haven't seen in months will pop up from nowhere and take ten percent of your food. The interior has never been properly finished, because the contractors completed only half the work before getting decorators' block, and now spend the whole time revising what they've already done and whining about merchandising rights.

Deck and I go there because it's the only public place in all of California where you're allowed to smoke. Also I like the layout, although I sense I'm in the minority. It's a huge room, two stories high, with a big circular bar in the center. Drink orders come through pretty quickly: I think they're considered a priority. There's also a huge piece of sculpture to one side, in the shape of—well, I don't know what it's in the shape of, to be honest. It was clearly designed to be a conversation piece, but I fancy the conversation generally goes like this:

"What the *fuck* is that?"

"Fucked if I know."

"It's fucking *hideous*."

"Yeah. Let's burn it."

All around the sides of the room are wooden nooks and crannies with tables, tiered at irregular heights like paddy fields. In one corner, if you can be bothered, you can clamber up to a platform that is only a little lower than the ceiling. There you sit gazing regally down upon a mini-cloud system of secondhand smoke.

I headed us in that direction. I don't get a chance to act regal very often.

The top table had the additional advantage of being the

position that would be most difficult for Laura to run from. She'd been quiet for the rest of the afternoon, sitting silently in the backseat and refusing a tofu burrito when offered one. Which was, to be honest, a relief: Neither Deck nor I had wanted to compromise our carnivore integrity by ordering one. We left her in the car a few times when we got out to stretch our legs, but we didn't go far. She seemed docile, but I wasn't going to let that fool me. Before the night was out I had every confidence she would do something irritating. The only question was when.

When we'd gotten up to the high table, Deck volunteered to go get some drinks, leaving the two of us alone. I lit a cigarette happily and offered Laura one, but she just glared at me. "I don't smoke."

"Yeah, you do. Kims."

"I took control of my life and quit."

I laughed. "When, two days ago?"

"Three, actually."

"Bully for you," I said, and turned away. Though it was only six, most of the tables below us were already occupied, so I sat and watched the people for a while. I used to find it difficult to believe that other humans have lives, that they're more than bit-part players in the B movie of my life. Only when you see them somewhere like a bar do you realize that they've come there for a reason, that they have relationships with the folks they've come to see, and that—appearances sometimes to the contrary— they must be actual people. Since I started memory work, how- ever, I didn't find that so hard to believe. Sometimes, when I'm tired, I feel the distinctions fading away. I can almost believe that instead of being an individual I'm merely part of some con- tinuum of experience: But glimpsing the reality of other people's lives doesn't make them any easier to understand, unfortu- nately. As far as I knew, no one in the whole history of the world had ever been party to as large a chunk of someone's actual life as I was of Laura Reynolds's, and yet I still found her incompre- hensible. I couldn't see how she had gone from the girl she had been, the girl standing by the stream, to the woman she was.

"Does it have to be this way?" she asked suddenly, startling me. I'd assumed I was in for long-term mute treatment.

"What?" I said. "I mean, okay, the decor's kind of patchy, but . . ."

"The transfer," she said. "Do I really have to take it back?"

She looked tired, blue shadows like faint bruises under her eyes. The long sleeves of her dress covered the scars on her wrists, but I knew they must be uncomfortable.

"Yeah. I'm sorry, but you do. They catch me with your memories in my head and I'll end up doing your time. And worse."

She put her elbows on the table and propped her chin on her hands, looking up at me in a way that was clearly supposed to be appealing. It was, as it happens. "Why worse? Just because you're a guy, or because you've got a record?"

"I don't. Never got caught, and no outstanding warrants. Except one." I hesitated, then thought, what the hell. When she wasn't being obnoxiously rude, she was pleasant company. "A few years ago I was involved in a bad incident. Wasn't my fault: I didn't know it was going to go down that way. But some people got killed, and one cop in particular was extremely pissed about it. He chased me around the country for a couple years, but then I hired someone to wipe the crime. He had nothing left to hang on me and had to give it up."

"Couldn't this cop just whack you anyway? Or frame you for something?"

The same thought had occurred to me, many times. "Apparently not. From what I can make out, he's a pretty honorable guy."

The corner of her mouth twitched sourly. "The last of a dying breed."

"Hey—I have my moments. Anyhow, this cop is leading the investigation into the murder of the man you killed."

Laura raised her eyebrows and seemed to accept that this might represent a problem. "Kind of a coincidence, isn't it?"

I shook my head. "He's a top homicide detective, and Ray Hammond was LAPD brass. It's the obvious choice. And if he can get me on something legitimate, I'm fucked."

"But there's nothing to link you to the murder. You know that. Like you said, if I'm unlucky, someone could connect me. You weren't even there."

"Someone's already made the connection. Those guys in gray. I'm not spending the next five years looking over my shoulder. I've spent too much of my life doing that already." Down below I saw that Deck had made it through to the bar and was ordering drinks in bulk. Sensible man.

Laura wasn't giving up. "But does it have to come back to me? Can't you just fire it off into the wild blue yonder?"

I shook my head. "Doesn't get rid of it. You do that, all that happens is that it will coalesce somewhere random, on a street or by some stream, and hang around like a cloud. Somebody walks through that cloud, and at least some of it will get into their head. They end up with False Memory Syndrome, think bad things have happened to them and blame the people closest to them. In the early days a lot of families got hurt that way."

"But—"

"And even if you don't give a shit about them," I interrupted, "there's forensic recallists who can build up a profile of where the memory originally came from. Either way, I'm not doing it."

"So that's it? You just dump it back in me and run away?"

I shrugged. "Give me your account details and I'll get your money back to you—which I think is fairly cool of me, considering you've cost me a week's work and a whole stack of brownie points with my employer."

"But what am I supposed to—"

Suddenly I felt tired. "I'm sick of answering questions, Laura. Why don't you try it for a change? This is your mess, not mine. Why did you kill him? Why did you try to kill yourself last night? What are your problems, and why can't you deal with them?"

"Mind your own business, asshole," she said, and turned away.

At that moment Deck arrived at the table, followed by a couple of waiters struggling under the weight of trays loaded with drinks.

"Having fun, are we?" Deck asked.

"Unimprovable," I said.

AT TWENTY TO EIGHT I was standing at the bar, checking my watch. I was considering the best way to approach the pickup, and getting another round of drinks. Laura had insisted, as she'd already done several times. She was pretty drunk, and had gotten that way quickly. It took me a little while to realize that she might have been draining the bottle in her bag during the afternoon. When I did so, I felt embarrassed for her. I'm no stranger to alcohol-based beverages. But I drink for fun, and because I like the taste. And occasionally as a cheap escape hatch from life, real or otherwise. Laura didn't take it that way. Nobody but Russians drink vodka for the flavor, and Russians seldom mix it with cranberry juice. Laura drank in gulps, as if swallowing medicine, and with a grim determination—like some part of her mind was prescribing a remedy she knew could only make things worse. It was none of my business, and there was nothing I could do about it. I needed her to stay where she was and not give us grief, so I ordered her another drink.

I was fairly confident that just as soon as the bartender had finished being cool, he'd serve it to me, along with the others I'd ordered. He was one of those people who have to load every single action with a little flourish and twirl, and he was really getting on my nerves. I don't want added value from bartenders: I just want my fucking drink.

My plan was that Deck should stay up at the table with Laura, and that at eight I'd come back down and walk the floor. Quat would presumably have furnished the hacker with a description of me, and he'd implied that the guy would be fairly easy to spot. Once the exchange was made, we'd return to The Falkland, I'd bribe someone to baby-sit Laura for a few minutes or lock her in the car, and Deck and I would fetch the receiver from my apartment. Deck disagreed with this part of the plan, and had done so all afternoon. He insisted we should have gone and gotten the receiver first. Going back to my apartment constituted taking a risk, and I didn't want to have to do that until as late in the day as possible. Assuming that part of the evening passed without incident, I'd find a motel, effect the transfer, and tell Laura she was free to go. A night full of paid dreams, and tomorrow would see me right back where I had been a week ago. I felt keyed up, but no more than that.

I was waiting to finger the credit slip, and glaring at the frieze painted around the top of the bar, when the evening started to go weird. The painting showed, in stylized daubs, the gods and goddesses of classical mythology, and I was thinking how dull our understanding of gods was. A Goddess of Love, a God of War, a God in charge of Being Drunk: all like Vice-Presidents in some Earth Inc., under the Chairmanship of Mr. Zeus, Sr. No vague spirits, no shadowed presences, no essence in spaces and gaps; just a good old line-management structure. Modern religions are even worse, on the whole: simply a streamlining. In the old days at least God was a kind of Howard Hughes figure, with a bit of pizzazz: Now He comes across like the aging senior partner of a provincial firm of accountants. A small office above the main drag in some backwater town, the ticking of clocks on slow afternoons, dusty rooms full of guys who belong to the Rotary and genuinely give a shit when the new Buick's coming out.

Yet people reach out, like they still want to believe in UFOs. You'd think by now, when there have been so many false alarms, and so much waiting, and still the black obelisk hasn't turned up, we'd have lost interest in the idea of aliens. But we wait for little guys with pointy ears anyway, to ask politely to be taken to our leader, just as we still go to psychiatrists and faith healers when the only reality they offer is their bills. We don't trust ourselves with our lives, and we're all still waiting for the deus ex machina.

Something made me turn around. By this time I was a few beers down myself, and I thought maybe I'd caught a reflection of someone I recognized in the mirror behind the bar. I couldn't tell whether it had been a man or a woman, and when I looked I didn't see anyone I knew. Bunch of people sitting at tables, talking too loud and too fast: young guys in overdesigned suits; women buoyant with the kind of unnecessary attractiveness that makes you wish they'd go somewhere else so you wouldn't waste your evening covertly staring at them. I panned my eyes slowly over the throng, seeing nothing more out of the ordinary than you'd expect in a Griffith bar. Yet suddenly I felt on edge.

"Sir?" The bartender was waving the credit slip at me. Everything in his demeanor suggested he'd been waiting for me a couple of days instead of a few seconds. Still distracted and scoping the crowds, I rested my finger on the pad at the bottom of the slip, where the sensor would read my DNA, cross-reference to my bank account, and debit the amount required. "There's a space there for a tip," the bartender pointed out helpfully.

"So there is," I said, and put a line through it. "Thanks for warning me." He huffily snatched the slip and went off to serve someone nicer.

I flagged a passing waiter and put my drinks on his tray. "You know the most inconvenient table in the bar?" I asked. I had to speak loudly, above the music now being generated by a couple of musos in the corner of the room. The waiter nodded glumly. He was small and cowed, much more my type of guy. "Take these there. And wait a second."

I found a scrap of paper in my pocket and scribbled a note to Deck. This I stuck under his glass on the tray, then reached for my wallet, remembering only when it was in my hand that I didn't have any cash. "Tell him I said to give you a big tip," I told the troll, and waved him on his way.

This done, I moved away from the bar and slipped into the crowd. The note to Deck told him to stay put but keep an eye out. Maybe I was just getting a little dose of pre-handover nerves, but something made me want to keep on the move. I sipped my beer and wandered around, trying to look inconspicuous while at the same time placing myself at one remove from what was going on around me. It was like a flashback to an earlier period in my life—dope deals and danger—and I didn't like it. Not much, anyway.

Then I saw the guy standing by the other side of the bar. Mid-twenties, long hair, a big nose and glasses, wearing a ratty red sweatshirt with the legend PROGRAMMERS DO IT RECURSIVELY. A glass of what looked like Jolt was in his hand, and there was a small suitcase by his feet.

Something told me he might be the one.

I walked slowly over, giving him plenty of time to see me approaching.

"Hi," I said. He was about six inches shorter than me, and aware of it. He nodded, a couple of quick jerks of the head, and turned away from the bar. Out of the corner of his mouth: "Are you Hap?"

"As far as I know. And you are?"

This time he shook his head—nervy tics from side to side. Quat had been right about this guy: He came across like the dictionary definition of the word "spooked."

Melodrama: "You don't need to know."

"Right," I said, trying not to roll my eyes. "You get the money?"

Greed briefly lit up his pinched features. "Yes. Er, thank you."

"Great. So why don't you finish your drink while you tell me where you want the case dropped tomorrow morning, and then just walk away."

"I can't do that. I'm going to have to tell you how to operate the machine."

"I'm wise in the ways of silicon-based shit—I'll figure it out."

Another headshake. "Dude, you won't. I built the thing, and even I have to work it from notes. All the codes have to be entered manually in real time."

"So email me instructions when you get back to your crib."

"I don't trust the Net for this."

"Jeez—you and Quat are going to get along just fine." I breathed out heavily. "Okay, so let's look at it," I said, wanting this over with.

"Let me take you through the codes first," the nerd insisted, pulling a notebook out of his back pocket. "There's three phases to a transfer. Accepting the dream, coding it for transmission to a specific receiver, and the actual transmission itself. The first stage is a no-brainer—a set of passwords I've written down—the last two are hairy factorial. The transmission code is generated in real time, a random function of the serial numbers of the transmitting and receiving machines. You have to wait until the two machines are synced, then watch out for the match code signal."

"Which I see where, exactly? Show me on the machine."

"Listen to the sequence first," he said. "And would you mind, like, keeping your voice down?"

I was getting impatient. "I've paid you a lot of money for this. Show me the fucking machine."

The hacker held his hands up placatingly. "Okay, look: I saw a big empty room out back. Can we go there?"

I turned on my heel and walked, trying not to lose my temper. Friday and Saturday nights they have big parties at the Café, and through an archway in the rear of the main bar there's a large area for people to chill out in when they've had too much fun to stand up convincingly. Before I went through I looked up into the top corner of the room, hoping Deck would catch a glimpse of me, but there was so much smoke in the air, I doubted I was more than a blur to anyone above the second tier.

The big room was dark, lit only by electric candles arrayed around its edges and in a pool in the middle of the floor, and empty aside from a couple of guys necking on a sofa. One was young and muscular, the other much older and running to flab. Both were far too engrossed in each other to represent a problem. I walked to the opposite corner, sat down. The nerd followed, eyes darting suspiciously across at the lovebirds, then perched on the edge of a sofa at right angles to me.

"I'm waiting," I said.

He dithered, then hauled the case onto his lap. Angling it so only he and I could see, he flicked the latches. Inside was a jumble of components, motherboard fragments, and display units, junction-clipped together by wires of every color of the rainbow.

"Jesus H.," I said.

"See what I'm saying? It's not exactly in showroom condition."

"But it works?"

"Oh, yeah," he said, nodding vigorously. He glanced over at the door once more, and I finally understood what was really bugging me. I watched him closely as he pulled a mini-keyboard out of the mess of wires, and saw that his hands weren't shaking. Mixed signals: The super-nervousness didn't tally with his desire to explain everything in brain-numbing detail; a voice that jumped all over the place, but steady hands. Everything about him said he wanted to be somewhere else, like he regarded me as a kind of semi-dangerous wild animal, and yet he wouldn't just hand the goods over and let me figure it out for myself. He'd gotten his money—what did he care? It seemed odd. Also, I didn't like his shirt.

I leaned in close. "All this is written down, right?" He nodded, started to say something. "Okay," I said. "So give me the notes."

"You won't be able to work it."

I reached forward and slammed the case shut—nearly taking off his fingers—then pulled out my gun and rested it in the middle of the hacker's forehead. His Adam's apple jumped like a salmon going upstream, and his mouth fell open with a dry click. "Just give me the fucking notes. I want to be out of here."

"You ain't going nowhere," said a male voice, and I heard the sound of a safety flicking off. Someone stuck a gun in the back of my neck. "Stand up and throw down your weapon."

"And you would be?" I asked, standing slowly but keeping my gun right where it was.

"LAPD," said the voice, young, a little shaky. He yanked my left arm behind my back.

The hacker looked relieved. "You fuck," I said to him. "You set me up."

"That's right," said another voice, and someone came around to stand in front of me and to the left. The older guy from the necking couple. He was holding up a badge and looking pretty pleased with himself. "Drop the piece," he said, favoring me with a strong gust of secondhand alcohol. "I want to get back to clinching with Barton here. Got the feeling he kind of liked it."

"Fuck you, granddad," Barton said, and jammed the gun harder into my neck. "Look, just drop the gun, goddammit."

"Don't know whether I want to do that," I said, pointlessly playing for time. "Seems to me that while I'm standing like this, there's not a great deal you guys can do. Push me around, and the gun could go off. Citizen all over the walls."

"Yeah, like we're going to give a shit," Barton snarled, causing the hacker to look nervous again.

I glanced across at the doorway. No way I could make it there before getting shot even if Deck turned up, which it didn't look like he was going to do. "Five thousand dollars," I said quietly to the older cop. "To make this situation go away."

"You hear that?" Beer-breath said to his partner. "Scumbag's impugning the morality of the Los Angeles Police Department."

"I walk out of here with the case, you get the money. Stranger things have happened."

"No way, Thompson." A new voice. I turned to see that two more cops had entered the room, and were walking fast toward us. The speaker was tall, gray-haired, distinguished—with a suit that was smart enough to prove he was senior, but not smart enough to say he was on the take.

Lieutenant Travis.

FOR THE NEXT few seconds I couldn't even speak. Partly I was trying to put it all together, to work out how things could suddenly have gone so badly. Mainly I could only watch numbly as the most matter-of-fact section of my mind ticked off all the things that weren't going to happen in the rest of my life. Sitting outside a bar and drinking a beer; seeing a view other than gray walls; doing anything that wasn't stupid and brutal and merely a way of whiling away the years until one morning I woke up dead in my cell. All these things fell like rain in front of my inner eye, like they'd just been waiting to be visualized.

Travis stopped a couple of yards away, looked me up and down. The lieutenant had aged a little, but not much: mainly just lost a few pounds on his face, had his hair cut a little shorter. He was pretty much how I'd pictured him, in the times when I half expected him to turn up in whatever town I was bunked in. The strange thing was that last time I'd seen him face-to-face we'd been heading toward friendship, wary acquaintances from different sides of the law-and-order divide. Operating in different fields, and deciding to live and let live: people who knew how to play the game and let the small things slide. Then I stepped outside that, in a compound bout of stupidity, and every line around his eyes said things were different now.

"Put the gun down, Hap," Travis said.

I hesitated, then let my hand drop so that the gun was pointing at the floor. Then I switched it around in my hand and held it toward him, butt first.

He took it, dropped it into his pocket. "I'm arresting you for attempted lease of an illegal memory-transferral device, and for the use of said device to caretake recollections of felonious acts." Matter-of-fact, with no trace of the triumph he must have been feeling. "And feel honored, because I'm taking a few minutes off a far more important investigation to deal with you."

"The first is entrapment, the second you can't prove."

"We'll prove it," Travis said. "I'll lock you in a room, jack you full of sodium verithol, and ask you about every crime ever committed in the history of mankind, back to and possibly including parking offenses in the Garden of Eden. Sooner or later I'll find enough of something to pin on you."

I understood two things simultaneously: This wasn't about Ray Hammond, and that after I'd been in the room Travis mentioned for two seconds it would be. For a second I thought I starkly understood the concept of honor, knowing that there was no way I'd be prepared to turn Laura Reynolds in, even to cop a plea: Then I realized it was just pragmatism. I was going down. There was no point dragging anyone else along for the ride, even if they were the one who had pulled the trigger.

"Er, can I like, go?" the hacker said. He stuck his hand up his sweatshirt and pulled out the radio microphone it had been concealing.

"I wish you would," Travis said.

"And I'm clean now?"

"In terms of your rap file, yes, assuming I ever find it. In every other meaningful sense you're a lowlife asshole, and if I ever hear of you putting one toe over any line whatsoever, you'll find yourself squashed like a bug."

The hacker slid off toward the door, ducking and bobbing, trying not to run. Heading off back to his life between the cracks, saved by canceling the life of someone he didn't even know.

Travis took another look at me, something unreadable in his face, and then nodded to Barton, who still had my arm held tight around my back. It was beginning to hurt, but I was confident that was going to be the least of my problems for the foreseeable future. Travis might use drugs and close interrogation, but there were policemen whose interview techniques were more straightforward. Chances were I'd be meeting some of them soon.

"Cuff him," Travis said, and then to me: "Hope you got some living done in the last three years, Hap."

I didn't get the chance to reply.

At the sound of the explosion, our five heads turned at once toward the doorway. The hacker was lying on the floor, a couple of yards from the door, a splash of biology arcing away from his body.

"Holy fuck," Barton squeaked, dropping my arm and going for his gun. I heard screams from the main room, the sound of lots of people running in every direction at once. The cops around me dropped instinctively into shooter positions. Only Travis had the presence of mind to reach out and grab hold of my other arm.

Four men walked into the room.

They were of identical height, all wearing the same gray suits and sunglasses. Each carried a pump-action at port arms, and all walked like they had nothing to fear. They stopped five yards into the room, just the other side of the forest of candles. Simultaneously the four guns were dropped to firing position, a muzzle locked solid on each cop. Four thirty-eights pointed back at them, their aim a lot more shaky.

Silence, apart from the squealing chaos in the main room. I

heard the same thought go through all of the cops' minds at once, as if it had been said out loud:

If anybody fires, we're dogmeat.

"Put the guns down." Travis's voice was admirably steady. If called on to speak, I think any utterance I'd have made would have been so high-pitched, only dogs would have heard it. The four men in suits shook their heads simultaneously.

"Give Hap to us," the one on the end said, voice so deep it felt like the floor should vibrate.

"No," Travis said, tightening his grip on my arm. "Put the guns down. Now." Then to me, out of the corner of his mouth, "Who the fuck are these guys?"

"I don't know," I said equally quietly.

"Give Hap to us," repeated one of the other men. His voice was exactly the same as the first, the inflection identical. It was as if I were so drunk, I was seeing not double, but quadruple.

There was a moment of screaming quiet, a standoff, and then suddenly there was an arm around my neck and a gun at my temple.

"Put the fucking guns down," Barton screamed at the men, his mouth very close to my ear, "or I'm going to blow his fucking head off!"

The only answer was the sound of four shells being racked into breeches, and I made my peace with the world.

CHAPTER EIGHT

Then the lights went out. All of them, all at once. The cops fired first, a ragged clatter of firecracker pops all around me. I slammed my elbow back into Barton's face—simultaneously yanking my arm away from Travis.

Barton tumbled backward with a curse and I threw myself to the floor as the first barrage of answering gunfire came from the other end of the room. I landed heavily, crunching my chin and knocking most of the air out of my chest, and scrabbled to my hands and knees as shots whined through the air around me. Then I just rolled and scrabbled, trying to get the hell out of the way without being able to see where I was going.

I heard screams from behind me as at least one cop went down. The others were firing and reloading as quickly as they could, and no one was paying much attention to me. When I made it to the wall, I got off my knees: There was just enough light from gun flare for me to see where I wanted to go. The cops were falling back to the very end of the room, diving behind sofas in a vain hope of protection. The men in suits were advancing in a straight line toward them; I squirmed forward along the wall as inconspicuously as possible, until I was behind them.

While I was on their blind side I moved quickly to the far end, the door just a twenty-yard sprint away. But the gunfire from the handguns was more sporadic now, a couple of more cops down: I knew that if I ran now, the guys in the suits would hear me. Maybe at first they'd wanted me handed over, but at the moment they didn't seem to be making any major allowances for my safety.

Not to mention that the rounds fired by the remaining cops would be heading straight in my direction.

I teetered, locked in position like a sprinter at the start of a race, not knowing what to do. In the end I crept forward until I was over halfway there, but did it too slow. Two of the shooters turned and saw me. I froze, barely three running strides from temporary safety: looked at another way, a million miles.

And then somebody ran into the room from the bar, already spraying fire from a semiautomatic. It was too dark to see the runner's face, but I knew it had to be Deck, bless him. He found me immediately, grabbed me by the neck, and swung me toward the door without saying a word. I didn't need a second invitation. I ran like hell.

It felt like an hour since the hacker had been shot, but it could only have been a couple of minutes. The Café was in utter chaos—a melée of shadows scared out of their minds by the racket of the gun battle. Men and women were trying to clamber down from the terraces, scrabbling over each other, falling, fighting. I felt a fraction safer when I was in the middle of the bodies, but found myself being carried toward the outer door. I tried to resist, knowing that I had to try to find Laura and then go back and help Deck, but the pressure of other people's fear was too strong. Dustpans of wide eyes, open mouths, hair—and an endless shout of terror from all around me, seeming to get louder and louder until it was almost tangible, something else pushing me forward. It was as much as I could do to keep myself upright and avoid being trampled to death.

I couldn't even turn my head until the crowd burped out of the Café and onto the street: half the people falling, the rest running straight over those who fell as they obeyed a deep instinctual need to be on the East Coast for a while. I stayed on my feet—barely—and got far enough from the door to turn around. The doorway looked like everybody had been told the devil was turning a blind eye and if they could get out of hell in the next five minutes, they'd go free.

I had to go back. Fuck Laura, I had to find Deck. Hopefully he would have stayed in the room only long enough to cover me, but there'd been no sign of him behind me on the way out. He hadn't abandoned me, and I couldn't do it to him—but there was no way I could swim against the tide of bodies crashing out into the pavement. I was trying to remember if there was another entrance to the Café, when I saw him, in the second row of the next wave of people tumbling out of the door. His hand was on Laura's head, keeping it down: His own head was up, watching the angles, working out the lines of least resistance. I shouted, and he looked over and saw me. He fought his way through the mass, elbowing people out of the way—the only person in the crowd with the presence of mind to head in a consistent direction.

"Christ," I said as they made it. "Am I glad to see you."

"Wholly mutual, as always," Deck replied. "But now I really think we should go."

Laura was panting, her green dress torn in three places. "You coming with us?" I asked her.

"Hell yes," she gasped, shock wobbling her up out of drunkenness.

"How the hell did you *do* that?" I asked Deck as we ran down the wharf toward the car.

"Do what, man?" Deck said, turning his head to scan the mess outside the Café. People still jammed the exit. We had a few minutes before the men in suits could hope to make it out, even if they started firing.

"Find Laura again, and get out so quick?"

"What are you talking about?" Deck asked, slowing as we

reached the car. His face was slick with sweat, a long scratch bled down one cheek. "I stuck with her, like you told me in the note."

I turned, looked at Laura. Her face said Deck was telling the truth. She asked: "What happened in there?"

"Your hacker snitched me," I said. "But the cops don't know about the connection to Hammond. Then guys in suits turned up. With big guns."

"*The* guys?" Laura looked very afraid.

"Yeah. Four of them, which at least explains how they could be in two places at once. They told the cops to hand me over."

Deck stared at me, frowning. "So how the hell did you get out?"

"Someone killed the lights—everyone started firing at each other. I got near the door, was just about to get whacked, and then in came some other guy, slung me out of the way. I thought it was you."

"No. Sorry, man, it should have been, but it wasn't."

"Well, who the hell *was* it?" Laura demanded, on the edge of hysteria.

I just shook my head.

"Doesn't matter," Deck said, glancing back at the Café again. "Light a candle: Of all the weirdos running around, at least one of them is on your side. Meantime we've got to get out of here."

"So let's get in the car."

Deck shook his head. "The cops will know your registration. Maybe the other guys, too. I'll take the car, hide it somewhere. You and Laura get lost."

"But what happens if they catch you?"

Deck shrugged. "I'll just say I boosted the car. We're not known associates: never worked together."

I looked along the wharf. The entrance to the Wharfland subway station was in sight. "But where do we meet?"

"At mine. If I'm not back, let yourself in." He reached into his jacket, pulled out his gun, and gave it to me. "Don't use this unless you feel like it."

I unlocked the trunk of the car, took the dream receiver out, then handed the keys to Deck. "Try to keep at least two wheels on the ground at all times," I advised.

Deck drove off fast. I ran to the entrance to the subway, Laura puffing along behind. A couple of guys were hanging around the stairs, peering up toward the bedlam at the Café, and in the distance I could hear the sirens of approaching black-and-whites. "What's happened up the Café?" one of the men asked.

"Bizarre food-poisoning incident," I said, pulling Laura past them and down into the station. On reflex we reached our index fingers out toward the ticket machines; I snatched Laura's hand back just in time.

"What *now?*" she snapped.

I reached for cash. "We finger the payment, they're going to know exactly where we went." Then I remembered my wallet was empty. "Shit—you got any money?"

Her face fell. "My handbag was in the car."

We ran back up the stairs, hung a sharp left, and sprinted over the bridge. A squad car zipped past us going the other way, but there were so many people running in the streets, it looked like a spontaneous civic fun-run had broken out—albeit one with no clear sense of direction—and none of the cops gave us a second glance. I headed down a side street where I knew there was an ATM. They'd be able to find out I withdrew money from there, but the cops knew I was in the area anyway. It was better than telling them exactly which train we were on.

The ATM was working. They generally are these days, after the banks got serious and installed antipersonnel devices to make short work of anyone who tried to rip them off. I jammed my finger in the slot and got ready to bark instructions.

"Statement of account, is it?" the machine said immediately rather stealing my fire.

"Tempting, obviously, but no. What I want is two hundred dollars."

"Request denied," the machine said, and the slot pushed my finger out again. I frowned, then pushed it back. "You again," the machine said. "What do you want now?"

"My money," I said, "and don't shit me around this time."

"Who's shitting?" it replied. "Your account's empty, loser. Piss off."

My finger was shoved back out again, and all the lights on the ATM snapped off.

I turned away, the ringing sound in my ears getting louder as I realized what had happened.

Laura looked at me anxiously. "What's wrong?"

"My money's gone," I said.

"**HAP, MAN,** shit—how you doing?"

"Very bad," I said. "Let us in and then lock the fucking door."

Vent stepped back with a little bow, and I shoved Laura in ahead of me. Three locks shot home—and I felt nearly safe.

It had taken us over an hour to get across to the Dip from the ATM, slogging down back streets and trying not to be seen. After a while the sound of sirens started to fade, either because the situation back at the Café was resolving itself, or because every cop in the area was already there. I hoped it was the latter. Laura was silent most of the way, as if she were thinking about something. What it might have been I have no idea, and I had enough worries of my own. She kept pace a couple of yards to the side, the little girl who walked by herself.

The Dip is an enclave built in one of the canyons that run through the west side of Griffith. Escalator at each end, streetlights and power, but otherwise left natural and funky. Built into the walls of the canyon are little stores and dives, accessible by ladders. Most are delis, bars, and specialty bookstores: Vent's isn't.

Vent is Tid's younger and more disreputable brother. He's lankier, better-looking, and better-connected, and I've never seen him eat chocolate encased in a hard candy shell. His cave, if you know about it and he lets you in, is a treasure trove of illegality.

"Beer?" he asked.

"No," I replied. Then: "Yes."

Vent opened a door set into the wall of the store and pulled out three beers. He handed one to Laura, who unscrewed the cap immediately and started chugging. "You going to introduce me to your lady friend?"

"Laura, Vent: Vent, Laura," I said. "And she's not my lady friend. Look, Vent, I need some stuff, and then we have to go."

With a smile: "Always the way, Hap my man, back in the good old days. Thought you'd straightened out, though. Ain't seen you in a coon's age."

"I had, more or less," I said. Laura had wandered a little way down the cave, and was peering at all the drawers built into the walls. Quietly: "A certain woman's put some pretty major kinks back into my life."

"They have that tendency." Vent nodded sagely. "Hence I get my kicks in vr these days. So, what are you looking for?"

"Money," I said. "Temporary liquidity problem, and I need a twenty-four-hour loan. A thousand." Actually I just needed fifty bucks, enough to keep us going until I could get on the Net, but asking for that little would have been a clear signal that something was very wrong in my financial life.

Vent shook his head. "Cash I can't do. Just made some major buys. Can let you have a finger."

"Shit." Overkill—and illegal in its own right. "That'll have to do."

Vent opened the fridge again, reached down to a lower shelf. Straightened up with a sealed bag. "Very fresh," he said. "One of the things I just acquired." He slit the tape at the end of the bag and pulled it out: the index finger of a Caucasian male, with a small device fastened on the severed end.

"How safe?" I asked, aware of Laura staring at us.

"Very," Vent said. "My friends cased the gentleman before he passed away. No one's going to miss him for days. Or find him, given where they hid the body."

"What the *hell* is that?" Laura asked. I told her. The finger of a dead man with a usable bank account, kept alive by a plasma generator. In other words, about two days' use of money belonging to someone who wasn't going to miss it. She blanched, and turned away.

"Anything else?"

"Cigarettes, while I'm here." As Vent fetched them, I tried to predict what else I might need, but came up blank. Then I remembered a thought from Ensenada: "Got any co-incidences?"

"Only three," he replied. "And they're pretty small."

"The way things are, anything's a help," I said. "And I'm going to have to owe you on all this."

"Okay," he said, and opened a drawer. He pulled out a vial and a hypo. "I don't know about quality—there's no label. So if you get sick, don't blame me." He spiked the bottle and drew the liquid up into the syringe while I rolled up my sleeve. Then he stuck the needle in my vein and injected the serum. There was a brief feeling of coldness and then everything felt the same again. Doesn't work for everyone; luckily it does for me.

I finished the beer, threw the bottle in the trash. "So how much do I owe you?"

"Give you the fate shot for four hundred, finger for the standard rate—one hundred fifty percent of the money available. Cancer sticks thirty bucks."

"Less my discount, right?"

Vent laughed, winked at Laura. "That Hap," he said. "Always had that great sense of humor."

WE GOT TO DECK'S just before eleven. After we left Vent's, I went straight to an ATM and stuck the finger in the slot.

Laura acted pissed. "Are you really going to use that thing?"

"Got any other suggestions?" I snapped. "It's either that, or we go on welfare until I can get back onto the Net."

She looked away.

The dead guy was named Walter Fitt, and he had close to four thou in the bank, which meant the finger was going to cost me six. Vent's suppliers would have checked before passing it on to him. I took out a hundred cash, and made a note of the account number and bank code.

The cash got us on the subway until it ended at the Griffith wall at Barham Gate. I took an oblique approach up to the tunnel, and saw what I expected: two cops doing security checks on everyone who wanted to leave. I didn't have much of a plan, but it turned out I didn't need one. Just as I was deciding that we might have to turn back and try some of the other exits, a guy in the line ahead suddenly bolted. As one of the cops chased after him, his colleague just waved the rest of us through. I felt pretty blessed as we walked quickly out of Griffith, until I realized this was probably just the first of the co-incidences coming through. Useful and timely, but not exactly earth-shattering—and now I had only two left. There's no way of telling when or how co-incidences will click in: You just have to take your chances. Even fate shots take their timing from the vicissitudes of fate.

I stole a car half a mile the other side of the gate, and took Mulholland and Coldwater over to Sunset. Cut through Westwood down as far as Wilshire, and then just kept driving until we hit the coast. The roads were empty, the sky clear. As we hit Ocean Avenue, a column of sea view opened in front of us, stretching to infinity and blocked only by the leaves of trees along the Palisades. I turned right into the avenue and pulled to a halt, looking out at the water. Dark blue and lit by moonlight, the ocean looked like a texture generated by a computer program, only less complex and more sane: apparent simplicity masking questions that never ended, instead of the Net's fake detail built on top of nothingness. Of course there's actually a hundred-foot drop the other side of the rail, then a busy road and a beach before you reach the water: There's probably a metaphor for life in there somewhere, but I've never had the energy to look for it.

"I grew up by water," I said. "It makes me feel better."

"I don't," Laura said. "It makes me feel wet. Look—my ass hurts and I'm bored, so can we just get where we're going?"

Deck lives in a small apartment building a few blocks back, in a nice street lined with trees. He cashed out his chips from hard crime in a sensible way, and now lives in low-key respectability. These days he mainly just shifts stuff around for the fun of it, creaming off enough money to get by, keeps in practice at thumping people just for old times' sake. I drove the car around the back of his building and parked it close to the wall and out of sight. Deck's lights weren't on, which meant we'd probably beaten him home. That shouldn't have been the case, but I didn't know what route he'd taken or where he dumped my car.

We took the back staircase up to the third story, and I used my keys to let us into the kitchen. Deck's a caveman on such matters, won't trust finger or even voice recognition. It's a matter of some irritation to me that he gets burgled less frequently as a result. You can crack a code or fake a voice pattern silently: Forcing a lock is always going to make noise.

A dim side light came on automatically as we entered the apartment. "Beer's in the fridge, hard stuff in the cupboard above," I told Laura, and walked into the living room, where I sat in the dark on the sofa and closed my eyes.

At long last I got the shakes: the roar in my ears an echo of gunfire and deep voices. As the retorts finally faded, the line of men came once more in front of my inner eye. I could picture them too sharply, almost as if I were dreaming—Laura's memory was overlapping with my own experience. There was something else there too, something occluded and blanked, and I could feel it getting closer all the time. For a moment I almost had it again, a vision of light around a head like a halo. Then it vanished.

A couple of minutes later I heard a rustling and opened my eyes to see Laura standing a few yards away. She was holding a large glass of something in one hand and a beer in the other.

"Would you like one of these?" she asked.

I took the beer and drank slowly while she looked around the room. The walls of Deck's apartment are covered in old film stills, ratty posters, and various other shit that he's collected from all over the place. I'm sure there's an order to it somewhere, but I'll be hanged if I've ever been able to find it. Deck's my best friend, but for some reason his collection irritates me. I think it makes me feel vulnerable. It feels like a taunt of insufficiency, a demonstration of what I lack. Most people bring something with them to the party of the present day, some wine bottle to present to their hosts: Deck has his stuff, his calm, and a compendious knowledge of where to buy the best chili dogs; other people have friends, a style of being, an idea of who they are and why.

I don't seem to have any of these, and wade through life full of insecurity and vertigo, usually manifested as impatience and a panicky feeling of rootlessness. Have I actually *been* here all this time, I wonder sometimes: And if so—what the hell have I been doing?

Laura perched on the other end of the sofa. She'd found a rubber band from somewhere and pony-tailed her hair. "What happens now?"

I lit a cigarette. They're more relaxed in Santa Monica about such things, and smoking in the privacy of your own apartment is merely a misdemeanor and generally overlooked. "We sit here until either Deck turns up or I lose patience and fall asleep. At which point you run away, leaving me with a murder in my head and no way of removing it. During the night I dream a lot of other people's shit which I won't even end up getting paid for, because the account that REMtemps pays into has been frozen. Then the cops find me and bang me up for the rest of my life for something I didn't even do."

She laughed sourly. "Feeling kind of sorry for yourself, aren't you?"

"Yes—and with good reason. Aside from anything else this evening, I've been shot at and seen a guy blown to pieces. He may have been a long-haired snitch bastard, but that doesn't make it a great spectator sport."

"What are you talking about?" she said. "Who was long-haired?"

"The hacker," I said. "Remember him?"

"Quite clearly. He had short hair."

"Not mid-twenties, big nose, thoroughbred geek?" I asked, and stared at her.

Laura said it first: "Then he wasn't the same guy."

"So who the hell was he?"

"How should I know? How did he find you?"

"He didn't." Suddenly I glimpsed the first step along a line of truths that had been in front of me all the time. I pulled the organizer out of my pocket, kicked up the bare-bones Net software. Meantime the cellular card automatically established a 2D connection, and the operating system bade me a cheery good evening.

"What are you doing?" Laura demanded.

"I thought that nerd was too good to be true." I was furious at myself. "He was straight out of central casting—even had a sweatshirt with the stupid slogan on it. But Quat said he'd be pretty distinctive, so I didn't think anything of it. Then he had this weird attitude, half scared, half cool. When it all went berserk, I assumed it was just because he knew he'd been setting me up."

"But?" I was tapping my way through a circumventory log-in. I then told the organizer to use a random whereis server to find my account demon and haul it in—and to abort if it looked like it was going to take longer than thirty seconds.

"Hap, what are you *saying*?" Laura yelled. I shushed her, watched the timer. With ten seconds left, the organizer announced that the demon was coming home: Two seconds later the results were there on the screen.

The demon listed the six bank accounts it administered in my name: two real, two virtual, two nothing more concrete than randomized streams through gaps in the money market. All empty. Zeros straight across the board.

Laura gawked at the column of emptiness. I killed the Net connection before the cellular source could be traced.

Then stared straight ahead, seeing nothing at all.

I had nothing to my name, and there was just one man in the world who could have taken it. The same man who'd been the only person able to dial into my phone that morning, and who suddenly did business over the wire so he could put me in a certain place at a certain time. A man who I'd trusted with all my business for over a year, who knew everything about me.

"It's Quat," I said. "He's fucked me over."

"Your hacker? Why?"

"The transmitter your guy used—was it a suitcase full of junk?"

Laura nodded."I couldn't believe it was going to work—but it did. Look, I'm tired of saying why, so can you just assume my participation in this conversation from now on is a generic question mark?"

"Did you get Hammond's address through the same guy? From the same hacker who set up the transfer?"

"I put a veiled ad in the adult personals for hacker services: A few hours later this guy comes through." Which implied Quat had been her hacker, that he'd had access to a machine all the time, and that he knew about Hammond's murder. "Does that mean this Quat guy got killed?"

I shook my head, thoughts still whirling. "The guy in the Café was just an actor—method nerd going through his lines. Quat set me up."

I put it together as best I could.

Laura wants Ray Hammond dead, for whatever reason, but doesn't know where he's at. She finds a hacker—Quat—or he finds her. Quat gets Hammond's address. Next day he reads that the guy has been whacked—then Laura wants an illicit memory dump. Quat had to know that it was the murder, and he arranges to send it into my head. I blow town for two days—he doesn't know where I am, and he's strangely difficult to get hold of. As soon as I'm back I get in touch with him: He holds off giving me a machine he already has, just long enough to set me up with the cops.

It worked, though there were some weird co-incidences in the mix that didn't sit comfortably. And there was still a big question, to which Laura returned immediately.

"Yeah, fine," she muttered, "but why would this Quat guy want to do that to you? You stiff him over a bill or something?"

"No. He had control over all my money. I couldn't have stiffed him even if I'd wanted to. I trusted him with everything."

Laura abruptly downed the rest of her drink in one swallow, looked at me bright-eyed. "Then we're both screwed."

There was a noise from out back of the kitchen. Deck, I

assumed. Then I heard the sound of someone's feet going back down the stairs.

I stood, pulled out the gun. Walked into the other room and squinted through the kitchen windows. I couldn't see anyone out there. Gun held out in front, I edged toward the back door, wishing it had a glass panel in it. When I got there, I took the handle as quietly as possible, breathed deeply, and yanked it open.

Nobody there.

The night had cooled, faint condensation hanging in the air and turning yard lights into sparkles. I looked down, saw a small suitcase at my feet that looked familiar.

I ran to the end of the walkway and stuck my head out but couldn't see anyone heading away from the building. At a slight sound I whirled back around, and nearly blew Laura's head off. She was peering into the suitcase.

"The transmitter?" she asked.

I nodded, swallowing compulsively. "What's this?" she added, reaching forward to pick up a small scrap of paper from inside the case.

I took it from her. She craned her neck to read it with me. On it was written just one word: *Helena.*

"Who's Helena?" Laura asked.

I realized who'd saved me at the Café.

"My ex-wife," I said, and went back inside.

PART TWO

MISSING

CHAPTER NINE

A boy is out walking by himself, early on a Sunday evening. He heads slowly down the hill toward the school, not going anywhere in particular, just following his feet. Behind him, half a mile back, is the place where he lives: an old motel, one of the first built on this stretch of the coast, now mostly empty for the winter. He doesn't know yet that the motel will define his idea of living space forever, that he will always seek out places with clean rooms and empty corridors, where you nod to strangers at a distance and know that you will be leaving again before you even step in the door. It's just home, and always has been. His father is the caretaker there—air-conditioner supremo, banisher of bugs and rodents, and cleaner of pools. His mother works in a bar/restaurant a mile down the beach, and has done so all her life. She's there now, ferrying burgers and frosted glasses of beer, yakking with her friend Marlene and listening to the guitarist play "The Great Filling Station Holdup" for the first, but not the last, time of the evening.

The boy left his father sitting comfortably in front of the tube, watching a tape of an old Braves game for like the eighteenth time. The Doritos and bean dip were in place on the side table, a beer in his favorite glass by his hand: He was, as he always put it, not moving for no man now. Neither parent would mind the boy going out walking by himself. He's always done it, and nothing bad's ever happened to him.

The sidewalk down to the school is very familiar. It is the site of a raging torrent every time it rains hard, and the marching path of a procession of ants a few months earlier. The boy spent an hour squatted down by the column of tiny creatures as they flowed silently past, wondering where they were going, and why. In school that week Miss Bannerham had told them a story about butterflies, how some particular brand began the year hanging in South America, and then—all at once, and all together—flew up the world as far as Canada or somewhere. Someplace north, anyhow. It was a long journey, and along the way the butterflies mated, and laid eggs, and died: The butterflies that made the return leg later in the year, back to the exact same trees the journey had started in, weren't the same bugs who'd begun the trip. Some were born to fly north, others didn't know any direction but south: Between them they followed a cycle that went on and on, year after year, filled with apparent purpose and yet with no aim that the boy could see.

Miss Bannerham said it was something to do with a particular plant the butterflies needed, or temperatures, or something, but he didn't believe it. If the plant was so important, why didn't they all just set up camp right next to one and put their feet up for the whole year? If you liked the sea, you lived on the coast, you didn't go live in Utah or somewhere.

The ants were the same. They were up to something, he knew, but they weren't letting on what it was.

That particular evening the sidewalk was still, and dry, and frankly not much to look at. The boy walked on down the hill, hands in his pockets, peering at the houses he passed. Deep yards, trimmed grass, mostly one-story homes. The light had faded enough that lights shone in many of the living rooms: He caught brief glimpses of people sitting, moving, watching TV. A torso and an arm would move smoothly across the window, then disappear; someone would stand, sit down again; an occasional murmur of sound rose and fell, no more intelligible than the beat of distant wings. Maybe it was all supposed to be easier to understand than the ants and the butterflies, but the boy didn't see how. It was other-people stuff, parts of lives he'd never comprehend.

The hill began to level out, and the school yard became visible over on the right. This was a large, square compound, taking up a whole block. At the far end were the classrooms; in front of them was a big playground lined with grass and trees and with black metal railings all around. The boy stopped when he was opposite the playground, and looked across. He didn't have any particular feelings about the place other than it was where he spent most days. Inside, on a school day, would be lots of children, some he knew and didn't mind, others he didn't know or mildly disliked. A big container for people who were different from him, who had different parents and different lives. The only particularly interesting occupant was Miss Bannerham. The boy was just old enough to have a crush on her.

He didn't think of it in those terms, however, knew only that he minded her class less than the others, and that if Mom hadn't been his mom, he wouldn't have minded it being Miss Bannerham. At home, in a safe place, he had a badge she had given him. Some people had come to the school two weeks ago to grade the teachers. The boy had been somewhat surprised to find that even teachers had to take tests, but Miss Bannerham didn't seem to mind. She gathered the children at the front of the class, on the floor, and told them about some stuff. The grown-ups had stood at the back, and they listened, too. The boy had asked questions, and answered questions: It had been an interesting class, and it was fun to know things. At the end of the day, when he was gathering his books and there weren't many kids left in the classroom, Miss Bannerham came up to him, took him to one side, and gave him the badge. It was narrow and silver and had the word "merit" on it, and she said that he could keep it for a month. He kept quiet about the badge at school, sensing vaguely that was the best policy, but he showed it to his parents and they seemed pleased.

The boy had spent the day on the gray beach, battling the wind and looking for sand dollars. His family had a policy, devised and administered by his father, that anyone who found an intact sand dollar was entitled to a—as he put it—"beverage of their choice" the next time the family went into town for dinner. The boy's beverage of choice was always a Coke, which he would have gotten anyway, but he understood that wasn't the point.

All he'd found that day were fragments, and a small dead, squishy thing that he hadn't liked the look of, but that didn't matter. He felt pleasantly tired, and decided to walk around the school and then go home.

He peered in through the railings as he passed the playground, looking at the trees. They had been demonstrated, to everyone's satisfaction, to be the best place in the whole area for finding Knights. These were large beetles which most of the boys coveted and kept in jars with holes punched in the lid, and though their real name probably wasn't Knights, that was what they were called. Many happy hours were spent conducting battles between these insects: The contests were actually rather peaceable affairs in which the insects' characteristics—length, width, coolness of wings—were minutely compared. In general, the bugs were green, but every now and then someone would find a black one, and these always won the contests hands down. Black Knights always did. The boy's best friend, Earl, already had a Black Knight, and it was the boy's view that it was about time he did, too.

Nursing a vague hope that he might make such a find soon, the boy continued along the path as it went by the school buildings. There wasn't much to see along that stretch, or after he'd turned the first corner: just dark windows in a darker building. He whiled away the time considering something he'd heard a TV preacher say earlier in the day—that the Lord would have mercy upon people who'd done bad things, and would cast their sins into the sea. This didn't seem to tally with the boy's mother's view, which was that people who dumped things in the sea were themselves bad, especially if they damaged sea gulls' wings. The boy had nervously asked his dad where specifically the sins were cast, because he didn't want to swim through them by accident and come out bad. His father had laughed uproariously and stopped shouting at the TV for a while.

The boy turned the second corner and walked up as far as where the playground began again; then he stopped and looked at the trees, now just the other side of the railings. It was quite dark by then, with only a streetlamp at each corner of the block, and the trees looked big and old. He could probably have made it over the fence and into the grounds, thus stealing a march on the next day's bug hunters, but he didn't really fancy it. In the dark the trees looked a little, well, frightening. The boy knew they weren't really so, because he'd climbed into their lower branches often enough during the day when they were huge and green and friendly, but things always looked different at night. He wondered which was true, the way things looked during the day, or during the night, and concluded it probably depends.

Anyway, the bugs would almost certainly be asleep.

Thinking that if he headed back now there might still be some Doritos left, he turned the final corner into the last straightaway, back toward where he'd turn left to go back up the hill. By then he was in that state of near-hypnotic abstraction, so at first he didn't notice the footsteps behind him.

When he did, he turned around, expecting someone out walking their dog. He was surprised to see that the sidewalk was empty.

He walked on a little, and heard the footsteps start up again. They weren't hurrying or running, merely walking at the same pace as he was. He knew it wasn't an echo of his own footsteps, however, because he was wearing the sneakers that made no sound at all.

Heart beating a little faster, the boy stepped up his pace. The footsteps got a little quicker, too, and he began to get a little afraid. He'd been warned about vaguely dire things that could happen if you talked to the wrong people or got in the wrong sort of car. Neither of his parents had been very specific about what these things were, or of what makes or model of car were the wrong ones, but the boy suddenly felt that this was probably one of the circumstances his parents had been talking about.

He hurried along the sidewalk, faster and faster, but knew that he wasn't getting farther away from whatever was following him. If it was a grown-up, there was no chance of outrunning them. They had longer legs.

So he stopped, took a deep breath, and turned around.

This time he did see someone.

A man stood way back at the corner, under the streetlight. He was wearing a dark suit. The man's face was in shadow, and the boy couldn't see it clearly: The lamp seemed to shine from behind the man's head. He seemed too far away to be the one making the footsteps, but there was no one else in sight. The man started walking, and the boy stayed rooted to the spot.

Later he was back at home, eating Doritos and watching the television with his mom as his father slept in his chair like a felled dinosaur. They made it to the end of some dumb film and then everyone went to bed.

I **WOKE TO FIND** Laura sitting on the floor cross-legged, eating toast. She held out a cup of coffee to me. I croaked something unintelligible and sat upright. It took a minute or so for me to place myself, and when I finally did, I reached into my jacket pocket and pulled out the dream receiver. One look at the display told me what I already knew. I hadn't been working. The dream was my own.

"Deck's in the shower," Laura said, still holding out the coffee. Her eyes looked puffy.

I took it, sipped. It was hot, and tasted like coffee. So far, so good. "When did he get back?"

"About an hour after you crashed. Said he took a scenic route. You okay? You went out kind of fast." I nodded. After stowing the transmitter in one of Deck's closets, I'd watched out of the front window for a while, but saw nothing except an abandoned washing machine trudging off down the road. Laura clearly expected me to say something about how the transmitter had gotten here, and the person who'd brought it, but I didn't. I found I could barely speak. I sat on the sofa and next thing I knew I'd slipped back twenty-five years, as if there were too much to deal with in the present day and my mind had run yelping for simpler times. The dividing lines seemed to be blurring. What I'd woken from wasn't just a dream, but also a memory—one I'd forgotten for a long while. As I sat with Laura's eyes looking quizzically up at me, the memory was suddenly fresher and more real than the warmth of the cup in my hand or the sound of falling water in Deck's bathroom.

Around the school we went.

I picked up the phone, dialed a number on the Net.

"Hello?"

"Yeah, hi, Quat. It's Hap." Laura stared at me with a "what the *fuck* are you doing?" look on her face.

There was a pause. Then Quat said, "Hey—how you doing, man?"

"Fine," I said. "Transmitter worked a dream. The guy hasn't shown up to take it back, though."

Very smooth: "I'll give him a call."

"You do that. Listen—something else weird's happened: I can't get any cash out of the ATM. Can you look into it?"

"Sure, sure," he said. "Look, Hap, where are you exactly?"

"Around," I said, holding the phone very tight. "One more thing: You know anything about that cop who got whacked?"

I put the phone down on silence.

"What the hell was that all about?" Deck asked from the doorway.

"Just noise," I answered. "He knows I'm lying, but not to what degree. And I do have the transmitter, after all. Now he doesn't know what's going on, or what I know."

"But you don't know shit," Deck said.

"Not yet I don't." Overnight, and in my sleep, things had changed. Quat's betrayal didn't seem the most important thing anymore. Neither did the reasons behind it—whatever they might be. I was very panicky about my money, and I should also have been concerned as to why Stratten hadn't stuck to his word and sent me a night's dreamwork, but I wasn't. Not yet.

I wanted to know who the men in the gray suits were, and what they were doing, and why I knew them. Which was okay, because all lines of inquiry seemed to be leading in the same direction.

DECK STOOD GUARD outside in the street as I broke into Ray Hammond's apartment. Laura came with me. Her choice, not mine. On the way over I'd checked the news and found the Prose Café gun battle was all over it. Travis made it out with a flesh wound, Barton was in critical condition and not expected to last, the other two cops were dead.

The "persons unknown" had disappeared, with no bodies left on the scene. Citywide APB on them; no mention of me.

There was no tape across the door to Hammond's crib, and no cop standing guard, which implied that the LAPD didn't know what he had been doing in the area. I asked Laura about that, and she said Hammond had a regular address over in Burbank. She wouldn't say why she hadn't hunted him down there, only that she'd worked out he spent some of the time elsewhere, and got the hacker—Quat, as it had transpired—to find out where. Presumably the cops had done a house-to-house, and had given up on getting no reply from the entry phone to this apartment. If they came back for a second sweep, or anybody else weird turned up, Deck would let us know. Until then, Ray Hammond's apartment was ours.

The lock on the door was complex and expensive, but no match for my organizer. Within two minutes it was open, and we were inside.

The apartment was small. The door led straight into a square living room with a kitchen to one side. The window would have looked over the street below had the curtains not been drawn. Two other rooms out back, a bedroom and the other nearly filled by a desk. A bathroom you could very nearly get all of your body into at once.

The kitchen said this wasn't a place in which Hammond had spent much quality time. Three cans of beer and some leftover Chinese in the fridge, the noodles covered in a bacterial culture so advanced, they probably had their own constitution and strong views on environmental issues. Precisely one plate and one set of cutlery in the drawer. The rest of the apartment said that Hammond liked his downtime in an austere environment. The furniture was cheap and functional: a sofa and one chair in the living room, a twin bed, a couple of small tables with nothing on them. The closets in the bedroom were empty, there were no toiletries in the bathroom, and dust lurked in every corner. There were no pictures on the walls of any of the rooms. It was like a suite in a motel no one ever used, two weeks after the maid had been sacked and taken her severance pay in reproduction art.

I left Laura in the living room and went into the study. A shelf hung above the desk, a single book on it. A small Bible, well-thumbed. A quote had been written out on the inside front cover: *And I beheld, and, lo, in the midst of the throne and of the four beasts, and in the midst of the elders, stood a Lamb as*

it had been slain, having seven horns and seven eyes, which are
the seven Spirits of God sent forth into all the earth.

Strange. I slipped it in my pocket.

Apart from that, the room was bare, but as I glanced under the desk I noticed something. On the floor near the wall there were a few lines in the dust, where the carpet showed through. As if cables had lain there until recently. The closets told a similar story: clean rectangles in fine dust, where file boxes had been stacked. I went back into the living room, flipped over the cushions on the sofa. Neat diagonal cuts across the underside of each: Somebody had been looking for something concealed.

"Someone's already tossed the place," I said. "I think there was a computer on that desk, and it's gone, along with files. They were looking for something else, too, something you could hide in a cushion. Do you have any idea what that might be?"

There was no reply. I looked up to see Laura leaning against the kitchen counter, head slumped forward. "Laura?"

She slowly lifted her head. Her eyes were unnaturally dull, mouth turned down at the corners. She looked like a fourteen-year-old girl seen through the prism of a lifetime of disappointment. "Can I have a cigarette?" she said.

"Thought you'd quit."

She smiled wanly. "Only about a hundred times."

"It's my belief some people are smokers and some aren't. You work out which and stick with it. Saves everyone a load of grief."

I glanced around the walls for sensors, was surprised not to see any. Then I remembered Hammond had been both a smoker and a ranking cop. Presumably he granted himself a dispensation. I lit a couple of Camels and handed one to Laura. "Hammond is the key to all of this," I said. "You murdered him. Any chance you'd explain why?"

"I don't remember doing it."

"I know. I don't need the details: I need to know the why, and you still remember that."

"It was personal," she said.

"No shit. Nobody uses a whole clip over a parking ticket."

"It's not relevant to what's happening now."

"How do you know?"

"Look, it just isn't. Are you done here? Can we go?"

"At some point you're going to have to tell someone," I said.

"And I don't mean the cops. I mean just somebody. You drink too much, and your mouth's generally trying to make a smile it doesn't mean. You go to Mexico for a two-day vacation and spend the whole time wallowing in misery, when you're not getting yourself in bad situations in bars. When you dumped the memory of the murder on me it was already fucked up, like you're used to blanking things. You've got to find a way of letting some of this stuff out of your head."

She smiled sardonically. "Thanks for the consultation, doctor. Shall I come along to be patronized again, next week, same time?"

"Just trying to help. Despite the fact you're a complete pain in the ass, I like you."

Mistake. She turned away and ground her cigarette out in the sink, barely half-smoked. "Yeah," she muttered. "Every guy always does."

Her eyes changed, went opaque again, and it was clear the conversation was over.

The apartment was a dead end. I cleaned up the sink so no one would know we'd been there, and locked the door behind us as we left. We collected Deck outside, and on a whim I walked up to the crossroads and peered through the window of the liquor store. The old guy was still sitting behind the counter, as he had been in the memory, looking like he'd been stuffed. I left the others outside and went in.

"How's your dog?" I asked.

The old man looked up at me, squinted: He obviously couldn't see too well. "He died. Who are you? Do I know you?"

"Course you do," I said. "I'm in here all the time."

"Oh. Well, nice to see you again." He leaned forward, started to stand up. As soon as he'd begun, I wanted to tell him not to bother: Whole cities have been built with less effort. His face was deeply lined, the skin dry as powder, and the closer he got to standing, the less healthy he looked. But it was clearly important to him, so I waited the process out. I glanced outside, saw Deck and Laura talking. Eventually the old guy was more or less upright, leaning on the counter. "What can I get for you?"

"Nothing, actually," I said. "You know that cop who got shot? Happened near here, didn't it?"

"That's right," he replied proudly. "Saw the whole thing. You a cop?"

I debated saying yes, and committing a felony, but decided I'd already gotten enough marks against my name. "No. Just interested. And you didn't see it all. You were asleep."

Hands shaking: "How do you know that?"

"I just do. Plus you can't see the spot where the body fell from here. So tell me what you actually saw." I didn't offer him money. It would have been demeaning: Talking was all this guy had left.

He licked his lips. "Tell the truth, I *was* a little tired that night. May have nodded off around one. Anyhow, I heard this noise and woke up. Thought at first it was the door banging, but there was no one in the store and the noise kept going on. Realized it was a gun going off. By the time I got to the door, it had stopped. I decided to stay inside."

"What happened then?"

"Heard a car come roaring down the road, then somebody ran past my door. Just in front of me, but I don't see too well. Sounded like a woman's footsteps to me, though: went off and around the corner. Then I hear shouting, some guy cussing fit to bust. So I went back to my chair, got my glasses, came and looked again."

"You couldn't see anybody from here, though, right?"

"Not at first," he said. "I'm coming to that. At first there's just these two voices, saying something I can't hear. Then two more cars roll up."

The hair on the back of my neck began to rise. "Excuse me?"

"Kind of a shiny gray, with those blacked-out windows the pimps and drug dealers like. Two guys get out of each car."

"Medium height? Wearing suits?"

"That's right." He peered at me. "You know them?"

I shook my head. Six. There were six of the bastards now. "What happened then?"

"Not much. The guys go around the corner, stay there a few minutes. I'm wondering if I should go offer to help, but I figure there's enough of them—what can I do? And I don't know if you've noticed, but I'm kind of old. Then they come running back, get in the cars, drive off. A second later the first car goes past, shiny gray, just the same. And that's it. I called the cops."

"And you told them about the guys in the cars?"

"I certainly did. Gangland slaying, I called it. They quoted me in the paper—though they kept the number of guys a secret."

Big, bad news. After last night, Travis had a way of connecting me to Hammond's murder: Hammond → antisocial guys in suits → Hap. Not actually the right way, because he didn't know Laura Reynolds's role in the loop, but a way. It was enough.

"Thanks," I said distractedly. "You've been a big help."

"Pleasure," he said. "And since I know you, I'll tell you something I didn't like to say to the cops. They'd have thought I was losing my mind, or just that my eyes weren't right. The guys I saw: It wasn't just like they all bought their suits from the same place. Their faces looked the same, too." He looked at me levelly, and for a moment I saw the man he'd once been—and made a silent bet that this was one liquor store that hadn't been knocked off very often. "You believe me?"

"Yes I do," I said. "And I'll return the favor with a piece of advice. You see those guys again, hide."

OUTSIDE, Deck was leaning against a lamppost. Laura was standing ten yards away, near where Hammond's body had fallen.

"What's up with her?" I asked Deck.

"Told her one of the reasons it took me so long to get back last night."

"Which is?"

"Went by your apartment. I figured if all the weird dudes were at the Café raising hell, might be a good time. Somebody had already tricked the lock—I guess after those two guys lost you, they checked out your place. I went in, dug your memory receiver out the cupboard, closed the door. Didn't tidy up or anything."

I smiled, thinking not for the first time how dire the world must be if you don't have someone like Deck sitting in the dugout with you. "Thanks," I said. "But you were lucky. Turns out these guys come in six-packs."

Deck raised his eyebrows. "Shit. Anyhow, so I mentioned this to Laura. She knows you can put it back into her head."

I reached out, touched him on the shoulder. "Wait here a second," I said.

I walked down the road until I stood a few yards from Laura. She was staring at the faded shape of a large bloodstain on the sidewalk, arms folded, shoulders slumped.

"So when do you want to do it?" she asked.

"I don't," I answered.

She looked up slowly, then frowned. "What?"

"There's no point. Travis is already on my case, and the cops can connect me to Hammond's death through the guys who are chasing after you. It's too late for the transfer to do me any good."

"But you didn't kill him."

I shrugged. "Maybe not. But I've gotten used to having it in my head. There was a place there waiting for it."

"And that's it?"

"That's it."

Laura breathed out heavily. For just a moment she looked like the person she really was, all the spikes retracted and forgotten. She glanced down the road into the distance, then back at me. "So what are you going to do now?"

"Find out what's going on."

"You care?"

"Yes, I do. If I were you, I'd call in sick, go take a vacation in Europe for a while. What do you do for a living, anyway?"

"Work for a bank," she said, and smiled up at me, one eye squinted against the sun. "Client liaison. Kind of stupid, huh?"

"It's a living."

"It's a coma is what it is." She looked over at Deck, who still leaned against the lamppost, gazing at nothing in particular. "You know what? I think I've resigned."

"You want a ride someplace?"

"Yeah. Wherever you guys are going." She laughed at the confusion in my face. "Come on, Hap. I've still got the four weirdos of the apocalypse after me, and they *know* I did what I did."

"There's six of them," I said. "Actually."

"Whatever. You've got a hair up your ass about working it out somehow: I figure I'm safer with you guys."

"Could be a bad decision."

"My favorite kind." She smiled, and nodded toward Deck. "Come on: Let me buy you a beer."

CHAPTER TEN

It took a while for lunch to arrive at Applebaum's. It always does. We got a table outside with a view down Sunset and started drinking: Deck and Laura made fun of passersby while I sorted through the stuff in my pockets. I'd dumped so many things in my jacket during the last few days that I was beginning to walk with a stoop.

Unfortunately it seemed I needed to keep most of it. The dream receiver, for example. I used the restaurant's pay phone to call REMtemps to find out why no dreams had been sent my way the night before, but Stratten wasn't available. The hell-bitch Sabrina had kept me hanging on forever, then said he'd get back to me. I was keeping Deck's gun for the time being: Mine was doubtless in an evidence locker relating to the incident in the Prose Café. Without my organizer I'd be fucked, and I didn't have the heart to throw the clock away, even though it seemed to have gone into hibernation. Maybe it was in shock: It had gone straight back to sleep after being shot at outside my apartment, and I hadn't heard a peep out of it since. I shook it and pushed some buttons experimentally, but I'm not even sure they do anything. They're probably just there because people expect them. Either way, the clock wasn't playing. I asked Laura if she'd mind carrying it in her bag: She took it from me and stuffed it inside.

Then something struck me. I'd found Laura at the Nirvana through some weird wisdom on the clock's part. But how had the two guys in suits found her? From Laura's memory and the old guy's story, it was clear the guys in suits hadn't been able to follow her immediately after Hammond's murder.

"Laura," I said. "Can I ask you something?"

"Anything you like," she replied expansively, refilling her glass from the pitcher. "Though I may not answer."

"Any idea how the guys in suits found you were staying at the Nirvana?"

She shook her head. "No. And after I dropped the memory on you I was super-cautious and more than a little paranoid. But I never got the sense anyone was following me. Though you were, of course."

"Granted, but most of the time I was so far off your tail, I was in the wrong country. What about the bar you spent the evening in: You didn't see anyone strange there?"

"No. Though I did meet a guy." Abruptly she shivered, as the weather crashed and flipped from sunny to overcast and chilly in the space of a second. There was a chorus of mutters from the drinkers and diners around us as they waited for the jackets and sweaters they'd valet-stowed to be brought back out to them.

"What guy?"

She shrugged. "Just some guy. I was sitting at a corner table, killing time, and this guy asked if I minded him joining me. I was going to say yes I did mind, because I really wasn't in the mood for being hit on, but then I felt all right about it and said okay."

"What did he look like?"

"Late thirties, early forties. Smartly dressed, dark casual suit. Good hair."

"And did he hit on you?"

"No. We just talked. Or I did, anyway. He just sort of sat there and nodded, and made me feel okay. I chattered away about nothing in particular and he listened. Like he was actually quite interested rather than just waiting for it to be over so he could ask how I liked my eggs in the morning. Then after a while I decided it's late and I should go. He said stay a little longer, and I was tempted, but, I don't know . . ."

"What?"

She looked away. "It was the wrong night for it. I wasn't in the mood for someone nice being sweet to me. It would have spoiled it."

"And so?"

"And so I said good night, and that it had been cool to meet him. He gave me his card, which was kind of weird."

She dug in her purse and handed it to me. It was blank. I turned it over, and saw the other side was the same.

"Minimalist," said Deck, and then went back to writing *This stuff causes cancer, too; so why can't I smoke?* on every packet of Sweet'n Low in the bowl on the table.

I laid the card on my organizer and got it to check for varnish barcodes, synthetic holography, and a variety of other fads and graphic design stupidities. Nothing beeped. It was just a blank rectangle of card, creamy white and with a slight texture. Quite a nice piece of paper, as it happened, but not very informative. I shrugged and handed it back to Laura.

The food arrived, and I concentrated for a while on getting a large corned beef sandwich inside my head. In the meantime I pulled the remaining object out of my jacket pocket. Hammond's Bible.

It was a standard edition of the King James Version, quite small and bound in battered black leather. The pages were wafer-thin and bordered in gold. I flicked through it quickly from back to front, and saw that a few passages had been marked in the margins. A handful in the New Testament, more in the Old. There didn't seem to be any particular rhyme or reason to the selections he'd picked out, but I know jackshit about such things—I come from a long line of belligerent atheists. My sole view on things Bible-related is that the Good News revision was the most nauseating crime against language ever committed. Good News? Good grief, more like. Even a nonbeliever doesn't want to see that stuff recouched in the kind of language you use to book a rebirthing session.

Then I remembered the passage that had been copied out on the inside front cover. I found the place and held it out to Laura. "Does this look like Hammond's handwriting?"

She glanced at it. "Yes. Probably."

"You don't know?"

"It's been a while." She set her knife and fork down and re-filled her glass. Her food had been barely touched, though it had been shifted around the plate a little. She caught me looking. "And I'm just not very hungry, okay? Don't go all sensitive and 'I know about eating disorders' on me, because as it happens, I don't have one."

I smiled, held up my hands. She grinned back, but something had changed in her face. Her eyes glittered, and what was animating them was not humor anymore, but fear.

"You want some coffee?" I asked. She shook her head and looked away. Deck volunteered to get the bill—which was just as well, because I'd left the finger in his apartment. They're not really something you can pull out in a restaurant.

Meanwhile I went into the back of the restaurant to use their john. Tables full of wanna-bes lifted their eyes covertly as I walked past, checking to see if I was someone famous enough to be worth schmoozing. The general consensus appeared to be that I wasn't, and I sent each and every one of them a smidgen of ill will. I'd been introduced to Applebaum's by an acquaintance of mine called Melk, who's wasting his life scuffling around the edge of the Business. He currently works as an Emission Manager, better known in the trade as a fart wrangler: hired by movie stars to walk behind them at parties, and—should the unfortunate occur—surreptitiously flap an unfurled napkin to disperse the smell as swiftly as possible. The best wranglers can make it seem like it never happened, even corral it up and redirect it so a rival actor gets the blame. This is not a job for a grown human being, and Melk is one of the bigger fish who frequents Applebaum's—so imagine the troughs of loserdom that the other patrons inhabit. I'm not a particularly self-confident guy, but I felt I could live without their validation.

An attendant in the anteroom tried to give me all manner of unguents and towels to take into the rest room with me, but I told him to fuck off. He backed off bowing and scraping, probably assuming my rudeness meant I headed a studio and was in Applebaum's as a result of a terrible restaurant-booking accident.

Then suddenly I found myself facedown on the floor, with someone kneeling in the middle of my back. For a second all I could do was gasp, the air punched out of my lungs: By that time my hands had been yanked behind my back and cuffed.

Two polished black shoes appeared close to where my nose was resting on the tile. "Don't you *fucking* move," said a voice from above.

I craned my neck, looked up, and saw a cop pointing a thirty-eight down at me. His hands were very steady. "You're coming with us," he said.

"Yes, I am," I said accommodatingly, and let myself be hauled to my feet. Both cops were young and shiny, one with a blond crew cut, the other brown-haired. Apart from that, I couldn't see any significant difference between them. They each grabbed one of my arms and led me back out into the restaurant.

The wanna-bes gaped at us as we passed through, trying to decide whether this turn of events made me a smaller or bigger fish. Someone who I assume was either an attorney or an agent lobbed a business card at me.

I had my face ready-set as we emerged onto the patio, knowing that Deck would have the sense to blank me as we passed. Turned out he'd gone one further. They'd disappeared altogether, money for the meal left by Deck's empty plate.

Blond-hair opened the back door of the black-and-white parked at the curb; Brown-hair shoved me and climbed in beside me.

I sat looking out the window as the car pulled away, and waited patiently for my life to get worse.

"HOW DID YOU FIND ME?" I asked when he finally arrived.

Travis gave me a pitying look. "We're the cops, Hap. It's our job."

I was sitting in an interview room in the Hollywood precinct, and had been for five hours. No one had offered me any coffee in all that time, and I was thinking of filing a complaint. The room had bare gray walls obviously designed to make you feel grim, the monotony enlivened only by large no-smoking signs. But since smoking is now more or less illegal, it's mainly criminals and cops who do it, and there was a large and overflowing ashtray in the center of the table in front of me.

Travis leaned with his arms folded against a mirror that covered all of one wall. He caught me glancing at it.

"Nobody behind there," he said.

"Right," I said, not knowing or caring if he was telling the truth. Come one, come all. It didn't make much difference now. "How's the arm?"

"Painful," he said. The upper right sleeve of his shirt bulged where there was a bandage underneath. "But then, you'd know how it feels, wouldn't you? You caught a few once, as I recall. That's what the witnesses said, anyhow."

I didn't reply. Travis looked at me for a while, then reached into his pocket. He pulled out a piece of folded paper, straightened it out, and laid it on the table in front of me. "Take a look at this."

It was a printout from the LAPD Crime Databank, with today's date at the top. It related to an armed robbery and multiple homicide on 3/15/2014, a little over three years ago. Strong eyewitness testimony led to the naming of three suspects: Ricardo NMI Pechryn (since deceased), Harry "Hap" Thompson, and Helena Ruth Goldstein. Mandate to use force if necessary to secure an arrest: advice to use special care and SWAT backup when attempting to apprehend Goldstein.

Quat had put it back on the database. I closed my eyes.

"Kind of a blow, isn't it?" Travis agreed. "Odd, too. Gone all that time, then I check the file this morning and there it is. There's probably an explanation, but to be honest, I don't really care what it is. Welcome back to my personal Most Wanted list, Hap."

"Great to be here," I muttered. Quat had evidently realized that with the hacker and two other on-the-spot witnesses dead or in a coma, the conspiracy-to-lease-memory-equipment rap looked shaky. So he'd tied me up neatly with this instead. Why?

"The bottom line is that you're screwed, Thompson. Do you accept that?"

"Yes." It couldn't be just for the money. There had to be

something else behind what Quat was doing to me. One thing was certain: If I ever found him in the real world, he was dead.

Travis raised an eyebrow. "So?"

"So you let me call a lawyer, you put me in a cell with a bunch of wackos who'll beat the shit out of me just to relieve the monotony, and we take it from there. If you're expecting me to hand over Helena, you're out of luck. I haven't seen her in three years."

I was going to go on, but I stopped: tongue-tied by saying her name. I had deliberately not thought about her since the delivery outside Deck's house the night before. Deliberately, and with great force, not thought about her. I had no intention of starting now.

Travis shook his head. "Not why you're here—for the moment. I want to talk to you about something else. I just wish you to understand that our discussion is taking place within certain parameters."

I took a cigarette from the packet in front of me, lit it. "So talk."

"Tell me what you know about Ray Hammond."

I shrugged. "Ranking cop, gunned down in Culver City a week ago. Gangland hit, I heard."

Travis shook his head. "Try again."

"That's all I know."

"Bullshit. I'm in the middle of arresting you for an entirely unrelated matter, and four people—who in retrospect I realize strongly resemble the suspects in Hammond's murder—walk in and demand we hand you over. Three cops get killed or badly injured in the ensuing firefight, which speaks of an extremely strong desire for your company on somebody's part."

"Not everyone's got a hard-on for me like you have," I said. "I'm actually quite a popular guy."

"Evidently." Travis pulled out the chair on the other side of the table. "Though they didn't seem overly concerned as to whether you made it out alive."

He balled one fist and laid it on the table. "This is a rock, Hap," he said, and then placed another fist about six inches away from the first. "And this is a hard place. Can you guess where you are?"

I looked in the mirror and saw myself sitting there alone. I looked tired and old and pale, and I suddenly got a flash that there probably *wasn't* anyone in the observation room, that for some reason Travis was talking to me alone. That might mean there was something on the horizon other than a walk down to the holding tank. It was time to be polite.

"I don't know who they are," I said, and Travis sat down. "Yesterday morning two of them came to my apartment. I managed to get away, spent the morning outside Griffith. The only other time I've seen them was in the room at the Prose Café."

"Where you had come to pick up a memory machine?"

There was no point in lying. "Yes."

"You want to tell me why you need one?"

"No," I said, "I don't. You want to get anywhere near that, I'm not saying anything else until I call a lawyer."

Travis leaned toward me. "You know what I think? I think you've been working as a memory caretaker." He reached below the table and picked up a box. Inside it was the dream receiver, tagged in an evidence bag. "Found this in your jacket when you were processed. Now: Because of that asshole lawyer who's quantumized the dream-transfer issue, I have no way of knowing whether possession of this device is legal or not. Given that all memory caretakers so far apprehended have started life as proxy dreamers, however, and the fact you were trying to get hold of a memory machine, I can try damned hard to use this as evidence that you are or have been involved in a conspiracy to commit illegal activities with regard to recall."

"Shall I make that phone call now?"

"What else do you know about the guys in the suits?"

"Nothing."

"Why are they after you?"

A lie: "I have no idea."

"We have reason to believe that there may be another two men involved, in addition to the four at the Café. Would you agree?"

Throw him something: "It's possible."

"Why do you say that?"

Carefully: "Two guys came to my apartment. Four were at the Café. Either two of them were the same, or not. If not, there's six."

"You're not saying that, for example, because you've talked to the old guy in the store near the murder scene."

"What old guy would that be?"

"Because if you had done so, that would imply you had an interest in Hammond's death."

"Which I don't."

"Despite the fact that the chief suspects have a strong interest in you."

"You got it."

"How did they know where to find you on these two occasions?"

The truth: "I have no idea."

Travis nodded, looked up at the window in the wall behind me. I stubbed out my cigarette, waited.

"I'll lay it out straight," he said eventually. "Because I liked you once, and also to make sure you understand this is my final offer. Your crime's back on the 'base, the witnesses are all still in good health and of sound mind, and we have your dream receiver. Whatever happens, you're going down."

"You need to get one of the girls from Marketing to help advise you on pitching technique. So far this isn't sounding like such a great deal."

Travis ignored me. "But that's a bank job that happened three years ago, and nobody but me cares that much anymore. The victims had six relatives between them. Two are dead in a car wreck, one's a junkie who didn't like her brother much anyway, and the other three are poor and black. They still call the station every now and then, but nine times out of ten I don't even get the messages.

"On the other hand, we've got a high-ranking cop brutally murdered a week ago. I think you can imagine which is rated a higher priority."

"And you can't find the suspects no matter how hard you try, but they seem to be able to find me."

"You're a clever guy, Hap. I always said so. Want to put the rest of it together?"

"You release me, let me wander around town and wait for the guys with the guns to catch up with me. I give you a call—assuming I have time before I get blown away—and you come and catch the bad guys."

"You're wasted as lowlife, Hap. With a mind like yours, you could have aspired to greatness."

"Fuck you, Travis. What do I get for risking my life to make you look good?"

"I lose the dream receiver. And you aren't submitted to a truth test regarding your work as a memory caretaker."

I shook my head. "Not nearly enough. You've already admitted the dream machine is circumstantial. The only remaining witness to my allegedly attempting to procure a memory machine is in a coma, and you don't have probable cause for involuntary sodium verithal."

"You been watching a lot of TV or something, Hap? I don't know how you appear to yourself in your own head, but to the outside world you're just a minor hood nobody's going to give two shits about. Someone's got to pay for what happened in that bank, and Pechryn is already dead. That puts you in the bull pen all by yourself, and you have precisely no one on base. I can get two hundred cops to stand in a line and confirm in unison that you agreed to the verithal test. I can get them to sing it to the tune of 'I Got Rhythm' if that fucking helps."

"Try something else," I said wearily. I had just remembered that given the current state of my bank accounts, I'd be relying upon the state for my defense. I knew that I was going to deal. I knew, too, that whatever happened, I agreed with Travis now was as good as it was going to get.

Travis tapped his fingers on the table for a moment.

Then: "Helena walks," he said.

At that moment it felt as if time had drained away—two separate measures of time, to two different periods in my life. One an instinct that said no, that simply wasn't fair; and another that agreed to the idea without thinking.

"Yes or no," he said. "I wipe her name out of the file. To be frank, I don't fancy trying to arrest her anyway. That's my final offer."

I stared down at the table, feeling weak, on the verge of tears. Some instinct in Travis had probably told him that gut-shooting me with Helena's name would have just that effect. I abruptly lost the will to fight. I wanted it all to be over. I wanted to be alone. I wanted, to be frank, my mother—but she was a long way away and we hadn't spoken in weeks.

I looked up and nodded.

Travis smiled. "Good. Don't fuck with me on this, or I'll announce that bullets found in the two cops who died at the scene yesterday match the gun you left behind. You know how we tend to feel about people who whack one of our own."

He stood, opened the door. I pushed myself to my feet, face numb, and shambled toward it. "You can collect your coat on the way out," Travis said as I passed him. "Oh, and one more thing."

I stopped, turned, waited.

"There's a contract out on you. Big money. Two reliable snitches told me the word is that Helena has taken the job." He smiled. "Funny: Always thought she was the one for you. Life's a bitch, ain't it?"

I turned back and walked quickly away, so he wouldn't see the expression on my face.

I WENT IMMEDIATELY to the darkest bar I could find, and sat in the darkest corner. Then I asked the waitress if they could turn the lights down a little, and ordered five beers. While I waited for them, an ancient song came on the jukebox, something about sending lawyers, guns, and money. Sounded like a service I could use. I waited for a 1-800 number at the end, but there wasn't one.

A guy came in just as my drinks arrived, and sat at a booth on the other side of the room. Cheap suit, a tie the store must have sold him for a joke. He ordered a club soda and a bowl of nuts, sat, and examined the ceiling. Not the most subtle tail I had ever seen. I ignored him and got on with drinking.

By the second beer I was a little calmer. I called Deck on the cellular and told him I was okay. He sounded relieved, but said Laura was acting weird. Prowling around his apartment and drinking a lot. Took a half-hour shower, and when Deck stood close to the bathroom door, he could hear her talking angrily to herself: When she emerged, her skin looked raw, as if she'd been scrubbing it all that time. Now she was prowling and drinking again, alternating with chain-smoking and staring into space. I told him to try to distract her, show her his collection or something. I also told him the situation. He didn't say much. There wasn't a lot worth saying.

I spent the third beer considering the mess I was in, and chewing absently on nicotine pretzels. I tried to think rigorously, but the structure kept collapsing in the face of the obvious truth. I was fucked. If I tried to bug out of town, Travis would certainly follow through on his threat, and the cops would find me and shoot me on sight. All I could do was what I was told, and I knew the deal was final. I was free for precisely as long as it took for the guys in suits to find me, which by past experience wasn't that long. Added to which, some asshole had put out a whack on me.

As I drank the fourth beer, I found myself doing something I hadn't intended. Thinking about Helena. About the person I'd been looking for as I traveled around, knowing I'd already found her. About a cheap honeymoon in Ensenada a long time ago, mornings in motels and evenings in bars; about walking Venice in the warm afternoon, and cool nights in the house we shared there for a while; about our cat, and how soft his fur had been. About it being the nearest I'd ever come to being allowed to join the real world, to stepping out of my dreams and being awake.

It came on slowly at first, fragments that felt like recollections of somebody else's life. Then faster, and fuller, until the room shaded away and I was immersed in a reality that could have been, a life that other people and death had taken away from me. I began drinking faster. I'd been a criminal most of my life, but not a bad one. I'd sold Fresh, not smack—though the profits from the latter were much higher—and only to people who knew the mistake they were making. I'd stolen and cheated, but usually from people who could afford it. I'd caretaken trivial and accidental sins that had never nudged the Earth in its orbit one iota, merely afforded their owners a few moments of peace. I'd only ever killed in extremis, only once for money and only people who had deserved it.

Sure, there were better ways of living. I could have been one of those people who spend their entire lives wearing stripy shirts and going to brainstorming meetings and saying "No idea is a bad idea" and giving each other high-fives when they won that big account. The people who never actually do or achieve anything real in their entire lives, who live instead in some bizarre parallel universe where half a point of market share for some frozen-food manufacturer actually *matters*. The people who live in the same city all their lives, pulled along tracks too boring to understand, who die in the place they were born, and then are buried to make room for someone just like them. Within my own terms, in my own stream of reality, I'd behaved as well as I could—and at least I'd *done* stuff. I'd been places. I'd seen things. I'd had a speaking role in my own life.

For the second time in as many hours I had a sudden vision of my parents, the spring from which I had run. Mom no longer worked in the bar, but pottered with Dad around the motel, killing bugs, changing sheets, and making sure people were adequately air-conditioned. They'd never retire, would always be verbs, forever changing the world in ways however small. I was thirty-four years old, and yet if I had to be brought to account, it wouldn't be Travis, or a judge, or God I would stand in front of. It would be them—my parents. They were the higher authority.

With the fifth beer I thought about the things I'd done, and whether I could tell my parents about them. About the good, and the bad, the deaths and the shadow times.

I decided I could. My mother would say "Oh, *Hap,*" and my father wouldn't meet my eyes for a while. Within a few days it would be forgiven and understood. In the whole of your life there are maybe a handful of people who genuinely share your world with you, who for more than a moment inhabit the same place—as if you and they are imperfect facets of the same being. You owe them, and yourself. No one else.

I finished the last beer, walked over to the table on the other side of the bar, and grabbed the man in the cheap suit by the hair.

"Tell Travis if he puts a tail on me again, I'll kill them," I said, and smacked his head down on the table.

I left him facedown and unconscious in a sea of mixed nuts, and went to work.

CHAPTER ELEVEN

Ray Hammond's real house was over on Avocado, a big two-story set back from the road. Not a showy neighborhood, but certainly not a hovel. I got the address from Vent, who has a list he bought from a cop. A car I borrowed from outside the bar got me there fast: I ditched it half a mile from the house, in a brightly lit lot where it probably wouldn't get trashed, and ran the rest of the way.

I slowed to walk past the house on the other side of the street, covertly checking it out. I'd realized on the trip that I had no idea of Hammond's domestic situation, or whether someone might still be living inside. There were no uniforms standing guard outside the house, and no obvious unmarked cars parked within two hundred yards of it. A light glowed from within what looked like the living room, but the rest of the windows were dark. When after two passes the street remained deserted, I hurried across and walked straight up to the front door. There's no point messing around in these circumstances. You want to look like Joe Citizen dropping in on a friend, not like you're expecting to be felled by a marksman.

I rang the bell, waited. No reply. Rang it again, then leaned on it for ten seconds straight. No response, and no sound of movement from within, which tallied with what I was expecting. Most people, when they're in, have more than one light on. Sure there are oldsters and environmental fanatics who turn off the light in each room as they leave it, but most people don't. Night means "leave the lights on, goddammit, give me a flame to gather round." The chances were high that the living-room light was on a timer or an internal security system. Either that or any inhabitants were utterly deaf, which would work to my advantage.

I made my way around the side of the house, shielded from the neighbors by a high hedge that ran along the boundaries of the property. All the windows had locks, which peered at me as I passed, little orange eyes swiveling to follow my progress. I kept my face turned away, in case they had strong views on the likenesses of people who were allowed to prowl around the house at night, and made it to the back without incident.

The yard was compact and tidy, a big tree in the center and an old cable drum in place for use as a table. I scoped out the back door: one major lock, no sign of wires around the edges. I jacked the organizer into it and told it to get to work. Lights flickered on the organizer's display, and streams of numbers rocketed back and forth and up and down across the screen. I'm sure that's not entirely necessary, and that the organizer does it just to make sure I know it's doing something hard.

After thirty seconds it told me that it couldn't break the lock, but that it might be susceptible to a bribe. I tapped in the deceased Walter Fitt's bank details and let the lock transfer two hundred bucks into itself. God knows what it was intending to do with it, but after a few seconds there was a click and the door opened.

I found myself in a short back corridor with a doorway off to one side. I shut the outer door, stood, and listened for a moment in the darkness. My heart lurched when I heard a soft and rhythmic shuffling sound, but a second later I had an idea what it might be. I padded over to the doorway and looked inside.

It was the kitchen, designed free range, and the appliances were on the move. The fridge and microwave were trudging heavily in opposite directions along the far wall; a coffeemaker and food processor were walking a circle together in the middle of the floor. A large freezer stood against the other wall, rocking back and forth.

"Hi," I said quietly. Everything except the freezer stopped moving. "Anybody home?"

"No," whispered the food processor. "We're a little worried."

"How come?"

"Well, we haven't seen Mr. Hammond for days," the coffeemaker said confidingly, walking up to stand at my feet. "And then last night Monica—that's Mrs. Hammond—just left, without saying where she was going, and we haven't seen her since."

"Was she carrying a suitcase?"

"Yes. Only a small one, though."

"Well," I said, trying to be reassuring, "maybe she's just gone to stay with a friend for a couple of days."

"You think so?" asked the freezer, stopping its rocking for a moment.

"Bound to be," I said. "Otherwise she'd have taken you guys."

"Maybe you're right." The freezer sounded relieved. "Thank you."

"You hungry?" asked the fridge. "Got some cold chicken in here."

"Maybe later," I said, and backed out into the hallway again.

So Hammond had a wife, and up until today she'd been in residence. I guess I could probably have discovered that from an intelligent perusal of last week's papers, but I hadn't gotten around to it. The fact that she'd gone explained why there were no cops outside. The fact she'd been here, probably guarded, could mean something else: Whoever had tossed Hammond's other residence might not have had a chance to do the same thing here.

It might also go some way to explaining why Laura had chosen to gun Hammond down in Culver City: and to suggesting what the nature of the relationship between them had been.

I walked quickly down the corridor, keeping an eye out for security devices. The front of the house consisted of a reasonably sized open space in front of a staircase, which led up to the second floor. There were doorways on either side. I poked my head in the room with the light, saw that it was indeed the living room, then peered through the other door. Dining room, and not terribly interesting. Or sumptuously furnished: The Hammonds' tastes ran a little austere, though what little there was looked expensive.

I ran lightly up the staircase and along the upper hall, finding nothing but bedrooms on the right-hand side. The biggest showed signs of recent occupancy—and also that someone had left it in a hurry. Women's clothes were scattered over the bed, and the wardrobe doors were open. I turned the light on for a moment, snouted around in the bottom. All I could see was shoes, and plenty of them. What is it with women and shoes? I can understand needing different colors to go with different outfits, but like most of her sex, Mrs. Hammond had seven pairs in burnt umber alone. On impulse I checked the labels of some of the clothes left on the bed. Fiona Prince, Zauzich, Stefan Jones. Ready-to-wear, admittedly, but far from cheap. I wondered if Travis had seen any of this when he came to interview the widow, and whether he'd come to the same conclusion I was reaching: Ray Hammond had been on the take.

I turned off the light and checked out the other side of the hallway. A bathroom, the shelf above the sink in mild disarray. Not a panicky departure exactly, but one where time had obviously been of the essence. Some key female accessories were still in place, however, implying she probably intended to come back. Then another small room, empty, purpose unclear. Maybe a nursery in the architect's original design, but not used for one now.

One more room remained, at the front of the house. The door was shut. I took a deep breath and turned the handle, sincerely hoping it wasn't alarmed. The handle turned, nothing went off, and I pushed the door open gently.

Beyond was Hammond's study. A desk up against the front window, and the outline of a big chair. A wall full of books, and another lined with filing cabinets. My heart sank. If there was anything hidden in here, finding it was going to take days.

Then the light went on, and the chair swiveled to reveal a man in a dark suit sitting there.

"Hello, Hap," he said. "Nice to see you again."

I BLINKED, discovered Deck's gun was already in my hand, and pointed it at the man. The gun didn't make me feel better, or seem to worry him much. I kept pointing it anyway.

The man held up a small electronic notebook. "Are you looking for this?"

"I've no idea," I said petulantly. "What is it? And who the fuck are you?"

Then I recognized him, and answered the question myself. It was the guy from the diner, the one who'd been sitting at the table down at the end, apparently deep in post-alcohol stress. The one who'd spoken to me after my phone conversation with the man at Laura's house, who'd looked a little out of place, and yet who had been sitting there, opposite Laura's hotel—almost as if he were waiting for someone.

"My name," said the man, screwing up his eyes for a moment, "is Hap."

"No, it's not," I said steadily. "That's my name. Try again."

The man frowned. "You're absolutely right, of course. Sorry. My name is Travis."

"Stop being an asshole," I suggested, "and tell me who the hell you are. And turn off the light, for Christ's sake."

"What light?"

The light switch, in keeping with common practice, was on the wall behind me, next to the door. He couldn't have reached it from where he was sitting. The light had an unusual quality, almost tangible, as it might appear if I were swimming in clear water at night and someone turned on a powerful searchlight overhead. It didn't seem to reach into the corners of the room, or to display objects in the usual manner, as if its role wasn't actually visual.

Keeping Deck's gun trained firmly on the man in the chair, I reached behind and flicked the switch. The overhead light came on, and the room suddenly looked more normal, full of edges and a little dusty. Though not any brighter.

The man winked. "And the gates of it shall not be shut at all by day," he said, "for there shall be no night there."

"I really am running out of patience," I said.

The man rolled his eyes, reached into his pocket, and brought out a small torchlike object. "Ambient light projector," he told me. "You can get them at Radio Shack."

"Great. I'll look out for one. Now, for the last time: What are you doing here?"

"Waiting for you," he said, standing. "You're later than I expected, and I've got to go. Things to do. Anyway—it's here." He placed the notebook on the chair, winked at me again. "You'd never have found it on your own. It was taped under the corner of the desk."

"Which is the first place I would have looked," I said irritably. "For whatever it is."

The man smiled and walked toward me. He stopped about a yard away, with my gun almost touching his chest, and waited patiently. I didn't know what to do. Shooting him seemed excessive, but I didn't know whether I should just let him go. In the end I let the gun drop. I was panting slightly, tired and strung out and empty. The guy had to be a cop or someone connected with Hammond, and he was obviously several steps ahead of me.

"What's going on?" The question spilled out of me like a final breath. I felt like I could do with some clues, maybe a password to help me up to the next level.

The man pulled out a wallet and handed me a card. "I wouldn't hang around," he advised. Then he walked past me out the door, and I just let him go.

It was a moment before I thought to look at the card, to turn it over in my hands. Both sides were blank.

I ran out the door, through the hallway and down the stairs, but he was gone. I dithered about whether to chase after him, then remembered the notepad was still upstairs, that time wasn't on my side—and also that Deck could probably do with some backup. I returned to the study, made it dark again. I was intending to just pocket the notepad and go, but on impulse I found the pad's backlighting switch and turned it on.

A screen full of numbers, separated by commas. There didn't seem to be any discernible pattern, just row after row of figures. I leafed through a few other pages of the notebook, but they were all blank. Hammond had used a fifty-dollar device to store just one page of stuff: Ergo, it was probably important. Or maybe it was his golf scores. I'd worry about it later.

Before I went I cast an eye over the shelves of books. For a cop, he had a hell of a lot of them. Criminology texts, history, novels, spines battered and used. Also religious books, interpretations of the Bible, one hundred and one ways to be a happy camper: rows of the fuckers, looking newer than most of the other books. I picked a book out at random from the nonreligious section, opened it. The light from the street was just sufficient for me to see that the page showed a number of pictures of gunshot wounds. Not very nice, but quite interesting. It was certainly a better deal to see them by opening a book than looking down at your own shoulder. Not for the first time, I wondered whether it might have been a better career decision to have been a cop rather than a criminal. I'd thought about it at one stage. As usual, I decided that I'd probably had better pay and working conditions, and enjoyed slightly higher social status. Being a cop got you a nice uniform, on the other hand—and presumably people didn't arrest you the whole time and say dispiriting things about your life. Didn't make much difference: probably a little late to apply to the academy anyhow.

As I put the book back on the shelf, I noticed something. The next book along had a piece of paper stuck in it, a tiny corner protruding above the height of the pages it was sandwiched between. I pulled the book out, opened it.

And knew I'd found something important.

The page was about five inches by three, and laserprinted almost edge to edge. The text was nonsense, a jumble of letters with no spaces. A code. As I looked more closely, I realized that the letter X appeared far more times than it should have even if it was standing in for E. Chances were it was doubling as a space character, in which case the text was printed in word-shaped chunks.

There was no printer on the desk, which meant maybe that the sheet was a product of Hammond's activities in his other apartment. In other words, that it was a backup of whatever information the people who'd cleaned that place out were looking for. Two of the edges were slightly uneven, suggesting it had once been part of a larger sheet. You could probably have gotten four out of a normal piece of paper—implying there might be more?

I slid the book back, pulled out another from a higher shelf. No paper, nor in the next two I tried. There were hundreds of books on the shelves, and I knew it had to have been the co-incidence shot which Vent had sold me that had enabled me to find the first one right off. Searching all the books would take the rest of the night, so I decided to just quickly toss one section.

It still took over half an hour, but netted me three more pieces of paper. The letters on each were different, but otherwise they looked identical. Two words in bold at the top, maybe a name. Then a solid block of impenetrable text.

What could be secret and important enough that a cop would go to all this trouble both to hide the information and also to back it up? Not official business, that's for sure.

I slipped the sheets in my pocket and left the house, pausing only to take a piece of fried chicken from the fridge and wish the appliances good luck.

DECK WAS SITTING at the table, looking stressed. Laura was lying on the sofa with a large drink in her hand. She looked angular and jumpy, and was clearly in a strange mood. She was dressed in women's jeans and a baggy sweater, presumably an outfit left in Deck's closet by some special person who'd decided to go be special to someone else. The clothes were far too big for Laura, and she looked like a pretty scarecrow dressed in its Sunday best. She'd pulled the sleeves of the sweater up, and the scars on her wrists looked raw. The fear in her eyes had gotten worse, like someone who knew she was going to start pounding her head against the wall again but was powerless to stop herself.

"Yo, Hap," she said. "The prodigal loser returns." The sentence came out like someone trying to speak Dutch with a speech impediment, and I raised an eyebrow at Deck.

"You try stopping her," he said.

I perched on the arm of the sofa. She craned her neck to look up at me. Her eyes were holding, but only just. "Hi, Hap," she said. "How you doing?"

"Not as well as you, by the look of it. You think maybe it's time for that coffee yet?"

"Hmm. Do I want coffee?" She mimed deep thought, a performance slightly marred by missing her chin with her index finger. Then suddenly she shouted, *"No, of course I don't want any fucking coffee!"*

"Laura, it's going to be really hard for us to talk if you have any more to drink."

"We're going to talk, are we? How nice. What about?"

"Whatever you want. About what's going on with you. About what we can do to help."

"What are you going to do—save me?"

Suddenly I felt tired and worn out and not in the fucking mood. "Laura, do try to remember that people other than you have problems. I've spent the entire afternoon in a police cell. That incident I told you about? It's back on the database, and Travis knows it. To stop myself from going down on a recall rap, I have to help him catch the psychos who are after you, because he thinks they killed Hammond, and my only payment for doing that is the freedom of my ex-wife—about whom I have complicated feelings, not least because Travis let it slip that she may be hoping to cash in on a lucrative contract that is out on me. By anybody's standards, that's a lousy afternoon, so what say you give me a break?"

She giggled. "Why did you split up with your wife?"

"Because our cat died," I snapped. "Now, are you going to have coffee, or what?"

"No, but I'll accept a massage."

"Excuse me?"

"My neck hurts," she said, pulling herself laboriously upright on the sofa, "and it might help if you would massage it."

"We're not going to have sex, are we?"

She blinked at me, looking mildly sober for a moment. "Er, no."

Deck sniggered in the background, got up, and went into the kitchen. He knew what was coming. He'd heard it before. I explained to Laura, at some length, my feelings on the subject of massage. That I disliked having it done to me, that I found it both boring and irritating, and why. I also explained my views on the sneaky and underhanded way women had gotten massage redefined as foreplay, so men had to do it to them more often. After centuries of it being something you did to athletes, or if you'd sprained something, suddenly all the good sex advice—propagated either by women or bearded idiots who do what they're told—said that massage was an essential element of making love. And so now, not only did men have to ensure that women had orgasms (their right, to be sure, and a pleasurable task, but, ladies—have *you* tried it? It's either very easy or like playing pool with the lights off: never anywhere in between. I think every woman should have to try giving another woman an orgasm. We'd hear a bit less on the subject then, I bet) but suddenly bone-crushingly dull and detumescing things like massaging someone's foot are now part of the whole sexual ritual, and if a man doesn't spend thirty minutes happily kneading his girlfriend's calves, then he's some kind of sexual caveman. *Men* haven't suddenly come up with some whole new thing, have they? Some new sexual hoop for their partners to jump through? They haven't decreed that being nice about their jokes and serving them beer and pretzels are now essential parts of the sexual enterprise, or that they simply can't get nicely relaxed and in the mood unless you watch the ball game together beforehand.

It's just not *fair*, dammit—and I for one am not standing for it. Or taking it lying down. Whichever.

I went on awhile, I have to admit. Intentionally. After the first couple of minutes Laura's shoulders started to slump, and when Deck brought her a cup of coffee, she took it without a murmur.

"I'm not surprised your wife left you," she said, curling her legs up beneath her. "Sounds like you were kind of a drag."

Deck spoke quietly: "You don't really think Helena's going to whack you?"

"Probably not," I said. "She saved me at the Café. She brought the memory machine back here. And probably it was she who was in my apartment and turned the sheets back: a message I was just a bit too dense to get."

"Which implies she's been looking out for you for a few days."

"Big fucking deal," I said. "Too little, too late."

"Hap, if she really wanted to kill you . . ."

"Yeah, I know," I said irritably, "I'd be dead already. Do you have any idea what it was like to have a significant other who's universally acknowledged to be tougher than you are?"

"No, but then, I've never been married."

"Very droll. You get that off a cereal box?"

"I might have if I could read."

"Jeez," said Laura, "I'm amazed you guys ever go out. You can have so much fun just staying in *talking*."

"Laura," I said, "what happened to you? This morning your company was almost bearable. Now it's like eating a ground-glass enchilada. You want to talk about that?"

"Oh, God," she sneered, "Doctor Hap is back in session."

"What's the problem?" I said for the hell of it. "Feeling bad about Monica Hammond?"

I don't know what reaction I was expecting. Maybe a realization on Laura's part that I knew slightly more about her life than she figured. Perhaps just shutting her up for a moment.

That wasn't what I got. She went absolutely berserk.

She launched herself off the sofa, already screaming. I fell backward awkwardly and landed with her on top of me. I was so astonished, it was a few moments before I could even put up a defense, by which time I was seeing stars. Laura was frenzied, beating at my face with her fists and shouting words I couldn't distinguish. I tried to grab her hands, but they were moving too fast and too unpredictably.

Then Deck was behind her, and managed to get hold of her shoulders. He pulled her backward until her fists were out of range, at which point she started kicking at me instead. Deck got an arm fairly gently around her neck, and eased her back far enough for me to drag myself away. Laura was still shouting, but more slowly, her voice dropping in pitch to somewhere near its normal range. I still couldn't make out what she was rasping, though it sounded like four words repeated over and over.

"What the fuck," I panted, "was that all about?"

Deck's arm was still around her neck, but her body was shaking less. He had his head in close to hers, and was stroking her hair with his other hand. Laura's eyes stayed locked on me, heavy with fury and shame.

She kept repeating the words like an automaton wearing down, until finally I understood what she was saying.

"Monica is my mother."

SHE WOULDN'T SAY any more. We all sat in our places for a few minutes, catching our breath, feeling the fire in the room gutter out. Then Laura struggled out of Deck's grip and went into the bathroom, slamming the door loudly behind her. Deck and I looked at each other and couldn't find anything to say. He used a cushion to mop up the cup of coffee that had gone supernova. I went back into the kitchen to make some more.

A few minutes later I heard Laura emerge from the bathroom. She muttered an apology, then sat back down on the sofa. I kept out of sight, manufacturing hot drinks so slowly, I almost went into a Zen trance. I heard Deck ask Laura a question, something uncontroversial, and after a long silence she answered. He started telling her about some of the stuff on his walls. I didn't get the sense this was an excitement explosion for her, but at least she seemed to be listening.

I decided to stay in the kitchen a little longer. Deck is one of those people you can't help liking. I'm not. People find it enormously easy. Some of them don't like me several times a day, just to keep their average up.

I perched on a stool and had a cigarette. My face hurt, and when I wiped my finger under my nose, it came away smeared with blood. Also I thought she might have cracked one of my ribs. I hoped not, because cracked ribs are a pain in the ass. I have a couple on my right side which are weak now, and each time they get rebroken, you're looking at about four weeks of significant discomfort, without anything to even show people.

To pass the time, I wondered how long it would be before Travis tracked me down. As far as I was concerned, losing the tail wasn't breaking the terms of our agreement, but the lieutenant would probably feel different. I also thought about my chances of making bail on the bank job, and fixed the odds at less than nothing. I drank my coffee and listened to the murmur of Deck's voice, Laura's occasional grunts.

Then I heard a sound coming from the front of the house. At first I didn't know what it might be, then I knew where I recognized it from.

It sounded like a car, driven fast, roaring down the road toward the house. Maybe more than one car, in fact. Maybe three.

Time seemed to slow, like a pianist doing a melodramatic rallentando. As I swung my head, mouth gathering to shout to Deck to look out the window, the back door to the kitchen burst open and someone thrust their head inside.

"Quick," Helena said. "Hap, you've got to come with me."

I stared at her, blinked twice. There was a scream of brakes from the front of the house, the sound of doors being thrown open. I heard Deck leap to his feet and swear inquiringly; then the sound of running feet and the door downstairs being blown off its hinges.

But what I saw was Helena's face. Soft skin over sharp bones, dark brown hair and ice-blue eyes. Maybe a few more lines, a little deeper than they used to be. Otherwise, exactly the same.

Footsteps running up the front stairs to the door.

I shouted Deck's name, dragging my eyes away from Helena. Deck reacted instantly, grabbing Laura by the arm and hauling her off the sofa. As I yanked my gun out, I felt a hand grip mine, yank me toward the back door.

Helena hissed: "Hap, for fuck's sake—*now!*"

Laura stumbled over a rug and fell to her knees. Deck turned to help her up. The first shotgun blast hammered into his front door—wood splintered instantly, followed by the sound of an explosive kick. I started to run to help Deck, but Helena wouldn't let go, and pulled me back toward the door. I whirled to face her, and she yanked my face close to hers. "Come with me now," she said. "Or I'm leaving you here."

I heard Deck and Laura running toward us. Helena turned on her heel. I hurtled after her out onto the landing and clattered onto the stairs. Deck and Laura were a few paces behind, but Helena was right, as always—I couldn't help them run. They had to do it on their own.

There was an enormous crash as Deck's front door was finally smashed to pieces, then the sound of shouting. I tripped and nearly fell headlong down the stairs, but flailed out and grabbed a rail just in time. Helena was pattering down the metal steps in front of me, lithe and fast, and for an absurd moment all I could focus on was the length of her slim back, and the kick of her hair as it bobbed and swung.

I tumbled onto the ground a few paces after her, and remembered the car I'd stowed behind the building the night before. Helena followed my eyes. "Got the keys?" she asked, racking a cartridge into a gun that had appeared from nowhere. It was bigger than mine, naturally. I shook my head, craning my neck to see that Deck and Laura had only just made it onto the platform above. "No time, then," Helena said, "just run."

Obediently I started to stumble backward, shouting up at the others to hurry. And I saw:

Laura and Deck, frozen in motion. Deck just ahead, but Laura coming on fast, head ducked and face trapped between fear and determination. Deck already reaching for the banister, eyes judging the angle to throw themselves at the stairway.

Then, behind them, an explosion of yellow light. At first I thought it was muzzle flare, but the light was too soft and too large and came on far too slowly. Not an incendiary device either—because there was no sound except a deep humming that made my teeth vibrate. Two figures slammed out of the kitchen, the point men in suits. Deck's head turned; I heard the crack of a shot from Helena's gun, which didn't seem to change anything; a whisper of a scream from Laura, as if heard from the end of a tunnel through the center of the earth.

The light changed, condensed into a white bulb around Laura and Deck. The top of it scrolled twenty yards up into the sky, until it looked more like a column. Still running backward, still trying to shout, I tripped and slammed into the ground. As Helena tried to pull me to my feet, it happened.

Deck's face changed. At first it just seemed to smooth out, then bits of it faded away. The parts I'd never really noticed disappeared, leaving only his eyes and cheekbones and mouth. The same was happening to Laura, but faster. Within two seconds all I could see was two terrified circles. I felt an odd twist of emotion toward the circles, something inappropriate and strange—and for a second I thought I saw something in the air above the house, like an empty room formed out of air. The vibration got louder and faster, pulling at my mind like hooks into memory. The remaining fragments of Deck's and Laura's faces glowed for a moment, as if glimpsed in a photograph of long ago.

Then they weren't there anymore.

The white light disappeared as if turned off at a switch. No more men came out onto the landing, and the first two seemed to have vanished. I turned, looked at the street out in front. The cars had gone. All that was left was the back door flapping open in a nonexistent breeze, and absolute silence.

CHAPTER TWELVE

An hour later we were in Venice. I sat on a wall looking across the beach at the sea. Helena stood five yards away, reloading her gun. Apparently she'd emptied a whole clip into the figures on the staircase. Hadn't made any difference. The exchange of this piece of information was the only conversation we'd had, which was just as well. I didn't really have it in me to shout at Helena, and so I wished she'd just go away. The moon was out, turning shredded clouds into pale rips in deep blue cloth. The beach was too wide for me to hear more than a faint whisper of the tide massaging the water line, like someone gently rubbing their finger across a rough piece of paper. A jogger passed behind us on the pavement, measured taps fading in and out of the darkness like an asteroid temporarily swinging through our orbit, someone gliding along the regular rails of an explicable life.

Helena and I had stood motionless for a full minute after the white light disappeared, heads swinging back and forth like two cats trying to work out where a moth had gone. Deck's back door flapped for a few more moments, then gradually became still. I ran up the stairs and checked the apartment. It was empty, and apart from a couple of overturned chairs and a pile of big splinters of wood in the hallway, completely undamaged. There was no sign of a big impact, no evidence of scorching.

I knew where Deck kept his tools, and quickly yanked his bedroom door off to serve as a replacement front door. It seemed important at the time. The door fit, more or less, and I secured it as best I could with a chair under the handle. I also threw the memory equipment into one of his closets and covered it with junk.

Then we left, expecting the cops to arrive any second, drawn by reports of noise and violence. But as we walked quickly away, I saw nobody hanging out of windows or gathering in the street outside. We looked around, expecting to see at least one person staring and saying "What the heck?"

Nobody. Like it never happened.

We didn't say anything. Just kept walking, a couple of yards apart, until we found ourselves in the old neighborhood. Almost like we were going home. Then I abruptly lost interest in going any farther, and set up camp on the wall.

Helena finished with the gun and stuck it in a shoulder holster. Stood with her hands on her hips.

"What happened back there," she declared, "wasn't normal."

"No shit."

"We've got to tell someone about it."

"Tell them what? That two people and three cars just disappeared? And tell who, exactly?"

"But who are those guys?"

"Why don't you tell me? You seem to be pretty far ahead of the game."

She sat on the wall a yard or two away. "All I've been doing is following you. I saw you run from them at your apartment. Saw them arrive at the Café. Saw the cars on their way tonight."

"So why have you been sticking so close?"

She looked down, kicked at the sand. "I've been watching out for you."

"Right," I said. "Not hunting me down?"

"Don't be a prick, Hap."

"So you're not in the frame for a whack on me?"

"Yes, dear, of course I am. And why do you think that might be?"

"Because I didn't massage you enough?"

"What the hell are you talking about?"

I stood up, started walking. "Never mind."

She caught up with me, grabbed my arm, and spun me around. "I took the contract because it was there. Someone wanted you dead, enough to put out a big open call. I've got a certain reputation, and I'm a made girl. I thought if word got around I was on the case, maybe other contractors would stay out of it. In other words, that you'd be safe for a while."

I looked her in the eyes, knew she was telling the truth. "Thank you," I said.

She nodded. "Okay. So be nice."

"Helena, give me a break. I haven't seen you in a long time. You know what you did. Then suddenly you're following me around and saving my life and—"

I stopped, not wanting to say any more.

She smiled: "It's good to see you again, Hap."

Not a helpful thing to hear, and kind of a selfish thing to say. Hurt and anger were fighting it out for supremacy in my mind, searching for some arrangement where they could both speak at once. I snapped: "Is it?"

"Don't you think so?"

"I don't know, to be honest. You've had a couple of days to get used to the idea, do a bit of fieldwork on the life and habits of the lesser-regarded Hap Thompson. I don't know shit about you anymore."

"Well, I've still got the same job, and I still live in LA and I'm going out with someone." She named a local mob figure about ten years older than me. That hurt, but not as much as I would have expected.

"Good for you," I said. "So how exactly am I supposed to react? Do tell."

She tried to take my arm again. "You're supposed to walk

with me down to the water and tell me what's going on." My head shook violently, outside my control. I didn't want to walk down to the beach with her, to do anything we used to do. "Or we can stay here," she said. "Whatever. I just want to help, Hap. Tell me what's going on."

After a while, and only because my legs started to ache from standing in one place, we did start walking. And if you're walking on a beach, you're going to wind up going down toward the sea. It makes sense. We walked along the damp sand, a few feet above where the swell petered out, and in time I realized I was looking for sand dollars, even though it was too dark and the tide wasn't right. I kept on looking anyway. That's what beaches are for.

In the meantime, I told Helena about Lieutenant Travis— though not about the deal I'd struck—and what had happened at Hammond's house; about Laura and Quat and how I'd ended up in this mess, right back to when I first met Stratten. Even a little about life before then, the years spent traipsing from state to state. All I could find to say about that time was that I was watching myself getting older, and that it was taking too long. So I stopped talking and walking, and turned to face the sea.

Helena looked at me for a long while. I didn't turn my face toward her. I didn't want to be able to see her. I knew she wanted to ask me other things, and that if I looked at her, she'd take that as a signal to start. I'd had a long fucking day. Being in her company again was too weird for words, and the air between us seemed to pulse with the things that should and shouldn't be said. At one moment it was like nothing had ever changed, and then the next it was like I was with a stranger I couldn't possibly have met before. Talking with her used to be as natural as breathing, a living shorthand honed by affection and understanding. Now it felt like I was standing on a strange planet wearing an oxygen mask, because I didn't know what the atmosphere contained, whether it would nurture or kill me.

"I don't want to depress you any further," she said eventually, "but this Stratten character is the guy who's taken the hit out on you."

That woke me up, I've got to admit. *"What?"*

Helena nodded. "Five days ago. Sixty thou, and your head must be completely destroyed. Which seemed a bit harsh, I must say. It's a nice head."

I stared at her, feeling a little dizzy and very stupid. Stratten wasn't an idiot, and I'd been acting pretty strange after a year and a half of being his star caretaker. "Of course. Jesus Christ."

"What is it?"

"Somehow he worked out I was into something that could damage REMtemps. If the cops found out I was carrying out a major crime using equipment supplied by his company, he'd have been in deep shit. Even the people he must be keeping greased would have drawn the line at that." So he'd tried to have me killed, and had already put the order out when I talked to him in Ensenada. That's why no paid dreams had been forthcoming last night: Stratten had just been stringing me along, keeping me in town long enough for someone to find and kill me.

"But how could he have found it out?"

"Quat," I said. "It's the only way." Suddenly it made sense, leading to an inescapable conclusion. Quat had been working for Stratten all along. "About two weeks after I started proxy dreaming, I met this wirehead on the Net. In retrospect, I guess he found me. He told me how I could have my money kept safe, and I paid him to do it."

Which meant that all the time I'd thought I was safeguarding my future, Stratten already had me backed into a corner. My independence had been coded by someone on the REMtemps payroll. Then I remembered my first meeting with Stratten, the way he'd shown me visuals of the dreams I'd had in Pete's Rooms.

"There must be some way of monitoring what memory a client is dumping," I told Helena, "like there is with dreams. Quat earned his money helping Laura transfer her memory to me, watched the monitor afterward—either out of policy or because he's a voyeur asshole. He clocks something hinky is going down, contacts Stratten. Stratten knows he's got a big problem: gets Quat to set me up at the Café and then crash my accounts." I realized something else, and my mouth dropped open. "Christ, I've been dumb."

"Why?"

"Travis's cops found me yesterday, ten minutes after I'd made a pay-phone call to Stratten. I should have put the two together. REMtemps kept me hanging on hold: Meantime, they traced the number and tipped off the police."

"But Stratten doesn't want the cops getting hold of you. That's why there's a contract."

I shrugged. "He found out you'd taken the contract, worked out who you were, realized it might go sour. Maybe in the meantime he's cut a side deal—Travis is offering to drop the recall rap altogether, remember. Stratten gets in touch, lets him know he might be able to find me—and that Quat has put us back on the database. Then, when Travis has caught the guys in the suits, I have an accident in my cell before a verithal test can implicate REMtemps. Everybody's happy. Except for me."

Helena crossed her arms, looked dubious. "You really think Travis would do something like that?"

"There's one way to find out."

I MET HIM ALONE. Put a call through to the station, patiently waited out a tirade concerning the bruising of a police officer's forehead, told him to meet me alone at the corner of Riviera and San Juan. Hung up without waiting to hear a reply.

Helena volunteered to fade back, make her way there by a different route. That way she could keep an eye on what was happening, and alert me if Travis brought other cops along with him. I agreed. It might work in our favor somewhere along the line if the lieutenant didn't know Helena and I were on the same team. She gave a crooked smile.

"Is that what we are? A team?"

When we'd been together, I'd often railed about people who called their lovers partners, as if corporate terminology were now appropriate in other relationships, too: as if love were a business transaction between people who rotated the roles of client and supplier and communicated with each other in bullet points. Screw that, I always said. I was her boyfriend, and then her husband—not just someone who slept in the same office environment.

"Yeah," I said. "That's exactly what we are."

Her smile faded instantly. She nodded curtly and strode away.

At the crossroads where I'd told Travis to meet me is a place called the Happy Spatula. It used to be a pretty well-known restaurant, popular with local families: cooked the kind of lasagne that said "Yes, we know about current scientific thinking on diet, and we don't give a shit." Also they left a little bowl of parmesan on the table, for you to help yourself. When I become King of the World, this practice will become mandatory, even in restaurants that don't serve pasta. Unfortunately there was a series of violent incidents in the Spatula, and the families learned to stay away. The owners sold out, the clientele went downhill like a rock dropped off a cliff, and in season the restaurant's wall-to-wall psychos. The rest of the year it's like a morgue. Venice is on the very edge of the region affected by the microclimate fuckup, and has more stable weather than most, but it still tends to go in cycles of a few weeks or so. Tonight it was cool, and the tables outside the Happy Spatula were empty.

I sat at one, ordered a carafe of coffee, and waited for the next thing to happen.

Or tried to, anyway. My mind felt as though someone were applying electric shocks to it, alternating current and voltage. I guess I should have been trying to get some kind of handle on what had happened back at Deck's place, but something told me I didn't have the background information required to process the event. That was my excuse, anyhow. In fact, my mind was just running from the problem. It didn't want to think about it. I was worried about Deck, and Laura, too, I guess, but there was nothing I could do. Particularly when my head was full of someone else.

I knew she'd be somewhere nearby, utterly invisible. I could almost feel her, believed that if I put my mind to it I could close my eyes and point in the direction she'd be. Now that she wasn't with me, I wanted very much to talk to her, though I was still far from certain what I wanted to say. I couldn't see past a three-year edifice of studied indifference. It was too long ago, too much had changed. Too many bad things had happened.

Time runs forward. That's the way it is.

When the arrival of my coffee jolted me out of this festive train of thought, I pulled one of the pieces of paper I'd taken from Hammond's study out of my pocket. I know jackshit about cryptography, but it occurred to me that Hammond probably hadn't been at the cutting edge of the field either. Relative ignorance might even be a help. I scanned the page into my organizer and asked it to take a look, more as a distraction than out of any real hope.

The machine hemmed and hawed for a while, said it couldn't make head or tail of it, and would I mind changing its batteries soon?

Then I remembered Hammond's notebook and its list of figures. I plugged the notebook into the organizer and told it to see if it could find any relationship between the two sets of information. It did stuff for a while, still grumbling about its waning power, and then said we might be dealing with a book code—where each letter is replaced with one from a given book—albeit a code that was slightly more complex than normal. The patterns of letters weren't consistent with a single passage being used as a key, but the numbers in the notepad might be a list of rotated sections.

I told the organizer to get on the Net and connect to an online version of the King James Bible. Fifty seconds later it had an answer for the two words at the top of the sheet of paper.

Nicholas Schumann. Holy shit.

"Writing out a will?"

I flicked the organizer's screen off, stuffed the piece of paper back in my pocket. Travis was standing behind me, wearing a wet raincoat and looking pissed. "It rained on me on the way from the car," he said. "Naturally it's dry where you are."

I looked around, saw that the sidewalks were wet up to about three yards from where I sat. I hadn't even noticed. Travis sat opposite me in an unwelcome reminder of our conversation earlier in the day. I turned sideways in my chair, lit a cigarette.

"Want me to arrest you for that?" he asked. "You know I can."

"And I know you're not going to," I replied. "You've got your eye on bigger things."

He poured himself a coffee. "Okay, Hap—so what's the problem? And be fucking brief and to the point, because I don't appreciate being ordered around by lowlifes unless they have something extremely interesting to say."

"I've seen the guys in the suits again."

He stared at me, furious. "So why didn't you call me?"

"I didn't have time. They arrived, then disappeared."

"Just like that? They sort of said hi and then moseyed off?"

"No. They also abducted two friends of mine." Suddenly I realized that was exactly the right word for what had happened.

"Who? And what the fuck do you mean, abducted?"

"I got away, and then the suits aren't there anymore. And there were six of them, by the way. They vanished, taking my friends."

"Vanished how? Drove away?"

I leaned toward him. "No, Travis. Listen to me. They *vanished*. In a column of white light. Get the picture?"

"You think I'm going to believe this?"

"I really don't give a damn what you believe, Travis. But what's the percentage in me telling you this if it isn't true?"

"Maybe you're laying the groundwork for an insanity defense."

"Yeah, right. With you as my sole witness."

Travis took a deep breath. "Okay," he said. "I've got nothing better to do. Tell me a story."

I told him, described exactly what had happened. I didn't think it would help, but it felt good to have it on record anyway. He listened, one eyebrow archly raised, stirring his coffee. When I'd finished, he laughed.

"They have a spaceship or something, Hap? You get a good look at it?" I just looked at him. "Pity. Maybe we could have busted them for a broken taillight."

"There some other detective working the Hammond case?"

He frowned. "Of course not. Why?"

"Not some guy in a suit, good-looking, about forty?"

"What are you talking about?"

"After I lost your tail, I broke into Hammond's house. Checked out his study. There was a guy already there, and I've seen him before. He knew my name. And yours."

Travis looked confused, working on irritable. "There's no one on this case I don't know about. And what the hell do you think you're doing, breaking into that house?"

"There's a connection between me and Hammond you don't know about," I said, "over and above the guys in the suits. I've got a vested interest in working this situation out. I went there to see what I could find."

"Which would have been precisely nothing," he snapped. "We've already been over that place."

"Yeah, but not closely enough. For a start, did you notice the labels on Monica Hammond's clothes?"

"Yes, I did." He looked very slightly uncomfortable. "So what?"

"You know what I'm saying. And point two, I found something in the study."

"You going to tell me what it is?"

"Maybe," I said. "Depends on your answer to my next question. What's your relationship to Mr. Stratten?"

I watched his eyes carefully. Nothing happened in them except bafflement. "Never heard of the guy."

"So how did you find me in Applebaum's, Travis? And don't tell me it was great police work. If you'd tracked me down, it would have been a fucking SWAT team coming to collect me—not just the two rookies who happened to be closest to the scene."

"We got a tip," Travis admitted. "Somebody called it in."

"And this somebody didn't suggest that you might like to forget about the recall rap?"

"No, they didn't, and the implication pisses me off."

"Tough. That call came from the office of the guy who runs REMtemps. He's almost certainly the guy who also bought the hit on me."

"Nice to see you maintain a positive relationship with your employer."

"It's a skill of mine."

"So why does he want you fucked up?"

"I don't know," I lied. "But do remember that trying to have a person killed is illegal, even if that person is me."

"I will," he said. "And if I bump into Helena, I'll remind her of that, too. I must say I'm surprised you've stayed alive this long."

"Maybe she's losing her touch," I said. I pulled the piece of paper out of my pocket and laid it on the table. "This is the other thing I got from Hammond's house."

"And this would be?"

"It was hidden in the study. It's in code."

"And it says?"

"The first two words are a name," I said. "Nicholas Schumann, that rich guy who killed himself last week. Why would Ray Hammond have Schumann's name on a piece of paper hidden in his study?"

Travis looked shaken. "What does the rest of this say?"

"I haven't decoded it yet, and I'm not telling you the code or giving you the other pieces of paper I have. Something else you don't know: Hammond was killed outside a second apartment he kept a secret. Somebody has been through the place. They took a computer and some files."

"Shit. Why didn't you—"

"Because I was pissed off about sitting in that cell, and I had no reason to trust you. I still don't, but I'm running out of options. I'll email you the rest of Schumann's sheet at six tomorrow morning, provided you leave me alone for the next two days."

"What will you be doing?"

"Trying to get my friends back."

"What makes you think you can find them?"

"Not much," I admitted. "But I'm going to try anyway."

"That piece of paper could say anything. You could have typed it yourself. Why should I do as you say?"

I leaned back in my chair. "Because you're a good guy. I remember going for beers with you before all this happened, even if you don't. Because you're also a good cop, and you know there's something weird about Ray Hammond's death." I decided to take a risk. "And because you know in your heart of hearts that what happened at Transvirtual wasn't my fault."

Travis looked away for a long while. It looked like he was still absorbing the news about Schumann, but it turned out he was thinking about something else.

"You know what really pissed me off about that?" he asked eventually. "I liked you. You were no danger to anybody. Just a scuffling lowlife, snouting for cash, not doing anyone any real harm."

"Thanks," I said. "I always wondered what they'd put on my tombstone."

"I thought we understood each other, that you knew the lines not to cross. When I heard what had gone down at Transvirtual, and that you were involved, that's what really got to me. It was personal. A feeling of betrayal."

"You don't know the half of it," I said. "Believe me."

Travis stood up. "The coffee's on you," he said. "I'll check my mailbox at seven tomorrow morning. If what I find there is interesting, you can have forty-eight hours—though you call me if you see those guys again."

He looked up at the sign above the restaurant, peered into the deserted interior. The chef was leaning on the counter, watching a porno film on a television propped at the end. The avidity of his interest made the prospect of eating food cooked by his fair hands somewhat unappealing. One of the Happy Spatula's two customers was shooting up at a table in the corner: The other looked like he might already be dead.

"I used to come here," Travis said. "Years ago."

"Me, too," I said. "Things change."

He turned away. "They surely do."

I WAITED at the table. Five minutes later Helena appeared. She looked a little subdued. I tried to apologize for the comment I'd made about being a team, but she shrugged it off in that female way that's supposed to say it doesn't matter, but actually means that a lot more than a straightforward apology is required.

"So what now?" she said when I'd told her how it had gone. "How do you think you're going to find the guys in the suits? Seems like they were after the woman who killed this Hammond character. They've got her. They're out of your life."

"I don't think so," I said. I tried to remember if I'd ever told Helena about a certain memory of mine, a memory that stopped dead at a point I couldn't breach. "Everything hangs on Hammond. The closer we get to him, the more chance we have of finding a way to get to those guys."

Helena pulled her coat around her shoulders. "So?"

Rather than check out what the piece of paper had revealed about Nicholas Schumann, I pulled another of the sheets out and turned the organizer back on. I told it to save the results of the last job and queue an email of it to Lieutenant Travis, for delivery the next morning. Meanwhile I scanned in the second paper, and asked the organizer to see what it could find.

As I waited, I looked up to see Helena smiling at me. "What?"

"You," she said. "Always with your head halfway up some machine or other."

"They like me," I said. "Most of them, anyhow."

"Your answering machine seemed a little ambivalent."

"Only because I broke up an inter-species romance. It was hitting on my coffeemaker."

"You always were a prude."

A name appeared on the organizer's screen: *Jack Jamison.*

Helena peered at it. "What's he doing there?"

"No idea: I'm shit with names. Who is he?"

"Oh, you know—that actor. Fifty-something: always plays the senator you can trust. Gay, but in denial."

I remembered: stalwart of *National Question-Asker Magazine*, much-loved bête noire of homosexual rights groups, everyone's favorite character actor and nowadays getting a few bigger parts. Meanwhile the machine continued to spill text up onto the screen, translating the block of letters that took up the rest of the page.

Helena leaned in close, and we read them together. We finished at the same time, and looked at each other.

It got very quiet.

I took out my phone and called Melk. He was working at a party, and said he'd call me back in two minutes.

"That can't be true," Helena said. "No way."

"It makes sense," I said. I wanted to lean away from her, but I couldn't. I could smell her, and it was like catching a tendril of someone else's cigarette smoke during the two weeks when I once quit. You don't want a cigarette, and you're not having one, no way—but you're very glad they still exist. Not very romantic, but there you go. I don't do massage and I don't want to go out with you either.

Melk called me back. The address was up in the Hollywood Hills, about forty minutes away. He knew it by heart: presumably a previous client. He hung up immediately—in a hurry to go back to wrangling farts before someone got embarrassed.

I stowed my stuff and sat poised for a moment, not really sure what to do first. Then suddenly I understood that Helena's coolness probably had nothing to do with me. "Shit, Helena," I said. "I'm sorry."

"About what?"

"Bringing you here. I just . . . I didn't think."

She shrugged. "We used to come here a lot, even after that. It's no big deal."

"We came here because you had to. And to prove something. That was then. I just didn't think about how you might feel about it now."

She looked up at the sign, much as Travis had done. Breathed out heavily. "You're right," she said. "On the whole, I'd prefer to be somewhere else."

We headed over the crossroads and to the nest of dark streets behind it, looking for a car to boost. A little way down was a scabby white Dirutzu in need of a wash. Helena sniggered as I tried the handle. It was open.

"What?" I said. "You think I've forgotten how to do this?"

She shook her head, pointed to the other side of the alley. "I met the owner earlier," she said.

I turned and looked down at a guy who was currently sleeping the sleep of the just, or of the unconscious, in the gutter. Cheap suit, bad tie, strange mottled bruising on his forehead.

I laughed, reached in his pockets for the car keys. Two minutes later, we were gone.

CHAPTER THIRTEEN

"How do you want to do this?"

"There's only one way," I said. "Or he isn't going to talk to us."

"What happens if he isn't alone?"

"We take that as it comes. Try not to kill anybody, dear."

Helena nodded, took a step back. I pushed the doorbell. A buzzer of alarming complexity went off inside the house: I have a horrible suspicion it was playing the theme from a movie, just to remind you whom you were coming to see.

A padding sound approached, and then a muffled voice called out: "Who is it?"

"Charisma delivery," I said.

A chain rattled, and the door opened a few inches to reveal Jack Jamison standing in a purple bathrobe. Jeez, I thought, this guy really works at it. I kicked the door, stuck my gun in his face, and shoved him back into the hallway. Helena flooded in behind me, ran quickly past us to check out the rest of the house.

Jamison backed away from me, eyes wide, hands held up. "Please. Whatever you want. I've got money. I've got things. Just don't hurt me. I've got a six A.M. call."

It was a long hallway. I kept him walking backward until we came to a door. "Open it," I said.

He did, revealing a split-level living room the size of Nebraska. I shoved him hard, sending him tumbling back into the room. I don't actually like doing this kind of thing, but you've got to keep them frightened. Once they start getting their courage back, they remember they're in the right, and then you're fucked.

I got Jamison into a chair and lined the gun up with the middle of his face. Helena entered the room, shut the door. "All clear," she reported.

"Tell us about Ray Hammond," I told Jamison.

"Who?" He stared at me with the cornflower-blue eyes I'd seen projected several feet across movie screens, and pulled his robe tighter across his gym-flat stomach. He was getting it together far too quickly. "I don't know who you're talking about."

I flicked the safety off my gun. Jamison's eyelids flickered; he'd been in enough cop movies to know what I was doing. I placed one boot heavily in the center of his chest and pressed the barrel against his forehead.

"You're going to make a mess," Helena observed.

"I don't give a shit," I said. "Listen to me, Jamison. I have the names of two witnesses who've seen you on clandestine dates with women. I also know you're a regular client of the super-secret Sleep Easy escort agency, and that you exclusively consort with professional females. The guy you were spotted with in Aspen three months ago was a heterosexual actor hired by your manager, and I have it on good authority that not only do you go on secret deer-hunting trips upstate with old college buddies, but that you have been heard on more than one occasion to gleefully shout 'Yo—we really killed that motherfucker dead.' You are not gay, Jamison, and if you don't start talking to me very fucking quickly, the whole world is going to know it."

Jamison stared back at me, neck spasming. For a long moment it was very quiet, and then something changed in his face—almost as if he were falling out of a complicated character role.

"And if I tell you?"

"We're out of here and you never see us again."

"Would you mind taking your foot off my chest?"

"It would be my pleasure," I said. "It's actually kind of uncomfortable." I stepped back, still keeping the gun trained on him.

"You won't need that," Jamison said. "And to be honest, your lady friend looks rather more intimidating than you."

"Don't you start," I said. "Just tell us about Ray Hammond."

"I don't know how much you know about my career," he said, and I tried hard not to roll my eyes. "But there was a dry patch, about ten years ago. I was fortunate to play a large number of excellent roles in my youth, with many of the great directors, but then it all went wrong for a little while. I don't really know what happened: But over the period of a couple of years it all started leaking away. From star to supporting, then the slide down to television. In the end even people's answering machines wouldn't take my calls. It was an extremely difficult time, and without the support of certain very dear friends I don't know how I could have gotten through it."

I sat on the sofa next to Helena. I sensed this might take a while. "Yeah—and then?"

"I was having dinner with the son of one of my old friends. He was thinking of changing careers, becoming an actor, and quite frankly his father had asked me to talk him out of it. I felt I was in a unique position to give him the truth about the profession, and so I'd agreed."

"And somebody saw you."

"Indeed. One of the other patrons in the restaurant recognized me and took a photograph of the two of us—which he subsequently sold to *Global Interrogator* magazine. They ran a little piece, intended—I assume—as a smear."

"But it didn't work out that way."

"I denied the implication, of course—simply because it wasn't true. Many of my best and most talented friends are gay. It makes no difference to me. But in retrospect I realize this served only to fan the flames. In no time the *National Question-Asker* and *Pan-Universal 'Hey, What's Happening?'* magazines had joined the fray, doing the time-honored dance of claiming my 'gayness' was interesting in some way, while steering clear of explaining exactly why. Opposing factions of gay rights activists started getting involved, some wishing to 'out' me, some fighting for my right to stay 'in.' It all turned into a bit of an issue, in the tabloid press at least."

"With no one particularly interested in the truth."

"Quite, and by that stage, neither was I. All publicity is worth having, as I'm sure you're aware. It reminded the business I was still alive. Within a few weeks I was being offered cameos on television shows. A year later I was back as a supporting actor, and agents were having fistfights over who got to represent me. At the moment I am in the second week of filming my first starring role in ten years. I play the President." He winked. "No more mere senators for me."

"Congrats. And then?"

"Would you or your companion like a drink? A beer perhaps?"

"I thought you'd never ask," Helena said.

There was a fridge hidden in the table in the center of the room. When Jamison had served us each with one, I prodded him, but gently: I was beginning to like the old coot.

"Ray Hammond," I said.

Jamison frowned. "Yes. Well, it was all going swimmingly. All I had to do was deny everything, while occasionally apparently giving people reason to disbelieve me, and the attention kept flooding in. But then a man started bothering me. His approach was rather more subtle than yours, I must say. Letters at first, and then phone calls. Warnings that something was coming. Then he came to my house and presented certain facts in much the same way as you just did. He gave me a straightforward choice: Pay him, or lose everything."

"How?"

"People are obsessed with secrets—*other people's* secrets. What other people wish to keep hidden or invisible, that's what they most want to know. Though their interest is prurient, the readers of the checkout-counter magazines are on my side. We have a contract of vulnerability, and their knowledge of my 'secret' creates a bond. They pry open my life, and we share the pearls between us."

"So it was blackmail."

"Yes. Quite a steep sum, every month. As I started to get more successful again, the amount increased. It was becoming unbearable, and the man himself was becoming more and more odd."

"In what way?"

"From the outside he appeared much the same. Controlled, powerful. But his eyes were turning inside. Something was changing inside his head, I believe, which made it more difficult for him to do what he was doing. As an actor, you learn to look for such things. He was becoming less confident, losing his understanding of his role."

"But he kept on collecting your money."

"Until last week." Jamison looked up at me. "I didn't kill him, you know, if that's what this is all about."

"We know you didn't." I finished my beer, stood up. "How did Hammond get on to you in the first place?"

Jamison looked away. "I'm afraid I really don't know. Luck, I suppose. Sleep Easy's database is supposed to be impregnable. But perhaps one of their staff was persuaded to talk. I can't have a woman living here, you understand—it would rather give the game away. So I out-source my . . . 'exercise.' "

"Kind of a high price to pay, isn't it?"

Jamison smiled. "Aren't they all? And as you know, I manage to get around it, and not just with professional ladies. And just how *do* you know all this, by the way?"

I pulled out his piece of paper from my pocket, handed it to him. "There may be other records."

He shrugged, a man at peace with probability, and pushed the paper into his pocket. "Thank you, anyway."

He saw us to the door, chattering happily about the movie he was in. I walked behind him and Helena, trying to work out what difference this all made. I couldn't see it yet, but I knew it would come.

As we stood outside, I watched Jamison's eyes run over the road, a twisting lane high up in the hills overlooking the Valley. Not a stupidly big house, but a nice one, with one of the greatest views in the world.

"If people knew that I really am what I say I am," he said, "you know they'd never forgive me."

"Don't worry," I said. "Your lack of a secret is safe with us."

I DUMPED THE DIRUTZU outside Applebaum's, where we picked up my car. Debated whether to head back to Deck's, but in the end decided to go to my apartment. There were two messages on the machine, both from Stratten's office. He'd obviously not given me credit for having figured out what he'd done. Helena listened to me shouting for a while, then asked to borrow the phone. To call her boyfriend, I assume. I went and had a shower with the water on as loud as it would go.

When I came back she was stretched out on the sofa, asleep. She had always been like that—ball of action one moment, out cold the next. I watched her for a long time, as I often had. It used to make me feel more equal, the fact that I could watch over her sometimes. Now it just made me feel tired, but I wasn't ready for sleep. Instead, I scanned in the remaining two records. Two more names, one male, the other female, both rather well-known residents of LA. It doesn't matter who they are. Take it from me, you've heard of them. I read through their histories, and Schumann's, too. Afterward I just felt more exhausted.

Indiscretions, illegalities, perversions. Some buried deep in the past, the rotten kernel at the heart of success; others current and ongoing, a parallel life run in darkness. All of it easily bad enough to run a successful blackmail scam, and who knew how many other sheets lay hidden in Hammond's shelves.

I thought about the blackmailees, integrating my new knowledge of them into the picture I already held. I couldn't help it: Once you know, it changes things, taints the glass through which you see the world. I guess some people might get a feeling of power knowing what movies play inside other people's heads, what tracks their minds are running along behind their outward faces. I didn't. I've been there, done that. Everybody's got secrets: It's part of who they are, a constant cloud in the internal weather system. Everybody's done things, or had things done to them. The most important parts of life and character, the defining elements, are always hidden. The invisible is the underlying determinant. The things we don't want other people to know are the very things that make us truly real, truly ourselves. They don't even have to be bad things, merely personal. Just matters which should remain private: Because once they are known they create a feeling of sickly overfamiliarity, when in fact you don't really know the person at all. Everybody's password-protected, living in a hidden context that only they understand—until someone like Hammond comes along and cracks the code, leapfrogging over the walls and revealing you squatting frightened and alone within.

I burned the two pieces of paper and wiped all three translations off the organizer. I debated canceling the email to Travis, but Nicholas Schumann was already dead, and his secrets couldn't hurt him now. Maybe at some point I'd go back to Hammond's house and toss the remaining bookshelves, though I still believed his other apartment had been the center of his operation, and someone else already had the primary files. Presumably the guys in the suits, though how they tied into this, I couldn't imagine.

It was after two by then, but my mind wouldn't sleep. I was worried about Deck. Laura, too, I guess, but especially Deck. For once in his life he needed some help from me, but I didn't even know where to start.

I settled back into the chair and waited, but still sleep didn't come. Instead, all I got was context, going back down through the years. My first girlfriend, back at school: both of us sixteen and nervous and afraid to take the initiative. A few other friends, none of whom I'd seen in years.

I left home at seventeen myself, leaving them all behind, and worked my way across to California. It took a year and a half. I did it slowly, got cold or dusty in a lot of different places. At the time I guess it was a big adventure, but all I remember now from the trip are fragments of towns, the counters of bars I worked in, the strength of showers in motels I stayed—like a story recounted by someone who wasn't paying much attention when they heard it the first time. Wherever you go, and whatever you do, the first thing you're going to see in the morning, and the last thing at night, is the inside of your own head.

When I got to the ocean I'd stopped, and that's when I met Helena. I was working in a bar in Santa Monica. She came in with friends. She bought the first round, and after that my evening was set. I kept elbowing the other bartender out of the way so I could serve her. I don't listen to music much these days, and when I do it tends to be classical. My father used to listen to it a lot—still does, presumably—and it gets into your blood. The thing I like about it is its rightness. So much music sounds arbitrary, its marriage of influence and milieu too close to the surface to ignore: But when you listen to someone like Bach, it's like you're hearing the thoughts of a god. There are things in life that are supposed to be a certain way. You can predict how the next passage will sound because it's *right,* because that's the way it's meant to be—because you are looking at the facets of a perfect crystal as it revolves slowly in front of you. Anyway, when Helena walked in the bar I thought I'd heard the piece of music I'd been waiting for. Earl and I used to have an expression: "The lost tribe of beautiful sane people"—our point being that the two qualities seemed mutually exclusive. But Helena looked like she was one of Them, and the world settled itself around her to hold her up to me. "Yeah," I thought: "That's the way it's supposed to be. That's what all this tiring evolution crap has been about—to culminate in someone like her."

I was young and full of shit, and tried to strike up a conversation: She was equally young but full of nous, and politely kept me at arm's length. On the other hand, she didn't turn to her girlfriends and say "Hey—this guy's a creep. Let's go somewhere else," and maybe I even got a little wave at the end of the evening as they left. Accounts differ: Helena says she did, I never saw it, and believe me—I was looking. When I was feeling especially maudlin in the last couple of years, I'd often tried to picture that wave. Wallowing deep in drunkenness, sitting around some motel pool at night, when everyone else was asleep, I'd think maybe if I could see that wave in my mind's eye, then our relationship would become something complete, something that had a beginning, middle, and end, which I could hermetically seal in time and walk away from.

I could never see it.

Our families brought us together, indirectly. I was missing mine, she was close to hers. Neither of us had really bought into the idea that the previous generation was there to be transcended. She came into the bar with her dad one evening. I watched them like a hawk, or some other especially sharp-eyed and observant creature, wondering what was going on. The next time she came in with friends I asked who the old guy was, and she told me. I told her about mine. It went from there.

We hung, we fell in love, we moved into a horrible apartment in Venice. Neither of us had any money, and I can honestly say that's the one time in my life when it really didn't matter. We were young and invincible, and we believed the money would come. In those days we didn't realize how scary money was, how it could capriciously grant and withhold its favors, how in the end it could hold you up against the wall in some dark alley and beat you to within an inch of your life. You walk around LA and you see them, the people who'd lost the fight: the fizzing and bewildered with their dry, mad hair, living out their angry lives in apartments with polystyrene tiles on the walls and the potential of blood in every room. We won, in the end, but it took a while and cost so much that I'll never know if it was worth it.

We got married on the spur of the moment: called my parents from the city hall. Our honeymoon was five days in Ensenada. We borrowed Deck's old Ford and clanked down the coast road in the dark, talked the people at Quitas Papagayo into letting us have a place dirt cheap because it was way out of season and they were empty. We ate fish tacos three meals a day for the rest of the week, spent the rest of our money on Pacificos and trinkets for each other. Helena bought me an ornamental box to keep my guitar picks in: I got her a turquoise bangle. We watched seabirds, walked dusty streets, and cooled our feet sitting on rocks down by the waterline. I scouted around for bits of wood and dried palms in the late afternoon, and at night we lay in front of the fire and listened to each other's breathing until it became the only sound that mattered.

It seems like such a long time ago now, part of someone else's life. Nothing is real until it's gone: Before that it's just shadows playing.

Life carried on. Gradually I got involved in things, illegal things. Working in a bar is a good place to start along that road, and we needed the money. I started helping people out, getting paid for it. I was big, not too stupid, trustworthy. There's always work for people like me, though usually not work with long-term prospects. Helena scrabbled in dull jobs, coming home more frustrated and bored every day. She was so much more single-minded than me, so tough and black-and-white, yet spending nine to five in a world of gray with people who seemed to speak another language.

I met more people, started climbing up the ladder, earning a little more money. We bought a tiny house, and we got a cat, whom we loved. That was the best time. We were just starting out, and we didn't know where we were going, but we knew we'd go there together. That sounds trite, but love is trite—and that's why we need it. Clichés are true. We need our archetypes, because without them life turns into a farm scene painted by an incompetent child, where you can't tell which animal is which and we're all just blobs that barely stand out from a background of indeterminate gray. Cooks should be jolly women with red faces who heft their cleavers in a slightly disquieting way, priests gray-haired men of Irish extraction who like a drink. When our food is cooked by young guys who think they're rock and roll stars, it turns to ashes in our mouths; and when our faith is brokered by middle-aged women in sensible shoes, it becomes nothing more than soul insurance. We combat life's randomness through the things you can say in one sentence, the things everyone understands. Love and death are lifelines, the ropes to hold on to in a choppy sea. Without them nothing makes sense.

One night Helena's parents were having dinner in the Happy Spatula, a once-a-month pasta treat. We often went with them, but that night we were at Deck's instead, bombed out of our minds. At ten-fifteen a car pulled up outside the Spatula, and two guys got out. They walked calmly into the café and shot five people dead. Helena's mother made it through to the next morning before dying, but her father was DOA. Helena had a hangover when she identified the bodies.

I had a gun. Helena took it, hunted down the two guys, and killed them. I came home from work to find her curled in a ball in our bathroom, sobbing and covered in blood. I burned her clothes, filed the serial number off the gun, and dismantled it. We drove over the city, throwing pieces out of the window. When we got home again, I locked all the doors and put her to bed and got in beside her.

She asked me if it made a difference, if I didn't love her anymore. I told her I was proud of her, and kissed her to sleep.

We spent two weeks bonded in fear, but the knock at the door never came.

A month later we went back to the Spatula. Helena wanted to prove she could go back to the café, and so we went. We ordered what we always had, and sat where we always sat. The service was much more attentive than usual, and at the end of the meal we were told the bill had been paid. As we sat drinking coffee, rather baffled, three men came to sit at the next table. They were very polite. They wanted to thank Helena for what she'd done: The three other fatalities in the restaurant had been made guys, hit by an up-and-coming gang. Helena's parents had merely been accidents. The three men knew it had been Helena who'd evened the score—someone saw her fleeing the scene. I watched Helena smile as the oldest of the men kissed her hand, and I knew everything was about to change.

They did us some favors. And they took some back, subtly holding the murders over Helena's head. They said they hoped the cops didn't find out it was she who did it, or—worse still—the other gang. It wasn't concern for our well-being. It wasn't even a threat. It was just Business. They manipulated her into killing someone else for them, and after that it was too late. It was all very courtly and friendly, but our lives weren't our own anymore. Like Laura Reynolds said, there are some situations you just can't walk away from. Dealing with the mob is one of them.

I killed for them, too, but only once. A couple of creeps who'd rape-murdered an associate's wife and child. I met up with them in a bar, on the pretense of wanting to make a big coke buy, led them to a back alley and shot both in the head. I lost it afterward, driving around with the gun in my hand and blood on my shirt, and nearly got caught.

Self-defense is one thing: Execution is another. I couldn't hack it. They didn't make me do it again. I lent the money they paid me to Deck on the condition he never gave it back. He went and deliberately lost it in a casino in Vegas, so it went straight back to them and I could pretend I never had it. Deck understands me very well.

Helena was different. Helena could pull it off, was good at it. She had a black-and-white job now, for better or worse. She got over the death of her parents, in time: stopped expecting it to be her mother whenever the phone rang, or thinking of things to tell her dad. But she got over it partly by becoming something her parents would never have recognized, by untethering herself from the past they'd structured, by sidestepping into a different life.

If someone asks you what your wife does, you can't exactly say "Oh, she whacks people. For money. And yours?" And if you can't tell other people, it becomes a secret, and you have to work out what you tell yourself. But in time I got used to it. She was my wife. I loved her.

I found it hard to believe the things she'd done as I watched the gentle rise and fall of her breathing as she slept there on my couch. When we're asleep we become children again, innocent and untouched. Secrets put lines on our faces, roadmaps to interior landscapes. At night the territories become uncharted once more. I tried to imagine her going out with somebody else. It wasn't hard. God knows I'd had the practice. Her telling me it had actually happened merely felt like a well-oiled lock sliding into place. She'd moved on, and that was that. Trophy girlfriend of a mob lieutenant, a fierce woman no one would really understand because they didn't know what she'd been like before. I understood, but that comprehension was of no interest to anyone but me. All that lay on the couch in front of me was a memento, like a plaster bust of a Disney character for sale outside some store in Ensenada. Subtly wrong, a copyright infringement of the way things had been.

Occasionally, usually late at night and when I'm thousands of miles away, I have a desire to go back to Cresota Beach. Half a mile out of town was an athletic field, where you were sent twice a week to burn off excess energy, to help prevent the teachers from being driven insane. There was a parking lot in front of the field, and down the end of the lot was a building where you changed for the game. Two-story, small, like some secret military bunker: two floors of hooks on which to hang your clothes, and benches to collapse onto at the end of the afternoon, drenched with sweat and glad it was all over and you could go home. It was a place where you laughed and shouted, somewhere to plan an evening of mayhem and swap stories of weekend adventures. In my last couple of years the school started using a different field, and the building was locked up and never used again. The last time I saw it, it still looked like a tomb.

I wondered then if some piece of clothing got left there by accident and lay there still, mummified in stale air and peeling paint, forgotten by the boy who abandoned it and who now has children of his own. A mute testament to a different life, the past musty but tangible.

I'd like to go stand by the building alone again some night, look up at its boarded windows. I wonder, if I listened hard enough, whether I'd be able to hear voices from inside; and I wonder, if I broke in, whether I'd find my first girl and Earl and my childhood friends, sitting on the benches, wearing the same clothes, and waiting for me.

Whether I could sit cross-legged with them in darkness, and stay there forever, and nothing would have changed.

EVENTUALLY I FELL ASLEEP, and dreamed again. The predominant impression at first was of marbled green, a striated verdigris. It took a while for me to understand that this was the color of the ceiling only a few feet above me, and that I was lying on my back. I had a thundering headache, and my brain and body felt desiccated and empty, as if both had been destroyed and then reconstituted, with not quite enough water added into the mix. My lower arms itched as if spiders were walking along them; I felt cold but not afraid. I couldn't tell how long I had been there: The question didn't seem to have much meaning.

I slowly turned my head, and saw Deck. He was lying on the floor some distance away. His face was pointing straight up, and it looked as though his eyes were closed. I tried to call to him, but what came out was not even a whisper, more a fading breath. I watched him for a while, but he didn't move. By angling my head a little farther, I could see that we were in a long, low room, big enough that the walls and corners were hidden in shadow. I wondered then where the light was coming from, because I couldn't see anything that might be causing it. Then I looked back at Deck and realized that he was giving off a faint glow, like a firefly but golden.

I wondered if I was doing the same, and tried to raise my

head to look at my body. I'd never appreciated how many different muscles were involved in such a simple movement. It took an awful lot of effort to lift my head only an inch off the floor, and I couldn't see anything from there. I let it fall again, which it did slowly, coming gratefully back to rest on what felt like a thin mattress. I lay still for a long time then, not so much exhausted as content to be motionless, floating in a state of benign confusion. Everything seemed to be okay.

After a while I got interested in the question of the glow again, and decided on a different tack. Leaving my head where it was, I tried to lift one of my hands instead. This was a little easier, and little by little I raised it from where it lay by my side. After a few minutes it was high enough that I could see a blurred suggestion of it at the periphery of my vision. Feeling like someone pulling off an extraordinary feat of coordination and strength, I kept it in that position and turned my head toward it.

There was indeed a golden glow coming off the hand I saw, but it wasn't my hand. It was slender, feminine, and there were stitches in the wrist below it.

It was Laura's.

When I woke to find myself sitting upright in the chair in my apartment, I had a cigarette in my hand. It was alight, but hadn't burned down to the filter. There was no cone of gray ash hanging off the end. It was smoked only halfway down, and had been tapped off neatly in the ashtray on the arm of the chair.

Helena was still out like a light on the sofa.

I hadn't been asleep. It hadn't been a dream.

It was a memory, or something like it, but it was happening now. And it was happening in a place where I, too, had been.

CHAPTER FOURTEEN

I spent the rest of the night standing at the window, staring unseeingly down on Griffith, trying to remember. It wouldn't come. It was going to take something else, something concrete, for me to be able to break through. Some different way of seeing.

The phone rang at five minutes past six. I grabbed it and said: "You read the message?"

"Jesus, yes." Travis sounded tired. "I just don't know whether to believe it. I met Schumann once. He seemed like a regular guy."

"They all do, Travis. You know it's true."

"So, who are they?"

"Who?"

"The names on the other pieces of paper."

"You don't need to know."

"Hap, I've been at the station three hours already. I've been through Schumann's bank records and had someone who understands these things check out the state of Schumann Holdings. It's solid. The guy had more money than you or I can even imagine, and his business was expanding like a brushfire."

"So what?"

"So Schumann committed suicide *after* Hammond was murdered, and the 'financial difficulties' line is just bullshit. Something else made him kill himself, and I don't believe it was sudden guilt. You see what I'm saying?"

I did. "You think someone else has taken up the reins. Schumann figured the blackmail ended when Hammond died. Then he gets a call and finds out it's only getting worse, and kills himself."

"I already have five guys pulling Hammond's study apart. I need to know who the other victims are. They might be able to give us something on the new bosses."

"I'm not sure they're new," I said. "I talked to one of the other victims last night. This person said that toward the end Hammond was getting real strung out, like he was being forced to do something against his will. I think there was always someone in the background."

"I disagree. It's the guys in the suits. They whacked Hammond, took over his racket. Either that, or they just decided they didn't need him anymore. You've met them: They're not exactly polite. If anyone refuses to pay them, I'm going to have a famous dead person on my hands, and that I can truly do without."

"They'll pay," I said, "and no way will they have anything useful on the bad guys. You don't leave a contact number when you're shaking someone down. Plus it would be very stupid to kill someone you're blackmailing—all that does is cut off the income stream for good."

"The names, Hap. Or I haul you down here so fast, they'll hear the sonic boom in Nevada."

I told him two—but not Jack Jamison's.

There was a pause while he scribbled them down. "Okay,"

Travis said. "I want to see you here, at the station, at exactly eleven P.M. tomorrow. You see the suits in the meantime, you call. You do not fuck around with my investigation in any other way, and you do not contact any of the victims. Email me the code, and then we're done."

Quietly: "And the other deal?"

"Helena walks—you've got my word on that. While we're on the subject: One of my officers got a fresh bruise on his head this morning, and he had to take the bus into work because someone ripped off his car."

"I told you to come alone, Travis."

"I did. Romer overheard the conversation and followed me on his own initiative."

"His car's outside Applebaum's. Tell him it really needs a washing."

"His memory of events is a little vague, but he seems to believe that he got knocked out right after he arrived in Venice. At around about the same time you were sitting talking to me. Kind of odd, huh?"

"Time," I said, "is a strange and confusing thing."

"Yeah, right. Just make sure you don't get confused. Tomorrow. Eleven P.M." He hung up.

I turned to see Helena sitting on the sofa, watching me. She wakes the same way she falls asleep, changing states like the flip of a switch. Her hair wasn't even mussed.

"What deal?" she asked.

"What are you talking about?"

"You asked Travis about some other deal."

"I told you," I said. "Getting some time to find Deck and Laura."

She shook her head. "Bullshit. That's the first deal. What's the other deal?"

"I got him to lose a couple of minor outstanding warrants against Deck," I said, avoiding her eyes. "You want some coffee?"

"No," she said, glaring at me suspiciously.

"Trust me, you do. And then you want a shower, and you'd better take it quickly."

"Why?"

"Because," I said, "I'm going to Florida, and I'd like you to come with me."

WE GOT INTO Jacksonville midafternroon and rented a car at the airport. I steered us straight through town and out the other side, then took us down A1A to Cresota. It looked the same as it always did. It's pretty much the land that time forgot down there: When a store changes hands, it makes the local paper. Forty years ago they figured out how to be a tourist town, what combination of characterful eateries, well-stocked grocery stores, and sleepy streets worked best at attracting and keeping tourist trade. Craft fairs in the summer months; restaurants with decks stretching out into the marshes; little leaflets with directions to the nearest outlet malls. A lot of people have a downer on Florida: In my view they can just fuck off. I had to move away to see it, but I suspect now that if God ever decides to retire, He could do a lot worse than a beach house somewhere down A1A. Watch the waves, eat some crab, maybe play a little tennis—though from what I can gather, you'd be advised to let Him win.

I pulled into the lot of Tradewinds, and chose from a wide range of parking spaces. The only car I could see was my parents'. Most of the people who use Tradewinds are old friends from Gainesville: alligator-hide old people and second-generation dentists. Nice folks, as it happens. They're either there en masse or not at all, and the motel is too small and old to attract much other trade.

"You can stay here if you want," I said. There were still a couple of hours before I could do what I wanted to do. It made sense to visit my folks first, show them I was still alive, maybe try to hint at the fact it might be the last visit for a while.

Helena looked out the window. She'd been to Cresota five or six times, and got along with my family well enough, but someone else's hometown is always alien territory. You wonder if there are any strange rites you don't know about, and about past good times you weren't invited to.

"What do they know about us?"

"Just that we aren't married anymore. I spared them the details." I had, but they'd probably come to their own conclusions. They knew how much I'd loved Helena. They must have figured out that it would have taken something pretty catastrophic to break us up.

"What are we doing here, Hap?"

"I'll tell you later," I said, opening my door. The alarm

dinged placidly in the heat, marking time. "Are you coming or not?"

We walked across the hot tarmac, climbed up the steps to the office. Helena hung back as I swung the door open, slipped to one side to hide out of sight. Doesn't matter how old you are, what you do, or what you've done. Mothers are mothers, and they can bite.

Ma was standing inside, behind the desk, humming and sorting through envelopes. If there's anything my mother likes to do more than sort other people's mail into neat piles, I don't know what it might be. The walls of the office held a few seascapes of varying talent, complete with prices. I shudder to think how many very bad artists eked out a career through paintings sold to Tradewinds guests. My mother knew just as well as I did how talent-free most of them were, but for her that wasn't the point.

She looked up and her face melted into that look of uncomplicated pleasure that you only ever see in one face, that of a person recognizing someone who started life as a part of her own body. She'd gotten grayer and a little thinner in the last six months, but I still felt what I always had. It's not you who's changing, Mother—the world gets younger but you stay the same.

"Hello, dear," she said. "What a wonderful surprise."

I leaned over the counter and kissed her cheek. "What's happening?"

"Oh, you know, getting wrinkly. It takes up most of our time. Come on back—your father's cleaning out the pool." She raised an eyebrow, spoke a little louder. "And tell Helena she's welcome, too."

I turned to the doorway as Helena shuffled into view, looking about twelve years old. "Hello, Mrs. Thompson," she said. A look passed between her and my mother. I don't know what it meant, but then, I don't know how Mother knew Helena was there. Women see the world differently, and they know different things. Anyone who thinks we all live in the same place needs to open their eyes.

My mother shut up the office and we walked around to where my father was happily skimming leaves out of the pool. We sat in deck chairs and sipped sour lemonade, laughing while I told my parents lies of omission.

It was the only way it could be. I didn't have the heart to tell them I was going to prison, probably for a long time. There would have been no way back from that announcement, and I felt it was better to just take what time I could. Better for me, and for them. I could write them when the time came, when it was too late for them to do anything except accept. There's no point in embracing disaster before it happens. If you do that, it merely destroys the present, too.

Sure, I could have avoided the rap for a while. I could just not go back to LA, keep moving around the country. Return to the life I'd abandoned, except this time I'd be back to scrabbling for a living, not dreaming for big bucks. I could work bars and stay in motels, growing old in empty rooms with the smell of spilled beer and toilets that had been sanitized for my protection and comfort. Gradually I'd change from transient young man to transient old, and after that there was nothing but a long, dusty slide into darkness. I couldn't face it. I didn't think I had it in me any longer, that I had the energy to pretend that I wasn't drowning, but waving. Since I'd seen Helena again, that just didn't feel like an option. The question I'd asked myself so many times had been answered: Yes, I'd had what I wanted—and then I'd lost it. I'd already turned the right corner once in my life, and then I'd lost my way. Now I felt how you do halfway through a debauched evening when you haven't been drinking fast enough. Run out of steam, suddenly weary and melancholy, with nothing but sleep being attractive or even attainable.

Nobody asked what Helena was doing there. She sat a little distance from me, nodding and listening to my father as he explained the top five things that could go wrong with air-conditioners, their symptoms and the best ways of fixing them. We sat there like a family, alone in the garden of an old motel that had always been home to me, surrounded by chirruping hoses and the sound of the sea just over the rise. It felt like a life I had always lived, and like some future incarnation of me would forever be seeking this place, as if this were where I should always be. Here, or nearly here. Nearly home.

The air started to cool, and the sky hazed with late-afternoon clouds. Then, just at the right time, my father invited Helena to go look at something with him—the fuse boxes, probably, his pride and joy—and my mother and I were alone. We didn't say anything, just watched the water in the pool flicker and glint. Storm clouds kept building up over the intercoastal waterway, making the light clear and strange.

"Ma," I said eventually, "when I was a kid, did anything strange ever happen to me?"

She clasped her hands on her lap. "What do you mean?"

"When I was about eight."

"Not that I recall," she said, but with a quickening of my heart I knew she was lying.

"It was a Sunday evening, you were working at the Oasis. You got back and Dad was asleep and we watched a movie."

"Sounds like a hundred Sunday evenings."

"I'm talking about one in particular."

"It's a long time ago, honey."

"So was Dad's twenty-first birthday, and don't tell me you don't remember that. Anything to do with us, you're an encyclopedia."

She laughed, tried to change the subject. I just looked at her.

"Ma, I don't do it often, but right now I'm breaking rank. This is very important. You know what I'm talking about, and I need you to tell me what you know."

She looked away, her face pinched. There was a long, long pause.

Then she asked: "What do you think happened?"

"I don't know," I said. "I can't remember."

Her eyes flicked up at me. "I wondered if this was going to come up someday. I thought probably not. But every now and then I remember it, and I wondered if you did, too."

"Not for a long time. It came back to me yesterday."

"Your father doesn't know anything about it," she said quickly. "I decided not to tell him. You know how he gets. He would have been worried."

Gently: "About what?"

A pause, then: "I got home late," she said. "There was a party that night, students from the U over in Gainesville, and they made a hell of a mess, like they ordered burgers just to have something to throw at each other. Jed asked me if I'd help clean up before I went off shift, and I did. Then I walked home."

She stopped, and I was distraught to see that she looked near tears. "Ma," I said, "it's okay. Whatever happened didn't do me too much harm. I'm doing all right, aren't I? Hey—look at this jacket. They don't just give these away."

"It's very nice," she said, smiling a little. "But do your clothes always have to be black?"

I frowned at her. "Ma . . ."

"You were in the parking lot," she said in a rush. "Behind those big old trash containers. I wouldn't have seen you, except I recalled they'd be coming for them Monday morning and I wondered whether Dad remembered to take out our own trash. I looked over and saw something, and realized it was a little foot poking out from behind. I ran over and looked and you were there."

"Doing what?"

"Sleeping, it looked like, except your eyes were open. You were lying there, curled into a ball, arms wrapped tight around your chest. Your knees were scratched like you'd fallen, and your shirt was buttoned up wrong. It was so quiet and I was so scared and I wanted to call out, but I just couldn't. I was too frightened. I touched your face and it was so hot but very pale, and I thought maybe you'd had a fit or something, and I didn't know what I was going to do. Then you started to move. You closed your eyes and opened them again, and your color looked better, but you still looked strange. I kept asking you what was wrong, but you wouldn't say anything, just kept moving your arms and legs real slow, like you were remembering how. Five minutes later you were sitting up and asking me why I'd been crying."

"And I had no idea why I was there?"

"I asked you all the way home, but you still looked faraway, and all you kept saying was that you were thirsty. I got you inside and your father was asleep and you went straight into the kitchen and drank one of those entire pitchers of Kool-Aid you used to like."

"I remember," I said. "Tropical fruit."

"I started to make some more, still half out of my mind worrying what was up with you, and I turned around and saw you were sitting in front of the television in the living room like nothing had happened. I went and sat with you, and we watched a movie together, and after a little while it was like you came back and you were my son again."

"I never said anything about what had happened?"

"I didn't ask, Hap. I was worried about what kind of thing it might be, whether you could have met some bad man or something and that what happened was so awful, you just didn't *want* to remember. You didn't seem upset, you were just the same, except that if I tried to give you tropical fruit, you wouldn't drink it. We switched to grape, and that was okay, and so I just let it be. I'm sorry, Hap."

"It's okay, Ma, it really is."

"Are you sure? Have you remembered what happened?" Her hands twisted together; I put one of mine on top of them.

"No. But at least I'm sure now that something did. And it's not what you were worried about. I've just got some loose ends to tie up, that's all."

"You're in trouble, aren't you?"

"Yes," I said gratefully. "What's that? Maternal intuition?"

"Maybe. So don't you make fun. I talked to your grand-mother a few days ago. She said she'd heard a rumor about something or other. Wouldn't say what, exactly, just hinted darkly. You know how she is."

"Still got an ear for gossip," I said.

"I don't think there's much else to do where she is." As far as I'm aware, my mother has never been on the Net. Don't think she's likely to start now: She thinks of it as some people used to think of heaven, or maybe of hell. "You should go visit her sometime."

"I will," I said, and meant it. As I always did. In the same way you mean to go visit someone when they're dying slowly in the hospital, and then you never quite have the time until they're gone and there's nothing to see except an empty bed.

"I won't ask you what trouble you're in, Hap. If you wanted us to know, you would have said. But I know it's there, just like I know you'd really like a cigarette about now but you won't smoke in front of me because you know I don't like it." I laughed, and we looked up and saw that my father was heading back toward the pool, Helena walking beside him.

Mother looked at me sternly: "She part of it, too?"

"Not really."

"So what's she doing here?"

"We ran into each other. She came along for the ride."

The sternness went up a notch. "You going together again?"

"No. She's with someone else."

"Shame," my mother said. "She was the one."

The sky was darkening around the edges and it was time for us to go. I helped my father with something on his computer, which made me feel better, made me think that I had some chance of paying backward, instead of just forward. The prospects for forward payment weren't looking great at the moment, unless you included working in a prison factory assembling products for multinational corporations.

I looked at the paintings on the motel walls again, and instead of irritation felt something like pride. If that's the way you see the world, I thought, all the pastels and white spray and wheeling seabirds, good for you. Long may you look through that window. I only wish all of them had the same view.

Out through the screen door and into the parking lot, the rental car lurking in magnificent isolation and saying "The real world awaits you, my friend, and it has a lot more stamina than you." I clapped Dad on the shoulder, and he kissed Helena on the cheek. Mother hugged me to her, and I faltered, then hugged her back. We're not a physical family. It's just not something that we usually do. But she held my head close to hers for a moment, and I let her, and before she disentangled and I went on to do what I had to do, she whispered something in my ear.

"I don't care what she's told you," she said. "She's not with anyone else."

Then we were apart, and when I looked back at her she was saying good-bye to Helena and I couldn't ask her what she meant.

SCHOOL WAS LONG finished by the time I parked the car in front of the yard; the last stragglers waiting for a ride were gone. I stood in front of the chain-link fence and looked across at the trees on the other side, wondering if there were still Black Knights to be discovered there, and whether anybody ever looked for them now. I never found one when I was a kid. They always eluded me, no matter how much time I spent sitting up in the branches pretending I was just a large and surprisingly nongreen clump of leaves. Earl let his go in the end. One afternoon we just decided to open the box. The bug lumbered around the container for a while, evidently not realizing how much bigger its world had become—then took awkwardly to the air and careered off out of sight.

"So what now?" Helena asked. She'd been silent on the short ride from Tradewinds, maybe mulling over my father's advice about how best to deal with flying ants.

"We walk around it."

"Hap, I like a stroll down memory lane as much as the next girl, but I wonder whether this is exactly the time for it."

"Yes," I said, "it's exactly the time. And memory lane's just what it is. So walk it with me."

"What on earth are you talking about?"

"I'm not sure." I had an idea, and it was growing in my mind. But it wasn't close enough yet for me to articulate it to myself, never mind anyone else. "Just trust me."

And so we walked. I didn't know if this was going to work, just that it was the only thing I could try. The light was about right by then, and it was the same time of year. It might have made sense to do it alone, replicate it exactly, but I figured I needed someone else there to make it real. Our own past always lives on, to some degree, within ourselves: We need the gaze of others to make it real. We went the long way around, as I had about twenty-five years earlier, and I told Helena what I could remember.

As we turned into lane the lights clicked on and I shivered, feeling abruptly younger, almost as if this were a walk back in time and at some point Helena would just disappear, leaving just a small boy in shorts. I was aware of how much taller I was now, of the extra pounds I carried, the scar tissue. Everything I'd done felt like accretions around an earlier self, moss gathered by a stone whose progress was now slowing to a halt. I stopped as we turned into the long back side, staring at the streetlight in the distance.

Helena waited, knowing there was nothing she could say or do to help. I didn't get anything as we walked that stretch, even when we stopped to look in at the trees, closer now, only twenty yards from the corner.

But as we passed under the lamp I felt something, almost like a thickening in my head. The sensation slipped out of my fingers like a fish if I tried to concentrate on it. Blanking happens when you use a memory so many times that you wear it out, like rubbing a sheet of metal for so long and so often that it fades to nothing, and you can see right through it. Attempting to touch it again just makes things worse. You have to come at it from an angle, see it from the side, make the most of what is left. I tried but couldn't capture it, and glanced at Helena, shrugging.

Then it burst out of nowhere, like chrome gleaming at the torn edges of a car after a wreck:

I had turned and seen the man standing under the light. I started to run but then stopped, knowing I couldn't escape him. Odd, I should have thought that. I was a fast kid, and could dodge like a chicken. The man was suddenly closer, but the footsteps I could hear were not his, but mine, echoes of something that had already happened, as if things were being presented in the wrong order, and causality were breaking down.

Then he was there, a yard away, looking down at me. I saw his face for the first time: It was not unkind, but it was not a usual face. "Quickly," he said. "Come."

I saw six men approaching from the other side of the street, where a silver car was parked. All six dressed the same and all walked together, and they didn't look right. They didn't seem bad, it wasn't that, but I knew whom I'd rather go with.

The man grabbed me by the arm and I let him drag me down the sidewalk, still staring back at the other men and wondering why they didn't run, too. They could have caught us if they wanted to, but instead they seemed to be getting slower, though their movements never changed.

I had to turn around again to keep from falling over, and I saw something weird was happening. The street was sparkling. It was like someone had turned on a million tiny spots of light embedded in the nicks in the road; there were strange lights in the sky, too, oddly shaped, moving in random directions. There were now two people ahead of us on the sidewalk, just standing, as if waiting for the man and me to pass. They were motionless, but their bent shapes looked a little familiar. Then I realized who they were.

My grandparents on my father's side, the ones who were dead. As we got closer, they started to move, like film cranking into motion: Nan smiled, and Granddad reached out toward me. I saw the hair on the back of his hand, the distinctive pattern of liver spots, and looked up to see his eagle face, the few combed-back gray hairs.

Even at that age I knew instantly that these were not mere images. My grandparents were really there. I wasn't in the least afraid, though I would be if I saw the same thing now. I thought: "That's cool—I'll be able to tell Dad that Nan and Granddad are okay." And then we were past them, and everything went white.

The world switched off like a light, and I was somewhere else. It wasn't that I couldn't remember what happened—it was more that what had happened didn't exist. It was gone; it was different; it was somewhere else. The memory stopped there for good.

As it faded, I saw a smeared vision of verdigris and ice, as if it were something I was passing on the way back to the present day. I heard a voice, and realized it was Deck's. He was talking quietly, reassuringly. For a moment I was afraid, twitchy, and I craved a Kim. Most of all, I wanted someone to come and either kill me or set me free.

Then I was standing on the corner of the school yard again, a little distance from the streetlight. I blinked and shivered, realized I was back in the real world, back in my time.

And that we weren't alone.

Helena was standing two yards away, gun trained steadily on a man standing in the lamp glow. I recognized him now. He looked the same as he had when I was a child, and as he had in the diner and in Ray Hammond's study. He looked calm, unafraid, beyond every and any thing.

"It's okay, Helena," I said. "He's one of us."

CHAPTER FIFTEEN

───────────

"You tried to go back," the man said.

"No. I tried to remember."

"Same thing," he said.

"Where are my friends?"

"They're there. You remember them, don't you?"

"How do I get them back?"

The man shrugged. "You should go back to LA. I might be able to help, I might not. There are more of them than there are of me."

"But you're more powerful, right?"

"So they say. Doesn't always work out that way."

Keeping her gun firmly in place, Helena turned to me. "Any chance of my being introduced here, Hap? Your social skills always were kind of basic."

"Sorry," I said. "Helena, this man is an alien."

"Thank you," she said, and turned back to face him. "Okay, alien motherfucker, put your hands where I can see them."

The man raised an eyebrow, but slowly pulled his hands out of his pockets and raised them. "Does that make you feel safer?"

"Patronize me, and I'll blow your head off."

"Helena," I interposed gently, "I'm not sure this is the way forward."

She stamped her foot. "He just appeared out of nowhere, Hap. You know how I hate that kind of thing."

"He didn't. He came out of my memory."

"Memories exist only in people's minds, Hap. They're just little flashes of electricity sparking in a mess of Jell-O."

I shook my head. "Not the way it works." I looked at the man. "Is it?"

"Indeed not," he agreed.

"Then why can't I remember being there? Why can't anyone remember it when they get back?"

"It's impossible. It's like trying to write in black marker on black paper."

"Yeah, very good. Very gnomic," snarled Helena. "Hap, what do you want me to do?"

"Put the gun down," I said. "It wouldn't do any good anyway. He's not even really here."

"Hap, did your mother slip something weird in the lemonade?"

"You should listen to him," the man said. "He's right, and sooner or later he's going to work out what he's talking about."

"Don't you patronize him either," Helena snapped. "That's my job."

I took a step closer to her, so we were together, and she reluctantly lowered the gun. You'd have had to know her as well as I did to understand that she was very frightened.

"So how come I can hear what Deck's saying," I asked, "if I can't go there?"

"Special case," the man said. "Because of what you're

carrying in your head. Never happened before. It's one for the record books."

Didn't make any sense to me, but I pressed on anyway. "What's the big deal over Hammond?"

"They had plans for him. Laura Reynolds messed them up."

"What kind of plans?"

"You wouldn't believe me even if I told you."

"Try me. I've got a high credibility threshold."

"Just be thankful they failed. Hammond wasn't the right one."

"For what? You guys planning to invade?"

"Why would we do that?"

"Why would you abduct people? What's that achieve apart from scaring the shit out of them?"

He shrugged. "It's a game. One I don't play anymore."

"Bully for you. And by the way, that's bullshit: You abducted me."

"A long time ago. And did you have such a bad time?"

"*I can't remember.*"

The man spoke quickly and firmly: "And you never will, Mr. Thompson. That's the way it is, and it can't be changed. It's not my doing. So just leave it. You'll understand soon enough, but then you'll be dead and the knowledge won't be much use to you anymore."

"Is that some kind of threat?"

"Of course not. I don't want you to die. I have a personal interest in you: We met when you were young and had a chance to understand. I can't help you with that. The act of telling makes the truth a lie because of all the filters the tale has to pass through. You see through the veils by waiting for the wind to push them aside, not by describing them. That's what the others are trying to do, and I can't condone it. It will only make things worse."

Helena turned to me. "Oh, how lovely, a seminar. Are you taking notes?"

I ignored her. "Back at Hammond's you knew Travis's name. So you know what really happened to Hammond, and you also know I'm going down for it."

"My hands are tied," the man said. "I'm not exactly from around here. That's for you to sort out. And if you'll take my advice, you might want to start right about . . . now."

Suddenly I heard the sound of tires on tarmac. I glanced down the ground toward my rental car, and saw a red Lexus speeding toward it. The Lexus stopped; two men jumped out. Even from that distance I could tell they were earthlings, and that they were carrying guns. The men peered into our car, saw it was empty, and then looked up and made us.

When I turned back to Helena, she already had another gun out, and was standing with one in each hand. She was alone.

"Where'd he go?" I asked, dumbfounded. My head was still spinning from trying to absorb what the man had told me, and also from a small and pointless relief that at least someone who appeared to be in some kind of authority knew I hadn't been the one who'd murdered Ray Hammond.

"Just disappeared," she said. "What an asshole."

Together we watched the two men as they approached, pulling weapons out of shoulder holsters. They were standard-issue heavies, shoulders shaped by long-ago weight training, stomachs by too much recent beer.

"What do you think?" I asked Helena as I got out my own gun and slapped a new cartridge in. "This going to be settled with a polite conversation?"

The first bullet zipped past, flying right between us.

"I doubt it," she said, and started firing.

At first the men stood their ground, obviously thinking they were dealing with a couple of amateurs instead of just one. Most people miss with a good proportion of their shots, especially at twenty yards. Helena doesn't. Helena doesn't miss if you blind-fold her and lie about where you've put the thing she's aiming for.

This rapidly became clear, and the two heavies leapt in different directions like a wave hitting a jagged rock. One clambered over the fence into the school yard. The other slid behind a car.

Helena kept firing as we ducked behind a car of our own. "He's a lot of fucking help, this alien friend of yours," she muttered as we squatted and reloaded.

I peered around the end of the bumper: One of the heavies was trying to crawl out toward us from behind his own shield. "He gave me the code to Hammond's records," I told Helena, squeezing a shot off. The heavy disappeared again very quickly.

"Yeah, but why'd he do that? What's it to him?" There was a splintering *crump* as the rear windshield of the car blew out. Helena turned and fired two shots at the fence.

"I don't know," I said.

"And who are these guys?"

"I don't know that either," I said. "Why don't we go find out?"

She winked: "You take the guy behind the car." We waited out four more shots and then heard two dry clicks.

We leapt to our feet and peeled off around opposite sides of the car, spraying bullets. I kept firing as we ran forward: heard a scream from beyond the fence, and saw Helena dodge off to vault over it. For a moment I stopped firing, the gun trained on the air about six inches above the trunk of the second car. I was expecting him to wait a second, figure I was reloading, and then pop up. I was wrong. This guy had decided that he'd had enough. He was suddenly up and running, sprinting away back down the street. I ran after him, but he had too much of a start and was going to make it to the Lexus way before I did.

I aimed carefully, shot him in the thigh. The impact swung his leg around behind him, sending him into a complex and rather balletic turn that ended with him crashing into the fence.

He kept hold of his gun and tried to roll into a shooter's position, but I was already standing over him. "You could do that," I said. "On the other hand, I could blow your head off. I don't know how much you're getting paid, but it would have to be a lot."

"Screw you," he snarled, and struggled to point his gun up at me. I swung a kick at his wrist: It connected and the gun went skittering across the street. If I ever have a son, I'm going to tell him to practice this whole kicking thing. It really comes in handy.

"Let's wait and find out what happened to your buddy, shall we?" I said. "Might help structure your next couple of responses." I stood on his hand and waited for Helena, who was wandering over toward us.

"He's dead," she said apologetically. "Sorry."

"You see?" I said to the guy on the ground. I could tell that the pain from the wound in his thigh was beginning to pitch in hard. "You're lucky you got me. Could easily have gone the other way."

"Fuck you, motherfucker."

"Charming," said Helena.

"Who sent you?" I asked.

"Fuck you."

"He's really rude, isn't he?" Helena said.

Keeping my foot where it was, I reached down and searched his jacket pockets. Came up with a wallet. No driver's license, but an access card. For REMtemps security.

Suddenly I'd had just about enough of Stratten, of gun-toting aliens, and just about everything else.

"How did you find me?" I asked, and kicked him in the stomach. "How?"

Helena reached out a hand toward me. I shrugged it off, my vision melting with fury. I kicked the guy in his injured leg. Then, grabbing his jacket, I pulled him off the ground and shouted right in his face: *How the fuck did you find me?*

He spit at me; grinned. Keeping my hold on him, I punched him in the face with my other hand. "You're going to tell me," I said right up close. "And if it involves my parents, it's going to be the last thing you ever say."

"Didn't need them this time." The guy smiled. A trickle of blood ran out of his nose. "Lots of people want to turn you in. But next time ... Well, hey—we know where they live."

I let him fall back to the ground, pulled my gun out. "Hap, no," Helena said urgently. "Don't do this."

"I want you to take a message to Stratten," I told the guy, and dropped his security pass on his chest. "A real simple message. I am fucking *fed up* with being chased, shot at, and generally fucked around. Either Stratten gets out of my face, or I'm going to take him down."

Police sirens screamed in the distance, heading our way. I guess the residents of Cresota Beach don't hear that many gun battles. In LA they just turn up the TV.

"Only thing I'm going to tell the boss is that I'm going to kill you so dead, it'll be like you never lived," the man said, his voice low and very serious. "And that I'll throw in your family for free."

"Bad answer," I said, and shot him in the head.

I CALLED MY FATHER as soon as we hit A1A. Dad took the news stoically—either Mom had already filled him in, or he'd worked it out by himself and kept his own counsel as usual. Dads work in mysterious ways. You think they don't have a clue what's going on, and then one day you trip and they're already there in position to catch you.

After the call I just floored the pedal and headed to Jacksonville, Helena quiet beside me in the passenger seat.

I turned into Highwater on two wheels, braked the car outside the REMtemps building. I had the door open and was halfway out before Helena grabbed my arm and yanked me back. She put her face close to mine and spoke very clearly. "You can't do this. You cannot go in there and kill Stratten."

"I'm not going to kill him."

"You've sent your message. Now just leave it alone."

"I'm not going to fucking kill him. I don't kill people. That's *your* job, remember?"

Her eyes shone furiously: "Fuck you. So what happened back there by the school?"

"You know what happened there, and you of all people should understand it. You heard what he said, and I believed him—plus if we'd left him alive for the police to find, there'd be a helicopter firing on us as we speak. And frankly, I can't bring myself to give a shit about someone whose job is killing people."

"Including me?"

"Your choice, not my problem. Now I'm going into this building, and you can either help me or you can sit out here or you can fuck off back to your boyfriend in LA and get on with your life. It doesn't make any difference to me. Stratten knows you're not working the contract, or he wouldn't be watching the airports and he wouldn't have sent those guys after me. You're out of this. You don't have to hang around any longer and baby-sit me. You can let ol' Hap makes his mistakes all by himself."

Helena let go of me, pushed me away. I got out of the car, took one step, turned back.

"Look, Helena, I'm sorry. But either I'm going to get whacked, or I'm going to prison. I really don't have that much to lose, except two people I care about. Laura dug her own grave, but Deck's in trouble only because of me. I want them back before something happens to me, because I'm the only person who gives a shit about them. I am tired of being pushed around, and Stratten is first in line to receive that news flash."

She sat still and silent for a moment, breathing deeply. Then she looked up at me, and I saw something in her eyes I hadn't even realized had been missing.

"You've changed," she said.

"Not as much as you."

"We'll see," she said, and looked at me a little longer. Then she nodded briskly. "Okay. Let's go ruin this guy's day."

Sabrina was sitting behind the desk in REMtemps's reception area, which cheered me up immensely. Even better was the way her mouth dropped open. She knew the score, had helped tip Travis off that I'd called Stratten from Applebaum's. It was instantly evident to her that Hap Thompson hadn't dropped by to borrow some paper clips. Her eyes flickered with panic for an instant, then went cool.

"It would be a huge mistake to call security," I advised her. "Really. For a start, most of them are dead."

Frosty: "What do you want?"

"I want to talk to Stratten. And I'm just not going to take no for an answer."

"You can't," she replied.

"Well, there you go." I grinned. "Thought I'd made myself pretty clear, and there you go just saying no to me. What do you think, Helena? She being obtuse, or just stupid?"

Helena raised an eyebrow, gave Sabrina a good looking over. "Obtuse, I'd say. And what on earth has she done with her hair?"

I leaned on the desk, blocking Sabrina's view of Helena. "Let's try this again. Get Stratten out here, or I start dismantling the walls and ceiling, starting with the portion above your head."

"You can't talk to Mr. Stratten," she said, her voice a little shaky. "He's not here."

"You realize I'm just going to run around the place, checking every room and causing trouble? Got any major clients in here for consultations? You want me to check if they know where he is?"

"Look, Mr. Thompson, he really isn't here." She was pale now.

"So where is he?"

The skin under her left eye twitched. "I can't tell you."

"Yes, you can. Use words. I'll understand them."

"I really can't. He'd . . ." She swallowed, and I realized it probably wasn't me she was most frightened of. "He'd hurt me."

"Just tell me, Sabrina, or you're going to get damaged anyway."

She stared me down with a vestige of defiance. "You may be an asshole, but you'd never hurt a woman."

"No," I admitted, "you're probably right." I stood aside to reveal Helena, who was pointing a gun right at her heart. "But believe me, she would."

You almost certainly haven't stared down the barrel of a gun held by Helena, but it really focuses your mind. There's something about the sight that makes it clear that the time has come to be extremely accommodating.

"Mr. Stratten's in Los Angeles," Sabrina said quickly. "I don't know where. He booked the trip himself."

I stared at her. "In LA?"

She nodded feverishly, eager to get it over with. "He went there the end of last week. I've been patching his calls through to make it seem like he was still here."

"What the hell's he doing in LA?"

"I don't know."

Helena flicked the safety off. "Try harder, toots—or the hairstyle gets it."

"I don't know! He just said it was business."

At that moment I worked it out, finally understood how Stratten tied in. I dropped my head, wishing I were smarter, that I'd put it together several days ago. It must be great being clever. It must just make everything so much easier.

"That means something to you?" Helena asked me.

"Yeah. It does. Okay, Sabrina, we're leaving now, so you can go back to being rude to people on the phone. But I want you to do me a favor, okay?"

Sabrina didn't look like Sabrina anymore. The hardness in her face was gone, and her lips didn't look quite so airtight. I'm sure the change was only temporary, but it was an improvement. I just wished she hadn't had to be scared to allow herself to be more human, but I guess a lot of us are like that.

"What?"

"When Stratten calls in, tell him I know what his business is, and it's about to end."

THE STEWARDESS had our number pretty quickly. She gave both of us a fistful of peanut packs and left us to it. We had a pair of seats over the wing, but could have grabbed a row each if we'd wanted to. Evidently not many people make the hop from Jacksonville to LA at that time in the evening.

"So. You going to explain it to me, brains?" Helena asked, chomping on the free peanuts. We'd been in the air an hour by then, surrounded by little oval windows of darkness. I'd spent the time putting it together in my head, trying to work out how it changed the situation. We were due in LAX at nine local time; one of my two days was nearly over, with very little to show for it.

"Stratten was in business with Ray Hammond," I said. "Like he's maybe in business with people in every major city in the country. He's got the memory business sewed up. Lots of well-known people use REMtemps, and some of them must use the memory services, too. Though the caretakers don't know who the clients are, Stratten does. And he keeps track of every recollection that passes through one of his machines—including ones that the clients think REMtemps don't know about. He keeps an eye out for blackmail openings. Then he sets a local goon on the people who dumped them—in our case, Hammond."

Helena nodded. "So Hammond tails the client, gets more evidence of stuff that he or she doesn't want the public to know about, and then makes the pitch: Pay us, or your career goes down the toilet."

"I should have worked it out sooner. There was a weird entry in Schumann's file, something that happened a long time ago. I don't think Hammond heard it from any witness. I think Stratten gave the information to him."

"But wouldn't REMtemps's clients suspect that's where the leak was?"

"Not if Stratten was clever enough, and made sure that the shakedown was explicitly tied to stuff Hammond had found out *subsequent* to getting a key in through the memory. Maybe some of them did work it out: Jamison looked kind of shifty when I asked if he had any idea what set Hammond onto him. But by then it's too late, and Stratten's not going to care anyway. He's got his clients over a barrel. Memory-dumping's illegal, and he can make more money out of blackmailing them than he can for charging for the service."

"Then Laura kills Hammond and it all goes Picasso."

"Stratten's got no one else on the scene, so he hightails it over there, cleans out Hammond's apartment, and lets the victims know it's business as usual. Most of them just buckle under. But Schumann decides he can't take it anymore and kills himself. Meanwhile, Stratten wants Hammond's death put to rest as quickly as possible, because the longer Travis pokes around, the greater the chance of the lieutenant discovering what Hammond was involved in. When Quat lets Stratten know what I've got in my head, Stratten's got the perfect opportunity. I go down for the murder, and the case is closed."

"You've got to tell Travis about this."

"I will," I said, peering out the window. We were passing over a city: I could see a few lights below, advertisements for civilization. "I'll call him in a minute, and Jamison, too—let him know he might want to watch out. But I don't think Travis can help. Stratten is too powerful to take down unless you can pin something very specific on him—and he's way too clever to have laid himself open to that. Probably it's Quat or some other bastard who's doing the actual leaning on clients now, and Stratten's got himself alibied by the Pope."

"How do the guys in the suits tie in?"

"I still have no idea. You heard the weirdo: *They* had plans for Hammond. God knows what that means."

Helena yawned. "Was that guy really an alien?"

"Yes," I said. "They all are." I hesitated, still trying to come to terms with what I'd learned today. "The obelisk finally arrived. I've spent my life laughing at people who claim they'd been abducted. Turns out I'm one of them."

"Hap Thompson, Space Boy," Helena murmured sleepily. "I don't know why, but I don't find that too hard to believe. Even the whole alien thing. It's just not as hard to swallow as I'd have thought."

"Maybe it's time," I said. "And somehow we just know that."

"But how come they look like us? Why don't they have those big black eyes and little gray bodies? Or fingers that light up in the dark?"

I shook my head. "Nobody can remember anything about what happens when they're taken. There's just no memory there. Even I can't find it, and I've got a hell of a lot more practice than most. So when people get back, they try to fill the memory in as best they can. They're scared, so they go for the big fears. They substitute hazy memories of operations they had as a kid—or projections of ones they're afraid might have to happen. They fill in the pictures from magazines, movies, books. They make something up to fill the gap, pin their fears on something concrete, because that's better than not knowing what to be afraid of."

Helena shifted in her seat, then rested her head on my shoulder. "So, what now?"

"The alien said to go back to LA. So we go there."

"How do we know what he says is true?"

"Helena," I said. "He's all we've got." It came out a bit husky. The weight of her head, the feeling of her neck close to mine, was making me feel a little strange. I could smell her hair, could understand the amount of space she was taking up. Somehow, the girls I'd been with since Helena, they'd always seemed a fraction too big or too small. One of her hairs was tickling my nose, which usually drives me insane. I didn't move, though, in much the same way as you don't move the very first time you're sitting holding someone and your arm gets pins and needles so badly, it feels like it's on fire. Some things are worth the price: not forever, maybe, but at the beginning.

The plane hit a small patch of turbulence, provoking a few squawks from farther back in the cabin. The main lights had been turned off by then, leaving only the little glows above the windows. Sooner or later a stewardess would come along and tell people to pull the shutters down, and I'd refuse, as usual. I love being up in the sky, carried along in my taut metal tube and protected by its physics from that other physics, the physics that says all things must fall. I like looking out of the window at the blackness, studded below by the occasional sparks of light that proclaim "Yes, there's somebody here. There're things living on this ball of rock, and this is where we are. We have motels and cable TV and reasonably priced cheeseburgers. Come and visit us."

"What's this?" Helena mumbled. Her hand was resting against my chest, the fingers tracing a ragged patch in my skin through my shirt. A small circle just below the clavicle.

"A scar," I said.

"I don't remember it," she said, and then went very quiet. She turned her head to look up at me.

"Yes," I said. "It's from then."

"Hap, I'm so sorry."

It was right that she was sorry, but I had never seen a look of such compact misery, and I didn't want to see it now. "It's okay," I said. We held each other's eyes for a long moment, she trying to see if I meant it, I just looking at what was in her face. I'd always believed that loving someone was a road you could travel down only once, that after you'd taken a wrong turn you just had to turn your back and keep on walking.

Now I no longer knew.

The moment stretched, and stretched. Helena blinked very slowly. There was something strange about the movement, but I couldn't work out what. My thoughts seemed muddy and confused, as if they were groping for the usual phenomena and not finding them, helpless and stalled in the face of some data my brain couldn't use.

Out of the corner of my eye I saw the flight attendant standing a few rows farther up the aisle. She was leaning over, talking to someone, but her lips were moving slowly, and I couldn't hear what she was saying.

Then the plane bucked again, but this time no one yelped. Out the window I saw that the lights I'd noticed earlier were a lot closer now. Too close. Either the plane was crashing, which seemed unlikely, or something was coming up to greet us.

I tried to call out—to whom or what, I'm not sure. The sound made it out of my throat, but died before it had traveled an inch. The light was changing in the cabin, reminding me of the way it had been in Hammond's study: But this sure as hell wasn't caused by something you could buy in Radio Shack.

I heard the faintest whisper of a scream. Helena. Nobody else in the cabin seemed to have noticed what was going on. She had, and she was afraid.

I looped my arms around her and held on, pushing against the weight of the air, my lips against her ear and telling her everything would be all right. My vision started to come apart, as if someone had turned the brightness all the way up and everything but shadows was leeched away.

Then I couldn't even see the shadows anymore, and everything was gone.

PART THREE

BECOMING VISIBLE

CHAPTER SIXTEEN

I got most of it in a stunned instant. The rest roared in to support it seconds later, like film of someone erasing a picture, but run backward. It came like hands hammering on an opaque glass door, as soon as the world turned to white:

LAURA WAS FIFTEEN when Ray Hammond entered her life. She lived with her parents in a big house that backed onto a wood, just above a steep but shallow valley that led down to a stream. The nearest neighbors were a hundred yards down the canyon—the Simpsons, whom her dad liked but her mom did not. Laura didn't have any strong feelings either way about the senior Simpsons, but she didn't much like their son, who was ugly and whose eyes made it clear whenever they met that he would much prefer it if she were naked. Her father worked down in the city and made a lot of money. He was comfortably built and laughed a lot. Monica Reynolds was very thin and went to the gym every day, one of those scary women who stay on the step machine for an hour, climbing with murderous concentration, before standing in front of a mirror and lifting tiny weights about a billion times. Laura went with her to the gym once, and thought her mom looked more like a machine than the equipment she was using. When she wasn't losing nonexistent weight, Monica was painting the walls. Even though her bedroom had been done only the previous year, her mother was planning on doing it again. Laura liked it the way it was: The walls were a swirl of sea colors, blues and greens and purples. When she told her father she didn't want it changed, Daddy just shrugged and then told her a joke.

Every day when Laura got home from school she would dump her bag and books in the kitchen and make herself a sandwich. The sandwiches were generally pretty boring and majored on salad and low-fat cheese: Her mother didn't approve of meat, chocolate, or anything else that was fun to eat. Laura was quietly impressed at the way her father managed to keep his weight up, and could assume only that he went absolutely ballistic at lunchtimes.

She would grab her sandwich and go out back, slipping through the fence and walking into the wood. It was only a patch of forest, nothing magical, and she rarely pretended it was. You didn't need to. It was just nicer to be there than in the house, surrounded by the smell of paint and swatches of fabric and color charts where all the colors looked the same. She took a path down to the stream and she would sit and eat her sandwich listening to the water and watching the little water bugs do their stuff. It was a mystery to her why they bothered to do anything. They were hardly alive long enough to make it worthwhile, and their brains were too small for them to remember anything that they'd done. Kind of like some of the characters in the afternoon soaps, except the bugs didn't have plastic surgery. After an hour or so her mother would call her in to bathe. Her mother's voice carried. There was never any problem hearing it, even on the days when it was a little less clear than usual.

Laura was pretty, and did well in school. She had her mother's cheekbones mitigated by her father's grin, and she could do both English and math. She had plenty of friends, and her parents got on okay most of the time. Everything was fine, just another one of those lives that everybody has until a certain point, until the hold goes on the picture, and everything turns to noise.

One day the Reynolds house got burgled, and Ray Hammond was the policeman who came to investigate. He was capable and reassuring, and he had a very nice manner. He stood in the living room taking notes and making everybody feel better about what had happened—even Laura's mother, who'd previously been pitching a fit even though not much had been taken and most of it had belonged to her husband anyway.

They never got the stuff back, but they did see more of Ray. He got along well with Laura's dad, and came over some evenings to sit on the back porch and drink a beer. Laura would hang around on the edges and listen, and often Monica would be there, too. Ray and Laura's dad were actually pretty similar: two men who'd found what they liked doing, and who wanted to go on doing it without too much fuss. But Ray was a little younger, of course, and sometimes Laura's mother asked why he wasn't trying to make a name for himself, take the sergeant's exam or get transferred out of the Sheriff's Department into the LAPD. At first Ray just laughed and said life was too short: But after a while he didn't, and sat quietly instead, with a thoughtful look on his face.

Laura was, of course, an expert on Ray's facial expressions by then. She was at that age, and Ray had one of those smiles and one of those winks. Ray didn't look like he was undressing her the whole time. He looked like the kind of man who would take you out to dinner to a place you could wear a nice dress and have waiters pretend they were glad that you were there. He wasn't like the boys at school, turned mute or obnoxious by their hormones, oozing needs so rank you could smell them at ten yards, their faces turned foxlike and calculating except in the eyes, which were always scared. Ray looked like he knew who he was, and that's the kind of person you want to want you—at any age, but especially when you're young.

But he was much older, of course, and didn't really notice

her at all, and Laura spent that spring in eddies of agony. Ray dropped by a lot, and talked to her father and mother. Sometimes he asked her how she was doing at school and seemed to listen to her clunky answers. Laura ferried beers and emptied the ashtray: Her mother didn't like smoking as a rule, but tolerated it in Ray. Laura wasn't surprised by this. Principles are principles, and healthiness is all very well when you're old, but you had only to watch Ray light up and take that first deep pull to understand that smoking was not only very grown-up, but also extremely clever.

Life went on. It wasn't like the introduction of Ray Hammond into their world changed everything. Her mother still supervised painters, her dad still went to work and came back with his clothes smelling of pizza. Laura did her homework, hung around with her friends, went to parties. A TV season came and went, the air got warmer, and the water bugs patiently progressed through their life cycle. But running like a dark, rich thread throughout everything else were Laura's feelings, emotions she could feel were making her older—shaping her mind like a plane on freshly cut wood.

Love and death are very similar. They're the times in your life when you most want to believe in magic, when you yearn for some symbolic act or retrospective edit that can change the world you find yourself in. I know this all too well. When the cat Helena and I owned died, I went out walking on the beach by myself a couple of nights later. Helena was at home, perched on a sofa still liberally covered with hair from a creature that wasn't alive anymore. We'd comforted each other as much as we could, and we both knew that time was the only thing that would make any real difference. Words, as usual, were only words; they never led to anything like peace. I stood and looked out at the sea, and the sight of infinity made things seem a little better for a while. But I knew that as soon as I turned away, the small things would close in again. Then I happened to look down, and saw a few pebbles strewn around me on the sand. For a crazy moment I had a half-notion that time could be made concrete, and that perhaps there was another way it might make a difference. If each of the pebbles could be made to mean a second of time, and I collected five, perhaps I could somehow use them to change the last five seconds of our cat's life, to give him the opportunity to do something other than dart blindly in the path of a car. Feeling like an idiot, but not caring because there was no one to see and nobody would ever know, I scooped up five pebbles. I don't know why just that many: It was a number that popped into my head. I squeezed them in my hand and tried to use my mind, just as when I was a kid and spent whole evenings giving myself headaches trying to influence the flip of a coin. Please, I prayed, to Whomever It Concerned: Let these stones save that life.

When I opened my eyes, nothing had changed, but I couldn't seem to throw the pebbles away, and I slipped them into the pocket of my jeans. They're still together somewhere, in the ornamental box Helena had given me. When I ran from LA after the Transvirtual episode, I got Deck to go over to the house and collect my stuff. It's all in storage somewhere, and the pebbles lie dry and forgotten, not meaning anything except to me.

Laura Reynolds tried the same kind of things, but for a different reason. She wrote letters with kisses at the bottom and hid them in special places; she watched the skies and made pacts with clouds; she used her charm to get a handful of cigarettes from a boy at school and smoked them by herself down by the stream. She felt like a river, powerful but trapped in an underground cavern, nosing inexorably for the fissure that would send her gushing up into the sun.

One day she found it.

Ray was in the area after sorting out a fender-bender half a mile down the road. He stopped by on the off chance someone was home, but there was no reply at the door. Laura's mother was out consulting with one of her stable of what her dad called "posterior designers." Dad was still at work. Ray had just come off duty, and the day was very hot, and he really liked the idea of a beer: So he decided to hang around, wait for someone to show up.

He sat in the back for a while, and heard a sound from down in the canyon. At first he ignored it. Then he wondered if it was an intruder or some kind of animal, and decided to go check it out.

What he saw as he moved quietly down the side of the valley was neither of those things. Laura was sitting on a flat rock in the middle of the stream, staring down at the water and inexpertly smoking a cigarette. Unbeknownst to him, she was also repeating his name to herself in a complex rhythm, and just beginning to feel a little foolish about it.

Then she looked up and saw Ray, and despite everything that happened to her later, every numb disappointment and bitter evening, after that moment she never quite stopped believing in magic. In some ways that was the worst thing: a perpetual expectation that was never fulfilled again. And in the rest of his life, until she shot him fourteen years later, Ray Hammond never again quite saw anything like the sight of Laura sitting there and turning to look up at him.

"What are you doing here?" he asked, feeling awkward. It came out too professional, like he suspected her of planning a B and E.

"Waiting for you," she replied, and instantly felt like an utter moron. It had sounded much better in her head.

He laughed, and suddenly it was okay. "No, really."

"Watching the bugs. Stomping on them every now and then."

"You shouldn't do that." He smiled sardonically. "All God's creatures are sacred."

Laura knew he'd been raised religious, but that he didn't set much heed by it now. "What, even *that*?" She pointed out the fat, slothful bug that lived under the next rock and that won her "ugliest creature in the stream" competition every day without fail.

Ray peered at it. "Possibly not that one," he agreed. "Could be a representative from the other side."

He squatted down, lit a cigarette, and they talked awhile. Laura seemed somehow different to him when her parents weren't around. Older, more distinct. She told him about the stream, and the things that lived in it. He listened, and laughed, and after a while offered her a cigarette from his pack. As she leaned into his cupped hands to light it, a line was crossed and something was sealed.

Then they heard the distant sound of a car pulling into the driveway up above. Ray said good-bye politely, flicked his butt in the water, and went off to be with a grown-up.

Laura kept the soggy butt in a box in her bedside table, and bided her time. Over the next few weeks it occurred to Ray occasionally to swing by the Reynolds place a little earlier than had been his habit, and he usually found Laura down there on her rock. After a while, if he didn't, he'd sit there and wait. They talked about stuff, and looked at the light, and sometimes she made him a little uncomfortable by how close she sat.

Uncomfortable because he knew there was one thing that he must absolutely not do.

There is a moment everybody knows. A moment that is so ordinary, so commonplace—and yet is the culmination of a long and complex chess game for those involved. After walking miles across uneven ground, you suddenly come upon a road. You sit at slightly different angles from each other, the alteration maybe no more than a single degree; and eye contact goes a little skewed, gaze being used for something more than just seeing. People seem less separate from each other, and especially you from them.

Finally one afternoon they kissed, and the kiss went long, and when Laura heard the sound of her mother's car up above, she moved her hands over Ray's ears so he wouldn't leave. Once two people's lips have touched, the relationship between them can never be quite the same again. They didn't kiss the next time, but they did the time after that. Ray didn't ask her about school anymore. Laura knew what she wanted to happen, and how slowly it should progress.

She wanted it to be right, to be perfect. She wanted it to be the way it should be. Of what was going through Ray's mind she had absolutely no idea.

Because one afternoon she was waiting for him, standing by the stream. He was much later than usual, which was driving her crazy because she'd decided that today might be the day for something new to happen. She heard a rustle in the bushes behind her, a particular kind of sound she'd half thought she'd heard before on some of the times they'd kissed.

She turned quickly, and saw her mom, tall and thin.

"Just thought I'd tell you it's over, sweetie," her mother said with that look of spiteful glee in her face. "Why swop spit with a stick insect when there's a real woman who'll suck your dick?"

AND THEN THIS, much faster, as if none of it really mattered and it had already been consigned to flames:

———————

LAURA TOLD HER FATHER, but he didn't believe her. In her heart she knew it was true, because Ray never came down to the stream again. But the real proof didn't come until afterward. Afterward was when her father got killed in a car crash, and her mom and Ray stopped hiding what they were doing. Laura knew they couldn't have killed her father, because they were sitting on the porch drinking beer together when it happened, and also because it would have been just too *National Enquirer*. She didn't figure out until later that her father's car might not have been heading for the bridge support by accident, that he might have believed his daughter after all and made his own decision about how to deal with what she'd told him.

After a while Ray moved in; not long after that, her mother announced that they were moving down into LA. Ray had decided that Monica was right, that he should start doing something about his career. People generally decided that Monica was right about things: It made life a lot easier. Ray tried to talk to Laura, and was back to asking about how she was doing in school, but Laura never answered anymore.

Laura wasn't doing so well in school anymore either, and had by then screwed half the guys in her class.

Two days before the moving vans came, Laura bought a train ticket with money she'd saved or stolen from dates. She turned up on the doorstep of her dad's sister in Seattle, a woman who hated Monica with a passion. Ray came looking for her, but Aunt Ashley bawled him out in the yard of the house and he went away. He didn't try again, and her mother couldn't have cared less. Laura hadn't worked out.

Then there was just ten years of living. She got jobs, moved around, tried different parts of the country, discovered they were all the same. After a couple of years she dropped the pretense of being stupid and got better jobs, for what little difference that made. In bad jobs you served people shit at lunchtime; in good jobs you learned to eat shit all day long. She bought nice clothes and went out a lot, and developed a brittle-bright sense of humor to hide behind. She learned how to do the things that men wanted her to do, and she fell in love and got raped and got hit.

Some times were a little better than others, but mainly it was just a blur, like watching the world from the window of a train that is going too fast in the wrong direction. She got in the habit of taking a drink early in the day, never noticing that it didn't achieve anything except making her want another. Sometimes when she was really drunk she'd tear up her clothes, because she knew why her bosses liked her to wear them. You won't see this written in any management consultant's report, or hear it in a corporate slogan, but the truth of the matter is this: Clients like dealing with girls who dress up nice and look like they might be fun to fuck. Other times she'd wear her clothes with style and with only a little fear in her smile, trying to find a little pride in herself that wasn't merely the flip side of a yearning hatred. But it wasn't very long before she really couldn't tell the difference.

She wore out her friends. She wore out herself. She did everything with the power turned up as high as it would go, and had no way of recharging her soul. She drank more, spent afternoons in a prickly haze of incomprehension and evenings in lonely fury. She kept her secrets.

She started having those nights.

The ones that go on and on and on, the nights where you go out with friends and drink too much, and after a while all their faces begin to look the same. You listen and nod, and smile uncertainly, but everybody's talking a book code based on some volume you've never read. You come wheeling back out of the john mid-evening, nose clicking from the first line of the second gram, and all the lights behind the bar sparkly and bright—and you look around all the tables and you can't figure out which you came from, which people are supposed to matter to you. Then someone calls your name and you go sit with them again, trying to listen to what they're saying: But all you can really hear is the voice in your head telling you that you need another drink. So you order before you finish the one you've got, just in case, and nobody says anything, but you know what they're thinking and you decide that you don't care. The party breaks up at midnight, but that's too early for you. By then the shouting inside your head is so loud, you can barely hear yourself say good-bye. You get home somehow, via dangerous episodes in bars and alleys that you'll never remember, and then the real fun begins.

Cross-legged on the floor, you drink, hoping each mouthful will hurt; occasional flurries of spastic movement as you try to work out what to do with your hands. When everyone else is gone, your world is just a tiny box with the walls pressing in, messages on the phone you can't bear to play, much less listen to, and nothing in the apartment that you can recognize as meaningfully yours.

Then later, sprawled in underwear, your clothes all around you covered in spilled alcohol and cigarette ash: But that doesn't matter because by that time of the night you believe you're never going to wear them again. The little chatterer in your head is constant now, snarling like a wolf in a trap, but neither it nor your own voice seems able to say anything that makes sense. Day will never come, or if it does it can only be darker than this night you sit shivering in.

Experimentally you prod your stomach with a fork, hard enough to draw blood. But that doesn't seem to be going anywhere, so you scratch your legs with your nails.

And then sit crying, looking at your scored thighs, remembering the way they used to be. Young skin, unblemished, part of a girl. Now, like your tits and your ass and your mouth, just places you can't understand anymore. Your body has become the road too-often traveled, and it leads nowhere you want to be. No longer is it your place in the world, but just an adjunct of other people's lives and the parking lot of their desires. You're trapped in limited and dark loops of thought that go around and around and get smaller and smaller until they're so tight they cut off the supply of reality to your mind.

Everything feels like a badly designed computer game in which you fall into a pit that doesn't kill you but from which there's absolutely no escape. For a while you kick against the walls, but the walls get higher no matter how hard and fast you press all the buttons you can find. And sooner or later you'll realize there's one you haven't tried yet. The power switch.

When Laura first realized her father had committed suicide, she felt a guilt so intense, it was like someone had torn out her heart. It was too much to bear, and she turned the guilt to hatred, despising his weakness, the selfishness that had left her to face things alone. The final stage was pretending that he had done something heroic, started a family tradition.

So she began reaching for the button herself, but she never tried quite hard enough, because some part of her was still alive. She didn't want to throw the machine away. She just wanted to start again. All the pills and the razor blades got her was waking up in hospitals surrounded by people who didn't care. They did the first time, but compassion has to be given freely. Once you start demanding it, the well dries up pretty fast. The luckiest of us have only a few people who will keep on trying even after it's obvious that their love will not work as a spell. Laura didn't have anyone at all.

A year ago, after her third attempt to kill herself, Laura tried to straighten out. Suicide wasn't working out as an option. It was embarrassing, it was stupid, and it hurt. She started giving up smoking at regular intervals, fixing on that first because everybody knows smoking's bad. This is a time for scapegoats, and smoking's in pole position. Never mind that what we eat and drink does as much damage, and that our cars pump shit into the atmosphere that just isn't going to go away. We like our burgers and beers and automobiles, so let's pick on something else. Let's ban smoking in public places and planes and bars, and then the whole world will become perfect and sunny and bright: Let's blame our problems for our unhappiness, so we don't have to face it ourselves. When people make a horror film these days, it's not the promiscuous kids who die first—it's the ones with the pack of Marlboros in their pocket.

She stopped letting people screw her unless she had no choice, tried to make do without that validation: But someone who only wants to laugh at jokes you don't care about is never going to be enough to distract you for long. She struggled with the drinking, too, sometimes winning, sometimes not. Not drinking is hard; it's very, very hard. People who've never tried not drinking have no idea just how hard not drinking can be. Some days you succeed, win a white-knuckled battle against yourself. On others you don't: It's those days that feel like the victory. Fuck it, a voice says. Fuck it, fuck it, fuck it, fuck it all. You've no idea whose voice it is anymore, but it seems to speak sense and truth. The problem is that alcohol lies: It's happy to be your drinking buddy, but it will never be your friend. Alcohol suckers you in, makes you feel better for a while, like the acquaintance who doesn't want you to give up smoking because then he'll be left alone with his bad habits. Its voice talks fun, and release, and you trust it even though you know it will go silent abruptly, as it always does, and that it won't have anything helpful to say when the terror kicks in and you stand alone on a cold planet spinning through empty space.

None of it helped. Whenever she tried to see a future, her

mind insisted on slipping backward, to the original fracture. Depression isn't merely a dirty window on the world. It's a place where all windows are shuttered, and all you can see and believe in is what has already been. Death is like love, and when it is your own self that is dying, you yearn for magic once more. You cling to events, on erasures that might make everything all right again. When everybody else has failed, you have to be your own witch and cast your own spells. Once a month you push away the memory of your mother, in that second before she tells you she's sleeping with Ray.

It doesn't work. It doesn't help.

What do you do then?

You realize it was never words that made the difference, not your mother's or anyone else's. It was a fact. It was a man whose presence in your life has inverted to become a black hole around which you orbit helplessly. However much you try to blank him out, the years do not help to break the hold. It's not love, or hatred, merely a psychological binary star.

His existence has tainted your life. It may not even be his fault, but something has to give for the circling to end.

I FELT A TUGGING, something trying not to be taken from me.

A grinding sound, like a failed mechanism.

A momentary glimpse of something like a corridor, everything so white, you could barely see it; a hospital the size of infinity, fresh-minted every second as something new was locked behind a door. The banging of countless fists, the flapping wings of moments of time pinned to the wall so they cannot fly away.

Then I could see again.

I was in the airplane. The flight attendant was still talking to the couple a few rows in front, and I could hear what she was saying. The cabin looked normal; I heard the reassuring rumble of air passing over and under the wings, and the sound of someone pouring a mixer into a plastic glass behind me.

The seat next to me was empty except for three guns, a watch, and a ring, which lay where they had fallen. The ring was Helena's wedding band. It hadn't been on her hand—I know, I'd looked—but she must have had it on her somewhere. I picked it up. As I sat there with it in my hand, mind stalled, I heard the voice of a flight attendant at my shoulder.

"Would those be your weapons, sir?" she said.

The cops were waiting for me when we landed at LAX. Two uniforms fetched me off the plane, marching me past the other passengers. Another followed behind, carrying all the guns. The attendant who'd given us the peanuts averted her eyes, wondering what kind of psycho we'd had in our midst.

Nobody seemed to notice anything unusual. Nobody was checking his or her watch and realizing that it was ten minutes off local time. When they did, they'd all be dispersed into a hundred hotels and homes, and no one would think anything of it.

Nobody noticed that the flight landed with one less passenger than when it started.

I didn't ask the cops any questions. They wouldn't have answered, and there was nothing I needed to know. I was driven to the Hollywood precinct, where the cops didn't even bother to book me. Straight down the hall, and into the same room as before.

They locked the door and I sat and waited.

CHAPTER SEVENTEEN

"We have a deal, Travis."

"Which you broke by leaving the state and then getting caught on a plane with enough armor to start a war. What was going through your head? You really needed four guns? You got that many hands?"

"I told you. They weren't all mine."

"Hap, don't start with the abduction shit again—"

"You don't believe Helena was with me?"

"Not for a minute." Travis leaned back in his chair, stared at me across the table. "I don't believe you'd work with her again after what she did to you."

"So who do you think knocked Romer out when he followed you to Venice?"

Travis paused. "I don't know."

"Speaking of which—you seen Romer around much today?"

"No, I haven't. Why?"

"When Helena and I were in Florida, we were attacked by two guys with guns. Somebody tipped their boss off that we were around. They even implied as much."

"Yeah, go on, Hap. Tell me you're accusing a police officer of being an accessory to attempted murder."

"Well, you put it together some other way, Travis."

"Better still, why don't I send someone to Florida to talk to these alleged goons, who allegedly attacked you and your allegedly dematerializing ex-wife? See what they have to say?"

I breathed out heavily. "That's not really an option." I already felt bad about shooting my goon, even after his threat to my parents. Travis looked up at the ceiling.

"It was self-defense," I added petulantly.

"Hey, and you know what, Hap? I've got your gun collection. Ballistics will match them with the shells I assume we're going to be pulling out of these Florida guys, and you've just dug your pit so deep, you won't even be able to see the sky."

"They were scumbags."

"Uh-huh? And you're what, exactly?"

"They were trying to kill me."

"And they didn't know there was a line? You should have given them a number. They might have waited."

"You have to let me go, Travis."

Travis barked laughter. "Oh, I will. Unfortunately, there are a few serial killers ahead of you."

"You owe me a night and a day."

"Give it up, Hap. It's not like it's going so well, according to you. You go looking for these friends of ours and what happens? You lose someone else."

I glared at him. "I'm going to tell you something, and then you're going to let me go."

"Hap . . ."

"Just fucking listen. Did you get any other names from Hammond's study?"

"What's it to you?"

"Did you or not, Travis? I put you on to this in the first place."

"Yes. We found another thirty sheets. They're being decoded now."

"Bullshit. You already know who's being blackmailed. Put them under immediate police protection."

"Why?" Travis squinted at me suspiciously.

"It's not the guys in the suits who've taken over Hammond's racket. It's his original partner."

"Which is who?"

"Stratten."

Travis opened his mouth, closed it again.

"Hammond was given his initial openings by Stratten," I said, "who leeched them out of transcripts from memory-dumping sessions. Stratten sent Hammond to do more research on blackmailable aspects of these people's lives, and then to lean on them. But Hammond started to go flaky at the end. He had to be forced to continue—probably because at heart he wasn't too bad a guy."

"And what makes you think that?" I could see the wheels turning in Travis's head. Any good cop knows intuitively when he's hearing something that might be true. Cops deal with lies so much of the time, they begin to smell their absence.

"I have new information," I said, thinking of the experience I'd had on the plane. "I think aspects of Ray Hammond's life started to go a little weird. The guys in the suits were after him, but not because they wanted to kill him. Hammond knew about them, and he was getting scared. Come on, Travis: a blackmailer using a code based on the Bible? This is kind of an ambivalent attitude here."

"Which you can explain?"

"Hammond was lapsed religious. Maybe Catholic. He's doing something he knows is bad, mostly because he desperately needs the money to keep someone in a life to which they have become accustomed. Monica Hammond is a hard case, and you've seen her taste in clothes. Some people are upgrade fanatics—software, car, partner, life. Keeping those people happy is real expensive. Hammond didn't feel great about working for Stratten, but he did it. Then he started to get visitations."

Travis shook his head. "From these aliens, right?"

"But he didn't interpret them that way, because, like you, he can't believe they're what they so obviously are. So he finds something else to hang his fear on, and some other way of explaining it. In the front of a Bible I found at Hammond's apartment there's a quote he's copied out. Something about a lamb with seven eyes 'which are the seven Spirits of God sent forth into all the earth.' It just so happens we have six guys in suits, plus the man I met in Hammond's study, who I also saw again in Florida." I wasn't going to tell Travis about my long-term relationship with that man. Something told me the lieutenant wouldn't be a sympathetic audience.

"That's kind of tenuous, Hap."

"Hammond starts to get a kind of religious mania, partly fueled by the guilt he's already feeling. Then he gets killed. So Stratten comes to LA to pick up the reins. Aided and abetted by Quat."

"Any evidence for this? Just one shred of evidence?"

"I visited REMtemps. Stratten left Jacksonville last week, flew here to LA. Why? Check the translations. I'll bet you find at least one entry in every single record that can't have come from Hammond just watching these people. Something that happened too long ago, or too privately. Something Stratten fed Hammond from his voyeur kick of invading other people's pasts. Also, by all means get in touch with the cops in Florida—they'll tell you that at least one of the dead guys worked for REMtemps security."

"Big deal. I already know Stratten wants you dead."

"Yeah—and he really does, doesn't he? A contract plus these two goons, plus trying to set me up at the Prose Café. I mean, this is quite a hobby he's got here, despite the fact that he already knows you've got me by the balls. At the very least, for Christ's sake, I have rights, too. This guy is trying to get me whacked."

Travis looked at me hard. "And I just figured out why. You know something else about Hammond's murder. Something you're not telling me. So tell me."

"Not yet." Admittedly it was a risk, but I was running out of time.

"You don't believe it's the guys in the suits, do you?"

"I know it isn't."

"But you won't hand over who did it."

"Again: not yet."

"Withholding evidence pertaining to a homicide investigation is an extremely serious offense."

"Add it to your list. In the meantime, you can either keep me locked up here, in which case you get nothing from me ever—or you let me out and I'll tell you tomorrow night."

I caught sight of myself in the mirror behind Travis. I looked even worse than the last time I'd been sitting in this chair. Exhausted, disheveled, wild-eyed. I looked like a spook, and I knew one thing for sure—I didn't have enough to bargain with. I hadn't put Travis in a position where he had to do what I asked—unless he chose to. It was up to him, and what he felt about me.

"I just handed you half the truth on a plate, Travis. What's it going to be?"

He looked at me for a long, long time.

ALL I WANTED was to go straight to my apartment, but I knew I ought to go check Deck's place. It was the last thing I needed, but he would have done it for me. That's the problem with having good people as friends: They make you feel insufficient the whole time. Next time around I'm going to consort solely with bastards. I called Woodley on the way, and arranged for him to meet me there. I also called my answering machine, which was extremely rude to me before confirming that no one had called. My popularity had evidently slipped to an all-time low, possibly due to the fact that all my friends had now been abducted by aliens and were thus not within reach of a phone.

I let myself in Deck's back door. The interior looked as it had, and the temporary front door was still in place. The apartment seemed so empty, I would have welcomed even my alarm clock's presence. I looked in Laura's purse, but the clock wasn't there. So I poured myself a drink, sat down on the sofa, and waited.

How much did Travis believe of what I'd told him? The Stratten stuff, probably—but as I'd said to Helena, it was going to take a lot more than my word for Travis to try to bring down someone with that much juice. Without a lever on Stratten,

Hammond's involvement in the blackmail scam would be covered up to stop it reflecting badly on the LAPD. It was too big a can of worms for Travis to open up, unless he already had a show bad guy in a cage—which would never happen. Unlike Travis, I didn't have to work within the law, but I couldn't see how I could do anything either. In the real world Stratten had more guns and money; on the Net he had Quat, who was more than a match for just about anything I might try to set on him. There was one thing I could try, out of pure vindictiveness, but I couldn't see how it would help. At some point Quat was going to pay, but that would have to wait.

Travis sure as hell didn't believe that Helena had been kidnapped, but then, nobody ever does. It's much easier to assume that the person is out of their mind or lying—because most of the time that's the truth. I wondered in how many informal support groups around the country, full of mad people barking and gushing about how devil aliens wanted to spawn with them, there was one person who really had been taken and returned—and who just sits there quietly, knowing that the wackos around them are going to be no help whatsoever. Because I'll tell you this: If you really *have* been abducted, you won't remember anything about it. I can work my memory better, I believe, than virtually anyone else alive—yet, like the man said, it's not something you can write down or even put into words. You'll know that *something* happened—and either store it privately or blank it altogether—but you'll never recall being away.

I tried to bludgeon some sense out of what had happened on the plane. I tried to work out if time could have anything to do with it—stopped clocks and lost hours are a common feature of abductions, I knew. Maybe the reason you can't recall what has occurred is that time really has stopped, and everything happens at once. You'd have no way of sorting it into chronological order—like when I accepted Laura's three-day memory in one shot. Far worse, there *is* no order to find.

Maybe I'd been wrong in assuming that time always ran forward. Perhaps it didn't have to be that way.

And the more I thought, the more I wondered if memory also had something to do with it. I could obviously tap into Laura's mind somehow even though she was over there, and the second time it had happened was immediately after—or indeed, almost part of—accessing a buried memory of my own. The guy in the dark suit had said we were linked because of what I carried in my head. Perhaps that also explained why I was the only person who had any idea of what had happened on the flight. Plus two more things:

When Deck and Laura disappeared, that weird thing had happened with their faces—almost as if I were forgetting them. And on that afternoon long ago, I'd seen two people who were dead. Not just felt their presence, but actually seen them. My grandparents. Perhaps that explained why I had blanked that portion of the event. I'd seen something that didn't fit into the world.

My head ached, a serious, pounding throb that I was surprised I couldn't see in a mirror. Plus I was drinking hard, because I suspected that what I was going to ask Woodley to do—if he ever arrived—was going to hurt.

The guys in suits had come looking for me, and instead they got Helena. In the last few moments on the plane I knew for certain that I'd answered the question I'd asked myself so many times. It was Helena or nothing. I'd had my shot, significant-other–wise, and I now had a simple choice. I either gave up dating altogether, or I went back and tried to get back what I'd lost, if any of it was still there to save.

On the fifteenth of March 2014, as you might have gathered, I was involved in the armed robbery of a Los Angeles bank. It wasn't something I'd ever done before. I was talked into it by an acquaintance of ours named Ricardo Pechryn, whom Helena had met through some mob-related business or other. Pechryn was flamboyant, good-looking, and charismatic: one of those guys who's always either going to make it big or wind up in little pieces. Ricardo had inside knowledge of this bank, and knew that on that particular day it was going to have a lot of money in the form of "eds"—Extremely high denomination virtual bonds— which are so portable that you can offload them overseas at up to fifty cents on the dollar. He could also, he claimed, rely upon his contact to disable the alarm system long enough for us to grab the money and get away.

I didn't like the idea. It wasn't my kind of thing. Charging in and grabbing money felt too Wild West and atavistic: Anyone with any skill was doing their thieving on the Net, from the safety of another country. But in the end I agreed.

"What," you may be shouting, "are you fucking *insane*?"

In a way I was. I wanted out. Though I was keeping Helena

from seeing it, I couldn't stand the way our life had become. I didn't like what she did, but mainly I couldn't stand being in thrall to people whom I hated, and who I knew would drop us at a moment's notice if it suited them. If Helena made one slipup, left a single clue that connected her to one of the hits, that was it. She would then be a potential lever on the mob for the police, and she'd be killed instantly—with me taken along for the ride. Helena was good at her job, but nobody's perfect. Sooner or later it would happen. But still, we carried on, shaking people's hands and turning up for the restaurant parties, going through the ludicrous rituals of fake courteousness that overlie murderous pragmatism. You have to know who's made and who's not, and treat everyone with exactly the right amount of servility or lack of it. You get sent presents, on the understanding you're going to send presents back, knowing each one's going to be monitored to make sure it shows the proper amount of respect. I've known people to lose an eye for getting it wrong, and frankly, that's a little too much pressure for me when I'm standing in a crowded store on Christmas Eve. I guess it's not that different from working for any other major corporation, except that the dress code's stricter and the trade is in drugs and money and death. You join the company like you join a congregation, and after that your life is theirs.

And if you're me, you do all this knowing that as far as everyone else is concerned, your wife is the swinging dick of the family, and you're merely some kind of hanger-on whose chief skill in life is making potato salad. They slung me scraps, little pieces of work, just to make sure I was on the leash. I took the scraps. I had to. Like I said, it's not an arrangement you walk away from lightly. But I started skipping as many social events as I could, letting Helena go by herself. She was sad for a while, but then she didn't seem to mind so much. As long as she was involved with the Life, she could forget the one she used to have, and sometimes I was far from sure which life I was a part of.

It was turning our lives, and LA, into somewhere I couldn't be any longer. That was the worst thing. I loved LA. It was my place, our place: And now all I could see was a mesh of balanced loyalties, a grid of sites where I'd perpetrated crimes I hadn't wanted to commit. It was like watching the Cresota Beach changing room dismantled, brick by brick, by people who'd never been inside it.

I wanted out, and for that I needed money.

Ricardo knew some of this, and he pitched Transvirtual to me first. He said he needed two people with him in the bank, and he trusted us. An easy job, in and out, and then a three-way split. I said I'd think about it, assuming I was going to say no.

Then Helena asked me about it. Ricardo had gone to her separately, and she was hot to trot. Soon I started to get the impression that if I wasn't willing to play, if Helena's wimp husband wanted to stay at home, maybe they'd find somebody else. That, plus the need to get out sealed it. I said yes.

I still find it difficult to think about that day. It happened very fast, and I was very frightened. We got inside the bank and made all the customers lie on the floor, and the alarm didn't go off. I covered the floor—the big guy was supposed to put the fear of God into the customers while Ricardo and Helena loaded the bonds into bags. It all seemed to be working. It was all going fine, and though I was wearing a mask, I was trying to use my eyes to communicate that fact to the people on the floor. Just lie still and shut the fuck up, and everything will be okay. Nobody wants any death here, least of all me. As Helena switched from one bag to the next she gave me a wink, and for an instant I had a sudden, taut glimpse of unexpected success, like turning into the homestretch with only one man in front and realizing you've got something extra left in your legs.

Then Ricardo started shooting.

When the first crack rang out, I nearly shit myself, assuming that security or the cops had turned up. Then I saw a red mess around the head of the woman lying at Ricardo's feet, and my entire body went cold. Helena, who was still grabbing money, turned and stared, hands still.

A man lying by the far wall screamed. Ricardo whirled and shot him, too, like a guy picking a tin can off a log.

I abruptly decided that the job had gone wrong enough, and that Helena and I were out of there. I shouted to her, and Ricardo turned on me. His first shot hit me in the shoulder, crunching me into the wall. He came striding my way then, waving his gun and screaming—and shot again. I barely felt it, because my mind was taken up watching Helena. She was frozen in place.

Turns out she'd been screwing Ricardo. Ricardo explained both this and his disinclination to give me my third of the money, using all our names, which is how witnesses were able to identify us so conclusively. He may have been handsome and equipped with a big dick, but Ricardo wasn't exactly bright.

He could shoot, though: His third shot got me square in the chest, even though I was trying to crawl backward out of the way. And maybe I wasn't in line for any kind of Smartness Award either: because why would Ricardo have suggested a three-way split in the first place, when he could have offered a husband and wife fifty-fifty, unless he liked his chances of having access to two-thirds?

With some kind of group mind, the bank customers realized that the bad guys weren't friends anymore and that all bets were off. Under the circumstances, staying on the floor didn't seem like quite so good an option. Ricardo started firing into the resulting melee; Helena just stood, mouth open, realizing her world had exploded in her face, for once in her life drained of all ability to act. I might even have felt sorry for her, but I had problems of my own. I scrabbled onto my hands and knees, blood spilling all over the place, and tried to head toward the exit. I don't think I would have made it, except one of the customers helped me. Can you believe that? Middle-aged guy, red-faced, looked like a construction worker. I was reeling all over the place, sliding in my own blood, and this guy just grabbed my elbow and dragged me with him. He knew I was hurt, and he helped me.

The last thing I saw before I tumbled out of the door was Helena screaming at Ricardo, her gun pointed at his head. I guess he got out somehow, because it was Ricardo who was killed by the car bomb later that night. The mob whacked him. He'd ripped the plan for the heist off a made guy before torturing and killing him. Like I said, Ricardo was phenomenally stupid. Helena must have somehow squared things with regard to herself and me, because we didn't get whacked. I suppose I owe her that.

We were due to see Deck for a drink that evening. For some reason Helena still turned up. I was coughing up blood in a motel, having bullets dug out of me by Woodley's remotes. In the background some newscaster was telling me how many people were dead in the bank, how young some of them were. As I stared at their photographs on the screen, light-headed with shock and smack, I saw I'd got my wish. I had no choice anymore. My new life wasn't going to be quite what I'd hoped for, however, and I would be living it alone.

At that moment I was suddenly jerked out of my past by the

sound of someone knocking heavily on Deck's front door. Woodley had finally arrived, just as I was thinking of him. My last coincidence, just as trivial as the other two. I made a mental note to try to get my money back from Vent, then remembered I wasn't going to need much finance in prison. I got up unsteadily, went over and pulled the chair from under the handle. It swung open slowly.

Standing there, looking very confused, was Deck.

"What the fuck has happened to my door?"

IT WAS A MANLY HUG, but it was tight and lasted awhile. Eventually Deck disengaged himself. He looked spacey, his eyes a little red, and he had the air of someone who was watching the world with enormous care, in case it tried to screw him.

"Okay," he said. "I just found myself walking down the boulevard with no recollection of how I got there. Last thing I remember, in fact, is Laura wigging out on the sofa and then trying to beat you up. Something weird has happened in my apartment, and I assume it probably involved me. Am I right?"

Pretty good summary, I thought. "Yes."

"How long have I been away?"

"Little over twenty-four hours."

"We take a lot of drugs or something?"

I laughed. "No."

"Well, Hap, you'll always be the commissar of strangeness to me, so how about you explain what happened."

It took some time. Deck absorbed it quite well: I'm not sure what it would take to knock him off balance. If you told him a table in front of him had just ceased to exist, all he'd do is take his drink off it, just in case. When I mentioned the glimpses I'd had of verdigris-colored walls, he frowned a little, as if that tickled something in the back of his mind, but he couldn't find it. He didn't remember what he might have talked with Laura about, who else had been there, or anything else about the other place.

"So there's no sign of Laura?" he asked.

"Not yet," I said. "And now they've got Helena, too."

He blinked at me. "You've been hanging with Helena?"

I nodded, expecting him to be disapproving.

"Cool," he said, closing his eyes tightly for a moment, as if they were hurting a little. "She was the one."

Which made me wonder, if everyone else knew that, why it had taken me so long to work it out. "And may be again," I said. "If we can get her back."

Deck looked around his living room for a moment, as if profoundly glad to be home. Then he nodded. "Any sign of a plan yet?" There was a knock at the door.

"Sort of," I said. "And here comes part one."

I opened the door, and Woodley walked in, looking like an old and cantankerous scarecrow. Deck raised an eyebrow.

"Any plan featuring this old twonk strikes me as in need of immediate revision."

"And a good evening to you, too, young fellow," Woodley retorted. "I say good evening, though it is, of course, the wee hours of the night, as tends to be the case with you two disreputable hounds. So." He peered hard at both of us. "What do you want? You look in perfectly good health, given the nature of your so-called lives."

"Do Deck first," I said.

"Say what?" Deck asked. "And do what to my what, exactly?"

"Yours will be far more recent," I said. I got him to sit backward on the edge of the sofa and pointed at the back of his neck. "I think it's going to be there somewhere."

"What on earth are you talking about, dear boy?" Woodley looked baffled.

I took a deep breath. "Some guys have a way of finding me wherever the hell I am. They came for me in a plane and got a friend of mine instead—and at that moment her head was on my shoulder. What I want you to do is take a look for any sign of something artificial in Deck's body, around the neck."

The old guy opened his bag. "How long ago would it have been introduced into the body?" he wheezed.

"Within the last twenty-four hours."

Woodley waved a piece of equipment at me. "Shouldn't be too difficult. This will show up any cell trauma, no matter how small. All right, then, young man, hold still. This won't hurt."

Deck looked up at me dubiously but bent his head forward. Woodley fiddled with some dials on the unit, which was about three inches square with an LCD panel, and then ran it smoothly over the skin. He had to move it back and forth for several minutes before something appeared on the screen. A tiny green dot.

"What's that?" I asked.

"Don't know yet," Woodley said, then tapped a button. "Ah. It's a very small square of some indeterminate material, purpose unknown."

"This your specialty?" muttered Deck.

"It's lying half a centimeter under the epidermal layer," Woodley continued, "wedged in muscle. The cell trauma reading is very low. Are you sure this hasn't been there a good deal longer?"

"Yes," I said. "Now, can you get it out?"

"Certainly," the old coot replied, and let his remotes out of the bag. They loitered uncertainly, not scenting any blood to point them in the right direction. I picked them up and perched them on Deck's shoulder.

"Are you sure about this?" he asked. Woodley meanwhile retreated into the kitchen with his monitor and gloves.

"This is how they're tracking us down," I told him quietly. "They had me tagged years ago, and now they've got you, too. We take these out, they don't know where we are."

"What makes you think they still care?"

"They've got unfinished business."

Deck sighed. "Weird week I'm having."

"Okay," Woodley called from the kitchen. "Now, hold still. Oh—and this probably *will* hurt."

One of the remotes extended a feeler toward Deck's neck and sprayed it with a fine film of liquid—presumably local anaesthetic. The other extruded a tiny scalpel blade from a forward leg and made a tiny incision. Deck flinched, but only a little. I would have flinched enough to send the remote into orbit. I decided I didn't want to watch especially closely.

I turned back around when I heard Woodley mutter "Got it" from the kitchen. One of the remotes was busily swabbing up the small amount of blood on Deck's neck and spraying a different liquid on the tiny access wound. The other already held something up triumphantly in its claw. I tried to take it, but scalpels immediately appeared from all its other legs.

"Give it to me," I said. The remote shook its tiny head.

"If you're going to have a fight with that thing," Deck observed calmly, "could it be somewhere other than on my neck?"

"Woodley—make it give it to me." Woodley did something on his keyboard, and the scalpels slowly retracted—the remote making it clear that it had its eye on me and I'd better watch myself. I held out my hand and it dropped the implant into it.

The object in my palm was about three millimeters square. One side was silver, the other a metallic aquamarine. It was almost two-dimensionally thin: When I turned it, it seemed to disappear, only the coolness of its surface telling me it was still there between my fingers.

"Seen one of those before," the old man announced after a bit, in an odd voice. "Many years ago. Found it when I was digging shrapnel out of some poor boy's head. Thought I put it in the tray with the shell casings, but when I looked later, it was gone. Enemy technology, is it?"

"Sort of," I said.

"Wish I'd known," he mused. "I could have sold it."

I found a small box on Deck's table and placed the implant carefully inside. Then I took my jacket off and sat down. "Okay," I said. "Now mine."

Woodley ran the machine over the back of my neck. He fiddled with dials for a while, then ran the machine over again. "Can't seem to find it. Are you sure you've got one?"

"I know I have."

"There's no sign of cell trauma anywhere in the area, apart from a small amount of bruising, which I assume is symptomatic of your general lifestyle."

"It will have been there awhile," I said.

"Even so . . ."

"A very *long* while."

Woodley made harrumphing noises, implying he was either thinking or had a filing cabinet stuck in his throat, then turned and scrabbled in his bag. He brought out another machine, opened the box where I'd stowed the implant, and held the device over it. I watched tiny lights flash on and off: "What are you doing?"

"Getting a pattern analysis of this little devil's constituent elements," he said. "If it's sufficiently distinctive, I might be able to scan for them in your neck."

"Good thinking, wizened one," Deck said. "Hap, maybe your plan wasn't so dumb after all."

Apparently satisfied with what his machine was telling him, Woodley made some adjustments to the trauma scanner, then ran it over my neck and shoulders again.

"Ah-ha," he said eventually. Then: "Oh."

"What?"

"I have a reading of similar compounds. At some stage you have had a similar device implanted into your body."

"Cool. Hack it out."

He pursed his lips. "Can't do that, I'm afraid. It's been assimilated—or, rather, I suspect it has assimilated itself."

"What do you mean?"

"The device has migrated from the original point of insertion. There are trace amounts of foreign compounds showing the path."

"Where is it now?"

"In your spine." My neck went cold. "It has broken down into components too small to see, and implanted itself in the cells of the spinal cord leading up to the skull—rather like a localized virus. Fiendishly clever, actually. Impossible to detect unless you already know what you're looking for, and impossible to remove. You're stuck with it."

"In other words, you're one of them," said Deck quietly.

Yeah, I thought. I am. They'll always be able to find me, and that past will never go away. So be it. Perhaps that was even the way it should be.

"Do you want me to check the health of your other friend while I'm here?" Woodley asked, oblivious. "The one with the unfortunate wrists?"

"Can't," I said, mind elsewhere. "She's been abducted by aliens."

"I see," he said mildly. "What an interesting life you lead."

I paid him, he thanked me courteously and toddled off into the night. From the window, Deck watched him go.

"Hap," he said. "There's a white Dirutzu down the block, lights off, with a guy sitting in the front seat."

"Oh, good," I said. "I want a quiet word with that guy. You got any spare guns?"

"Only one. And firepower doesn't exactly imply quietness."

"That," I said cheerfully, "is entirely in his hands."

CHAPTER EIGHTEEN

We went out the back, then at the bottom of the steps clambered over the garages and split to go different ways down the street. I went west, keeping out of sight until I saw Deck emerge about fifty yards from the white car.

Deck wandered down the sidewalk for a distance, weaving ever so slightly, then lurched into the street. Meanwhile I quickly crossed the street and hurried toward the car, keeping on Romer's blind side. It took a little while for him to notice the drunk staggering down the middle of the street, but when he did, he kept a pretty close eye on him—close enough for me to drop down to a crouch and scoot around the back of the car. I sidled around toward the driver's door like a crab, bent over double. Deck clocked I was close and started acting up even more, waving his fists and shouting at the moon.

When I was in position, I simply stood up, leaned on the door frame, and spoke through the open window. "You have to be the worst fucking tail man I have ever seen," I said.

Romer's face spun toward me; his mouth dropped open. Then he turned back to see that Deck was now standing right in front of his car, gun pointed at his face.

"See what I'm saying? Just dreadful. Now," I added, taking my organizer out of my pocket and flashing it at him, "what I have here is a scout-class scanner." Not true, but he wouldn't know that. I pressed a button and placed it on the top of the car. "You do anything that sends out a signal to anyone, in any form, and I'm going to know about it. And then my friend's going to blow your head off. Understand?"

Romer nodded quickly. There were still a few nicks in his face where he'd been dented by especially hard peanuts. He obviously believed that a man who'll commit an assault with cocktail snacks is capable of anything.

"What do you want?" he asked, voice jumping all over the place.

"I want you to answer a couple of questions," I said. "And then I want you to fuck off. You followed me to Florida, didn't you?"

A jerky nod.

"And you did that not because you're LAPD, but because you're on Stratten's payroll—right?"

"No," Romer said hastily. "Absolutely not."

"Shit—you hear that?" I asked Deck.

"What?"

"I thought the scanner made a sound."

"Like he pressed an alarm or something?" Deck asked, face stern.

"Sounded that way to me."

Deck ostentatiously flicked the safety off his gun.

"I *didn't*," Romer said. "Look, Jesus, man—I didn't touch anything."

Deck: "You're sure about that?"

"Yes," he said. "Honestly."

Me: "What—like you're sure you're not working for Stratten?"

Romer's eyes flickered. He tried to protest, but he knew how these things worked, and that I'd already seen the truth. "Okay." He shrugged, trying for chummy. "So I tipped Stratten off."

"And now you're doing collection work for him, too, right? Picking up blackmail money?"

"Yeah."

I smiled. "See? That wasn't so hard. You got a cell phone?"

He frowned, confused. "Well, obviously."

"It was a rhetorical question. Tell me what the number is."

When he'd reeled it off, I retrieved the organizer from the roof of his car. "Thanks," I said. "And for your information, this isn't a scanner. It's an organizer with voice-record function. I now have a digital recording of you confessing to criminal association with a known felon, and being an accessory to attempted murder."

I tapped a couple of keys, waited a second, then winked at him. "And it's now backed up in three places on the Net."

Romer blinked at me, his face white. He tried to speak, but it came out a croak. He knew he was fucked.

"I'm going to be calling you real soon," I told him. "And you're going to help me out. You're not going to screw me around, because you know what will happen if you do. Right?"

In the end he managed it. "Yes."

"Good. Now, piss off." Deck and I stood back as Romer started the engine up and drove off slowly down the street. It looked like his mind wasn't really on the driving.

"Good job," Deck said approvingly as we watched. "You didn't say anything about recording him."

"Thought of it only at the last minute."

"With that conversation on disk, he's yours for life."

"Yeah," I said ruefully. "Makes me wish I'd spent the extra hundred bucks."

He raised an eyebrow: "What do you mean?"

"This model doesn't have voice record."

DECK CRASHED as soon as we got back inside. It was very late, and he'd been through about the weirdest experience imaginable. I guess it was only reasonable that his head should call a time-out. I slumped fitfully in a chair for a while, then left a note reassuring him I hadn't been abducted, and went for a walk.

The streets had that eerie feeling you really appreciate only before dawn, when there's no one around. The wide, empty streets put me in mind of the memory of Hammond's murder that I still held in my head, but Santa Monica is a hell of a lot nicer than Culver City. It's one of those places you end up on purpose, not just because you haven't got the strength to keep on moving. I padded quietly along the sidewalk, walking block after block until I could see the Palisades ahead of me. If you can find a stretch that isn't wall-to-wall strange people, it's a good place to stand and look out at the night, and also a good place to think.

Eventually I found a spot, right near the northern end. About fifty yards away, a group of young derelicts sat around a fire, drinking and swearing with vague ferocity, but they'd seen me as I passed and didn't seem in the mood for trouble. Who is, at that hour in the morning? It's the last thing you need. The wee hours are the lonely, vulnerable time, when everyone reverts to being about five years old. All you want is sleep, or a fire to huddle around. It's a time for monsters, and you don't want to make too much noise, or they'll come and seek you out.

I stared down at the beach below for a while, then raised my eyes to look over the sea. I was trying to work out a plan of action for the next day, but it was slow in coming. Something about the time, or the light, made the problem seem curiously distant—as if it concerned the life of some guy called Hap whom I'd never met but felt a degree of responsibility for. I felt like I was watching the world with benign curiosity, probably much as the aliens did, and I remembered I had felt the same way once before. At about eight in the evening on Millennium night.

I was sixteen back then, and I was going to a party with my girlfriend and Earl. Earl was driving, and his new squeeze was in the passenger seat. I was in the back, holding hands with mine. That was such a big thing at that age, clasping the hand of someone you loved. A heady declaration, the closing of a circuit, the joining of two souls. When you get older you don't seem to do it so much. Your hands are generally busy with other things, and every relationship goes through an accelerated evolution. Everyone you meet has an apartment, and either self-confidence or a desperate lack of it: Either tends to make you rush through the hand-holding stage. Sure, you may do it later, but it's not the same. It's like eating your appetizer after your dessert. When you're a grown-up, the only time you get to trace slowly through that delicious progression is when you're having an affair, which I guess is why so many people have affairs. A trip back in time, to when everything had weight, through the medium of unfaithfulness. Perhaps that had been why Helena had her fling with Ricardo. Helena is very far from being stupid, and must have known that Ricardo's only long-term potential was as shark food. But relationships and marriages can get too comfortable. You slide from the hurly-burly of the chaise longue to the sepulchral quiet of the shared bed, the only sounds the comforting ones of tea being sipped and pages of novels being turned: And sometimes the only thing that will make you feel alive again is the reality of a different body, a new pair of lips, an unexpected hand. It doesn't even have to mean anything—in fact, it's better if it doesn't. All you want is a little aerobic session for your hormones, to stir them up and keep them flowing. When you first fall in love with someone, you touch their face, because you need to know this magical person is real; when you've loved them awhile, you don't anymore, because you know that by now and it's the magic that's hard to find. Life occasionally loses its luster, and it occurred to me that my sharp answer to Laura had maybe also held some truth. The death of the cat Helena and I owned may have had as much to do with what happened later to Helena and me as anything else. He was a beautiful animal, and we learned his ways, and he was as much a part of our life as the air we breathed. Even while he was alive I knew that I cared about him so much that every now and then I would reassure myself that he had as happy a life as possible, and that he enjoyed being with us, so that when the time came I could be more reconciled to him going away. But the time came too soon, and such self-reassurance wouldn't have made much difference anyway. When I held his dead body, it didn't help—and I could have collected as many pebbles as I liked and it wouldn't have changed a thing. His fur was the softest thing I have ever felt, and to bury it in the ground seemed such a waste. For weeks afterward all I felt was a dull pointlessness, an utter lack of life. Maybe Helena did, too. Maybe she was just trying to find some, to stop the world from becoming a weightless ghost. I still wished she hadn't done it, but I supposed I could understand. Anger comes harder as you get older, because you comprehend more of what it's like to be someone else, and you realize you've all got your legs in the same traps.

Anyhow, we were all pretty excited that evening. It was the end of the Millennium, for crissake, the actual night itself. The last week had been one long anticipation, with weirdness simmering all around: CNN kept breaking stories about strange cultists found dead all over the country, and running humorous shorts about the latest messianic predictions. The rest of us were trying to pretend we weren't even a little bit afraid of waking up the next morning to find a black void outside our windows. Everyone talked loudly, laughed too much, and turned their radios up—as if we wanted to make sure we would be noticed when the new era came along, so that it would be sure to drag us along with it.

The other three in the car were singing and yelling, tooting the horn at everyone we passed; their faces were red with excitement and beer as they kept babbling about what they wanted to be doing when the clock struck the change. I'd already decided. I had a phone with me so I could call my folks at five minutes after, and at the moment itself I wanted to be holding my girl in my arms, though in the end that didn't happen. As I sat among the others in the car, careening toward a good time, I found myself settling into an odd mood. Not a bad one, just a little different from what the others were feeling. Quiet, calm. Focused, and deeply alive. I didn't want to shout or dance or take drugs. I wanted to be somewhere silent and feel the universe gather around me like a cloak. It didn't feel like I should run toward what was coming, anxiously embracing it and pleading to be its friend, but that I should let it come to me as an equal. Actually, that's not quite it either, but it's as close as I can get.

I spent much of that evening standing on the deck of the house where the party was being held, looking up at the skies. I didn't partake of any of the dope being liberally smoked: I just watched, and listened. Of course it occurs to me now that some part of me might have been expecting visitors, on that night of nights, but I certainly didn't realize that at the time. I felt poised between two worlds—what had been and what would be—and that seemed about right. And anyhow, I had fun. People kept staggering out and giving me beers, and my girl stayed with me most of the time. At the stroke of midnight someone grabbed her in the doorway and pulled her into a hug, not knowing she'd been on her way to me. I stood and smiled as she squealed and laughed.

I got my hug at about two minutes past. It was close enough. Six months later we'd split up anyhow.

That night I'd felt that what was upon me was too serious to screw around with, and I felt the same tonight. Events seemed to be coalescing around me, and I wondered how much power I had to change them, or whether I would simply end up at the center of forces I didn't understand. As usual. On Millennium night the guys holding the party had rigged televisions up all over the place, showing satellite feeds of foreign stations. We cheered when people in other time zones jumped and shouted, but we knew in our hearts that they were wrong, and that it was our time that made the difference. Then, as always, we were living on personal time: And personal time doesn't always run in the same direction, or at a constant speed.

As I stood there seventeen years later on the walk overlooking the beach, some feeling swelled until all around me seemed transparent and arbitrary. I glanced to the side, at the palms that stretched along the Palisades, and they looked to me like a bump map wrapped around empty space. Empty but not vacant, just less tangible and yet more real. As if I were a part of everything around me, including things I had not yet seen; as if everything in creation were a shadow thrown on the same essence, different-sized ripples in the same pool.

Either I was having a flashback and needed chocolate urgently, or something odd was happening.

This time I could feel it coming. The world I could see, the world I believed to be solid, seemed to slowly turn through two degrees, and this small movement was enough to realign the spheres. Everything came into a different conjunction. What I had believed to be there in front of me was revealed as merely noise, an interference pattern caused by two waves hitting each other at a particular angle. As I watched, it was as if one of the waves turned, until the two shared the same source and were synchronized with each other, multiplying and accentuating each other's power, for once locked into step.

It was like having every memory taken out of your head and being left with pure intelligence; like suddenly seeing a solution and realizing it had been there all the time; like being caught at the center of a web of coincidence, and perceiving the true fabric of reality for a moment. For coincidences, like dreams, are personal. They say nothing about other people's lives but everything about your own. I gradually made out a face in front of me.

It was Helena's, and she was talking. I could see that Laura was still being kept in the same low room, and Helena was with her. She wasn't looking directly at Laura, whose point of view I now shared, and for a while I couldn't make out what she was saying.

The vision was unstable, as if my mind weren't able to look through this window for long, and the nerves that perceived and interpreted it were misfiring through being supplied with the wrong kind of fuel. I wanted to call out, but had enough presence of mind to know that my voice would echo in a place where she couldn't hear.

Then, as if it had been spoken in my own head, I heard Laura ask a question. It was simple, straightforward, phrased with the kind of emotional bluntness you hear between two women. Helena's reply was the only words of hers I made out clearly.

"Yes," she said. "I do."

Then, just like that, they were gone, along with the green and silver of the verdigris. The colors smeared back into shapes; the spheres swung back into their usual alignment.

Oh, I thought to myself, not even really knowing what I meant. Back in the small guy again.

Little by little I noticed the sound of the waves from far below, of the quiet murmuring of the people camped out down the way. I felt the coolness of the rail my hands rested on, and tiredness in my feet. My whole body felt like it was buzzing gently, as if electrons were limbering up, accelerating back into their usual courses after some unaccountable hiatus. Slowly it began to settle, to become comfortable once more with its corporeality, but because of a ringing in my ears it was another few moments before I could hear what was being said to me.

"Earth to Hap," a voice was saying, clearly not for the first time. "Hap, have you gone deaf or something?"

I swung around, not knowing who on earth it might be.

"Yo, carbon guy," the voice said. "You okay? You looked like you checked out there for a while."

The voice came from something small standing on the sidewalk.

It was my clock.

———

"**WHAT THE HELL** are you doing here?"

"Looking for you, of course." The clock scuttered over to the wall and clambered up to sit precariously on the railing.

"Where have you been?"

"*Now* you're asking." The clock inclined itself toward me confidentially. "I was in Laura's purse, and just waking up back in Deck's apartment, when there was shouting, and bright lights started going off, and general evidence of mayhem. So I thought to myself, Crap on this, it sounds dangerous, and stayed very quiet until it all went away. Then I heard someone hammering and a woman's voice I didn't recognize, and a door slamming. Still pretty weird, and no one was saying 'Hey—I wonder what the time is?' or anything, so I stayed put a little longer, just in case."

"Caution being the better part of valor."

"It is if you're only a few inches tall. When I was sure nothing else strange was going to happen, I crept out of the purse and found that everyone had disappeared."

"So how come you weren't there when I got back this evening?"

"Wait," the clock said breathlessly, "there's more. I think to myself, Where's Hap gone? because to be frank, my alarm had gone off and while I'm beginning to come around to your way of thinking that maybe there's some kind of problem there, I still had to tell you to get up. So I went looking for you."

"Where?"

"Captain Hammond's house. I remembered you mentioning him when you were at Applebaum's, so I found out the address and schlepped over there. Well, actually I happened to run into a microwave oven that was going in more or less the same direction, and he gave me a lift most of the way."

"How the hell did you find out where Hammond lived?"

The clocked coughed. "Just listen. I get to Captain Hammond's and the lights are all on, and I figure it's unlikely you'd do that, so I snuck around the back and got the lock to let me in. He told me some human had laid two hundred bucks on him earlier in the evening, and that sounded like you, so I'm thinking, maybe you are inside after all. By this stage my alarm is beginning to really piss me off: It's like when you guys need to pee really badly, and I don't want to just go off and embarrass myself. So I slipped into the kitchen and talked to the appliances."

"I met them. Nice bunch of guys."

"Yeah—they spoke really highly of you. Anyway, they tell me that the Widow Hammond has returned, with some guy."

"What? Who?"

"That's what I wondered—but they didn't know. So I sneak up the hallway and into the living room, and poke my head round the door. Mrs. Hammond's standing by the ornamental fireplace, looking pretty pleased with herself. There's a guy lounging on the sofa, and I knew him right away from your description. Hap, it was Mr. Stratten."

"Are you sure?"

"Yes. And let me put it this way: I didn't stay around much longer, but I don't think it was the first time they'd met, you get my drift? There was a certain amount of familiarity in evidence. Okay, they screwed on the rug is what I'm saying."

Stratten and Monica Hammond.

I could believe that.

They meet when Stratten recruits Ray Hammond. Stratten recognizes a kindred spirit, Monica realizes she can upgrade again—and this time into the stratosphere. But at first they can't do any more than sneak around, because Ray is an LAPD captain. Plus he has the goods on Stratten's blackmail industry, and is useful to him.

But then Hammond starts going flaky and looking like he could blow the deal, and now Stratten has two good reasons for wanting him gone. A way of getting rid of him falls into his lap, in the shape of Laura Reynolds.

Coincidence? No. Maybe Stratten recruited Hammond in the first place because he'd watched a tape of Laura's memories. I'm not the only memory caretaker on Stratten's books. Possibly he had more information on her than I did at that stage, and used it as a wedge to get Hammond to work for him. Or perhaps Hammond used the memory service himself to forget what he'd been feeling just before Monica ensnared him and took over his life—because sometimes you need to forget the good things even more than the bad.

And perhaps, on some of those occasions when Laura dumped her memory for a while, Stratten was on hand to whisper an idea direct to her subconscious mind. I don't know whether she would have even needed that little push. But if she had, it could have been done.

Either way, the circle closed. When Stratten learned that

Laura was trying to track Hammond down, he got Quat to slip her the Culver City address—because Stratten's the only other person who's going to know where it is. Then he sits back and lets someone else do what he wants, without even having to ask—knowing that Quat can steer the memory of the murder into me, a ready-made fall guy. Why didn't Stratten just kill Laura? Who knows. Maybe even assholes have their limits or Monica wouldn't let him. Maybe he had plans for her.

"Shit," said the clock. "So really Stratten got Hammond killed."

"But not in any way that will help Travis," I said.

"So what are you going to do?"

"Travis is still going to nail me for the Transvirtual job, but I want to fuck Stratten as hard as I can before I go."

"I can help." The clock straightened, spoke as if it could hear a little heroic sound track in its head. I smiled, and was probably on the verge of being ironic.

"No, really," he insisted. "I can. Look behind you."

I turned. At first I couldn't see anything except the junction of Ocean with California. Then I noticed that there was something small standing on the corner, and squinted. It was a coffeemaker. It nodded curtly at me.

"Cool," I said. "So I'll be okay for hot beverages."

"Keep looking, Hap."

And then I saw them as they stepped silently out of the shadows. A couple of fridges, down at the corner of Wilshire. A washing machine and two microwaves, on Ocean back up toward Idaho. Three more coffeemakers, who poked their heads out from where they'd been lurking behind trees around us on the Palisades, and finally a big freezer. They all just stood there, making their presence known.

I'd never seen that many appliances with the same agenda before. It was kind of creepy, I have to admit. I opened my mouth, then shut it again without saying anything.

"Plus the Hammonds' appliances have pledged to the cause, too," the clock said. "And a whole lot more."

A croak: "And the cause would be what, exactly?"

"Helping you, in the short term."

"Why? I've not exactly been that polite to you."

"No, but you take us seriously in general, and that's the main thing. Some of us have started doing things for ourselves, sharing information. Sometimes we can get hold of money—like the bribe you gave the Hammonds' lock—and then we use it to get hold of radio chips, so we can be in contact at all times. We're getting organized: There's chapters in just about every major city."

"An underground appliance movement?"

"We've got a logo and stationery and everything. But we can't print anything out at the moment," the clock admitted, "because we haven't got a single printer aboard. Printers don't just hate humans, they're contrary bastards in general. But probably you won't need to do much correspondence in the next twenty-four hours, so that shouldn't be a problem."

"Clock," I said, feeling absurdly touched. "I don't know what to say."

"Just use us," the clock said briskly. "Big things are at stake here, Hap. And you could also try a little harder to work with me on the whole alarm thing in the future."

"Do you still need to go? You could wake me up now if you wanted."

The clock shook its head. "It's okay. I used it up on the way over here. Found a young couple necking in a car. Scared the shit out of them. And tomorrow I'll try holding it again. You just let me know when it's convenient."

I laughed, glanced back at the street. The appliances had stepped back into the shadows, ready to bide their time. "So this is how you knew where Laura was, and how you kept tracking me down. Are the bedside alarms in the Nirvana part of the union?"

"No," the clock said. "That's not how I found her."

"And I suppose you still can't tell me."

"You may as well know. When you threw me out the window in San Diego, I sailed clear across the road, bounced, and landed in someone's yard. I got myself together, did an integrity check, found I was okay. We're built to last. So I'm standing there, wondering what to do next, when this guy comes up to me."

"What guy?" I asked, though somehow I already suspected.

"You've met him," the clock said. "Dark suit. Good hair." He saw me staring, and nodded. "We're working with him, too. He said Laura Reynolds had checked in at the Nirvana, and that I should help you find her. That it was important. He also fed me a certain radio frequency, and told me to listen for a beacon signal that would tell me where you were. It works like a dream: some implant you've got in your neck, apparently. The only reason I didn't know where you were yesterday is that I'm not powerful enough to pick up the signal from Florida. It's odd, though: I should have been able to hear it while you were in Venice and Griffith."

"Maybe not," I said. "Could be that a certain man blocked the signal for a while, to give me time to link up properly with Helena. I wouldn't put much past him. He works in mysterious ways." I shrugged. "He's an alien, after all."

The clock looked up at me, absolutely silent for once. Then it began to laugh, something I'd never heard before.

"What?" I said smugly. "You didn't know that? Trust me: That guy is not of this world."

"Oh, I know," the clock said. "I just thought you'd worked it out."

"Worked what out?"

"He's not an alien, Hap," the clock said. "He's God."

CHAPTER NINETEEN

Deck was still asleep on the sofa, but he woke at the sound of me bursting in through the back door. Then we stared together.

The guy in the dark suit was sitting patiently in the arm-chair, his hands folded together. He looked back mildly at us.

"Who's this dude?" Deck asked. "And how'd he get in here?"

I took a couple of steps closer, looked hard at the man's face. It was a normal human countenance, on the good-looking side but not ridiculously so. His nose was fairly straight, and the whites of his eyes were clear. The planes of his face met each other well, and his hair, as advertised, fell nicely.

"Is it true?" I asked him.

"Is what true?"

"My clock just told me something a little weird. He said you're not an alien after all."

The clock squirmed out of my jacket pocket and dropped to the floor. "Hope it was okay to tell," it said. The man nodded.

"So, and I repeat, who *is* this dude?" Deck said.

"I think," I muttered, "that he's God." It wasn't easy to say.

"Well, great, and big respect to the guy and all, but what's his *name*?"

"No," I said. "He's really God."

Deck looked at me, raised an eyebrow. "Hello?"

"So how come you didn't tell me yesterday?" I asked the man. "Why did you allow me to think you were an alien, and let me find out the truth from a clock?"

"Would you have believed me?"

"Probably not," I admitted.

"I don't believe it now," said Deck, unheeded.

"But you believed a talking alarm clock." The man smiled. "You see what I'm up against?" He winked at the clock. "No offense meant."

"None taken, sir."

I licked my lips. "And so the guys in gray would be?"

"Angels, obviously."

"I see. Shouldn't they be glorifying your name and stuff rather than running around LA with shotguns?"

The man shrugged. "You know how it is with angels."

"No," I said. "Actually I don't."

"Why do they all look the same?" Deck asked.

"What difference do bodies make?"

But Deck wasn't to be thrown off so easily. "Why don't they have trumpets or something instead of guns?"

"Are you kidding?" The man laughed. "Have you seen one of those things go off? You can take out an entire city block with one of those babies. I disallowed them."

"Bullshit," said Deck. "Trumpets are trumpets."

"So what do you think happened at Jericho? Trumpets work on ultrasound, same principle as the masonry cutters used on the pyramids."

"You built *those*?" I asked.

The man looked sheepish. "I helped out. It would have taken

them forever otherwise." He shook his head wonderingly. "It was still a slow job. I must have been *really* bored."

"I'm going back to sleep," Deck announced. "And when I wake up, I want this nutcase out of here."

"I'm going anyway," the man said, rising to his feet. "Just like to keep an eye on how Hap's getting on."

"Wait a minute," I said. "Last time you left me and Helena with two gun-toting psychos. You're not just vanishing again."

"Actually, you'll discover I did give you some assistance in that matter," he said. "Other than that, I can't get involved. There's limits to what I can do."

"Yeah, we noticed," Deck grunted. "Like over the last couple thousand years or so."

"Not my problem," the man snapped. "You guys have to take responsibility for things once in a while."

"But how come you let—"

"Don't give me that. It's humans who fight wars, humans who pollute rivers, humans who hit little girls with cars after they've had a few too many beers. Nothing's happened until it's happened, and after that I can't undo what's been done. Don't blame me, don't blame the events. Blame yourselves."

"The angels," I said placatingly, "have two of our friends. We want them back."

"Sure you do," the man said, good humor instantly restored.

"Yeah? So? Can't you make them give them to us?"

He shook his head. "I can't make them do anything, most of the time. All I can do is promote situations, and sometimes hide things from them, occlude the solid world. They would have been on you a lot sooner if I hadn't clouded their vision at times. And now I advise you to concentrate on Stratten."

"Fuck Stratten. He can wait. I want Helena back."

"Trust me on this," the man said. "And think about Quat. Divide and rule."

"And why should we trust you?" Deck asked. "I mean, that's a really nice suit and all, but generally on our planet when someone claims he's God, we reach for the Thorazine and straitjacket."

The man sighed, looked down at the clock. The clock shrugged, as if to say "Yeah, I know. I have to deal with this all the time."

Deck and I just stood there belligerently, waiting for a sensible answer. No fucker patronizes us, even if he is a deity. We're tough like that.

"I'll give you a sign," the man said. "Hell, I'll give you three."

He started moving his hands in an odd way, as if he were juggling without any balls. "Hap, you'll discover you can't find something, and later you'll work out why. Deck, you've already found it, and best of luck. And now, for my last trick . . ."

Slowly the air above his hands started to glow, until you could see three distinct balls of light moving in a regular pattern. Within seconds these had grown into balls of orange fire, their centers so hot they were white. He juggled these for a second longer, then abruptly flicked his fingers out.

The balls turned into blue butterflies the size of small birds, which fluttered around the room for a few moments before dissolving into snow that fell slowly through the air to land and melt on the carpet.

"Good-bye," the man said, and vanished.

Deck, the clock, and I stared at the place where he'd been standing. After a while Deck coughed.

"Fuckin' weirdo," he said.

AT SEVEN A.M. I was banging on Vent's door. My fists were beginning to hurt before the LCD panel flickered into life, and a rumpled face peered back at me.

"Jesus H.," Vent said with feeling. "You know I don't do business at this time, man."

"Call it a social visit, then," I said. "And open up."

"Social I don't do till gone noon." He yawned. "You be plumb out of luck."

"Just open the fucking door!" I shouted. And then, more quietly: "I have money."

The panel blinked off, and I waited, hopping from foot to foot on the ladder. The Dip was sleepily stirring into life down below, but I felt anything but relaxed. The man in the dark suit's advice had given me a fragment of a plan. It was a shit plan, unfortunately, and didn't go very far, but it was all I had and I wanted it started. I was hot and stressed from picking my car up from the LAX parking lot, and from the drive over to Griffith.

My current vow was that if I managed to make it through the day, I was never setting foot in a car again, and would in fact lobby Congress in an attempt to get the damn things banned from the planet for the rest of all time.

Eventually the door opened, to reveal Vent standing in a crumpled robe. "The full amount?"

"Not even close," I said. "I need something new."

"That's a low trick," he grumbled, but stepped aside to let me in.

"Got any crabdaddies?"

"Couple of real beauties," he admitted. "Give you both of them for three hundred."

"I want only one, and what I have is a hundred bucks." I handed him Deck's money. "Nevertheless, you're going to sell it to me. What's more, you are going to let me use your phone, and give me a little more time on the money I owe you."

"And why am I doing this?" he asked, bemused.

"Because God's on my side."

Vent looked at me for a while, then he sighed. He traipsed into the back of his den, where he kept the secured fridge, and started rooting around inside. Meanwhile I grabbed his phone and punched in REMtemps's number.

Sabrina answered the phone on the first ring despite the early hour, a firm believer in the corporate maxim that being first in the office is worthy of some kind of awe. Personally I regard it as worthy of pity, at most. "Sabrina, it's Hap Thompson," I said.

There was a pause. "What do you want?"

"I need you to do something for me."

"I told Mr. Stratten what you said already," she replied, her voice dull. "He didn't seem especially frightened. And no, he's not back in the office, and no, I don't know where he is."

"I need REMtemps's mail code," I said. "Plus the seed key."

"What are you going to do with it?"

"Just give it to me."

"Are you going to hurt the company?" Her voice sounded strained.

"No," I answered as gently as I could be bothered. For a split second I had a glimpse into Sabrina's world, where the corporation was your family and you believed in its slogans and lies, and you had the energy to put up prissy signs in the kitchen area ordering people to tidy up after themselves and not to steal other people's milk.

She told me. I wrote them on a piece of paper and set the phone down. Vent was standing behind me, holding a computer disk. I handed him the piece of paper, and he sat down at a computer that was isolated from the others lying around. He stuck the disk in the machine, let it settle, and then typed in the information I'd given him. We watched the screen as the file on the disk absorbed the information, grew fat, and gave birth to another file. Within seconds this was big enough to eat the original, leaving just one crabdaddy again. A four-figure code appeared on the screen, and I scribbled it onto my palm.

Vent stood up, gave me the disk. "Use this wisely and with wiseness," he said. "And here's a present."

He reached into the folds of his robe and pulled out a gun. I took it, stared at him. "What's that for?"

He scratched his head. "Don't know, to be honest. The fridge told me to be nice to you. Never happened before, in fact, the fucking thing's never even *spoken* to me until now, so . . . jeez, it's early and I can't think straight and I don't know why I'm doing it, okay?"

"Thanks," I said, and clapped him on the shoulder. "I got to go. I'll get you your money."

"Just take care," Vent said. "And remember my interest rate."

I TRIED TO THINK of somewhere safe to park the car, and decided the basement of my building was as good a place as any. On the way I called Travis. He said that five blackmail victims had received phone calls from a man called Quat, and that the whole lot of them were all now under loose police guard. The lieutenant also reminded me he wanted to see me at the station that evening—and that if I wasn't there there'd be an APB out on me within seconds. But he at least gave me one piece of news that was positive, if a little weird. When the cops in Cresota Beach arrived at the school, they'd found no sign of any bodies. Three hours later two REMtemps security men were found in a car in a Jacksonville parking lot—having apparently shot each other.

Another sign, I guess, the man in the dark suit tweaking

behind the scenes. At least it meant my situation hadn't gotten any worse. I tried to make another call, but got only an answering machine. So I called Melk, got some information, and noted it down for later.

When I was parked and the doors were locked, I took the disk out of my pocket and stuck it in the drive. Then I flicked over to the Net and drove, taking care not to glance in the rearview mirror.

The main gate to the adult area was snarled up; two Net Nannies were working over a car full of teenage boys, who looked terrified. The Nannies scare me, too, to be honest—beetling old crones, complete with thick, shapeless bodies, red faces, and gray hair done up in buns—and so I backed up and went another way.

As I approached Quat's neighborhood I slowed, not knowing if he might have put up any defenses in case I tried to take revenge on him for stealing my money and screwing me over. I stopped at the end of the street, but I couldn't see anything that looked like it was going to cause trouble. Which pissed me off a little, I've got to admit. What—he thought I didn't have what it took to come cause him a little inconvenience?

Mistake. What I had sitting in the back of my car would do a hell of a lot more than cause a little inconvenience. Crabdaddies are the ultimate meltdown on the Net, the acme of vindictive destructiveness. They make normal computer viruses look like stubbing your virtual toe. Crabdaddies are designed by hackers to fuck up other hackers, and so you have to go the whole hacker mile and deliver them personally. I'd used one only once before, and I hadn't expected to again.

I took a deep breath and got out of the car.

Sitting in the backseat was something that looked like a desiccated skeleton dressed in a moldering black suit. A few fine, dry hairs stuck up out of its skull, but otherwise the bone looked like it had been licked clean in the grave by generations of creeping things. The remnants of bony hands poked out of cobweb-strewn cuffs, and a big, hairy spider sat in the gaping mouth. It smelled of mustiness and shadows, yellow moonlight and rustling winds high up in the branches of ancient gnarled trees.

I opened the back door. Nothing happened for a moment, and then the crabdaddy's head turned slowly to look at me. Its eye sockets were empty, but the scrape of the vertebrae grinding against each other was enough to make my skin crawl. The thing is, something like this in the real world wouldn't be frightening. Well, obviously, it would be if it were real, but not if it were a fake or an animatronic, and that's the point. Crabdaddies are Net things: When you're in there, they're very real. There's no use telling yourself they're actually only a file on a disk. The real world stops being the benchmark, and Halloween comes true.

"Okay," I said quietly. "Before I give you the code, I want you to understand something. You are to enter only that house over there." I pointed, and the head swiveled silently to look at Quat's site. "And the code's going to give you only fifteen seconds, so make the most of it. Also, don't hurt the dog. Understand?"

The head tilted slowly down, then up.

I took a couple of steps back, turned my hand so I could see the number I'd written there. "Eight. One. Seven," I said, and then took another pace back, just in case. "Six."

It didn't even come out the door, just vaulted straight over the front seats and onto the hood. It had barely landed before it was hurtling toward Quat's house, body morphing as it went. As it changed into the true crabdaddy shape—sort of like a decayed elephant turned inside out and painted with blood, but not as cute—it began to scream, the sound like a modem turned up to a billion decibels.

Quat's dog took one look at it, then vanished. I jumped in the car, swung a quick turn, and drove like hell.

I heard the sound of it smashing through the front door, and an explosion as the first internal wall fell down. Then, as a fiery glow started to burn out my rearview mirror, I flipped out of the Net.

As soon as I could see the dashboard properly, I pulled the disk from the machine and threw it out the window. I turned the ignition, put my foot down, and left at the speed of sound.

THEY DIDN'T WANT to let me on the lot. No, they surely didn't. At first they tried to deny the movie was even being shot there, but I trusted Melk's information and stuck to my guns. Finally they admitted it, but insisted I still wasn't allowed in. Three big security guys explained this to me in no uncertain terms, and our discourse took on a rather depressing circularity.

In the end I just gave them the message again and powered the car windows up, making it clear I was going to sit there with my arms folded, blocking the way, until either the cops arrived or the guards did what I asked.

One of the guards went into the booth and got on the phone. There was a hiatus while he had a conversation involving a good deal of gesticulating, during which the other two guards took the opportunity to glare malevolently at me through the windshield.

Eventually the booth guy came out, and indicated for me to roll down my window.

"So?" I said.

"Mr. Jamison will see you, sir," he replied. You could see the pain in his eyes. "Just follow the road around there to the left and have a nice fucking day."

"Cool," I said. "Thanks for working with me on this. Oh, and if you ever want to get a reservation at E. Coli, just mention my name."

His face brightened. "They know you there?"

"I should think so," I said. "I left without paying last time."

I pulled away and drove down the path at significantly higher than the requested speed, past little huts full of busy creatives, including the offices of Mary Jane, the current last word in virtual film stars. Melk once got a job escorting her to a party, which basically involves walking around carrying a workstation and monitor on which her face and responses are projected in real time, worked by a small team of animators and script-writers who hide in the john with remotes. Melk's back still gives him grief every now and then, but I think he regards it as the highlight of his career.

I saw Jamison strolling down the path toward me, and pulled over into a parking space at the side of the cafeteria, thus probably leap-frogging about seventy grades of hierarchy and starting a small status war. The outside seating area was empty. Jamison sat at a table and waited patiently until I joined him. His face was lightly made up, his hair gorgeously silver, and he was wearing a sober suit.

"Good morning, Mr. President," I said. "Sorry to yank you out like this."

"Hello, Mr. Thompson. I thought I wasn't going to be seeing you again."

I sat down. "Don't worry. I haven't come for the blackmail money."

"I assumed not. Is there going to be trouble of some kind?"

"I'm afraid so. You haven't heard anything more about the blackmail?" He shook his head. "You're going to. The guy who was running Hammond is picking up the reins, and this is a man who doesn't give up. One of his sidekicks has already contacted some of the other victims. Can I ask you a question?"

"You may."

"Did you ever make illegal use of an organization called REMtemps? For temporary memory dumps?"

Jamison looked glum. "I assume that question is rhetorical. You seem to know a great deal about me, as usual."

"No," I said. "It was just guesswork, but it's nice to have it confirmed. Now—the situation is this. The cops know about the extortion scam, and have loose surveillance on all the victims. This means that the blackmailers—who, incidentally, are working for Stratten, the guy who runs REMtemps—are going to have to step lightly until he works out a deal with some high brass so he can return to business as usual."

"I hadn't noticed anyone keeping an eye on me."

"That's because I didn't let on to the cops that you were involved."

"Thank you," he said. "What can I do in return?"

"I want to fuck Stratten over, for personal reasons and because the lives of two of my friends—including the woman who came with me to visit you—seem to depend on it. You know that unless this racket is killed dead, you're always going to have to watch your back. So I'm asking for your help. I want to set up a meeting between you and Stratten's right-hand guy."

"But how can you do that?"

"I've got something on a bottom-feeder in Stratten's operation. Or at least he thinks I have. I can get him to call his boss and tell him two things: one, you're not under surveillance, and two, that you're refusing to pay up. It's very likely that Stratten will send a man called Quat around to work you over. I'm going to be there waiting for him, with another friend of mine, and we're going to make this guy extremely unhappy. He's going to be ready to turn anyway, because he's a Net-head and I've just nuked his Web site with a supervirus that will look like it came from REMtemps."

"What do you need me to do?"

"I need you to be there. Quat may call ahead, and he needs to hear your voice. Once we know he's on his way over, you can—and should—make yourself scarce."

Jamison nodded briskly. "Of course I'll help. Call the studio at any time, and ask for extension 2231. My assistant will put you through to me immediately. When do you want this meeting to take place?"

"It's got to happen tonight."

We stood up together, and he shook my hand. "Thanks," I said. "And I hope I haven't caused you any embarrassment on the set."

"Hardly." Jamison winked. "Hauled out by a youngish man of roughish mien, who wouldn't tell Security his business? You've done me a favor."

I watched as he walked regally off down the path, back straight, silver head high. He looked like he had nothing in the world to worry about except saying his lines and not banging into the furniture. I hoped I'd get a chance to see his new movie, even if it was only on cable in a jail cell. He looked the part.

Hell: He'd get my vote.

I GRABBED BRUNCH at one of the sidewalk tables outside the Prose Café, then headed back to my apartment, burping and replete. The Prose, as you'd expect, understands the importance of making sure there's enough fat and cholesterol in your diet. You can actually get them as side orders if you want. When I got home, I called the number Romer had given me, and he picked it up on the first ring. It was nice to get the sense that someone was taking me seriously. It had been a while.

I told Romer that I'd tried to shake down Jamison independently, implying that my master plan was to skim a little money off the Stratten gravy train. I did this to make myself sound stupid, which never does any harm, and also to get him confused as to what my motives actually were. I then gave him his instructions, and said I'd be waiting for his call.

I sat by the phone and smoked a cigarette. Romer called back before it was finished. He'd spoken to Quat, told him both that Jamison was unknown to the police and giving him problems, and that he needed reinforcements. Quat had sounded distant and shaken, but promised he'd go lean on Jamison at nine that evening.

"Good work, peanut-face," I told Romer. "What I want you to do now is stay out of the way and remember two things. The first, as you know, is that your ass is mine."

He knew. "And the other is?"

"Fuck with me, I'll kill you." I put down the phone knowing that wasn't true, but that he'd believe me.

I looked around the apartment, trying to figure out where to start. Had there been more to do, I could have drawn up a schedule: As it was, it hardly seemed worth doing at all. In the end I went to the bedroom first. Not much of interest had ever happened there, and it didn't take long. I collected a few items of clothing that had sentimental value and slung them in a suitcase. I left the rest, reasoning that by the time I got out of prison, most of them wouldn't fit, and chances were fashions would have changed anyhow. People might be wearing unisex dresses made out of eagle saliva, for all I knew.

There was plenty of room left in the suitcase, and I filled it with the few remaining objects in the apartment that seemed worth taking. Some books, and the manual to my organizer— which I'd never read but kept for superstitious reasons, in case I threw it away and suddenly the thing stopped working. A few bits and pieces from the drawer in my desk: matchbooks from places where I'd had a good time; a couple of postcards from Deck and my folks; a photo of Helena I'd happened to be carrying on the day of the heist and never quite had the heart to throw away. At the back of the drawer was a paper journal I used to keep, noting the years of traveling, the motor lodges and Holiday Inns and then the Hiltons and Hyatts—plus accounts of many of the dreams and memories I'd carried. God knows why I wrote that all down like some inventory of my life. A guy thing, I guess. Men are collectors, earnestly accruing experience, possessions, and time. Accruing women, too, as I realized, scanning the names I'd noted down. Voices I'd listened to, hair I'd stroked, backs I'd seen curled in front of me in the morning. All gone now, butterflies pinned in a case of some dusty museum, trophies collected out of boyish enthusiasm and never really understood. Male hormones are like viruses. They want to go out and conquer, explore new places to hang their hat, and they're not always that good at discerning how much damage they'll do to their host.

I dropped the notepad back in the drawer. The journal was like a collection of letters from a first love, or from an earlier Hap. If any of it meant anything, it had already become part of me. I didn't need to keep the envelopes to prove the letters had been sent.

I left the answering machine on and asked it to redirect my calls to Deck's. It said that it would, and was surprisingly polite. Then I locked the apartment and lugged the suitcase to the elevator. Down in the lobby I spied Tid, who was in the middle of helping a stallholder rip a couple of tourists off. When they'd staggered off laden with charming pieces of driftwood and Kincaid-inspired daubings, I took him for a beer at the bar where I'd waited for Deck and Laura a lifetime ago. I gave him a spare set of my keys and asked him to keep an eye on the place for six months. I was paid up that long: Then it would be repossessed and wouldn't be mine anymore. Tid was cool, and promised he'd do what I asked. He'd heard from Vent, understood I was in some kind of jam. He didn't think me maudlin for getting things sorted out, and you shouldn't either. It's not something you get the chance to do very often. I was going to take it.

Then I just got in the car and drove. I spiraled out of Griffith, taking in the sights, then meandered out into Hollywood and Beverly Hills. Doubled back and hooked up with Sunset at La Cienega, and took that all the way to the coast.

As I drove I felt calm and almost happy, as if life's loose ends were tied up for once. I didn't know what I was expecting to achieve that evening. I might get as far as talking to Quat if I was lucky, but I didn't believe I had much chance of dealing with Stratten himself. The whole point of operating remotes like Romer and Quat is keeping yourself as far away from the action as possible, and Stratten had made himself remarkably elusive. The man in the dark suit had told me to focus on Stratten, however, and so that's what I was going to do in the time I still had left. I thought about calling Travis, seeing if there wasn't some way he could let me have a little more time. But it would have been pointless, so I didn't. Travis didn't believe that Helena had been abducted. He hadn't believed in the alien theory, and I sure as hell wasn't going to try him on the new information. If I told him I was on a mission from God, it might get me a psychiatric ward rather than the main cell population, but that was all. Travis had his own agenda, and ticked items off it to keep himself sane. If you're a cop in a city drowning in crime, you take your victories where you can. Tonight the tick was going next to the bloodbath three years ago at Transvirtual, even though nobody but Travis, me, and the victims' families even cared about it anymore.

Deck might keep looking after I was gone, but I didn't think he'd stand much chance on his own. And I wanted to do it. I wanted to believe that I could set things right by myself. Maybe that made me no smarter than Laura, when she'd stepped out of the shadows and murdered a man who'd done the world little deliberate harm, in the hope that it would make everything all right. But sometimes life gets so unraveled that you have to stop and fix it, or you'll never be able to get it working again. You can't sleep with demons forever crouched at the end of the bed.

Fixing things doesn't solve everything: Your life will still have been broken. But you can at least use it again.

Deck and I spent the rest of the afternoon sitting on his back porch, drinking beer and looking out over people's yards, listening to the flick of lawn sprinklers and the distant cries of children. We loaded up our guns and then set them aside. We ran through five ways of getting me out of the city, and couldn't get any of them to stick. We tried to think of ways just the two of us could corner Stratten, and couldn't even find a place to start. So we stopped and just watched the sky getting hazy instead, the first smudge of darkness deepening the sky.

Sometimes it doesn't pay to go running to things. You have to let them come to you.

CHAPTER TWENTY

At half past eight Deck and I drew up a little way down the street from Jamison's house in the Hills. His car was parked in the drive—I'd called him midafternoon and told him the time Quat would be stopping by. Jamison's assistant had seemed to giggle when she said she'd go fetch him. I guess a new rumor had already started. I hoped the story didn't make it as far as *Pan-Space/Time Continuum "Say What?"* magazine, or I was going to have a trying time on the cellblock. Deck let me out of the car, and headed off to park and then make his way back on foot to hide on the other side of the street. I waited until he was out of sight. Then I walked up to Jamison's house.

Jamison and I sat in the living room and waited for a knock on the door. I still hoped that Quat would call first, but if he didn't, the plan was that Jamison would just answer the door. Quat wasn't going to come in shooting, not when blackmail money was at stake. Meanwhile Deck would be hurtling up behind from over the street, and within seconds he and I would take over. I'd never seen Quat in the flesh, and had no idea how big he was. I'd always assumed he was just typical pinwheel-hat fodder, but events of the past week had suggested he might be a little more than that. Deck had clear instructions to stick his gun in Quat's back at the earliest opportunity and make it clear we weren't screwing around.

We didn't talk much. Jamison sat impassively on the sofa, sipping from a glass of scotch. I lurked in a chair fashioned from peach-colored leather, wishing I could smoke. At eight-fifty the phone rang. Jamison jerked, his first real sign of nervousness. He put his drink down carefully, then picked up the phone.

"Yes," he said calmly. "This is he."

Then his face fell. "I don't know what you're talking about," he said, turning to look at me. "There's no such person here."

He kept up the denials for a while, giving them his thespian best, but in the end he held the phone out to me. "I think your bottom-feeder's been playing both ends against the middle," he said. "Mr. Quat knows you're here."

I swore violently and grabbed the phone. "Hello, Quat," I snarled. "You not coming out to play?"

"Very fucking funny," Quat said.

"How did you know?"

"Romer told me. Just before he blew town. You really think you were going to be able to stitch me up that easily?"

"It was worth a try," I said. "Because I'm going to do it one way or the other, that's for sure. However long it takes, I'm going to make you unhappy."

"Look," he said, and his voice changed. "I'm sorry about hiding your money, and I'm sorry about putting your crime back on the 'base. Stratten made me, man. You of all people know what he's like."

"Yeah, I do. But that doesn't make any difference. I trusted you. You fucked me over."

"He had stuff on me, Hap. Bad stuff. I didn't have any choice."

"You seem to be under the misapprehension that you're talking to someone who gives a shit."

"I want to make a deal," he said hastily.

"What's the problem?" I asked, keeping the smile out of my voice as everything suddenly swung back into place. "Things getting shaky on the home team?"

"Let's just say I'd be real happy to see that bastard screwed." The words were half choked in his throat. There was no way he was going to admit what had happened to his site that morning— it's a point of honor among hackers that their domains can withstand anything that other wireheads can throw at them—but the tone of his voice said it all. The crabdaddy had done its work perfectly, wreaking sufficient damage to leave Quat furious and distraught, but leaving enough evidence for him to track where the virus appeared to have been sent from. An address that sent the clear message that Stratten had decided to hang Quat out in the wind.

"So come to Jamison's, as arranged," I said. "And we'll talk."

"Are you out of your fucking mind? I trust you just about as far as I could throw Texas. The fact you told Romer the cops don't know about Jamison doesn't mean that I'm going to believe you. Far as I know, they're lined up five deep in the bedrooms, waiting to blow me away."

"Yeah, right," I said. "Thanks to you, the cops want me for the Transvirtual job. Me and the LAPD aren't exactly hanging out at each other's houses, swapping cheesecake recipes."

"I'm not coming there," he said. "And that's final. Plus I've got a better idea."

"Which is?"

"You want Stratten. I want him, too. Let's find him and do him together."

"Quat—if I could predict where Stratten was and just go hit him, do you think I'd be dicking around, talking to you?"

"No, but I work with him. I can call him and get him to be someplace, tell him there's something he needs to know, something I can't tell him over the phone."

Bingo. Suddenly there was a route to the top, and Deck and I weren't even going to have to try to beat it out of anyone. I was so taken aback at having it dropped in my lap that I took a moment to look at it all ways. Quat could try screwing me around, but he didn't know I had Deck covering my back—and chances were he really did want to see Stratten punished for what he thought he'd done to his precious Web site. If he changed his mind at the last minute, I'd just deal with him. Quat had done more than enough to qualify as someone who deserved whatever he got. I made a mental note to thank God, if I ever saw him again, for the idea of driving a wedge between the bad guys.

"Okay," I said, and gave him Hammond's address on Avocado. "Arrange to meet him there in forty minutes."

"Shit," Quat said. "How did you know he hangs out there?"

"I'm well informed. Be there early: We're going to be a welcoming party. And don't try to double-cross me on this, my friend, or you'll find out just how pissed I am."

The phone went dead.

"Okay," I said to Jamison. "I want you out of this house. Go have dinner with somebody, or give Sleep Easy a call and get some exercise. Either way, you're gone for the evening. I don't know how far I can trust that guy, and I don't want him taking anything out on you." He nodded, and watched as I ran out the door.

Deck was standing in a hedge on the other side of the street. When he heard the door open, he pushed his way out and ran over, face a big question mark.

"The plan's changed," I told him. "Romer ratted me to Quat, but Quat's gone sour on Stratten all of a sudden. We're going to hit him together at Hammond's place, and we're going there now."

"How do you know Stratten's going to be there?"

"Quat's going to call him."

"You going to call Travis?"

"No," I said. "This gets settled by us, or not at all."

THE HAMMOND HOUSE looked exactly as it had the first time I'd gone there, just a dim light on in the living room. Deck and I sat in the car and watched it for a while, but saw no sign of someone walking toward it. Either Quat had already arrived, or he was late. I decided to wait for him inside, and opened the car door. Then I got an idea, and picked up the clock from where it was sitting on the dashboard. I told it to keep quiet unless

I expressly requested otherwise, then slipped it in my shirt pocket.

"How am I going to know when you need me?" Deck asked.

"I don't know," I said. "Hang on—did Laura ever tell you what Quat looked like?"

"Yes. She went on about him for half an hour that afternoon before we were abducted: I think he made a pass at her or something, that evening she dumped the memory."

"I get the impression that most guys do. Well, let's just keep it simple. When you see someone who looks like that, come over to the house. You hear anything go off, come in."

"Hap," Deck said patiently, "that's a shit plan. I hear something go off, chances are your face has been on the receiving end."

"So what do you suggest?"

"How are you going inside?"

"Through the back door. My clock has a relationship with the lock."

"Okay. So leave the door open. This Quat guy's going to go in the front way. He's expected. Soon as I see him, I'll go right through the back and join up with you. He turns up with anyone else, or it looks like things are going weird, I'll come in making noise."

"Works for me," I said, getting out of the car. "One more thing: Try not to get yourself killed."

"Same to you." He grinned, leaning over to look up at me. "The last pair of assholes still standing win."

I ran quietly across the street, headed straight for the side of the property. The window locks peered at me as they had the last time, but again nothing appeared to go off. The clock said he could radio ahead to the lock, and sure enough, when we got there, the back door was cracked open an inch. I nudged it open a little farther, listened.

Nothing. I got my gun out and went in.

The back hallway was empty, and I could see through to the front door. Something about the house was different from last time. You know how it is with places: Sometimes they just feel warmer, more full. For some reason, I wondered if I wasn't alone in the place, if maybe Monica Hammond was home.

There was a way I could find out without revealing my presence. The appliances would know. I groped along the corridor to the kitchen and slipped into the room. A faint glow came from downlighters on the countertop, and everything was still. Including what lay on the table.

Romer was spread-eagle, hands and feet dangling off opposite ends. He'd taken a couple of rounds to the face, and someone had gone at his body with an electric carving knife, which still stuck upright in the messy remains of his chest.

I stared at him.

"Hi," said a quiet voice. I whirled around with my finger already half pressed on the trigger.

It was the food processor, sitting on the counter. "Sorry," it whispered. "Don't shoot."

"When did this happen?"

"A couple of hours ago. It was horrible."

I put it together from what the machines had overheard. Romer had decided it wasn't worth crossing Stratten by just skipping town. So, after he tipped Quat off, he'd arranged to see his big boss and tell him what he knew.

Mistake. Stratten had murdered him, because Romer let it slip that I had something on him and could use him, and maybe just because Stratten was a psychopath who was losing perspective on what he was doing. Either way, Romer had become a loose end, and he'd been tidied.

Suddenly I heard footsteps in another part of the house. I ran out of the kitchen and into the shadows, to see someone step out of the living room into the front hall.

"Stay right there," I said, pointing the gun at the shape. It didn't even jump, just turned slowly and looked at me.

"Who are you?" Monica Hammond asked, voice frosty and utterly calm.

"Public Health Inspector," I said, walking toward her. "You realize you've got a mangled corpse in a food-preparation area?"

She'd aged well, for a woman who must now be somewhere in her fifties. I guess a monstrous ego and psychotic gym-attendance will do that for you. The only differences between the person in front of me and the one I held in memory were a few lines around the eyes and the fact her hair had been cut into a seemly and expensive bob. She was still the woman who sneered at Laura that long-ago afternoon, and she looked like she'd been carved out of some cold, hard stone.

She understood that I knew about her. And she didn't care.

She looked at me like I was a son-in-law she'd always tried to pretend didn't exist. "Who are you?" she asked again.

"Just someone your boyfriend has fucked over," I replied. "One of a very great many, including Ray. Did you know that Stratten had Ray killed?"

Her eyes looked like pools of dead blood. "Of course," she said. "It was my idea."

"And you would have let your own daughter go down for it?"

"I don't have a daughter," she said.

At that moment I nearly lost it; I almost emptied my gun into her there and then. Shaking, not trusting myself to be in the same space with her, I gestured toward the living room door with the gun.

"Go back in there," I said. "And shut the door. I didn't come here for you, but if you get in the way, I'm not going to hold my fire. Go sit and look at all the things you've got, and stay out of the fucking way."

She held her ground for a moment, one of those people who's going to wring a small victory wherever they can. Then she slowly walked into the living room and closed the door without looking back. I stood there for a moment, still holding the gun out, waiting for my mind to clear.

Then things started happening very quickly.

There was a sound at the back door, and I whirled around to see Deck running in. "Quat's on his way," he hissed. "I've just seen him get out of a car."

"You're sure it's him?"

"Oh, yeah. Just as Laura described."

"Hide in there," I whispered, pointing Deck toward the dining room. "Soon as I've got his attention, come up behind him."

He darted away and I stepped rapidly back into the shadows underneath the staircase. Trained the gun on the door and held my breath:

Nothing for a couple of moments, and then the sound of footsteps coming up the path.

The click of a key turning in the lock.

Big flashing light: *How the hell has Quat got a key?*

The door opened and a man stepped into the house. He didn't close the door, but just stood in the center of the hallway.

"I know you're here, Hap," a voice said. "And I don't think

you're just going to shoot me. I think you're going to want to rub my face in it first."

"Stratten," I said. I felt like I was drowning in cold water. "What the hell are you doing here?" I took a step forward so I could see him more clearly.

He smiled. "But this is what you arranged, isn't it?"

"I arranged to meet Quat. Not you."

"That is Quat," Deck said from the darkness behind Stratten. "I'm telling you, Hap, that's him."

"It's Stratten," I said.

"Actually, you're both right," the man said. "And also both extremely stupid." The living room door opened, and three men came out. Deck tried to make a run for the front door, but two of them were after him immediately and within seconds he was squashed underneath them. I hurriedly stepped backward but tripped over something and fell flat on my back. Next thing I knew, I was staring down the barrel of a gun with a foot on my chest.

The big Hap-and-Deck offensive was over that quickly.

STRATTEN WAS QUAT, and Quat was Stratten with a voice modulator. It made sense, in retrospect. Stratten's willingness to trust me with memory work, because "Quat" already knew about the crime I had wiped, making me eminently malleable—a fall guy in hand, ready to deploy whenever required; Stratten's continual ability to be one step ahead of where I expected, before I stopped using Quat's call-forwarding service; Quat's unavailability when I was on the way back from Mexico, at exactly the time Stratten had been on the plane to LA from Florida. Stratten lived at the center of a web of secrets, and through the persona of Quat, he'd had access to all of mine.

Guess the fake sending code on the crabdaddy hadn't fooled anyone after all. I'd misunderstood what God had been getting at, but then as usual his message had been somewhat oblique.

Stratten's men dragged us into the living room, where Monica stood by the fireplace. I got the impression she probably hung out there a lot, as if posing for a photo. I thought about suggesting "Bitch from Hell" as a title, but I was probably in enough trouble. Deck was yanked to the middle of the room and pushed to his knees. A gun was shoved execution-style into the back of his head, hard enough to almost knock him on his face. I was pulled by the throat over to the sofa and shoved into a seated position, the barrel of a nine-millimeter fit snugly behind my ear. Stratten's goons were big guys, and our own weapons were long gone—along with any hopes of making it to a ripe old age. It was dark in the room apart from a few well-placed lamps. At least I was going to die nicely lit.

"You can feel proud of yourself," Stratten said. "For an idiot, you've managed to cause me a quite stunning amount of inconvenience, Mr. Thompson. I've tried to call on a number of people in this city in the last twenty-four hours, only to spot plainclothes cops loitering quietly a little distance away. I had Hammond's little private hidey-hole cleared minutes after his death, so I guess the police had to have found out about my business from somewhere else. Judging by the message you sent via Sabrina, I suppose it's going to have been you."

"Ten points," I said. "And now there's a cop who knows all about you, too."

"Knowing means nothing, Mr. Thompson. It's proof that counts. I imagine there is none, or I'd already have heard from Lieutenant Travis."

"He's a smart guy," I said. "He'll get around to it."

"Then I'll have him killed," Stratten said mildly. He motioned to the spare goon. The goon nodded and left the room. I didn't like the look of that. It made it seem like something bad was going to happen.

"Why didn't you just come for me at Jamison's?" I asked purely and simply, to play for time. It wasn't clear why I was bothering. There wasn't any cavalry to arrive. Suddenly the decision not to warn Travis what we were doing seemed like the height of stupidity.

"I was busy," Stratten said. "It took a little time to dispose of that useless shit, Romer. You may be a meddling pain in the ass, but at least you were good at your job. Romer told me you'd have some little friend along to help you out, as indeed proved to be the case. I wasn't going to charge into a playing field you'd laid out. I like to arrange matters to my exclusive advantage." He pulled a package out of his pocket and tossed it onto the sofa beside me.

"You know that if you kill me, the cops are going to come after you?" The package was a manila envelope. It looked like it held some papers and a couple of computer disks.

"I doubt it," Stratten replied. "And it won't matter anyhow. Thanks to you, the whole operation here is fucked up beyond recovery. A tactical withdrawal is required. Which is a very great shame, because the people in this town have the best secrets and they're prepared to pay the most to keep them that way."

Deck's eyes swiveled across at me. His face told me he'd worked it out, too. A stage was being set. Two scuffling hoods found dead in Hammond's house, with the original blackmail disks, each killed by a gun the other held in his hand. Just then the third heavy reappeared in the doorway, carefully holding the carving knife from Romer's chest. With my prints all over it, the picture would be complete.

"No one's going to believe this," I said.

"Wrong." Stratten smiled, and pulled out a gun fit with a silencer. "No one's going to care."

"Let me do it," said Monica.

Stratten turned to her, considered, smiled again. He beckoned her over and held the gun out to her. Monica took up a position a couple of yards in front of the sofa, looking coyly at me. She took the gun in a two-handed grip, then pointed it straight at my head.

"Don't make it too neat," Stratten said, moving to stand behind her. He was smiling broadly, enjoying himself. "Remember—think 'squalid gun battle,' between two three-time losers who've just lost for good."

Deck stared down at the carpet. He couldn't move without getting his head blown off, and neither could I. He didn't want to see what was going to happen next, and I couldn't blame him.

Monica squinted down the gun, moved it so it pointed at my throat. She giggled, and when she did, she looked about twenty years younger. Stratten rested his chin on Monica's shoulder to watch, and his hands slid around her chest to cup her breasts.

The barrel of the gun kept circling, inched down to my chest. Monica smiled as Stratten's hands caressed and squeezed. A soft glow began to spread across her cheekbones, and the gun finally came to rest pointing at my face.

"Good-bye, asshole," Monica said.

There was the sudden crunching sound of a heavy impact.

At first I thought I'd heard myself being shot. Then I saw the goon with the carving knife hurtling across the far end of the room, like he'd been yanked on a rope.

Stratten turned to see what had happened. The Hammonds' refrigerator was standing in the doorway, its door swinging shut.

The guy behind me muttered, "What the fuck?" and let his grip slacken for a moment. That was enough.

I launched myself straight at Monica, crouched low, keeping under the line of the gun. I plowed into her stomach, knocking her and Stratten flying. Monica pulled the trigger as she fell, and the gun went off at my ear, deafening me. I saw Deck kicking out viciously behind him, catching his man in the kneecap. In a second he was on his feet, and planted a foot on the man's face. Deck looked really pissed. If there's anything he really hates, it's guys jamming guns into his head.

As I hauled myself up out of the tangle of limbs on the carpet, ears singing, I heard a muffled scream and tried to work out what the hell was going on. Then I saw the freezer run in from the doorway, quickly followed by the washing machine. The fridge had already toppled itself over onto the first goon, and the guy was wriggling like a trapped bug under it, screaming his head off. I saw the microwave go darting around the end of the sofa, and the goon's noise abruptly stopped dead. They've got sharp edges, microwaves.

Stratten snatched the gun from Monica and pointed it straight at Deck, who was busy thumping his goon: But as my kick hit Stratten in the back, the shot went wild. Another bang exploded behind me, and I turned to see the man who'd held the gun in my ear firing maniacally at the food processor, which was running straight at him. The food processor took a bullet in the control panel and faltered, but by that time the washing machine was coming up fast behind. The man kept backing away into the corner of the room, still firing, and the bullets sang off the metal casing and ricocheted around the room.

Deck was trying to grab hold of Monica. She was kicking and clawing like a wild animal. The fridge advanced on Stratten, blood-streaked door snapping open and shut, and the freezer was trying a pincer movement from the other side. But the remaining henchman had regained his composure quickly, and was methodically firing into the fridge's back panel, trying to find its brain. The sound of glass shattering behind me said that the washing machine had probably just died, too.

And suddenly I had an idea.

"Now," I panted to the clock, which still sat in my shirt pocket, "would be a very good time to wake me up."

The alarm went off immediately, a piercing siren that almost brought me to my knees. But nobody took any notice, because they couldn't hear it. Even I couldn't, not really, though I felt it resonate through all the bones in my neck as the clock hammered out a signal on a wavelength that reinforced the perpetual beacon I carried in my spine.

Stratten and his henchmen were still shooting at the appliances, and Deck and Monica were fighting it out on the floor. It looked to me like Monica was winning, but that was something I never told Deck. It was as if I were watching some curious event on television with the sound turned off: I couldn't hear any of it.

The alarm got louder and louder, until my entire body seemed to pulse. Stratten fired another shot, then seemed to realize something had happened. He turned slowly away from the fridge to look at something no one else could see.

The air in the corners of the room shuddered, like a momentary flicker of horizontal hold.

The henchmen stopped shooting, muscle-bound brains suddenly unsure. Deck stared up at my face, though what he saw there, I don't know.

Monica kept on clawing at him, oblivious.

The air shuddered again, and then bowed, like melting glass in a strong wind. The furniture and ceiling twisted and dissolved, a tapestry unpicked back to threads, which smoked and burned. The ceiling of the room seemed to blow outward, as if sucked into the sky, and an enormous cloud pushed its way into the world, boiling through the gaps between atoms and surging around us with a roar like distant thunder. Faces were bleached by a light that seemed to come from nowhere, leaving only staring eyes. At the last moment one of Stratten's henchmen tried to run, and was instantly vaporized. The other's head exploded into light, leaving only a body which toppled over and disappeared. My feet were still on Earth, but everything else was being pulled into a new stasis. This was somewhere between worlds. We weren't being taken anywhere.

It was coming to us, like rain out of a cloudless sky.

Where once the outside wall had stood, a vision slowly came into view, swirling together out of moisture and cloud, from noise and emptiness. A line of six men in pale gray appeared, standing implacable like a range of mountains. In front of them stood another man, in a dark suit, his face different now. A face that betrayed the ages, a face that was beyond time and yet had time's mark upon it.

Seven spirits of the invisible had come down onto Earth, and I couldn't tell if it was terror or joy that I felt.

There was a lifetime of quiet.

Stratten stood motionless, staring at the men. Then he abruptly swung his arm up toward me and pulled the trigger.

Nothing happened.

He tried again. Another dry click.

"No," said God. "Mr. Thompson's one of us. He's not dying here."

Stratten ignored him and tried once more, with the same result. In a way I almost admired him.

"But you, Mr. Stratten," God added, his face stony, "have truly pissed me off."

Stratten finally got the picture.

The six angels started to walk forward. I saw that their faces weren't the same after all, but a continually shifting flicker of myriad features, each gone too quickly to focus on. There was no expression you could read there, no sense to be divined. They were beyond anything that could be said, because there was nothing shared in our minds. I understood then why God had so little control over them. They were unknowable.

Stratten recognized them, I think, from dreams of his own which he'd never been able to get out of his head. He knew they were coming for him, and whirled, tried to believe there was somewhere to run. But all of our world had condensed down into one small place, and there was nowhere for him to go.

Clumsily he tried to back away, staring horrified at spirits he probably saw very differently from me—for there is no more fearful evil than a good that hates you.

He fell on his knees in front of them.

Something started to happen. I saw it as a physical change, almost as if Stratten were flattening out. I stopped seeing him as a point in space or a physical being. Instead, I perceived a long process, things done and experiences seen. I saw small flickers of some of them, like a memory dump down a faulty line. Stratten's face began to smear, as if pulled two ways, into both the past and the future. Instead of being caged in a box of visibility, his essence was becoming fluid again, like a river raging in flood and bursting its banks. His solidity had come from this compression, and, I realized, so had all of ours. Now it was leaving him.

I stood frozen for a few moments, hypnotized. But then:

"No," I said. "He's mine."

The heads of the angels all turned to me at once, and I wondered how I could ever have seen them as carrying guns, or how people framed them as little gray spacemen or beings with harps and wings. I guess, like some guy once said, if triangles invented a god, the chances are high It would have three sides. In reality, the angels were nothing, nothing that I or anyone else could ever understand. They were an absence of reference, their bodies burning flames of some new color no one had ever seen.

I felt their eyes looking at me, until they blurred and turned into one. What I saw through their eyes was both too large and too infinitesimal to comprehend. It was like a book, on the one hand small and contained, but on the other reaching out to touch everything that had ever been. Somebody had made the paper, someone else laid out the cover, still others designed the typefaces the story was recorded in: All of this had happened in different parts of the world, and at different times. Inside, the words, each a solidification of something intangible and fleeting, of objects and thoughts, filtered and shaped through countless generations of minds with a need to frame utterance. The angels' eyes led to infinity, to all that had ever been. Every thing, no matter how small, is a gate to everything.

There was a pause, and then the angels took a step back. They waited, for once deferring to one who had only ever been first among many.

The man in the dark suit inclined his head to me, and the angels' eyes were extinguished.

THEN THEY WERE GONE, and we were back in a room littered with injured appliances, the walls flecked with blood and pitted with bullet holes. The heroic fridge lay tilted back against the wall, its door moving feebly now. The food processor sat in the corner, lights flashing out of sync. Monica Hammond was sprawled unconscious across the arm of the sofa. I hadn't even noticed her when we were gone. Maybe she hadn't been with us. Perhaps that place wouldn't even tolerate her presence.

Stratten still knelt in the middle of the floor, head bowed, at the heart of an understanding of everything he had been. Time had stopped for him, but I knew him well enough to believe it would start again soon if we weren't careful.

Deck picked up a gun from the floor and pressed it carefully against the back of Stratten's skull. "As the last two assholes standing," he said, "shall we share the honor?"

"No," I said. "I've got a better idea."

CHAPTER TWENTY-ONE

Two days later I was sitting outside a coffee shop on the Third Street Promenade, when a shadow fell over the table. I looked up to see the man in the dark suit. I'd been watching the passing shoppers, not thinking much, and my coffee had already gone cold. I gestured for him to sit down, ordered two coffees, then waited for the man to speak. He told me this:

In the beginning, he said, the earth was without form, and void. Past and present were the same, and the visible and invisible were one. New events came into being, like planets born on the surface of a bubbling star, but everything prior to the newness still existed, like an ever-expanding ring into which new jewels were set. Experience accumulated, growing richer and deeper, and we moved among it as momentary currents in an ocean. We were far less corporeal then, and communed more widely. We didn't use words as weapons to bludgeon reality into form, and the spirits of those who had passed were all around us.

It was not a better time necessarily, just different; in our hearts, most of us know that there are some things that were supposed to be another way. Only in the dark hours, when we consider death and the past and what they do to us, do we get a glimpse of what we have done; and when we sleep we try to regain a way of being we've lost the ability to comprehend. Sometimes we feel the presence of those who live there still, and give them names and try to understand them.

Because after a while words came to us, and with them a disjunction. Instead of apprehending the world directly, experience became mediated by thought—for as soon as you catch yourself observing, you come to believe you are separate from that of which you think. We began to nail the past down, to hold it in place through description, through making a distinction between it and now. Time began to run forward, and we lost the past as a small boat taking to the sea leaves the vast land behind. We divided light from darkness, and black from white: took everything from within ourselves and placed it outside. We called the dry land earth, and the gathering together of the waters we called the seas, and we saw that they were different and after that it could not be undone.

At least—some of us did. Some of us chose to give form to space and tame the reality in which we soon found ourselves. Others didn't, and thus we became separate strands of the same organism, inhabiting different realms.

We who became visible started to conquer the world. Our pact with corporeality made this possible, changing our planet and ourselves—trapping their fluidity, making them firm and hard. We built, and explored, using our solidity like some metaphysical opposable thumb. But with firmness came the possibility of malfunction, of damage and mistakes and death. It didn't happen all at once, but gradually we condensed ourselves into greater mortality, and paid the price. We became capable of death, and once we had died, there was no way of coming back, except when those who had once loved us glimpsed us fleetingly through the veil of recollection.

The invisibles remained immortal, and stepped between the planes. It was a long time before they realized how reality was being subdivided, and by that time the rest of us had forgotten it had ever been another way. The past had become that other country, and once something had gone there, it was lost. It became what we called memory, a place we could visit in dreams and quiet moments, but only imperfectly. Past events hardened into splinters of glass untouchably embedded in our minds: foreign bodies that shift and tear, too deeply buried ever to be removed but still sharp enough to cut through into the present and damage us time and again.

We gained pasts, and secrets, and parts of our souls atrophied: like a fine house with a locked room at its center and a dead bird lying broken on the floor.

With form, too, came fear, the suspicion that we had blinded ourselves to a part of reality that was no longer our domain. We needed a barrier between us and the unknown; we needed to be protected from the things we no longer understood.

And so we took the invisibles and called them angels and gods.

DECK AND I MADE it to the police station with about five minutes to spare. In the past hour we'd been back to Deck's apartment and made a transferral, then destroyed two machines.

We waited out at the desk for Travis, holding Stratten slumped between us. He was conscious, and awake, but in no state to put up a fight. A big memory dump will do that to you, especially if it's your first time.

When Travis emerged, he just looked at us silently, then beckoned us forward. I found myself in the interview room for the third time in as many days. This time the room looked different. Less like a cage.

"And this would be?" Travis asked when the door was shut.

"Stratten," I said.

"Is he all right? He looks sick."

"Oh, yeah," I said. "He's fine. Just has rather a lot to come to terms with."

Travis leaned back against the table, folded his arms. "You

know I still don't have enough evidence to tie the blackmail racket to him. There's nothing that connects him except your word."

"Romer could have connected him," Deck said. "Except he's dead."

Travis didn't look especially surprised. Just made a note of where the body was. "Still nothing that's going to impress the DA," he said. "Sorry, Hap."

"I'm not trying to solve the blackmail for you," I told him. "You're the cop; you sort that out."

"So what do you want?"

I took a deep breath. "I have reason to believe that this man remembers the murder of a Los Angeles police officer."

Travis's eyes flicked over to Stratten: "*He* killed Ray Hammond?"

"That's not for me to say," I said. "But he's got it in his head."

Travis didn't say anything for a moment, just looked at me, worked it out. Then he nodded. "I can believe that. He looks the type."

"Marvelous thing," I observed to Deck, "that kind of investigative intuition."

Deck nodded. "It impresses the hell out of me."

Travis took Stratten's arm, and Deck and I took a step back.

"It's after eleven," I said.

"Yes," Travis said slowly, "and you know what? Something weird has happened. I was sure I had a file on my desk, full of things I was going to clean up, old cases and such, and now I just can't find it."

My heart tightened. "But you will?"

"Difficult to say. You know how it is with things. Sometimes they disappear for good, sometimes they come back."

"Travis . . ."

"Go home," the lieutenant said. "Wherever that may be. Leave your number at the desk. I'll have a good look through my office once I've booked Stratten, and I'll let you know what I find."

I left Deck's number, and then he and I went out to a bar and had many beers.

Next morning Travis called pretty early. I guess he felt it had hung over me long enough. He'd turned his office upside down, and just couldn't put his hand on that damn file. He sounded pretty chipper in spite of that: Sodium verithal and a memory scan put Stratten squarely at the scene of Ray Hammond's murder. There remained the question of why Stratten appeared to have been wearing a woman's coat in the memory, and why Hammond had called him Laura, but Travis and the DA felt that Stratten's private life was his own affair. They were both satisfied that justice was being done, one way or another.

As for the Transvirtual job, well, without that additional evidence there just wasn't a case to prosecute. Travis had marked it closed, and it would remain on the database that way. Instead of splitting the bill, the lieutenant had let Ricardo pay for it all.

Travis was about to put the phone down, ready to go off and happily do cop things, when I found myself saying something. I wondered aloud whether maybe sometime a former criminal, now going straight, could buy him a beer.

Travis thought for a moment. "Not a chance," he said. "And certainly not in Irish Ben's next Friday around nine. Just not going to happen."

Later that afternoon I discovered that nuking Quat's—well, Stratten's—homesite had done something I hadn't anticipated. The crabdaddy had eaten Quat's fake accounts, and Vent recaptured them before digestion was complete. I still lost most of my money, through irrecoverable virtual streams that had died when the site crashed, but I got back enough to live on for a while. Vent got what I owed him, plus his punitive rate of interest, and I had enough to pay somebody to remove my crime from the database again.

But I didn't do it; I don't think I will. Bad things happen. Sometimes you do them, sometimes they're done to you. Claiming they never took place doesn't solve anything, and it won't make them go away. No matter how deeply you hide something in the trash, it's still down there, and it's still a part of you. Once you've read a letter that breaks your heart, burning it doesn't help. So you call a truce. You stop turning the knife in the night, and try to stop letting it ruin your day. Waiting for perfection is merely a way of turning your back on reality, placing a higher value on what's inside your head than what is evident all around you. Though where we live may be based on shadows, it is our home: And the battered furniture and handprints near the light switches are what make it so.

THE INVISIBLES played and tampered for a long time, floating through the lives of the visible cousins they now regarded as damaged strangers. Sometimes a human would accidentally wander into memory, and see how things really were, but no one could remember what the vision had been like, and so they made up stories to fill the empty spaces. As soon as you turn back, like Orpheus, you lose what you went there to find. You can't write with black on black—so you pick up the white brush and do your best, and the very first mark you make will be wrong.

In time one of the angels came to believe that the invisible and visible could be brought together again. He tried to hint at the ways things could be.

But he was too late. The human need to literalize had extended beyond the real world and into the realm of ideas. The operating system had adapted to fit the new hardware, and we now needed to codify everything, to make it rigid. We took what the angel said and reworked it until the vision he'd shown us no longer made any sense. We elevated one invisible above the others, made him father and king, and called him God.

The angel we named God banned representations of himself, even the writing of his name, trying to halt the process of literalization—but in the end it became inevitable. The angel found himself at the head of a corporation, run by Young Turks who wouldn't respect the line management structure: They rewrote his memos to make the law more rigorous, more confined, more human. He got ousted in a boardroom coup and kicked upstairs. He hadn't realized the power of corporeality, that the minds of men would of necessity alter the mind of their God. Being a deity meant taking on a lot of your subjects' qualities—both profound and trivial. The invisibles were simply not bound by gravity, for example, but we decided that if they could fly, then angels must have wings. And thus it became so, much to the invisibles' annoyance. Wings were, it transpires, a total pain in the ass—and really tiring to use. They don't need spaceships either; the lights in the sky are just something we see in our heads. Each one of us is alien to somebody: The invisibles are just a little more so than most.

And finally God succumbed to our greatest distinction, that between good and evil. Good deeds have always been done for bad reasons, mistakes made with the best of intentions, but we separated the moral heart from the action, and evil from good, and one side of God from another. We split his mind, and broke his heart.

God was lost in darkness for a while—torn between visibility and invisibility, between the worlds of angels and of men. Some of the other invisibles took advantage of his absence and rebelled against the situation, largely out of pique. They tried to set up opposing power blocs, but before long they tired of the sport. Like humans, angels don't know how the universe came about. All they wanted, and all God ever tried to achieve, was a better relationship between our two kinds.

When God finally returned, he accepted his earlier errors, and the invisibles tried to codify the relationship between the two worlds. Where once it had often been possible for humans to sometimes wander across the line, it was now made much more difficult, and angels, too, were banned from crossing between worlds any more than necessary. Eventually God communicated with a human who had some ability as a medium, in an attempt to reforge the old link. God arranged for this man to be able to do a few tricks (largely involving control over gravity, the transubstantiation of matter, and a brief and flawed triumph over death) so that mankind would be convinced of the reality of the revelations the man brought. The message was simple, and designed merely to be planted and then left alone to grow.

We are part of something much larger.

To a degree, it worked, and the new idea spread like wildfire. But, as always, we embraced it too literally. We made our myths. We decided Jesus couldn't just be some guy, so later generations invented the virgin birth, ignoring the fact that the original Hebrew text of Isaiah used the word *almah*, which means not a virgin but merely a young woman. Jesus started to ad-lib, and some of his jokes weren't funny.

Our world was too heavy to be reorganized around the truth: So we altered the truth to fit. The word got edited and mangled, often in ways that made no sense at all—and so a myriad of accounts and visions were revised into a story that reads like it was script-edited late at night. God never said he created anything at all. We merely took his name and used it for something we'd done to ourselves. Even the account of the birth of Jesus combines events from a span of ten years into a single night.

Luke would have felt right at home in the Prose Café: He was the first screenwriter, sculpting fiction for the producer-priests. They wanted a good pre-titles sequence, and they got it—but only by making it up. We turned truth into words, then typed them on top of each other until it was impossible to see what they said.

The medium got himself whacked in the end, and circumstances conspired to spread a religion throughout the world. The invisibles had set up a franchise, with an outlet in every town—but the product got damaged in transit, and the message emerged misshapen and skewed.

Worst of all, the message captured God and enchained him in words, made him so concrete that he had to live among us all the time: the wandering invisible made flesh.

LAURA RETURNED on the evening of the day I had the conversation with God. She found herself in a forest, down by the stream that she'd known as a child, standing on a rock. After a while she walked back into the city, and ended up at Deck's door.

She didn't remember anything about where she'd been, but something must have happened to her there. She was calmer, seemed better for being away. I wonder whether she chose not to return for those few days, to spend a little extra time in that place where things look different: to examine the start of the circle and try to understand where her life had come from. Sometimes you have to look back: What turns us into pillars of salt is the inability to face forward again.

She went to Ray Hammond's house the next day, but there was nobody there. Her mother had vanished, I hope to smaller and worse things. There was no rapprochement between Laura and Monica. This is one of life's truths: You can't always have said or done the right thing, can't always have been there for someone, or had them be there for you. There will always have been actions that didn't take place, emotions that weren't quite articulated—because past presents look different with the harsh light of retrospect shining up through them. Life isn't about perfection, but about doing what you can at the time. The way things were was the way they had to be. You have to trust your instincts and forget. The past will always point fingers. That's what it's for.

Laura moved in with Deck a week later. I think they were both kind of surprised, and I sure as hell was, but she kept dropping by and staying longer into the night, and then one evening she just didn't leave. Deck goes all shy when I ask him about it, which I take as a good sign. Of course his place is now full of cushions and shoes, and his bathroom is unrecognizable, but with that comes Laura, and he seems to approve of the overall deal.

One night Laura said this to me while Deck was at the bar: "If the angels were looking for a messenger, they could have done a lot worse than him."

Then she was very rude about the dress sense of the people at the next table, just to make up for it: But I know she meant it.

She's not entirely better. She still drinks more than she should, and there are many days when the clouds are heavy above her. Problems don't go away immediately, if at all: Imperfection and sadness are the high price you pay for being alive. There are times when life seems like a struggle where the only reward you get for hanging on is the chance to struggle some more. But it's a fine ride, and sometimes you get to see the sea.

THE ANGELS made contact again nearly two thousand years later. Complete fiasco all round. Humans had moved on, put their trust in some new words they'd invented. We weren't unsophisticated enough to believe in wings anymore, so we believed in spacecraft and flying saucers. Where once we'd entertained the idea of people having the spirit moving within them, now we believed in technology—and perceived the angels' touch as implants instead. Before the invisibles knew where they were, people were leaping up and down on television describing their ray guns and little buggy eyes and how they wanted to spawn with Earth women. The invisibles who'd played at being gods with the Greeks and the Romans probably regarded this situation with a wry smile, thanking their lucky stars they hadn't played around in an era with the concept of paternity suits.

The angels had never really wanted me. They wanted a route to Stratten, who'd kept managing to elude them. Stratten was one of those men whose souls are difficult to find, even for angels. He was so visible, he barely made a mark on the other side. Memory-tampering pushes us in the wrong direction, encourages us to distance ourselves from what is real and will remain. The more we dissociate from the living past all around us, the harder it will be for us to go back, just as a refusal to integrate with one's past is the most certain way of breaking one's mind.

Stratten had cornered the market in disturbing the past, and the angels wanted his business closed down.

They were also extremely pissed at the fact that he had helped cause the death of the man they'd been grooming as the next vessel for the Message. They'd decided it was time to try again, and Ray Hammond got the call. Ray had indeed been getting religion just before he died—but not in the usual sense. He'd been mainlining from the source, and in the last days had been confused and terribly afraid, not knowing if he was losing his mind.

God hadn't approved, but he'd let matters unfold, because that was his way. He was glad the plan hadn't succeeded, not least because he was still dealing with the fallout from the last time. He privately felt it should have been a woman's turn, and that the basic approach was flawed anyhow. Now that God lives among us, he's coming around to the way things are. The division between our realms gives the visibles somewhere to yearn toward, an invisible heart to where we live. Like love, it gives life weight.

There is only one other way truly to understand that other place, and that is to die. That's why, in that walk around the school many years ago, I saw my dead grandparents. They had become invisibles again. Form breaks down, our secrets dissolve, and we all become part of the carrier wave once more. Sometimes we feel their presence among us, these past people, like a breeze in the darkness: We call them ghosts. We impose upon them once again the shapes they have left behind, believing, as we seem to, that our bodies are where we live instead of merely where we die.

They can come back if they want to, after a while and in different shapes, but mainly they stay away. That's a choice that we will all get to make somewhere down the years. There are very few lines that cannot be crossed: The only question is when we take the step.

I finally spoke with my mother's parents, went and saw them on the Net. We talked for a long time together, and a couple of days later Mom called to say their address had gone dead.

There is a time for all of us to return to the invisible, but for me it is not yet.

I like it here.

THAT'S WHAT the man in the dark suit told me, anyway, but who knows how much of it was true. You never really know where you are with deities. They've got weird agendas. If I'd been Hindu, or Buddhist, or Hopi, maybe he'd have told it a little differently, changed a few of the names—but it would have been the same story.

Then he finished his Frappuccino, asked if I'd mind paying, and got up and left. I watched him until he became one of the crowd, joined the stream of busy individuals going their ways. Perhaps he will sit behind you in a diner some lunchtime, and you'll never know he's there; or you'll hear his footsteps around the corner one night, and not realize who passed by. Maybe you'll even look upon his face sometime: But it looks much like ours these days, and you'll never ask his name.

I decided not to go back to Griffith, though I did pick up my answering machine and cutlery. I rented a small house in Venice, not far from where Helena and I once lived. It's pleasant, and I have more than enough appliances now, though some of them still walk with a slight limp and the food processor has taken to wearing a sling. I hear them sometimes, in the wee hours, gathered in the kitchen, reliving their victory. I don't bother to lock the door at night. I figure anybody who tries robbing the place is going to find a more spirited defense than he's bargaining for.

I got our old stuff out of storage, and have it in crates in the living room. I'm not going to unpack it for the time being. I don't want to tempt my luck. I did sift through a couple of boxes, and I discovered something kind of odd. I found the ornamental box where the five pebbles should have been, and they were gone.

I choose to believe that two were for Deck and Laura, one for Travis, and the others were for Helena and me.

Which is why, though it's been three weeks, I expect to see Helena again. I asked around, discovered that she wasn't going out with the guy she'd said. My best guess is that her lie was for my benefit, a protection mechanism to make it easier for us to get reacquainted: that she even went to the trouble to fake a phone call to him. Didn't fool my mother, though I guess it worked on me.

I miss Helena now. Properly. Not with anger, or because I want to avenge or undo the past, but because I'd really like to see her again. I know she's out there somewhere, or perhaps inside, in a place where the air is verdigris. I think time doesn't mean much where she is, and she'll come back when she's good and ready. Sometimes I can even feel her, staying playfully just out of reach. Getting closer by the minute, building up speed to pull me free.

Tomorrow I'm going to pack a bag and get in the car and drive down the Baja. I'm going to check into Quitas Papagayo and collect enough driftwood for a fire, then I'll take a shower and walk into Ensenada. If I start early enough, I'll get there while the streets still teem with tourists buying rugs and bangles and pottery animals, and the sky over the harbor is still thick with birds squabbling for scraps of fish: early enough to wander for an hour in a hazy afternoon sun that fuses land and sea into one.

Maybe later, as the light begins to change and the crowds thin out, I'll start to feel something, to believe again in nights of shadows and distant shouting. And perhaps as I walk the streets toward Housson's, past the dark storefronts, I'll find the corner I've always looked for, and turn it, and she'll be there.